By Gigi Levangie Grazer

The After Wife

Queen Takes King

The Starter Wife

Maneater

Rescue Me

The After Wife

The
After Wife

A NOVEL

Gigi Levangie Grazer

Ballantine Books Trade Paperbacks
New York

2013 Ballantine Books Trade Paperback Edition

Published in the United States by Ballantine Books,
an imprint of The Random House Publishing Group,
a division of Random House, Inc., New York.

BALLANTINE and the HOUSE colophon are registered trademarks
of Random House, Inc.

Originally published in hardcover in the United States by Ballantine Books,
an imprint of The Random House Publishing Group,
a division of Random House, Inc., in 2012.

Library of Congress Cataloging-in-Publication Data

Grazer, Gigi Levangie.
The after wife : a novel / Gigi Levangie Grazer.
p. cm.
ISBN 978-0-345-52400-3 (acid-free paper) —
ISBN 978-0-345-52401-0 (eBook)
1. Widows—Fiction. 2. Grief—Fiction. I. Title.
PS3557.R2913A68 2012
813'.54—dc23   2012007064

Printed in the United States of America on acid-free paper

www.ballantinebooks.com

2 4 6 8 9 7 5 3 1

For my boys, Thomas and Patrick.

We are in this together.

The After Wife

Prologue

"Hi, my name is Hannah . . . and I'm a widow."

Three in the morning. Again. Like any good therapist, my bathroom mirror has infinite patience.

"Before I was widowed," I say, "I was born. Then I had boobs. Then I had relationships. My relationships were all in L.A., a magical place where the men have less body hair than the women. Then, I fell in love. Then I was pregnant. Then I was married. I do things backward, it's my way."

I haven't slept in weeks. Tears come to my eyes. Eyes I no longer recognize. "Then, I was the happiest woman on earth," I whisper.

Being a widow in Los Angeles is not as easy as it sounds (*I kid.*). I found out the hard way. No one talks about death. A dead "civilian" is as unpopular here as crow's-feet and fat kids. But if a celebrity dies, you must literally beg people to shut up. You won't find Top Ten Non-Celeb Deaths on TMZ. Civilians don't die from a phenobarbital injection administered by a personal anesthesiologist, or from ingesting Vicodin and champagne with a crack chaser. When our time comes, it's without bells and whistles, pomp and circumstance, vodka baskets and tranny hookers.

Try this L.A. party trick. At your next soiree on a Malibu deck— or in a Los Feliz garden next to a koi pond, or like me, attempting a downward dog at a Santa Monica hip-hop yoga class saturated in tramp stamps—drop the line: "My husband just died, thank you," when someone asks how you've been.

Then watch them scatter.

"And now," I tell my reflection, my captive audience, the one who listens. "Now, I'm at a loss."

1

The Last Time

September. Saturday. Time? *Frikkin' early*.

"Now? Really?" I said. "But, I'm so tired . . ." I pulled the covers over my head.

"I just want to sleep in," I said, my voice muffled. Work had been brutal this week. My producing partner-in-crime, Jay Oleson, and I had shot a reality show pilot in five days, watched helplessly as our director stormed off, were at the root of a possible lawsuit from a competing production company, and had been fired and rehired twice in three hours by the network head.

But who was I kidding? My acting chops are on par with Snooki's.

"That's what all the girls say at six in the morning," John, my husband, said, in his hoarse morning voice as he tried to slide my pajama bottoms off without untying them. Well, guess what, my hips are actually bigger than my waist. This is where we consistently run into trouble.

"I hate you," I said, as I frantically slipped the pants to my ankles. I was already wet. My hands grabbed the headboard and held steady.

"I hate you, too," John said, his unshaven cheek against mine, his breathing heavy. He was already inside me. Our routine had been going on for a good . . . how old was Ellie? Our daughter, our curly-haired, chubby, nearsighted daughter. Born Valentine's Day three years ago. So, over four years.

"Ouch," I said, shifting my hips. Pain and pleasure brought me back to the bed, which hadn't known a quiet moment since John moved in. My hands were still holding on to that headboard. We'd cracked it long ago. There was no plan to fix it. What would be the point?

John wrapped his arm around me, squeezing me tight and grinding his hips against my rump, the one he encouraged to grow by throwing things like linguini with duck sausage and truffles at it.

"You could gain a few," he'd say, slapping my bottom. There are no sexier words in the English language. "You could gain a few." And to me, not a small person. Not a person who looked like she missed a meal. Ever.

"No," I said, "no, no, no . . ." I liked to protest, though I wouldn't go so far as a painted sign or a bullhorn. Just enough so he wouldn't think I was easy. I mean, even though we were married and all.

On Saturday mornings, John liked to be at the Farmer's Market on the Third Street Promenade early—before the regular customers, the crowds, the crazies—to show off Ellie to his old chef buddies, smell the fresh produce, bag some grapes, pears, figs, haggle over the price of bison, down oysters perfumed by the Pacific, and grab an espresso.

We'd be eating something amazing tonight. Something with figs. Figs, a brown sauce, a roast guinea hen? Of course, we usually ate something amazing for dinner—even if it were a simple, perfect omelet. John had been a chef until he retired to stay home, raise our daughter, and write his cookbooks. I encouraged him. He'd mesmerized me from the get-go, using his powers of mind control, his slight pooch, his manly forearms, and his penis-wand.

Goddamn, my husband's hot. I bit his shoulder. Like biting into a ham.

You've probably heard of them—John's books, I mean—the Cooking for Bachelors series. He'd been a busboy, waiter, sous chef, head chef, then private chef for various celebrities before *Mexican for Bachelors*, *Italian for Bachelors*, and *French for Bachelors* took off. No, no. John's not a bachelor. If he were a bachelor, I'd know about it. But he had spent a long time—forty years—being a bach-

elor . . . so he'd done his research. That is, before I pinned him
down one sunny afternoon in my front yard at Casa Sugar.

Back to the marital bed . . . I came, a small shudder and release,
then again, a deeper orgasm. Not like when I'm on top, rubbing my
body against the arc of his belly. Those orgasms go back centuries.
They're my favorite, even though I complain that I'm doing all the
work. I'm gyrating, rocking, whipping my hair like Tina Turner. It's
a whole show. You'd think I was getting paid.

God, I love a belly on a man. I didn't know how much until I met
John. Not a huge Budweiser gut, but not one of those manorexic
18,000-packs atop android legs running on San Vicente. That nice,
warm tummy on my man tells me a couple of important things:

    a. That he's enjoyed food and wine.
    b. That he's not in an unhealthy relationship with a Bowflex.

John came inside me, with my leg over his shoulder. How it got
there, I have no idea. I loved watching him. His bright hazel eyes
glazed over, like he was in a dream state. And me, Hannah Marsh
Bernal, I was making it happen for him. We were still trying for the
next baby. We'd probably still be trying well into our nineties. I had
read a study that stated women who used condoms with their long-
time mates were more depressed than women who didn't. Sperm,
apparently, was human Prozac. Good news for me. We'd gotten a
baby and years of me walking around in a drugged stupor out of it.
I truly believed there was something stored up in his body that
settled me. If we hadn't had sex in a few days, I would tell him
people's lives were at stake.

I would tell him the angels would cry if we didn't make love.

Close to two hundred pounds of masculinity slowly rolled off my
body. And there I remained, breathless. I closed my eyes. "Let that
be a lesson to you," I said, barely above a whisper.

John kissed my cheek and nuzzled my neck. I felt him swing his
legs over the bed, humming all the way to the bathroom. He
was still humming when he came out of the shower. Good God, it
was ABBA.

"I'm fucking starving!" he yelled, giddy. He stood over the bed with a towel wrapped around his waist. He would stay there, staring at me, until I opened my eyes. Finally, I looked up, and thanked the gods for his chest hair. L.A. was full of men who looked like giant-sized infants with the advent of the hairless package.

Ellie hadn't awakened.

"I love you, Hannah Banana," he said, his eyes wide, as though making a discovery. I knew exactly what he was thinking. I thought the same thing. "How did I wind up here? How did I wind up with this person who makes me so happy? How did I get this beautiful life? This beautiful daughter?" And I would add: "How am I the best fed woman on the planet?" Sometimes, I thought, just sometimes . . . good things happen to good people, or at least people who don't engage in road rage.

"You're staring," I said, as I opened my eyes.

"I want to remember you, just like this," he said.

"You see me like this every single day," I said, closing my eyes again. "I love you . . . but we have to do something about our sex life."

"Remember," John said, "listen for the doorbell. We're supposed to get our new patio chairs today. Remember, baby, okay? Tell Ellie I didn't want to wake her up—I love you!"

And he was off. The Farmer's Market beckoned.

I woke with a start. I reached for John's pillow, and breathed in his scent. On the side table was a cappuccino, with blocks of brown sugar on the side. And a note.

I am one lucky bastard.

xxxxxx J

The doorbell rang. The chairs. Our dog, Spice, barking at the front door.

Then, the phone rang.

2

Bad News Has Its Own Ring

A Timeline:

Doorbell ringing. The delivery of the patio chairs. Disoriented. The phone next to our bed ringing. I grab it, hoping it doesn't wake Ellie.

"Hello?" I say. Things go through my head, a work issue, talent gone mad, a deal falling apart, network boss having an early morning "best idea since Viagra" moment, John discovering the first organic persimmons at the Farmer's Market.

The doorbell is still ringing. I am naked. I can't open the door naked. Where're my pajama bottoms? I find my top and slip my arms through.

"Am I speaking to Hannah Marsh Bernal?" a woman asks. She sounded serious.

"Who is this?" I respond. What was this phone call?

"I'm sorry, but I need to speak to Hannah Bernal." Pajama bottoms, floor, angled at 10 o'clock.

Doorbell ringing. Pajama bottoms on. Check.

"Who is this?" I respond. "This is Hannah, who is this?" Why did my stomach feel weird all of a sudden?

"My name is Dr. Rogan," she says, "I'm calling from Santa Monica Hospital."

My fingers go cold. My knees start to shake. I wait, and listen. What did my body know that I didn't?

"I'm sorry, I don't understand," I say. Just like me to apologize for not understanding. It's something I've been doing since first grade.

"Hannah, your husband, John Bernal. He's been in an accident." My heart freezes.

"No?"

"Hannah, is someone there with you?"

"No? Where's John? Where is he?"

"Hannah, Mrs. Bernal—"

"Where is my husband? I need to speak to him! Please! His . . . his chairs are here!"

"Hannah, please," Dr. Rogan says. She's so calm. I hate her. "You need to come down here. You need someone to bring you to the hospital. John was hit by a car. I'm afraid he's—"

"I can't! No!"

("Mommy?")

"No? NO?"

("Mommy?")

"Mrs. Bernal," Dr. Rogan says, "I'm so sorry. I'm afraid John didn't make it—"

"Where is he? I need to see him!" I beg. "He's alive. Ellie's here, he can't—"

"Your husband died in the ambulance. He wasn't alone. I'm sorry . . ."

"Mommy!" Ellie appears, somehow, in front of me. Her huge, round eyes stare up at me. John's huge, round hazel eyes.

The phone rolls out of my hands. I grab Ellie. I look into her eyes, those eyes, John's eyes. Grab her to my chest and hold her tight. I sink my face in her hair. John had washed her hair last night, in the bath. For the last time. John did everything Ellie. John was Ellie, and Ellie, John. She was his shadow. Were they ever apart?

John always took Ellie to the Farmer's Market on these crisp Saturday mornings. He hadn't taken her today. Today was different; Ellie wasn't awake when he left.

Ellie lived.

"I . . . I hate God, Ellie," I say. I start to wail.

"What's wrong, Mommy?" she asks. "What did God do? Why are you crying?"

"I love you, Ellie. Mommy loves you so much."

Now, Ellie was starting to cry.

"Mommy has to call Uncle Jay and, and Auntie Chloe and Auntie Aimee, okay? I'm okay, really, Ellie. I'm okay . . ."

I start dialing Jay. The numbers dance as my fingers fumble.

"Can Daddy make me pancakes?"

My heart stops beating.

"Mommy will make pancakes," I say.

"Mommy doesn't know how to. Daddy knows how to!"

"I'll learn. I promise. I'll learn everything," then, into the phone, "I'll learn everything. Jay. Come here. Come here. I know it's early. Come. Now. It's John . . . please."

Externally, now I am calm. I keep hysteria at bay, away from my voice. To this day, I don't know how.

First five minutes post-worst-case scenario phone call:

Ellie followed me as I checked our bed. I checked it and re-checked it. Spice, our dog. John's dog, circling me, watching.

"Mommy, what are you looking for?"

I threw off the covers, then threw them back on, and looked under the mattress. Then, I went through our closet. Ellie stood there in the doorway.

"Mommy, where's Daddy?"

I ran and checked the kitchen, Ellie's bathroom. I looked in the backyard. The garage.

John?

I scooped Ellie up and squeezed her so tight she started crying again, and then I took her, still in her pajamas, to my neighbor's house, Home-of-The-Extremely-Loud-Comfortable-Using-Swear-Words Children. Four patio chairs, wrapped in plastic, were sitting on her porch.

"Can you . . . feed Ellie?" I asked the tall, sturdy mother-of-thugs, dressed in sweatpants, as she opened the door.

"Oh, Hannah, I signed for your chairs—"

She stopped.

"Can you feed Ellie, please?" I asked. "I'm sorry—"

I heard the familiar, comforting SpongeBob theme song. Proof that the world is normal, and that the phone call was wrong. All wrong. Kids were settling down with cereal bowls in their laps in the living room.

"Are you okay?"

We didn't know each other well. I'm ashamed of this fact. She was friendly with John. I was the third wheel in the neighbor equation.

"I'll be back," I said. I put Ellie down. Hugged her again. She's my everything in last year's Christmas pajamas. The neighbor took Ellie's hand; both stood watching me. The chairs would wait. I ran back to my empty house.

I pulled John's jeans, T-shirts, jockey shorts, socks out of our laundry basket and put them all in a garbage bag. Preserve his smell. Right Guard and aftershave. The dent in his pillow. Don't touch the dent. His notepad. His note to me. The bedcover had ink stains from where he fell asleep, his pen still in his hand. His slippers where I could trip on them. Yesterday's sports section tossed on the rug. I picked it up. John was still alive. Evidence was everywhere! He had to be alive.

I slid back under the covers. And screamed. Spice put his paws on the bed and barked.

A car screeched to a halt on the street, a door slam, another door slam, a voice calling my name. Best Friend Chloe rushed in, breathless. "Hannah, oh Hannah . . . I came as soon as Jay called—what happened, where's John?"

She went down on her knees and kissed my head, then crawled into bed and wrapped her arms around me while I clutched John's pillow. The dent, gone now. Just like that. Chloe smells like motherhood. John's pillow smells like him.

"Accident," my voice is saying.

Next Best Friend Aimee rushed in, *click-click-click*, boot heels and keys and big jangly purse. "Motherfuck, baby—motherfuck—"

She climbs into my bed, too. She smells like an exotic bird.

My Third (and last—I promise) Best Friend Jay is lifting me out of bed. He hasn't bothered shaving. Jay hasn't appeared unshaven since a long-ago Halloween, where he dressed as a scruffy Al Pacino. He holds me, basically carries me to the car. Somehow, we make our way to Santa Monica Hospital. Somehow, we find the room, below ground level, where John lies, waiting. But he's not waiting. He'll never wait for me again. Somehow, I manage to identify his body. He is still warm. He looks . . . perfect. Perfect. His brain, inside his skull, broken.

"But . . . there's nothing wrong with him," I say to the man wearing glasses, dressed in white. We are surrounded by white—white walls, white slabs, white floors. *Are we in heaven?* (It's cold as hell.)

"I'm sorry," I say, apologizing, but for what? Tears make it hard for me to talk. My throat is closing up. Jay is holding me up, his arms literally around my waist, as though I'm a puppet. I'll collapse if he lets go.

"I don't understand. He looks perfect," I say. "John? John?"

John is unmarked, but the brain is like that. Fragile. One blow directly to the back of the head. *Intraparenchymal hemorrhage.* I learn this term. I know it so well, I can spell it backward. Bleeding within the brain tissue.

"I'm sorry, I don't understand," I say. I'm apologizing again.

"I'm sorry," the man says. We are polite with each other, as though we are both mistaken.

"I can't leave him here," I say. "It's too cold. Can I take him home now?"

Jay pulls me away from the white room with the white slabs.

This is the last time I see John.

Until the next time.

3

September Mourning

"This is what we're going to do, my angel," Jay, my partner and first call in joy and tragedy, said. Sadness looked spectacular on him, with his tall, lanky frame, white-blond hair, and cheekbones for days. We were ensconced in my closet, which, prior to today, had been our favorite hideaway, our place to share a glass of wine, analyze shoes, bitch about work and his train wreck of a love life.

Jay sank down next to me in his gunmetal Tom Ford suit and stroked my hair. "Uncle Jay's putting the 'fun' back in funeral," he murmured.

Jay had called the rabbi. Jay made all "the arrangements" as per Jewish custom. Jay had called John's father in New York to tell him his beloved son had died. Jay held me for two nights as I screamed and cried, as my knees and hands shook uncontrollably, as I clutched my stomach and threw up, so many times there was nothing but bile, then so many times there was nothing at all. I wept through Jay's crisp new Prada shirt, ruining it with yesterday's mascara. I dug my nails into his skin, begging him to get John back here, NOW. I heard him, from the next room, as he entertained Ellie, telling her Mommy wasn't feeling well. I heard him pause when she asked for Daddy.

"Come here, Ellie," he said, his voice cracking, "Uncle Jay needs a hug."

And Jay insisted on dressing me for John's funeral. I was too weak to resist his styling overtures. Payback for ruining a Prada shirt is a bitch.

"Here's what I'm visualizing," he said to the heap on the floor. That would be me. This was the first time I'd seen him in the last three days without Ellie attached to his hip.

"Elizabeth Taylor at Mike Todd's funeral," Jay said, then put his hand to his chest. "It's going to be hard, I'm not going to lie to you, but I think we can pull off the bouffant—dream big, darlings."

We weren't alone. A petite blonde clutching a bundle of sage shook her hand; her Buddhist bracelets (or Hindu? I can never remember what religion bracelets are) stirred. Chloe Clybourne Lew wore an Indian prayer shawl and a floor-length tie-dyed silk dress, with no discernible makeup on a face Avedon would have stood in line to photograph. We'd been very close since my first official day of pregnancy in Dr. Scofield's office. Now she was not having it. "Bouffant is another word for cancer. You know, of course, that hairspray causes global warming and birth defects." In the background, I heard dogs barking and whining at my back door. Chloe had not arrived unattended; rescue dogs were her gay male escorts. She took them everywhere.

"Birth defects?" I asked. This didn't sound right.

"Babies don't even have hair," Jay sniffed.

"The science is right there on my blog," Chloe said.

"Whatever. I'm not going to let the planet get between my girl and her 'do," Jay said.

Chloe was tirelessly concerned for everyone's welfare—stray dogs, Planet Earth, the homeless, Darfur, and me. *And would not let any of us forget it.* Even after her husband, Billy the Asian Republican, lost his investment banking job, she had to be reminded to stop writing thousand-dollar checks to Doctors Without Borders or the American Cancer Society, as if the checks were parking change.

I met Chloe the day I learned I was pregnant. Seven months along, she was Westside P.C. from her Bolivian peasant blouse to her sandals made in a women's shelter in Kenya to her almond-eyed children, who had jumped out of the Benetton catalog and were reading, drawing, and occasionally questioning Chloe in their "obstetrician voices." I watched them, in awe. I watched her, in awe. *People like this did not exist.*

"How many do you have?" she'd asked me.

"How many what?"

"Children," she said, looking at me cradling my tummy, as though keeping safe whatever was in there. "Which number is this?"

"Kids? Oh, I don't have any kids," I said. "You're looking at a miracle." Since John, my whole life had become a miracle. I had a warm, sweet home, a man who loved me. And now . . . a baby. *Me*.

Little did I know, I had just become Chloe Clybourne Lew's latest Very Special Project.

"Jay, drop the teasing comb," Chloe said. As Jay's eyes pleaded with me, we heard a *click-click-click* . . . and Angelina Jolie's slightly used older sister rushed in on five-inch heels, smelling of cigarettes and drinks with a Romanian spy in a Parisian bistro.

"I feel like shit," Aimee Le Fleur said. "How's my girl?" In her fishnet tights, diamond stud earrings from Disappointed Suitor, Spring 1996, and sleek black dress, she looked like Ms. Jolie working undercover. *In other words, impossible to miss.*

I'd met Aimee a hundred years ago, when I was a young buck casting assistant and she was a young buck actress. She came in to read, and I demanded to know where she got her shoes. She demanded a callback, and she would tell me. A draw. We both won. She nailed the gig, and her shoe size is the same as mine, so I borrow what I can't buy.

"Is this your first funeral, Aimee?" Chloe asked. "You know this isn't about you, right? Fishnet stockings, really?"

"Eff off, Princess," Aimee said. "We can't all rock the burlap look."

"Can we not fight, children?" Jay pleaded. "Mother's under enough pressure here."

To my knowledge, this *was* Aimee's first funeral. Aimee studiously avoided all things potentially unpleasant—children, dogs, plants, Renée Zellweger comedies, and love. She folded her long legs under her and I snuggled onto her shoulder.

"Indira Chloe raised her voice first," Aimee said, pouting.

"Jay wants to turn John's funeral into a Broadway musical," Chloe said.

"And that's bad, how?" Jay asked, waving the teasing comb. "Wait, before we go any further. Just . . . take a look."

He pulled a hatbox out of a shopping bag. "Florence of Miami sent her." Florence, Jay's mom, had hopes that her 6′4″ Nordic god progeny was going to be the world's most famous drag queen. That's the kind of mother she was.

"Jay," Aimee said, "this is not the Kentucky Derby."

Jay opened the hatbox . . . and brought out a veil. I am not kidding.

"I'm not wearing a veil," I said.

"Don't you want to be fashion-forward?" Jay asked.

"I didn't even wear a veil at my wedding," I pointed out.

"To my eternal dismay," Jay said.

"Wedding?" Aimee said. "Standing in line at the courthouse behind a guy with prison tats and a girl with shaved eyebrows—"

"I don't know why you didn't have it in my backyard," Chloe said. "I had a Hindu priestess, a certified vegan caterer, Native American four-piece band . . ."

"And I just lost hearing in one ear," Jay said. "Girls, you know how I love a white wedding. Well, Hannah's was the most romantic wedding I've ever been to."

I looked up at Jay, and he grabbed my hand. Aimee checked her Cartier watch from Disappointed Suitor, Fall 2007. "Ten minutes, people. Let's get this show on the road."

"Aimee," Jay said, "this is an iconic moment in Hannah's life. Let them wait."

"After all," Chloe said, "it's not like John's going anywhere."

We all looked at Chloe, who clapped her hand over her mouth. Jay burst out laughing. It was so absurd, choosing the right shoes and hairstyle for my husband's funeral. I wondered whose tragic life I had stumbled into. I had to laugh, too, through my tears. Even Aimee tried laughing, though it looked like a struggle. In the midst of my grief, I thought Aimee could lay off Professor Botox for a couple weeks.

The 405 freeway was suspiciously uncrowded. Where were all the normal people—the "norms," Jay and I called them—rushing to normal events? I looked out the window at gray skies. I couldn't take the thought of rain. John hated rain.

Where are you? I thought. *Why did you leave me?*

"I wish we'd have brought Ellie," Jay said. "I feel like I'm lying to my little darling."

I had been to funerals before. Mom and Dad's funeral—that was a biggie. Emotionally, I mean; there were no attendance records broken. I'd decided not to bring Ellie. This could have been a bad call. But look, when you are forced to decide whether to take your preschooler to her daddy's funeral, then you can judge.

"She had the perfect dress," Jay said.

"Ellie's way too young," Chloe said. "Check my mommy blog."

"Please don't talk about your mommy blog," Aimee said. "I beg you."

"Ellie would have looked exquisite," Jay said. "I'm just thinking of the photographs." Uncle Jay had bought Ellie the perfect two-hundred-dollar dress for a kid who's going to a fancy wedding, high tea, or, you know, Daddy's funeral. Ellie had opened the big box with the rope handle and squealed. It was a Jenny Kayne midnight-blue silk dress with an empire waistline.

"She makes children's clothes?" I had asked, pulling John's old gray robe tighter and wiping my nose with the sleeve. I had slept in this robe for two nights.

"Where do you think the money is?" Jay said. "Kids and dogs, sweetheart." He was slipping the dress over Ellie's chubby arms, held high above her head. It was their personal *Dancing with the Stars* routine.

"Divine!" Jay said, as Ellie twirled, pausing before the heavy an-tique mirror in the living room, placed to give the small room a feeling of depth. "Look at my angel—she's Audrey Hepburn!" he said, then whispered, "It's perfect for the f-u-n-e-r-a-l."

The truth about Ellie, my glowing, effervescent daughter, is that she has a little weight problem. Okay, she's a chunk. I feel terrible even talking about this. She's chubby, cute, but at certain angles, chubby, uh-oh. Like Michelle Obama could come after her with a calorie counter. In my neighborhood, the kids are thin as knives.

"Ixnay on the uneral-fay," I said.

"Fine," he said. "I'll take her to the MOCA opening for Murikami."

"Please don't turn her into the girl from the Grinch."

"God no. That kid looks like a walking STD," Jay said. He refused to believe there was anything "wrong" with "his" child. Since her six-month half-birthday, he'd taken her to breakfast at the Polo Lounge, sushi at Katsuya, charity balls at the Beverly Hilton, fund-raisers in Brentwood mansions, and premieres at Grauman's Chinese Theatre. He dressed her like royalty, or, you know, Suri.

Jay had an ongoing one-sided rivalry with Suri Cruise.

"We wore that last week!" Jay would yell at a picture of the littlest Cruise in *People* magazine. "That whole sailor look—Ellie's already played that, sister!"

I'd look over his shoulder, and indeed, there'd be Suri, wearing one of Ellie's outfits.

"Suri is gorgeous and sweet and she's being raised by people who are very close to seemingly human," I'd say. "What about that Jolie-Pitt brood?"

"Well, I adore me some Shiloh. She knows exactly who she is. Flannel has a name and that name is Shiloh. I say, more power to her. Own it, girl! You do you!"

We'd left Ellie at the neighbor's house, watching loud cartoons, as though the world was still making good on its promises.

The limo turned onto Hillside Memorial driveway and parked in front of a big white building. "You look beautiful, honey," Jay said. "Like Kim Novak beautiful."

I pulled the veil over my face. I understood why widows wore veils. Grief changes a face. You're unrecognizable, even to yourself. Your facial geography is redrawn, as though gravity has struck, suddenly and indelibly.

I teetered into an auditorium filled with faces, familiar and unfamiliar. Whose life is this? *Why?*

"Goodness," Jay whispered, as he held me up. "Standing room only."

"John was so beloved," Chloe said, as she started weeping and snapped pictures with her iPhone.

"No," Aimee said, snatching the phone. "You are not twitpic-ing John's funeral."

"Are memorial services the new singles bar?" Jay asked.

I focused; the attendees were 25–45, in the warm-to-on-fire range. John's fan base was young and included gay men and single women. Based on his series, they must have thought he was single, or didn't care that he was married. L.A. Moral Standards = Champagne Bentley + Malibu Colony beach house minus wife and kids.

"They're dressed like they're going to Vegas to see Sting," Aimee sniffed. Aimee was not ready to hand over her "Prettiest One in the Room" trophy. These Brookes and Jasmines would have to pry it from her cold, dead hands. *Pardon the expression.*

"Facebook," Jay said, as though Facebook were the explanation for everything. "Hold your head high, Hannah. You're Liz Taylor, remember? Let's give them a show."

He kissed my hand. With as much dignity and balance as I could muster on Louboutin stilettos (a funeral gift from Uncle Jay) I made the most glamorous entrance of my life, as though this were the movie version of "My Husband's Funeral" starring Hannah Marsh Bernal.

Sophia, Ava, Ingrid, and La Liz, herself, would have been proud.

* * *

The Grief Team and I had agreed to let Chloe speak for me at the funeral. Chloe was the earthy, poetic one. She would choose the right words to capture the man who was my husband.

I still couldn't find those words. I tried. I didn't have any sonnets in my head, no poetic verse I could conjure up. I couldn't do it then, couldn't do it now. Maybe when I'm very old, and have distance over time and space, distance and memory loss.

Chloe made her way to the podium. I waited for her to tell everyone how wonderful John was, in every single way that I could think of. Even the ways that made me crazy. She would tell them he was a giving husband and father, kind to animals, plants, and made magic with crushed garlic . . . and I was going to die without him.

"I've always had a crush on John," Chloe said, into the microphone.

After that, I blanked out. Jay finally raced up and wrestled the microphone from Chloe, who was rhapsodizing about John's veal piccata for an uncomfortably long time (especially for a vegan).

"So," Jay said, into the microphone, "I've always had a crush on John."

The most popular boy had married me, the geeky girl. Without him, I was nothing. Without him, I would disappear.

Jay had planned a small memorial for a few select people at my home. "Let people give you their condolences," Jay said, when I objected. "Let people say goodbye."

"I don't want to say goodbye," I wept. "I never want to say goodbye."

I sat on my couch, Spice at my feet, and received the sad faces, the nervous smiles, the plates of homemade squash risotto, the tears rolling down big men's faces and the shaky grips of slender women. That night, after the "festivities," Aimee and I relaxed outside in John's new patio chairs, under my avocado tree, and shared a cigarette. I hadn't smoked in a decade. Chloe came out with a pile of laundry under her arms. She'd been cleaning house since the last mourner had left.

"Everything's under control," Chloe said. "The dishes are out of the dishwasher. I have raw, organic vegan meals for two weeks in the freezer."

"Discomfort food," Aimee said. "Sit, Chloe. You're making me crazy. More crazy than usual."

"Chloe, what are you doing with those clothes?" I asked.

"Laundry. I brought my own nontoxic detergent."

"No!" I said, shooting up from my chair. "No . . . no laundry—"

"But it's just dirty clothes," she said. "They were all in a garbage bag."

"They were in there for a reason," I said, as I tore through the basket. "I have to keep John's scent, don't you see? I have to keep him." White and black T-shirts. Calvin Klein jockey shorts. Socks. I grabbed the basket and ran into the kitchen. I could feel Chloe's and Aimee's eyes on me.

"No laundry!" I said, slamming the door behind me.

4

Wife After Death

Beyond the shock and the horror, there's just so much . . . stuff. That box of Sweet'N Low in the cupboard? No one drinks coffee with Sweet'N Low. No one except John. I always told him that one day, that stuff would kill him. *Way to prove me wrong.*

"Does the Salvation Army take Sweet'N Low?" Jay asked, as we cleaned out cupboards in the kitchen. John's kitchen. His wood chopping block marked by pot burns and oil spills, nicks from his set of Henckels knives.

"Chrysalis won't take it," Chloe said, talking about an "exclusive" homeless shelter in Santa Monica. "They only allow Stevia. It's natural."

"Of course," I said. "What do I call John? Is he still my husband?"

"Of course, he's still your husband," Chloe answered.

"In a year? Will he be my husband in a year?"

Chloe and Jay exchanged glances. Here's the thing about death—it's unlike any other game you've played (unless you've played gin with Aimee)—there are no rules.

"What about my wedding ring?" I ask. "It makes me feel like I'm lying. But if I take it off, I'm really alone."

"You want me to make you some grieving tea?" Chloe asks. *How do I tell her that I am all tead out?*

"No thanks, baby," I say. Chloe and Jay are helping me sort

through John's belongings. What to keep, what to donate, what to toss. So far, I've kept everything. I stop Jay when he's about to throw out a small jar. "What if I need fish stock base?" I ask. I'm not even sure what fish stock base is.

"It's expired," Jay said, "September."

"The fish base went at the same time as John," I said. "That means something. I have to keep it."

Grieving is difficult in a world where bad news doesn't exist, a world known as Santa Monica, California. Every day is a sunny 72 degrees, except in the early mornings, when the fog rolls in. I'm up early to spend quality time with my fog. The fog and I, we have an understanding; the fog "gets" me. But soon enough, here comes eight o'clock, and it abandons me, surrendering to blue skies and fresh, ocean breezes. And that sun, that damn sun. Santa Monicans act like they can "catch" bad news. I think it's because everyone's so healthy. Grieving widows, a living sign of human vulnerability, are as welcome as chlamydia. (Unless, I imagine, you're a vegan, recycling widow.)

I live in NoMo, the fashionable side, North of Montana Avenue, in a Spanish-style bungalow. NoMo has wide, tree-lined streets curving toward the ocean, large, expansive homes, and swimming pools. SoMo, South of Montana, has apartments and condos, small homes, a few anemic-looking trees, and the dreaded parking issue. In these parts, Montana Avenue is our 8 Mile.

"Fashionable," however, doesn't describe my home. Casa Sugar has two bedrooms, almost two baths; it's what's known in real estate parlance as "charming." Charming, if you like old, spotty plumbing. Charming, if you like raising mice. Charming, if you want to get to know drywall specialists. Casa Sugar is a 1920s vestige from when wealthy people built beachside bungalows to live in during the summer months. These homes are a dying breed; they're rapidly being torn down and replaced by marble and cement "Mediterranean" monoliths.

In my little backyard is a beautiful hundred-year-old avocado tree. My Realtor—who knew Trish, the widow who'd lived there close to fifty years—told me the tree was the reason she'd bought it. I believe her. Monet would have painted this tree had he lived in NoMo instead of Giverny.

Over the years, I had saved a reasonable amount of money for a down payment, and had been searching for a charming (small, extreme fixer-upper) bargain. I'd almost given up when my Realtor called, and in her gravelly New Jersey accent, intoned: "We got somethin' here, geez, you better come see it. It's nothing to look at, frankly, but it's cheap. They got it on the historical registry, you won't believe it."

Historical registry. Music to my ears. The price would be more reasonable, as developers wouldn't want to swoop in—there was no upside to buying a tiny house where the lot was worth more than the structure.

Walking into Casa Sugar was like taking a trip in a time machine. A step-down living room. Original moldings. Antique lamps and ashtrays. A Japanese screen from the 1920s. Hard candies in carnival glass dishes. Silver-framed eight-by-ten glossies of a black-haired beauty with bow lips and arresting eyes. The widow Trish had been some looker, way back when. On the counter in the tiny kitchen, a notepad with careful cursive writing.

Trish's heirs were looking for a quick sale. Anyone with half a brain would have walked away. Well, apparently, I don't possess half a brain, because I loved Casa Sugar. She was like me, outmoded and in need of cosmetic work.

My daughter, Ellie, named our house when she was barely two (proof of Ellie's genius). Casa looks like a big sugar cube, with thick white walls and deep blue accents. I'd seen some crappy movie shot in Greece with Daryl Hannah, a French chick, and the actor with the eyebrows, in a tame ménage à trois. I don't remember the sex (I don't think about sex anymore); what I remembered was the architecture, the predominant colors: dazzling white and sharp, almost severe, blues.

Casa Sugar became my Mykonos.

John and I had plans for a trip to Greece next summer. We'd be quaffing ouzo and eating fried octopus under a blazing Aegean sun. He was going to finish up *Greek for Bachelors;* I was going to take a month off from work. We had our itinerary mapped out. I still can't bring myself to call the hotel or airlines to cancel. Maybe I'll take Ellie. I can't tell you how screwed up it is that I won't make it there with John. Unless I bring his ashes with me.

(Note to self: *YouTube "How to pack your husband's ashes for romantic trip to Greece."*)

Build it and he will come. It turns out that all I had to do to attract the right man was to spend all of my life savings. When John showed up, I was like a male peacock, but instead of flashing tail feathers, I wooed him with hardware. He didn't fall in love with me so much as my doorknobs. Don't laugh. Those brushed brass doorknobs are very special. I receive a Christmas card from Restoration Hardware every year. And do you think I bought copper pots for my health? I don't think so.

Ellie had missed her preschool's field trip to the Santa Monica Aquarium on the pier. Basically, I had neglected to fill out the field trip form. John had been our designated field trip form filler-outer.

"Don't worry, Ellie," I said, after I realized my (hundredth) slip-up. "Mommy will take you to the pier."

The Grief Team wasn't about to let me drive yet, so Chloe volunteered her services. She'd be spending the morning working at the Santa Monica Animal Shelter, which was just up the street.

"Today might be a good day to tell her," Chloe said, as she dropped us off on Ocean Avenue, just east of the pier. Ellie was standing on the grass, under a palm tree, just outside of earshot.

"Great idea, why don't I just ruin the aquarium for her?" I said.

I turned to look at Ellie, who was concentrating on a dandelion she'd pulled out of the ground.

"Children know a lot more than we think," Chloe said.

"Go blog yourself," I said, joking, then called out to Ellie, "C'mon, sweetheart, let's go see some fish."

Ellie had closed her eyes and was blowing on the dandelion. She was making a wish.

I knew what it was.

* * *

We wandered into the small, open, bright blue building with a sign that read SANTA MONICA AQUARIUM. I was happy to see it wasn't crowded. Ellie shied away as an older woman, a volunteer wearing a blue shirt with a nametag that read JUDY, approached.

"Welcome to the Aquarium," Judy said, then smiled at Ellie. "My, you have a pretty sweater on." Ellie stared impassively back at her.

"We're just going to look around," I said. "Ellie wants to touch the sea stars, and maybe see an octopus, isn't that right, honey? And she is really excited about the seahorse exhibit."

Ellie frowned.

"Oh, the seahorse exhibit is very special," Judy said. "If you have any questions, I'm here to help."

Ellie and I cruised the aquarium, from the shark egg tanks to the moray eel exhibit. I could feel her relax as we observed the sea life around us. She became more verbal, less anxious. Ellie sat on my lap as she drew a picture of a humpback whale at the children's art table, and looked back at me, smiling. When we spied an octopus at the bottom of a big tank, camouflaged as a rock with goggly eyeballs, she laughed out loud. My daughter and I were experiencing a glimmer of normal life.

There was no way I could introduce the concept of a dead father into this near-perfect morning. I shoved the idea, along with my guilt, to the back of my mind as we pushed on to the seahorse exhibit.

Ellie pulled me over by the hand. The seahorses were out in force, gliding like water fairies on the current, their tails loosely attached to long strands of sea grass.

I squinted and read the information card on the tank, then paraphrased for Ellie. "Honey, the female seahorse, the mommies, lay the eggs, but the male seahorses, the daddies, carry the babies until they're born. Isn't that amazing?"

Ellie pressed her nose up against the tank as Judy appeared at our side. "Are you enjoying your tour?" she asked.

Ellie nodded and smiled at Judy this time, a big grin. "The daddy seahorses are like my daddy," she blurted out. "My daddy carried me around when I was a baby all the time. Right, Mommy?"

She turned her little face up to me, her round eyes accentuated by her wire-rimmed glasses.

"Yes, Ellie," I said softly. "I don't think Daddy put you down for a whole year."

"Your father must be very special," Judy said.

"Oh, he is. He's not here right now," Ellie said, as though she were reassuring Judy. "He's visiting somewhere. But he's coming back. Soon."

Judy's eyes skipped to mine momentarily, then back to Ellie. "I'm sure he is, dear," she said.

"Very soon, like at dinnertime," Ellie said. Judy smiled at her, patted her shoulder, then left to help a family full of kids find the touch tanks. Ellie and I sat back on a bench in front of the seahorse exhibit.

The seahorses were mesmerizing, with their rainbow sherbet coloring and their quiet domestic contentment. I found myself wishing I could climb inside the tank and gaze soothingly at disquieted humans.

"Ellie, do you think seahorses talk to each other?" I asked. "Like, do you think they discuss the weather, or who they played with at school?"

The biggest one of the brood of seahorses was staring me down. "Ellie?"

I turned. Ellie was gone. I looked around. I stood and whirled around—Ellie wasn't on the other side of the tank. I couldn't see her anywhere.

"Ellie?" I called out. "Ellie!"

The aquarium was starting to get crowded with kids. The sound level was rising.

"Ellie? Where are you?!"

I couldn't possibly have lost my daughter. "Ellie!" I yelled. I was starting to lose feeling in my hands. My knees were getting weak. "Ellie!"

I was spinning. Where was she? I had looked away for one second.

"Ellie!"

Oh, God, I'm the worst mom ever—oh, God, oh God—"Ellie! Where are you?!"

"Miss?" Judy appeared, and grabbed my shoulder. "Miss, your daughter's fine."

"Mommy, I'm fine." Ellie was standing next to Judy.

"She was over by the octopus."

"Mommy, I was over by the octopus," Ellie repeated, and took my hand. I grabbed her to my side.

"Are you okay? Do you need some water?" Judy asked.

"I'm fine, sorry. I'm just . . . I got so scared," I said, then bent down to look my daughter in the eye. My knees were still shaking. "Ellie, please don't ever do that to Mommy again. Promise Mommy."

"I promise," Ellie said. "I promise I won't leave you forever."

She hugged me. I buried my face in her hair. When Chloe picked us up, I informed her that we had a great time, and we would never be going anywhere again.

Have you had a loved one die? A family member? A child? God forbid, don't even think about it. *Ptew, ptew*—wave your hands over your head. Okay. How about a husband or boyfriend or wife or girlfriend?

Here's what you don't realize when it happens. You're going to walk around for days, weeks, calling his name, and getting annoyed when he doesn't answer. Like he's ignoring you instead of what he's doing, which is being dead. You're going to leave a message on his voice mail and wonder why he didn't return the call. Then, you're going to call just to hear his voice. You're going to forget something at the grocery store and think, well, he'll pick it up for you. You're going to wonder what he's making for dinner tonight. Because he always made dinner. You're going to hope he's not experimenting, like the night he made sand dabs with licorice glaze. The pharmacist will call to have you pick up John's new prescription for Ambien. You're going to wonder why he needed Ambien. What was keeping him up at night?

You will pick it up, because you need to sleep. You're not sleeping at all, but when you do finally, finally fall asleep, you see him in your dreams and he's so alive in your dreams, you make love to him, he holds you, you talk. You will be crying when you wake up. Waking is the enemy, yet dreams are torture.

The September sky was ink black and dotted with stars. As Spice stood sentry at Ellie's bedroom door, Jay and I snuggled on the ground in the backyard like lovers under a blanket, sharing a second bottle of Trader Joe's seven-dollar pinot. We weren't in the State of Lucid.

"I see the first guy I slept with," Jay said, staring at the stars. "The Constellation Cyrus. Look at the size of that celestial body."

I thought about Ellie, fast asleep in her room. "Kids are so resilient," I said. "I don't want her to forget . . . When she laughs, I feel like she's forgetting . . ."

"They're not that goddamned resilient. I remember every bad moment of my childhood. Ask your therapist."

"I don't have one," I said. "I have you, I have my Grief Team."

"A crazy dog lady, the poster child for narcissistic personality disorder, *et moi*, Miss Lonely Hearts."

"When do you need me back at work?" I asked, changing the subject. Jay hadn't brought up work, but I know it had to be wearing on him. Jay shifted. I could smell his signature scent above the jasmine. If I had to guess the name, "Rodeo Park Men's Stall" might be about right.

"Whenever you're ready," he said. "I could definitely use your people skills—but take as much time as you need. Within reason. Tomorrow morning good?"

I laughed. I was the wrangler. I was good at coddling talent (using the term "talent" loosely), making them believe I was listening to their complaints when I was actually thinking about lunch.

"Tell me a story, Uncle Jay," I said. "Are Kevin and Karli still together? Have they had a baby yet?" Kevin and Karli were the married, D-level stars of our semi-successful reality show. Think Tori and Dean, lite. Yes, I said *lite*.

"They'd have to have sex—with each other," Jay said. "He's not a fan of the punany. He has a T-shirt with a circle around a punany, with the punany crossed out."

"Even money says they hire a surrogate," I said.

"Too easy," Jay said. He looked at his BlackBerry, then started to get up.

"You're leaving?" I whined.

"Hidalgo," he said.

"Married," I intoned.

"Hello? Green card. His wife understands."

"This is you talking," I said. "This is what I hear—blah, blah, blah, wife."

"I love you, despite your lack of respect for romance," Jay said. "Don't stay out here too long. Cold."

He kissed the top of my head. I held on to his hands.

"I love you more, despite your romanticism," I said, stumbling over the "cism" part. *Hi, Wine Tongue.* I listened as the screen door shut. A moment later, I heard Jay's MINI Cooper as it rolled down the street.

I reached for my glass. My eyelids were getting heavy. Did this mean I would sleep? *How about a pleasant dream? How about we leave Salvador Dalí at home tonight?*

"Well," I said, "tonight I sleep." I shivered. The night had suddenly turned frigid.

"It's not true, you know," a woman's voice said.

I sucked in my breath. Maybe it was the neighbor. Her kids still up?

"Hello?"

"What they say," the voice said. It sounded like an older woman.

"Oh my God," I said. Someone was toying with me. *Ellie!* How many steps to the door? Where's my phone? Why didn't I bring my phone outside?

Slowly, I rose to my feet. My knees were shaking.

"So . . . what do they say?" I said, trying to seem calm. I moved toward the door, jumping as I knocked over my wineglass.

"That you can sleep after you're dead. Not true."

I lunged for the door. It was jammed. I jiggled the door handle. Spice barked from inside.

"I love what you've done with the house, by the way," she said.

My eyes were on the kitchen counter. The knife I'd used to cut open a bag of frozen cauliflower was still there. No one eats cauliflower, it turns out. I had to get that doorknob fixed. Nothing would ever get fixed again. Faucets, doorknobs, cauliflower, my life. *Oh, John. Where are you?*

"Thank you?" I said. I felt a cold rush of air behind me. The door would not open. Finally, I summoned my courage, and turned around. I saw no one there, but the swing hanging from the avocado tree was swaying in the breeze.

5

The Town Crier

I am trying to remember to do two things: eat and sleep. Per Chloe's advice (also posted on her blog at NoMoMama.com—named for our neighborhood), I'd started leaving Post-it Notes for things I've forgotten. Like where my daughter is. Or did I eat breakfast? Or where did I leave those darn Post-it Notes? Widowhood was sort of like Alzheimer's, without the funny. I put Post-it Notes with the words EAT and SLEEP in big black letters on my bathroom mirror. I'm bone tired but I don't sleep at all. My brain is on overdrive, tracking every memory of John and pinning it down, saving it to be filed, alphabetically and chronologically. I'm beyond the point of exhaustion, but still I strive to remember; I'm in a waking coma, but am afraid to forget. I'm desperate not to forget.

Remember caring for that first baby? Remember utter fatigue? Same feeling, same recipe, but add loss. My girlfriend was on an overnight flight to London with her four-week-old baby boy, who wouldn't stop crying. She sat in the dark, with her wailing baby. And prayed for the plane to crash.

Metaphorically, I'm not far from there. I'm scared as hell, and braced for impact as I lie wide awake, holding Ellie in my arms.

My brain switched on early this morning. The faintest light emerged shyly behind tall palm trees, which appeared like skinny old ladies wearing outlandish hats. Late September now. The air has changed. The Santa Anas are kicking in, tossing palm fronds and pinecones from the skies, leaving my lips parched, carrying the elusive promise of the Big One. Oh, how I pray for the Big One.

Soon, the sky is so clear, the outline of the palm trees against the blue is etched and almost painful to behold. The world is in HD, but I don't want to see clearly. I need my fog. Bring it back, my mind says. Blur the lines of my reality until there's nothing left to see, nothing at all.

The day John wandered into my life—wait, he was hopping on one leg—I was dogsitting. This is a story that ends well. Which is more than I can hope for me, now.

Jay has a dog. I'm using the term "dog" loosely because Ralph is not a "dog" to Jay. He is a child, a gift from God, the sole inheritor to his estate—if you call a restored craftsman near Main Street in Santa Monica an estate—which I do, by the way.

Ralph has all the attributes of a child—if that child has received every Snickers bar, every Grand Theft Auto game, every iTouch app his little mean heart desired—in a bichon frise body. Jay feeds him organic, grass-fed filet mignon and strains his morning mango juice. He sleeps with him on a hypoallergenic pillow. If you are reading this and you are a dog, quick, find a gay man to raise you.

Ralph has his own website, Twitter feed, YouTube videos, Facebook fan page. And book deal. Ralph is a horror film with a Swarovski collar.

Fool that I am, I agreed to babysit Ralph. I lost him after twenty minutes.

Ralph, the Paris Hilton of canines, was gone for two days. Fortunately, Jay was in Miami. There's no reaching Jay once he hits South Beach. It's fifty-fifty whether anyone will ever see him again. Jay falls deeply, madly, for-the-last-time-ever-I-mean-it in love about as often as Madonna changes identities. And sometimes, it seems, with the same men Madonna falls in love with.

Gay Cuban men are his Kryptonite. Who can resist a gorgeous

man with a 28-inch waistline who can samba? I don't want to meet the person who can.

I had five days to find Ralph. I put up flyers (next to "OLD DOG NEEDS ARTHRITIS MEDICINE" and "DECLAWED CAT," oh, and the "TURTLE MISSING" flyer—*how far could it possibly get?*). I hired two pet detectives. One was a high school girl who dressed like an anime character. I fired her after fifteen minutes. The other was Sheila, a fashion-defiant lesbian (overalls) with a van and a jones for conspiracy theories. Sheila warned me that Ralph could have been dognapped for ransom. (Ralph did have Internet stalkers.) Or, he had been eaten by coyotes.

"Coyotes don't go where there are green tea soy lattes," I said. "They know the rules."

"Dude, they're right on your street, at dusk," Sheila answered, as we stood in my front yard. "You'd better find Ralph before they do." Apparently, my safe, quiet, palm-tree-lined street was a molten river of teacup poodle blood (and Swarovski crystals).

In the midst of this discussion, a convertible VW pulled up in front of the house. "Hi," a man said as he exited the car, then winced as he hopped toward us. "Are either of you 310-555-1314?"

In my head, Jay was saying, "This man is Shit Hot."

Chloe would say he looks like he would be a good father.

Aimee? *He's too good-looking. Don't trust him.*

I had read a dozen relationship books while bathing in an Epsom salt bath, wearing a flowered shower cap. *Sexy, huh?* I was not exactly a cougar, or even a lemur. I read: *Love Your Man Despite Everything, Seven Steps to Getting Him* and its sister book *Seven Steps to Keeping Him,* and *Lasting Relationships: Why You Won't Have One.* Different from my usual fare, Gabriel García Márquez, Philip Roth, Raymond Chandler. And that Churchill biography I've been meaning to crack. For ten years.

Apparently, when it came to men, I'd been doing everything wrong.

The books claimed I was too assertive. From forty on, I would not make the first move. Upon meeting an attractive man, I was not to speak first, under any circumstances (even a natural disaster). This would be my Kilimanjaro.

I was too loud. Now I would speak softly, and without a hint of sarcasm. I hoped I wouldn't strain a neck muscle.

I tended to be overly enthusiastic. *"Hi, I'm Hannah do you like scary movies I hate scary movies I'm not crazy about the Lakers I love the Dodgers I don't understand jazz I hurt my wrist doing Pilates you want to go out sometime like tonight?"* The men who found me attractive were most likely deaf in one ear. If I were to meet an attractive man, I was not to make suggestions on where to eat, what movie to see, or what the names of our children should be.

I WAS NOT TO SLEEP WITH A MAN ON THE FIRST DATE. Trust me, this needs to be in all caps. These books wanted me to wait not three dates, but three *months*.

No problem. I had not met anyone (schizophrenics spinning in their underwear at the Promenade don't count) in six months and had not had sex in about seven. Or more. (Why are we arguing about this? Don't be mean.) It was the longest dry spell of my adult life. I was in a race with the State of California for longest drought. Let's just say, when John hopped into my life, he looked like a rib eye in faded jeans and a black cotton T-shirt.

But now I knew the rules. He'd have to speak first. Which he did. Sheila looked at me while I stared at John, the man who would impregnate me, marry me, and then, die on me.

"That's her," Sheila finally said.

"Ah, okay, I think I have her dog," he addressed Sheila. God knows what he was thinking about the mute with the wild hair (that would be me).

"Ralph?" Sheila lit up.

"I think it's Ralph," the man said. "Honestly, it was hard for me to get him in the car. He bit my shin when I tried to pick him up."

"Are you single—I mean, bleeding?" I snapped to, just in time to humiliate myself.

"I'm fine. I'm used to it. I grew up with a lot of cousins. Someone was always getting bit, usually me. I must taste good. Let me just get him out—"

He looked at me. "On second thought, you do it."

I strutted to his car, channeling Naomi Campbell on her way to court. I worked it like RuPaul, sweetheart. Ralph was sitting on a folded towel in the backseat, assessing me imperiously. Every morning, like a prayer, I spritzed on L'Instant de Guerlain. It made me feel like a svelte Parisian without all the hard work, like sneering and dieting. John sneezed.

Great.

I picked up Ralph and took quick measure of John's looks. Solid. Lush eyebrows. *(I'm an eyebrow obsessor—if there were an eyebrow porn website, I'd be on it daily.)* Thick dark hair, a few grays. Those serious hazel eyes.

"Nice house," he said, looking at his future home. "You know, I've never met a dog that didn't like me. Women, yes. Dogs, no."

This nonassertive thing was getting exhausting. I'd need a nap if I kept it up.

"What was Ralph doing at the time he bit you?" I asked.

"I don't know, nothing really. He was just sitting outside a sushi restaurant."

"Interesting. Ralph loves sushi." I looked at Mr. Gorgeous. "And how did you address him?"

"Uh, I said . . . hey, ah . . . hey, doggie. Hey, little doggie."

"Oh, see. Ralph hates that. He finds it patronizing. First of all, he doesn't think he's a dog. Ralph, in fact, is larger than life. He has a website, thirty-three hundred Facebook friends. He tweets. He likes and expects recognition. Did you offer him a tuna roll?"

Now it was John's turn to be mute.

"Where are you from?" I asked.

"The city."

"I figured that. Manhattan."

"Guilty."

"Do you smoke or drink?"

"No . . . and . . ." (PLEASE GOD. Don't make him an "I'm in recovery" guy. I always wonder if I'm supposed to look for scars.) "Yes." (THANK YOU.)

"Own anything?" (At this point, a skateboard would do.)

"This car. No, scratch that—I lease it. Oh, wait, I have my saxophone—"

"Musician?"

"I wouldn't call what I do music."

"Jazz?" I scrunched up my nose. Three things I don't understand: jazz, the Dallas Cowboys, and thick-bread sandwiches.

"I'm sorry," he said.

"Drugs," I concluded. It wasn't a question.

"Advil." He smiled. "I got it bad." Ooh, that smile. He still had human teeth. Westsiders go to the cosmetic dentist for horses. I know women whose veneers make them look like Mr. Ed, but less attractive. If these toothy broads ask me a question, I answer by banging my foot on the floor, twice for yes, once for no.

"Gayish or straightish?" I asked. Better get this out of the way now, trust me. He laughed, showing off distinct crow's-feet, which I had the sudden urge to lick. *The perfect response. He was straight! Yay, me!*

"Last meal?" The Final Test. L.A. men don't eat. They're all watching their waistlines. If I actually dated, I'd starve to death.

"Tie between Joe's Stone Crab and a margarita or Baby Blues in Venice, washed down with a couple Red Labels. I'm a chef, so food is, I don't know—let's put it this way, my last girlfriend was jealous of all the attention I gave my meat loaf."

My breath caught in my chest. "You're a chef?"

"A private chef, but I'm thinking about writing a cookbook series."

"What a coincidence," I said, "I like to eat. You want to come in, see my doorknobs?"

"I usually don't do that on the first date," he said.

"This isn't a date," I said.

"But I brought you a dog."

"That would be the worst thing to bring me on a date."

John laughed. "This is never going to work out, you know."

"You haven't even seen my hardware." I sashayed past Sheila.

"You need me to hang out?" Sheila asked, eyeballing John.

"It's okay," I said, watching John hop toward my house. "Unless he's wearing La Perlas under those jeans, I'm going to keep him."

"You don't know him, dude," Sheila said, grabbing my arm. I smelled patchouli on her, mixed with dog shampoo. Or is that the same thing? "He could be a dognapper. They're all over the place. Along with the coyotes . . ."

"I'll take my chances," I said. John and I spent the afternoon admiring my door handles, restored cherrywood floors, and, yes, my office's textured walls. We locked ourselves in the office, away from the demonic Ralph, to steal our first kiss. (I was talking. I don't think I ever stopped the whole time we were together. Even when I slept. I just couldn't believe I had found someone who loved me enough to listen.)

John took my face in his hands and kissed me.

"You just want me to shut up," I said, coming up for air. Our foreheads touched, his eyelashes playing with mine.

"Yes," he said. "Apparently, it didn't work."

So, he kissed me again. Oh, oh . . . oh.

"I'm never going to be quiet," I said, after catching my breath, "if you keep that up."

We made love. Well, furious, high-school-but-a-hundred-times-better sex. I'm surprised either of us survived. I threw out all my relationship books the next morning, when John went to get his things.

Dead bastard.

After John's death, Jay sets up shop for me outside in the backyard, under our beloved avocado tree. Jay has a theory that the sun is good for me, that lying in my darkened bedroom with the shades drawn is, somehow, unhealthy. Tell that to mushrooms.

Chloe makes me chamomile tea. She feels I'm not ready for Starbucks, and she's probably right. Aimee makes sure my patio chair is wiped of Santa Monica morning dew, which tends to hang around through the afternoon. She buys me little sandwiches and salads, which look perfect and delicious and as appealing to me as eating clay. Complete thoughts escape me. All I can think is one word: Why. Why? Why? Why.

"Why" is my mantra.

I say it so many times, that one night, as I sit under my avocado tree's protective canopy, I hear an answer.

"Why not?"

It was the old lady's voice again. Then . . . nothing.

The wind. A distant howl. Someone playing the new Mariah Carey CD two streets over.

But the words rang clear and true in my mind, and echoed in my soul. This simplest of answers gave me solace. That night was the first I'd slept longer than an hour since John left.

Why not.

One quiet Sunday night, Jay and I were sitting in the kitchen, when he asked me if I'd announced John's death on Facebook. This was like asking in Latin if I knew Swedish. I am a techno-Luddite. I don't know what uploading, downloading, or streaming is, but it sounds like farm porn.

"I'm not even on Facebook, you know that. I don't Twitter, Linx, or Plaxo. What is a Plaxo?"

"John was on Facebook," Jay said.

"Yes, I know," I said, getting annoyed. Like I didn't know everything about John. "He had a fan page. For his books."

Jay pursed his lips.

"What's that look?"

"That look says, 'Do I tell my widowed best friend that her husband had a personal page on Facebook?' "

"I don't like that look," I said. "Where's my laptop?"

"How are you going to get on his page?" Jay asked. "It's not like he's around to friend you."

I found my laptop. "Go on your page," I ordered. "You were Facebook friends, right?"

Jay gave me another look.

"That look says . . . 'I'm not sure I want to be a party to this. It could ruin my night, or, at least, the ability to raid your refrigerator for limes whenever I need them,'" I said.

"You're good," Jay said. He logged on. Jay's page came up. Jay's profile picture? A half-naked photo of Jay, taken in Cabo over a fourteen-day weekend.

"Photoshop!" I said. Jay had great abs for a forty-something, but those were NOT his triceps. Somewhere, a twenty-five-year-old Cuban was missing his guns.

"Do I judge you for sending out the same eighteen-year-old photo to the trades whenever we get a new production deal? You look like an Aniston sibling, for Baby Jesus's sake!"

"Okay, okay," I said. I looked up John Bernal on Jay's list of 1,438 friends.

"Where'd you find all these people?" I asked.

"Terrorists . . . trannies . . . ," he replied. "They just find me. I don't friend chunky monkeys."

"What if you get a terrorist who's a fat tranny?"

"Then, I have a moral dilemma," Jay said. "Okay, there's John."

John had posted a picture taken in our kitchen, grinning over a perfectly golden-brown deep-fried turkey.

"Thanksgiving . . . ," I whispered. Tears sprang to my eyes. I got that same sick feeling in my stomach, clawing its way into my throat. Would I be sad forever?

John's "wall" was filled with sorrowful messages. An endless stream of "sorrys" and "sadness," "sorrow," "goodbye," and "love" and memories old and recent.

I scrolled through older posts.

There he was, alive and cheerful. Virtual high fives and how are you doings? and how's your family? Good to "see" you here! "Nice to meet you, too" . . .

Jay put his hands on my shoulders and whispered into my ear. "You okay, baby?" he asked. I just nodded.

"You don't think he had another family somewhere, right?" I asked Jay.

"God, no," Jay said. "That's only neo-conservatives and Charles

Kuralt. That one surprised me. But you know, I always thought he was sexy. A total 'bear.'"

"John's 'friends' with Gwyneth Paltrow? He knows how I feel about those 'I Am Africa' posters! And those radio spots for Estée Lauder?"

"Estée Older?" Jay asked.

Jay shut the computer down. "Enough," he said. "I've seen this movie . . . remember Harrison Ford and Kristin Scott Thomas in that airplane crash movie?"

"The one where they find out their spouses were screwing each other, and then they screw each other?"

"I black out when it comes to Harrison Ford French-kissing," Jay said.

"We had no time to screw anyone else," I said. "Jay, do you realize . . . for the rest of my life, I'm going to have to tell people about his death."

"Remember this, pudding," Jay said. He put his finger under my chin and gazed into my eyes. "When you feel sorry for yourself, that you are the bearer of this terrible news. Remember that you had the ultimate privilege. True love."

I watched Jay tear up, and nodded, silent, as salty tears descended into the corners of my mouth. Salty? Who am I kidding? They tasted more like pinot.

"Don't be jealous," I said. "Someday you'll love somebody with all your heart. And then, he'll die on you, too."

"If I'm very lucky," Jay said, crossing his fingers.

On the long list of people to tell. You have to tell your child.

6

How to Tell Your Kid
(Pour yourself a drink, first.)

On second thought, pour two. You won't be driving tonight. You got somewhere better to go? Go ahead. Pour another. Nobody's carding.

John loved kids. Even before Ellie was born, you could find him at his friends' kids' Little League playoffs, Pee Wee football games, or ballet recitals, cheering from the sidelines. Not that he knew anything about football, or ballet, or much about baseball. Didn't matter. He'd cheer on every child—kids from opposing teams, as well. He owned a padded seat for long waits on the cold metal stands. He bought a folding chair that looked like a La-Z-Boy recliner. Kids loved him, too. They'd spot him in a crowd of parents. Maybe it was his smile, his boyishness. Maybe because he'd remember their names. John was always up to play catch, to guess Silly Bandz shapes, to hold one end of a jump rope.

I loved children, too—on other people. Since college, I'd been so busy with my career I couldn't even keep my Yoplait from going bad. The point is, I'd forgotten to have children. Or, you know, date.

And then I met John. I spent eight of my nine months of pregnancy seasick to give John the one gift he'd never received: Eleanor

Parker Bernal. She weighed 8 pounds, 3 ounces, was born at 5:38 in the morning after twelve hours of labor . . . and the first person to hold her was her daddy.

"Eleanor," he said, putting his nose to her tiny one. "Ellie . . . I've been waiting for you . . ."

"Can I see her?" I said. I was still groggy from the drugs, but I was pretty sure I'd just given birth.

"You're gonna love Mommy," John said, as he handed me this squirmy bundle in a pink blanket. "Mommy's the funniest girl I know. Just don't ask her to cook anything, ever, okay, El?"

The baby yawned. Already, she was bored with me. Then, she started crying. Mother and daughter were getting off to a great start.

"She doesn't even know me well enough to hate me," I said, as I handed her to John, who pressed his face to her cheek and started singing softly. Meanwhile, my seasickness had ended and the thought of French toast had begun.

The baby stopped crying.

"Oh, he's good," the nurse had said. "Daddy has the touch."

Weeks later, I was sitting in our backyard under our avocado tree, nursing our baby. Nursing was the only thing John couldn't do with Ellie, but trust me, I think he tried when I wasn't looking.

John was feeding me rigatoni bolognese, to keep up my strength to breast-feed; even I was jealous of myself.

"What were you singing to Ellie the morning she was born? 'You Are My Sunshine'?"

"Um, no," John said, putting a forkful of pasta in my mouth. Sometimes, he fed me just to keep me quiet. Worked.

" 'Hey, Jude'?" I said, my mouth full.

"You're not going to guess," John said. "Eat."

" 'Don't Worry, Baby'?"

" 'I'm a Flirt,' " he said. "R. Kelly. Told you you couldn't guess. It was the first thing that came to me." He stuffed another bite of rigatoni in my mouth, making it impossible for me to object.

From birth, John took his little shadow, Ellie, everywhere. Whole Foods, the library, bookstores, corner market, post office, the Brentwood Country Mart for BBQ chicken, Montana Avenue for a stroll and an espresso, the Promenade to watch a matinee. Was I jealous? No. I was relieved. John was born to raise Ellie; she was born to complete him. Me, I spent her first three years petrified that I would choke her with a half a grape. I needed a buffer.

Then there were Mommy and Me classes, which should have been renamed Mommy, Hot Daddy, and Me. African Music Mommy and Me, Pre-Ballet Movement Mommy and Me, Cooking Lebanese Mommy and Me—in every class, there were a dozen young moms and John. The few classes I attended scared me back into my jar of Ponds. How did I miss the middle-aged-mommy wave?

"I blame the latest wave of starlets," Jay had said one day after I cried to him sitting in our favorite coffee shop. "Instead of normal young starlet activities—smoking meth, driving the wrong way on the 405, flashing their baldies, screwing bad manager/boyfriends—"

"There must be a bad manager/boyfriend outlet store. There's so many of them."

"Starlets are popping out babies," Jay said.

"One after another," I said. "Babies are the new drug of choice. And the Mommy and Me girls are following in their pedicured, heroin-pricked footsteps."

I took Ellie to her ballet class after John had passed away. A new Mommy asked me, in my desiccated, elderly state, "So, are you Ellie's grandmother?"

New word for me and my kind: *Grammommy.*

If I had been the one to die, Ellie's life would continue relatively smoothly. But I wasn't. I was left here to pick up the pieces. And endure Mommy and Me classes.

Life is cruel.

Ellie attends Bunny Hill Preschool, in an old two-story just south of Sunset. Remember when there were "nursery schools"? Perhaps they still exist out in the Valley, but not here. Oh, no. Here there are "preschools." "Preschool" sounds much more important than "nursery school." In preschool, your toddler learns "pre-reading" and "pre-math." Don't get me started on pre-K. I just like my K straight, thank you.

Why are we in Bunny Hill? Every big life decision I make is based on a quotient: Time + Distance divided by Parking. Thus, Ellie's pediatrician, Dr. Bob, located seven minutes from Casa Sugar, has ample parking; Dr. Jim (the "surfing doc" who's always on CNN hating on vaccines, because, like, "science" is, like, not "cool") is closer, but parking is impossible. Bunny Hill is 8.2 minutes from Casa Sugar. Parking is great. Done and done. Also, Chloe had insisted on Bunny Hill.

"I don't want to be an alarmist, but like my blog says, preschool is the new college. You don't want Ellie going to prison, do you?" Chloe had said.

Our interview with Rhoda, Bunny Hill's seventy-year-old matriarch (matriarch is to Bunny Hill as Castro is to Cuba) went something like this:

1. Have you ever spent quality time with any of the Real Housewives of Beverly Hills?
   (I thought this was a trick question. It wasn't. The right answer was "yes," not my answer, which was snort, laugh, cough.)
2. Can you offer a Four Seasons Maui cabana for our Spring Auction?
3. Can you get letters of recommendation from Bill Clinton or Whoopi Goldberg?

By the time John and I were ready to turn tail and run, Ellie was emotionally attached to Fred, the school mascot, a tired old bunny kept in a cage in the dusty backyard.

"Did you realize," Rhoda whispered, her eyes wide, across her crowded desk, "Ellie is already a pre-learner?" Of course, we signed over our life savings.

Now, guess what? Bet you can't. I'm the only widow at Bunny Hill, including elderly Rhoda, who's vacationing in Greece this summer with her husband, Abe. I feel about that how I feel about everything that's unfair—wars, poverty, starvation, the price of almonds, John dying, Nic Cage's hairline—there is no God.

Oh, and none of the *moms* of the other Mommies are widows, yet, either.

So. My child.

They sell grief books for parents. Well, when bad stuff happens, the last thing you want to do is drive to Barnes & Noble, and ask an English Lit major working minimum wage for a how-to-tell-your-kid-dad-is-dead book.

A week went by. Almost two weeks. Aimee and I were sharing a bottle of pinot noir as I tried to roast chicken à la John. Crispy skin, juicy breast. Truckloads of garlic.

Ellie danced through, then stopped as I sweated over the bird. "Mom, that's Daddy's job," she said.

"You're right," I said, "it is Daddy's job."

"You're not a cook, remember?" she said, her hazel eyes huge in her chubby doll face. "Daddy really needs to come back and cook." She was wearing a new outfit, via Uncle Jay. I wasn't totally sure about the leopard tights. The beret seemed fine.

"That's right, Ellie. I'm not a cook," I said. "Just ask this chicken."

"Daddy's the Mommy Daddy. And you're the Daddy Mommy. You go to work and he stays home with me." She waltzed off, wiggling her bottom. I tried to avoid Aimee's glare by hiding behind my undercooked chicken.

"I'm trying to find the right moment," I said weakly. "I'll do it. After I make these vegan cupcakes for Ellie's lunch."

"Step away from the spatula," Aimee said. "I'll roast the salmonella out of the chicken. There's no time like the present."

"And there's no present like time," I said. "But we don't have that, do we." Now and then, Aimee made sense. I had to be the adult, even if I just wanted to lie around in my pj's and watch cartoons and eat cereal out of the box and generally avoid everything.

"I'm going in," I announced, and went to find Ellie.

I hadn't stepped foot in John's office since he died. My books are there. Various pens I like. I just can't seem to cross the threshold.

See, if I walk in and he's not bent over his desk, mumbling he's got "nothing in the tank"—then he's really dead, isn't he?

Ellie had wandered into his office. I watched her from the doorway, hopping around, peeking behind the bookcase, looking through his scribbled recipes.

"El," I said, finding my voice, "I want to tell you something."

El's usually the one who wants to tell me something—that's what she always says, very serious. "Mommy, I want to tell you something."

I sat on the love seat from his old apartment. Ellie snuggled close to me. She'd been clinging to me lately, without even knowing the bad news. I'd wake up to her little fingers entangled in my hair.

"I don't want you to tell me something," she said, whispering.

"El, it's important."

"No."

Ellie is three. Three's a stubborn age. But more than that. Three is smart. Three knows. This three, she knew. Her daddy had never been away from her. I had an epiphany. *Luke the Goldfish.*

"El, you remember Luke?"

John had won Luke the Goldfish at an arcade game at the Malibu Chili Cook-off, from a toothless carny. Luke was a bargain at three bucks. *(And $120 at Petco for the tank, food, chlorine drops, light-up rocks . . . goldfish are a money pit. You know the drill.)*

Luke the Goldfish was effervescent and full of life. He had a little Joel Grey in him, now that I think of it. He really enjoyed greeting us in the morning, swimming right to the surface and blowing goldfish kisses. Ellie loved Luke. I loved Luke.

A week later, Luke went belly up. At first, I thought he was sleeping. I've never had a pet, forgive me for not knowing that goldfish don't sleep. I tapped the bowl, then screamed, dropped his food, and ran out of the room.

"Luke's dead," I said to John, who was making French toast. *(Oh, his French toast—browned edges and sifted powdered sugar on top—you don't even know.)*

"Well, I'm not surprised," he said. "We did win him from a guy with no teeth."

"It's like a bloodbath in there!" I said. Ellie was still asleep. "Go, get him out, please, before Ellie sees—I can get a goldfish twin later. Maybe say a prayer—what's a prayer for the dead?"

"You want me to do a prayer for Luke?"

"Luke. Was. Special."

"I'll do the kaddish," John said, wiping his hands on a dish towel. I followed him, then listened in the doorway as he recited words in Hebrew, and as the toilet flushed.

"I love Luke," Ellie said, bringing me back to the (horrifying) present, in John's office.

"El, you know how Daddy hasn't been here in a few days?" I said. Lying. Few days? Kids have no sense of time, scientists say. Like dogs, a year will go by and feel like hours. They'll just pick up right where they left off. I don't buy it.

"No no no nonononononononononono . . . ," Ellie said, putting her hands over her ears.

"Ellie, Daddy loves you so much—"

"nonononononononono—"

"He loves you so much but you're not going to see him—"

"nonononononononononono—"

"Ellie, please—even though you won't see Daddy anymore, I mean, in his office, or cooking—"

"NONONONONONONONONONONONONONO!!!!!!"

"El, El, Daddy's in heaven—"

"NONONONONONONONONONONONONO!!!!!!!"

"You'll feel him forever, in your heart—he's there, he's still there—we just can't see him—but you can still talk to him—I'll never ever stop talking to him—"

"No no no no! NO, MOMMY, NO!" El said. She hit me.

"Please don't be mad at me," I pleaded, going down on my knees. "Please, El—"

"NO, MOMMY, NO!"

"I'm here, Ellie. I'm not going anywhere. We're going to be okay. Daddy wants us to be okay. He doesn't want us to be sad. I'm here. I'm here!"

How could I lie to her? I wasn't there. I was gone. Could I even say

I would survive? What if I got sick? Died of grief? People die from a wounded heart.

I couldn't write the how-to book on telling kids their father is dead.

And if you've written it, you haven't done it. Think back to the hardest conversation of your life: "I want a divorce." "Princess has to be put to sleep." "Mom and Dad, I'm gay." I win "Most Difficult Conversation." I get first place.

And when the wailing and sobbing and sniffling finally came to an end, I sat on Ellie's bed and held my exhausted, red-cheeked daughter in my arms. And around us, Casa Sugar was silent, holding us in its embrace.

7

Dead Men Tell No Tales;
Dead Women, Either

One clear Saturday morning, Jay somehow got it in his head that it would be a good idea for me to take Ellie to Pacific Park for the day.

"You can take her on rides, play games. She needs alone time with you," he'd said in my bedroom, as he instructed me on how to dress myself. I'd lost the will to accessorize.

"She'll have a whole lifetime of alone time with me," I'd said, as I slipped into old Juicy Couture sweatpants. I could see Jay blanch. "Jay, she wants her dad, not me. I was the third wheel."

"Nonsense," Jay said. "Ellie adores you. More important, you adore her. Now, let me get you down there early enough to avoid gang shootings."

With that, Jay drove us down to the pier, with instructions to have fun, and that he'd pick us up in two hours. We looked around. The ocean was flat, the sun glinting off its surface like a new set of knives. I stared out at the endless sky and sighed. I'd forgotten my sunglasses. Of course.

Ellie clasped my hand and looked up at me, giving me a wan little smile. There were circles under her eyes.

"Ready to have some fun?" I said. I smiled back—or at least, a close facsimile of a smile.

Ellie nodded. The sun shone on her curls. We walked down the pier, into the park.

We'd eaten cotton candy, rode bumper cars, won a stuffed Sponge-Bob toy at the water cannon, got carried away at Whac-A-Mole, and I'd lost about twelve million dollars at the basketball hoops (which John could win in a heartbeat).

Hip-hop music blared as the Saturday crowd filled up the lines, and though I was done before I began, Ellie was desperate to ride the Ferris wheel. We were running late, and Jay would be waiting for us, but Ellie wouldn't take no for an answer.

"I'm not a big fan of heights," I informed Ellie. "And the fact that it's solar powered just makes me nervous."

"Mommy, it's okay," Ellie reassured me. "See?" she said, as we were strapped into our cart. "See? We'll be okay."

She slipped her hand over mine, and laughed as the Ferris wheel floated lazily toward the sky. I felt light-headed as the ground drifted away from us.

Suddenly, Ellie got squirmy. "Mommy, make room," Ellie said.

"Ellie, stay," I said. "What are you doing?" The Ferris wheel continued to circle up. Ellie scooched her bottom away from me, toward the other side of the cart.

"Ellie, stay next to me—"

The view was breathtaking, a postcard for Southern California days. I could see the entire coastline. All I wanted, though, was for the ride to stop. I was feeling woozy. I needed solid ground beneath my feet. My palms started to sweat.

"Mommy, when we go to the top, Daddy can jump in!"

"Honey, no," I said. I felt stunned. "Daddy's not going to jump in."

"Mommy, Daddy's in heaven . . . he's right up there." She pointed to the sky. "He can see us—he'll see us and jump in!"

Ellie tried to stand up—I grabbed her and screamed as she leaned over the rail. People below started staring and pointing.

"Ellie, stop!"

"Daddy!" Ellie yelled. "Daddy! We're here! Daddy!"

The ride operators took notice. I held on to Ellie, who had started to cry, until we reached the bottom. Jay, pale, a worried look on his face, was waiting for us. A ride operator, an older woman, shook her finger at a sobbing Ellie as she raced out of the cart into Jay's arms. I stumbled as I walked toward the exit.

"Mommy!" Ellie said, her eyes red, tears running down her face. "Why didn't you let Daddy in? Why?"

"I'm sorry," Jay said softly, holding Ellie in his arms, his hand over her head, as we made our way back to the car.

Five-fifteen in the morning. The wind blows through an open window. I get up to close it. *October*, I think. The air is changing. Chilly. A sweet smell, the promise of rain. I sit in front of my mirror, and stare at myself. Stare at all the ways my face has changed. I'm forty-three-and-a-half years old. *Only*. Too old to fully appreciate Lil Wayne, too young to be a widow. This is around the time I start lying about my age, but I lie older. I look much better for forty-four than forty-two. Especially since John died.

I've lost twelve pounds. I can't coax it back on. I've tried everything, except, maybe, eating (*where's that damn Post-it?*). I know what you're thinking. You're mad at your husband or boyfriend, the guy who takes up most of your bed and the last piece of crispy bacon. "I could drop these saddlebags? Just by losing *this* guy? Done and done!"

Listen, don't get too excited. Like love and marriage, death is complicated, as complicated as life. But back to me. Because this is my story. When you lose the love of your life and twelve pounds, you can write yours.

I've always had a little extra. Extra in the boobs, waistline (what waistline?), the Big Three: hips, thighs, and tushie. I was born with a little extra. Never bothered me except on tropical vacations, where girls forget to wear the bikinis along with the strings. But when I go to Eastern Europe or Orlando, Florida, I'm a beauty queen. Croatia is my Oahu, Disney World is my Bahamas.

John fed my little extra. He fed me, I mean, really fed me. In every sense of the word—spiritually, emotionally—and, this is important—physically. He was a professional chef. I'm a professional eater. When my sweetheart was alive, if I grabbed a roll around my stomach, or complained that my breasts made a backhand an impossible dream (not that I ever played tennis), John would speak up in their defense:

ME: I hate my boobs.

JOHN: How can you say that about Lola and Michelle?

ME: I wish you wouldn't call them by name.

JOHN: Those are my boobs. If we ever break up, I get custody. Or, at least, visitation rights.

ME: You can have them. As long as I can have Roger and Degen.

JOHN: Who are they?

ME: Your balls.

Pause.

JOHN: We're never breaking up.

Now, I look older than my "lying up" age. My Grief Team tells me I look great. They're lying. I look like a hard forty-four, a forty-four who's had a few too many, too many times. A forty-four who steals her kid's Adderall. I can't sit on my newly bony ass more than a few minutes at a time, and yet, that's all I want to do. Sit, and lie down. My breasts, proudly established since the mid-eighties, are deflated. I look like what I am. A grieving widow. All I need is prayer beads and a black lace scarf over my head and I get to be an extra in *Godfather 12*.

John's toothbrush tortures me. *What do I do with his toothbrush?* There's no handbook for this stuff. I would trade all the frozen 3 Musketeers bars in the world, the entire eighties music oeuvre—George Michael, Madonna, Duran Duran, even INXS—vanilla lattes, the Oakland Raiders, and that good European butter, to hold John's hand *one more time*.

"And dear God, dear, dear effing God," I say. I'm sobbing. "What I wouldn't do for our Saturday morning quickie . . ."

* * *

The first ghostly "conversation" happened when I was drunk; the next, I was crazy. I hadn't mentioned what I wasn't sure was real to anyone, not even the Grief Team. Now, I felt (relatively) sane, but then again, maybe not: I was raking Casa Sugar's backyard one evening when its poltergeist returned to lecture me on home décor.

"I've been meaning to ask you, the blue tile in the kitchen—you think that's too much?" the old woman said.

Exactly when did it became apparent to me that I was speaking to a ghost? Well, generally speaking people stand on the ground, the floor, or steps. This woman was floating. Plus, she had a translucent quality. Floating, translucence—*dead giveaways, if you will.*

"I like blue," I croaked. "I'm just going to . . ." I had to sit. Sit or faint. These were the choices.

"Who doesn't?" she said. "But, why so crazy with the blue, I wonder."

"Um . . . who are you?" I asked.

"Trish, of course," she said. "This is home sweet home. I mean, before you moved in and brought the whole blue thing." I could see her more clearly, now that I was no longer blinded by fear. Her black hair was braided, accented by silver streaks. I recognized the beauty queen in her cupid's bow mouth.

"Do you mind?" I asked, motioning toward the wine bottle on the small patio table. She shrugged. I was planning on having a glass when I'd finished raking, but now I picked up the bottle, sat back down, and drank right from the source.

"It must be a shock," she said.

"Well, kinda, yeah," I said.

"Losing your husband. So young." She clicked her tongue. "Such a shame."

"It's all kind of a shock," I said. "I'm talking to a dead person. That's kind of surprising."

"I've talked to you before," she said. "You asked a question that needed an answer."

I thought about it. "My God. You're Mrs. Why Not."

"Why not," she said, nodding her head. "I thought you might appreciate that."

"Why me?" I asked. "Why are you contacting me?"

"It's obvious. You need me," she said. "Look, you wouldn't hear me, or see me if you didn't want me here. We're around all the time—but no one pays attention, past, you know, like age two."

"I'm surrounded by dead people?"

"Spirits. Sounds better, no?"

"I'm not sure I'm comfortable with this—"

"A gust of cold air. That's a sign. You know, they keep it freezing up here. The ones in charge, they've got the AC on full blast. Or, you walk into a room and smell vanilla. But no one's in there, the stove isn't on. How many times have you misplaced your car keys?"

"Those are all signs?"

"Sure. We used to use chimes more, bells, too, but with all the cellphones—doesn't work anymore. We had to update our system."

There was so much I wanted to know. *Was there heaven and hell? Was Anna Nicole Smith sorry she missed the reality show craze? And John, where was John?* Trish wouldn't answer any of my questions. She claimed she'd get in trouble if she got too detailed. "Who's going to come down on you?" I asked. "I mean, you've made it, right?"

"Kid," she sighed, "there are rules for this, rules for that, there's the Special Communications Committee, the Office of Other-worldly Affairs, the Committee to Oversee Overseers—and the politics! Don't get me started. Washington has nothing on this place."

"Is John coming back?"

"I can't tell you that, sweetie," she said. "I have to go now. Don't want to overstay my welcome."

I'll tell you this. Dead people sure are nosy, but ask them a question? They shut right up.

And Trish faded away.

* * *

I was surprised to find Jay in the kitchen, his arms folded across his chest. "Who, may I ask, were you talking to?" he asked. "I was watching you from the kitchen window."

"Don't you mean 'whom'?" I said, stalling for time using grammatical diversion.

Jay didn't go for it. Was it better to lie or tell the truth? *Always, always tell the truth.*

"No one," I said. "Why?"

"You appeared to be talking to the avocado tree," Jay said. "What does one talk to foliage about?"

I tried another tack. "You look like the actor from *True Blood* in this light."

"I do?" Jay said, momentarily distracted. "Wait. No. You, my best friend. My business partner. The 'practical' one. The anchor, remember? You were talking to a tree."

He sat on a kitchen stool, put his elbows up on the chopping block, and stared at me.

"I thought you were hitting Main Street with Hidalgo tonight," I said.

"We met up. I gave him money. That was our date." Jay hid behind his brave face, which looked like a six-year-old eating a lemon.

"I see a lip quiver," I said. "And you promised you'd never let him make you cry!"

"The money's not for him," he said, his eyes watering. "Damn these lilac contacts. The money's for the baby."

"Baby?"

"Yes. Hidalgo and his wife—guess what—they're having a baby," Jay said, his voice cracking. "Isn't that sweet?"

"Oh, honey," I said. I wrapped my arms around him. "I'm so sorry."

"Sweetie, I'm the one who sews outfits for his dog. Can you please not be crazy, too?"

"I'm not crazy, Jay. Look at me. I'm not crazy."

"I'm looking. The eyebrows have me a little upset."

"I have to tell you something," I said.

"Give it to me straight, no chaser, no ice. In fact, just give it to me uncut on a mirror."

"I was talking to a ghost."

Jay put his head on the block. "I just can't," he said. "I just can't . . ."

"Don't you want to hear about the conversation?"

"I'm sure this is normal. *Not.* I'm sure that a lot of new widows go through this. *Never heard of it.* I'm sure that you will be fine. *I'll visit you on weekends.*"

"Fine. I'm going to check on Ellie and go to bed. I'm sleepy."

"Night, night, crazycakes," Jay replied. "I'll see you in the morning. Unless you're having breakfast with your ghost friend."

"Do they eat in heaven?" I wondered. How happy would John be if he could at least cook? I walked toward my bedroom, feeling Jay's gaze on me.

"Not crazy," I said.

"Like Teri Hatcher's eyes," Jay said.

"Mean!" I said.

I woke up to Jay and Ellie and five giant pumpkins (and one little one) in various states of evisceration on my kitchen chopping block.

"I love the smell of pumpkin guts in the morning," I said. Ellie, scooping seeds from the little pumpkin, had an apron around her red cashmere robe (that Jay had bought to match his).

"Never too soon for Ellie to learn family traditions," Jay said, working his Obama pumpkin. "This Halloween, I'm getting my Katy Perry on. I'm thinking Lady Gaga for our little miss, here." Jay doesn't just carve pumpkins; he designs "squash art." If you had seen the Lindsay Lohan Mug Shot he carved last year, you would have wept. Someone actually stole the Liza Minnelli pumpkin from his front porch.

"Over my dead—," I said. "Oh, wait. I meant, no, never, *nein.*"

"Mommy," Ellie said, "who invented purple?" Purple was John's favorite color.

"The Tiny Artist Formerly Known as Prince, sweetheart," Jay said.

"What does Ellie have today?" I consulted the calendar, taped to the refrigerator. "Wait. What day is it, again?" John had written Ellie's schedule through the end of the year. It was disconcerting (understatement) to read his scribble every morning, reminding me where to go. Reminding me he wasn't here.

"Mommy, it's Wednesday. I have school today. Monday, Wednesday, Friday . . ."

"Right. Wednesday," I said. "No Mitt Romney pumpkin?"

Jay shot me a look while concentrating on Obama's mole. "Pumpkins are Democrats, everyone knows that," he said. "I'm taking Ellie to school this morning. Isn't that right, child?"

Ellie smiled and nodded, her mouth full of scrambled egg. Spice waited at her feet for anything dropped. No need to vacuum!

"I can take her," I said. I heard dogs barking in front of my house, and a second later, Chloe strode in, wearing the NoMo Momzilla uniform: lululemon tights, Harari flip-flops, and a twelve-year-old boy's ass.

"Why isn't she ready?" she said, looking at me, then Jay.

"Why aren't I ready for what?"

"Power Yoga," Chloe said, over the dogs barking outside. "You need a break. You need peace. You need warrior one. Oh my God, *be quiet*!"

"You guys decided this?" I said. "Last night?"

"Yes. Come on, we're running late. I've got the dogs in the car." Chloe's frantic meter was rising. "I can't leave them at home, my dining room table is missing a leg now, and I think there's a litter somewhere . . ."

"Already, yoga is stressing me out," I muttered.

Chloe's hybrid SUV was covered in bumper stickers. Iraq, Non-Violence, Anti-War, Obama, Obama–Biden, ObamaMama, HOPE, Arms are for Hugging . . .

"How's Billy?" I asked, as I got in, trying to ignore the dog glut.

Chloe is separated but living with at-some-point-ex-husband Billy. In this "new"—read "shit-ass"—economy, they can't afford a divorce. Billy Lew Superstar was a big trader with Bear Stearns until the company evaporated overnight. He still shakes his head, as though it's a magic trick he can't figure out.

"Billy bogarted my yoga practice. He spends hours on YouTube learning crow pose and bird of paradise. He's even walking on his hands," Chloe said, turning to me. "Hannah, he's thinking about becoming a Democrat."

"Now I know the end is nigh," I said.

Chloe and I pull up on San Vicente, outside her favorite studio. Yoga studios in Santa Monica are like hookers in Las Vegas—there are ten on every corner. Wait, come to think of it, there are ten hookers in every yoga studio in Santa Monica. Talk about parallel universes. In the entry, I navigate Ugg and Croc Mountain, vying for ugliest footwear ever invented. I'm overcome by the smell of dank yoga mats and feet.

"So this is what staph smells like," I said to Chloe, who's on a mission to find the best floor spot in the sea of tramp stamps, bandannas, and Hollywood divorcées. I follow, and set my mat down between her and a woman of indiscernible age and race. Eminem started blasting. The instructor, a hot, shirtless guy with a booming laugh, called out the first forward bend. I touched my toes. Well, okay, I touched my knees as my eyes wandered into Silicone Valley. "It's like Frank Ryan's memorial in here," I said, referring to the deceased plastic surgeon. Chloe stuck her palms under her feet. *Bitch.* As we moved through our first down dog, I recalled a death at the serious (i.e. no fun) yoga class on Main. A bulimic yogini went into shavasana and never got up; it ain't called "corpse pose" for nothing.

It was just after we moved into triangle pose that I started to experience the Five Stages of Yoga Grief.

Denial: My triangle feels good. I'll whip through this class, no prob. In fact, I'm so relaxed and confident, I almost feel normal.

Anger: Sun salutations. I've lost my breath. Shit. I'm a grieving widow surrounded by hairless, nubile bodies. Why is everyone else able to touch their toes with their tongues? And why aren't these

people working at ten on a weekday? (Porn isn't a 9-to-5 job, I remind myself.)

Bargaining: Holding warrior two. Dear Lord, Mary, Dear Baby
Jesus, if you get me through this pose, I will devote my life to helping others. (I'm not sure how, maybe I can find something that
doesn't take time away from my breakdown.)

Depression: I am not the skinniest, sexiest, richest, bendiest,
down-doggiest in this class. I may be the funniest, but that's only
because the porn twins, or T-Rex, the tall guy in the corner who
wears the ski cap, or the good-looking, creepy guy I call "Bundy"
have no idea how funny they are. I could be the widowiest, but I
don't think I qualify as the depressed-est: Crazy loves yoga.

Acceptance: I accept that I suck at yoga.

I'm rolling up my mat when a woman with matted hair and a
Pillsbury body squeezed into neon tights bounds over. Her silvery
eyes are going off like the Fourth of July. *(She does yoga three times
a day. Which begs the question: Yoga or Muffins?)*

"Oh my God!" she says, grabbing me in a sweaty, neon hug. *I
can't think of her name. Morgan? Marianne?* "How are you? I
haven't seen you in ages!"

"I'm . . . okay," I say, as I watch Chloe weaving her way through
the crowd. I ache to be away from this person.

"How's that handsome husband of yours?" she asks. "How'd you
get so lucky, huh?"

I really just want to leave. Do I lie and say he's fine?

"Um," I said, "he's . . . he passed away. He died."

"Oh!" she says, her eyes popping out like a Tex Avery cartoon
character. "Oh my God. Well . . . no wonder you look so skinny!
You look amazing!"

L.A. is no place for widows.

Aimee was in my driveway, smoking a cigarette, wearing a leather
jacket, and leaning against her black convertible BMW. She looked
like she belonged in the Brentwood traveling company of *Grease*.

"We're late. You smell like wet cat," she said, as I limped up with my yoga mat. Chloe coughed at Aimee, then sped off in her dog car toward the West L.A. shelter. Her Pomeranian, Bakasana, had refused Doggie Dramamine and vomited in the backseat.

"I'm just relieved I don't smell like rescued Pomeranian vomit," I said.

"They don't really have Pomeranian Rescue?" Aimee asked, wrinkling up her nose, the only part of her that can wrinkle. "That's just going too far."

"So, what are your orders for the day?" I asked. "Apparently, there's a lot of concern about me."

"Concern?" Aimee said. "Concern is putting it mildly. I was right there with you when you got knocked up. I was right there when you got hitched. But crazy, I don't know if I can do."

"Reassuring," I said.

"Marriage and babies is bad enough." Aimee shook her head. "Look how it ends."

"So . . . where are we going?"

"To the spa. There's a new treatment I want to try."

"There's a treatment you haven't done?" I said, in mock horror.

"State of the art," she said. "Don't ask questions."

Aimee is "I don't know how much over forty." That number is buried, like Jimmy Hoffa's body and Vanilla Ice's career, where it can never be found. She loses her driver's license whenever the urge to change her birthdate strikes. Usually after a bad audition. The one thing Aimee's worked for her entire life—The Role: Nicole Kidman in *Dead Calm*. Jessica Lange in *Frances*. Julia Roberts in *Mystic Pizza*—has been denied. She's put everything aside for that phone call. No boyfriend lasted more than six months, no plant more than three. There's nothing on her walls in her studio apartment on Ocean. There's no food in the fridge, just numbing cream and Stoli. She's never even subscribed to a magazine.

Aimee has been waiting to go on location for twenty years.

"What are you thinking?" Aimee asked me.

"We're going to have to fit your BMW with cosmetic surgeon

GPS," I said, looking closely at her. "Did you do something with your . . . ?" I touched my earlobes.

"No," she said, "Do you think I need to? They belong on an eighty-year-old named Si."

"Your earlobes are perfection," I said. "You could be an earlobe model."

"You were so smart to stay on the kind side of the camera," she said, looking at herself in the rearview mirror. "I look in the mirror now . . . it's not the same, is it?"

"Aim, you are more beautiful now than you ever were," I said. "Lay off the needles. Pretty soon, I'm going to look like your mother instead of your best friend."

"I don't need help," I said, as we sat in the waiting room in kimonos and slippers surrounded by Brentwood momsters texting like drunken teens. The spa décor was "if a little Asian influence is good, a lot is money"; bamboo meet bonsai meet giant laughing Buddha head. So far, this spa experience was giving stress-inducing yoga a run for its *namaste*.

"Hannah, cut the crap," Aimee said. "You had an entire conversation with an avocado tree. What's next? You get engaged to a ficus?"

"Aimee, hi," a busty, brunette attendant bounced (her hair extensions bouncing a beat behind) into the waiting room. "So good to see you! Come this way, okay?"

"How'd your *Two and a Half Men* audition go?" she asked Aimee, as we followed her bouncy self.

"You went on a *Two and a Half Men* audition?" I said.

"It spoke to me," Aimee said. "There were a lot of colors to play in the scene."

"Aimee, I want you to know," the attendant said, stopping at a door, "this is my last week."

"Oh . . . are you going back to Ohio?" Aimee asked. "This town is so tough."

"No," the girl said. "Hawaii! I got a part in the new Michael Bay movie. They're saying I'm the new Megan Fox! I'm sooooo excited!"

This is how I know Aimee's a great actress. You couldn't tell she wanted to eat the girl's liver with a rusty spoon.

"There's an old Megan Fox?" I asked. "She's like . . . twelve, right?"

"I'm so happy for you," Aimee said.

"Thank you," the girl said. "Oh, and good luck to you, too!" *God bless the children,* I thought. *Who speak in exclamation points.*

"Your V-Steam attendant will be here in a moment. You're going to love this! I just had one this morning. My vagina feels brand-new!" she said, then bounced off. I held Aimee's arm back as her hand formed a fist.

"What's this about her . . . stuff?" I asked. "I'm not interested in a brand-new vagina. I like my old, pre-owned one."

"It's called a V-Steam. You sit on special stools, they bring in giant bowls with Chinese herbs in hot water—and you steam your vagina."

"Like a clambake?"

"Well, yes, I suppose so," Aimee said. "A clam, or a mussel."

"Aimee, I love you, but I'm not steaming my vagina for you. I don't even like to say the word 'vagina.' I boycotted the *Vagina Monologues* for ten years." I pulled my kimono around my waist and got up to leave, stepping over the elegant older man who had taken a seat next to Aimee.

"Excuse me," I said. Then, I realized. He was a man, a man wearing a tailored suit and a hat. He wasn't here for the vagina steam.

"Who're you talking to—"

"Sitting next to you," I said. "That man, there."

"Hannah. You're freaking me out. There's no one here."

"Look!" I said, pointing. "Look! You can see him! He's right there!"

"Hannah!" Aimee said. "You're scaring me."

"He looks so sad," I said.

"Hannah, you need help." She was holding my shoulders. "You need to relax. You need a break. You need a V-Steam. Do it for Ellie."

"Why is he so sad?" I said, as the man faded from sight.

* * *

Maybe I *was* losing my mind.

"It's the Ambien," Jay said later, as day turned to night. "Some people have the Faustino reaction."

"You shouldn't be taking Ambien," Chloe said. "Read my blog. You could wind up in rehab or dead."

"Or, you know, with a proper night's sleep," I said.

"She shouldn't be drinking so much," Aimee said, as she poured more vodka into her glass. "Did you drink before the steam?" Aimee had forced me to steam. And no, I don't feel like I have a new anything down there.

"I survived porn yoga and poached my bits for you guys," I said. "Can you all just . . . leave me alone?"

"Leave you alone?" Jay asked. "We're supposed to go into the studio with an entire season of titillating episodes. Hannah, if we don't wow them, we could be canceled."

"Canceled?" I asked. "How is that possible?"

"They're cutting way back on programming," Jay said. "Even our cheap little show."

"I'll figure out the season. I mean, even though it's reality."

"Reality is the greatest fiction, you know that," Jay said. "Where should I sleep tonight?"

"Jay, you've been here every single day—you need to concentrate on your own life. Halloween is around the corner; you've got barely a week to get your Katy Perry on. And Chloe—you've got kids, dogs, and a sort-of husband—"

"Wasband," Aimee said.

"You want us out? You like dead people better than us?" Chloe asked.

"Never," I said.

"I'll come by in the morning," Jay said.

"No," I said, "if it makes you feel better, I won't talk to any dead people tonight, no matter who drops in."

"What's Ellie wearing tomorrow?" Jay asked, as I escorted them

to the front door. "Let me put something aside—fur vest and jeg-
gings?"

"That fur vest made in China?" Aimee said, then winked at
Chloe. "Woof."

"Don't say that!" Chloe said, as I closed the door and turned to
my quiet, empty house. I listened for Ellie's soft breathing. The
truth? I was scared—scared to be without my friends. And scared
to be with them, denying what I saw. Times like these called for
swift, forceful action.

I headed for the medicine cabinet. And found an expired bottle
of NyQuil. I gave myself a shot, and shuffled off to bed.

8

Coyote Ugly

In the fairy-tale land of NoMo, the houses are bigger, the residents are all in training for the imaginary Olympics, the children are blonder, the cars are shinier, and the dogs, even the rescues, are purebred and walked in threes by professionals. The plant life, itself, gives off a richer bouquet—jasmine, pine, rosemary, lavender, olive trees, English roses . . .

"Landscaping," Jay has said, "is what separates civilization from 'Oh, hell no!'"

Even NoMo's crazies are a cut above SoMo crazies. Take the mad movers—or peregrinators, if you will. Rollerblade Bob, a sixtyish hippie in tie-dye T-shirts Rollerblades to Whole Foods, Starbucks, the cliffs, and back; Hazmat Harriet, who basically wears a hazmat suit to run San Vicente every morning; there's Corkscrew-Loose Lizzy, with a head of blond curls, who forces her hapless shepherd to run for hours on end. Goggles Gus is the old man who jogs so slowly past the date palms on Marguerita at dawn, it looks as though he's moving backward. SoMo only has the homeless population, which occasionally wanders north from its designated areas south of Wilshire. They might show up on the doorstep of a double-lot Cape Cod, or peeing in the bushes of a regal Spanish Revival.

Coyotes, both two- and four-legged, are another issue. The four-legged leave bloody tracks on the NoMo streets—Binky's spine on 15th, Tinkerbell's ear on 20th . . .

But the two-legged are more sinister.

After a peaceful night's Ny-coma, uninterrupted by the living or the dead, I got Ellie off to school, and decided to take Spice for a walk. He and I needed fresh air and a fresh start. Spice is the color of John's favorite seasoning, cumin, and is not only of indeterminate origin, but indeterminate age (like Brentwood divorcées). Don't kill me, but Spice is not attractive. His legs are stubby, his body long. His nose smushed, his ears lopsided. Spice is Bert Lahr in my little Oz. He's the Cowardly Lion, afraid of everything. He must have been traumatized as a puppy, but does he have to run from a floral arrangement? What is it about the guy on the oatmeal box that makes him shiver?

Our relationship has not been smooth. The first night in my house, Spice peed on my brand-new Cosabella panties. What's the message? How about "I hate you" in Bark.

Now it's me, the baby . . . and Spice. And two of the three of us merely tolerate each other.

I put on Spice's leash and plied him with liver treats. Finally, miracle of miracles, we were walking, moving west toward the beach. The morning was frigid, even for late October; palm trees and blue fingertips. I should have worn gloves. Did I own gloves? I should have worn a hat. Did I own a hat? I'd need more Post-its. I was so busy berating myself as we passed a woman with a tangle of gray hair, tugging at a yellow Lab the size of a linebacker (NoMo's number two canine, after the omnipresent labradoodle), I didn't notice her pointing at something in the gutter.

"This is the work of Cheney!" she said, her eyes sending out messages from Planet I Need a Hobby. Her long wrinkled skirt and blouse with no bra set her fashion clock at Woodstock, between the hours of midnight and two A.M. The older women in the neighborhood (well, older than I am) were bohemians; they could afford it.

In any other neighborhood, people would be handing them singles and half-eaten sandwiches. I pulled at Spice, who was barking and whining, mirroring my inner life. The huge Labrador paced and sniffed at the ground.

"Poor baby!" she said. "You see what these animals did!"

I peered into the street as Spice wheeled and leapt, pulling me away. I saw a heart pendant, fur, and dried blood. I focused on the nametag. Something had made dessert out of "Cupcake."

"Coyotes?" I said. "I've never seen one." I'd heard their cries, their staccato, high-pitched yapping—a war party where the prey eats organic, wheat-free dog biscuits. Because it's a pain when your dog is allergic to wheat.

"They're right here, on this very street! They're rampant. They live in abandoned homes, and roam, hunting for victims, just as the sun is fading."

I had walked into a Gothic novel. I needed to walk out. "I don't know anything about wildlife," I said. "I mean, mold won't even grow in my house." Just keep talking, Hannah. Keep babbling. You'll end up like Woodstock Wanda, here.

"There's a pack," she said, buoyed by my nonsense. "Dick Cheney, the big one, he's bold. I've seen him wander the streets in broad daylight. He chased my husband and Sammy, here, just last Tuesday—it must have been six o'clock . . . Cheney tracked him for three blocks—thank God, my husband's a triathlete—"

"A coyote named Dick Cheney chased your triathlete husband." Were there any other kinds of husbands in Santa Monica? What was everyone in training for?

I wanted to remember this.

"He's got Cheney's eyes—pure evil, cold, heart of darkness." (*This is the Socialist Republic of Santa Monica, after all. The latest City Council mandate has labeled every third Tuesday "Validate Each Other's Feelings Day."*)

"I keep Spice in the backyard. It's fenced in," I said, as Spice continued to whine and pull. *I am right there with you, buddy,* I thought.

"They'll hop it. Six, ten feet, they drag off dogs the size of Great Danes—and God help the little ones . . . I'm glad I don't have small children," she said. "Do you have a child?"

"Yes," I said. "Ellie is three and a half. She's not allowed to put toys made in China in her mouth."

"Oh, good Lord!" she said, her eyes bright. "Don't let her outside. Until she's nine or ten and can carry a bat." *NoMo was getting less appealing by the second.*

"Thanks for the advice," I said. "We'll be going now."

"You live down my block," Woodstock said. "I've seen your dog. Your husband walks him."

"Well, yes," I said. Every day, John had walked Spice to the palisades overlooking Santa Monica Beach, where he could gaze out at the Pacific past the Malibu cliffs, take iPhone photos, send them to his Facebook fan page, and call it the *Cote D'Mercedes Benz.*

Spice was a different dog with John by his side.

"I see him all the time," Woodstock said. "Such a nice man. He always waves. . . . What a smile."

Upon our return, a silver Range Rover was parked halfway in the street, blocking my driveway.

"Oh, no, Spice," I said with a sigh. "We have another coyote problem." A haystack-haired blonde with huge white sunglasses, clown lips, white jeans with feathered pockets, and a tank top pulled over authorized flotation devices, was jabbering into her BlackBerry on my little front porch.

"Oh my God! I know, right?" Blondezilla was saying, loud enough for SoMo to hear. "He's divorced, he's got a Cialis prescription, his house is all paid for—*oops*—gotta runski." She pulled her sunglasses over her head, appraising me. "See you tonight at the Penthouse." She hung up the phone.

Dee Dee Pickler, head of the SMCA, what Jay and I refer to as the Santa Monica Coyote Association, rushed at me on platform flip-flops, locking me in an embrace with Big and Bigger. The SMCA is Westside Real Estate, and they're coming after your sons and your Gillette Regent Square two-story Spanish colonial. They're an Army of the Night, living in SoMo apartments, driving leased Range Rovers, and hanging at the Huntley Penthouse on 2nd. They have big dreams harbored in their big bosoms: star on the "Real House-wives of Anything," live in a NoMo McMansion, and land one of the Wilson Brothers. If Owen and Luke aren't available, the Un-known Wilson Brother will do.

"I brought something for you!" Dee Dee said, diving into her fake LV tote. Dee Dee had the first tramp stamp in SoMo and is not afraid to use it; she did not laugh when I asked if she's a Maori. Word is, she likes gummy bears on her Pinkberry and doesn't al-ways remember her child's name.

"Just a minute," she said, sorting through her purse. Then she handed me a small package, wrapped in silver.

"Thank you, Dee Dee," I said, taken aback. "I appreciate it."

"Not a thing, honey . . . I was so sorry to hear about John," she said. "He was so cute. Like what was he, six feet? Six one?" She sized me up, as if thinking, "I never knew what he saw in you." "I'm sorry I didn't come by earlier, I thought I'd give you some space. So . . . it's been over a month. What's your time line?"

"Time line?"

"To sell your place."

"I'm not selling," I said.

"Property taxes are skyrocketing. Public school doesn't come cheap in NoMo."

I kept forgetting to pay bills. I knew, in theory, that bills wouldn't stop coming because John died. One of the more shocking things about his death is that time hadn't stood still; people still shopped and worked and watched *America's Got Talent*. And sent me bills.

"Thanks for paying your condolences, Dee Dee."

"I'm just trying to do a favor for an old friend," she said. "If you sell now, I can get you into a one and one-and-a-half off the 10."

"I have enough to cover my property taxes," I said. John's life insurance check was coming in soon. To avoid living right off the freeway, I'd return to producing in the next week or so. Really, I would.

"Well, no pressure, you know who to call," Dee Dee said. "Your pal Dee Dee." She teetered off toward her Range Rover. In Santa Monica ("SaMo"), the fewer kids you had, the more car you drove. I went inside with Spice, sank onto the living room couch, and stared at the gift. "Should I open it?" I asked Spice. "It could be truffles." Spice just sighed.

"You're killing me!" someone said. "Don't keep me waiting. I love gifts!"

Spice started barking at John's favorite armchair, an old, cracked leather piece we bought at a garage sale. Trish emerged, seated in his chair, her dark braid around her shoulder, delicate hands clasped, a child's great anticipation on her old, lovely face.

"Did you ever go all white?" I asked, circling my head.

"Never," Trish said, stroking her hair. "I kept my color right up 'til my last breath." Spice calmed down, sitting still as a statue, completely focused on Trish. Did he see Trish? Or just feel her? Smell her? Her scent reminded me of citrus and sunshine, like the Farmer's Market on a June morning.

"What a nice dog," Trish said. "Not a handsome one, that one. But he's smart. Now, open the gift!"

I picked up the silver box, then hesitated. Maybe I was just hearing and seeing things, as my friends feared. Maybe I was losing my mind. After all, Post-it Notes were the only thing keeping the S.S. Casa Sugar afloat.

"No, I'm sorry," I said, putting the box down. "Ghosts don't exist. I mean, it's understandable that I would be experiencing these kinds of hallucinations . . ."

"I'm as real as the granola you almost ate for breakfast," Trish said. I know I poured granola, then changed my mind. Granola's a lot of effort, let's face it.

"I've never been so insulted," she huffed.

"I'll open it, but then, do something," I said. I tore open the wrapping; inside the box was a gift card for three months of storage. "What an ass. Listen, don't freak me out by pulling your face over your head and screaming."

"What? You want me to tell a joke? Dance?" Trish said. She stood and started tap-dancing. "I'm not real, huh! I would cook but I'm not allowed to use a stove. One time, someone up here figured out how to make pancakes, ruined it for everybody. Keys, funny noises, doors slamming, cold air, that's all okay. But no pancakes."

"Trish. My sanity is at stake. If you don't exist, I've lost my mind. And I'll lose everything . . . ," I said. "And, by the way, you do have a scent. It's nice."

Trish was becoming even more clear, like a painter's vision come to life—here was light, there shadow, here color . . .

"I still don't understand." I asked, "Why me? Do you have unfinished business down here? Is this like a CBS show?"

Trish leaned back. "God, no. Children have the ability to communicate with the dead, until around age two," she said. "After two or three, all of the external 'stuff' takes over. 'Do this, don't do that. Stay inside the lines, don't climb that tree, don't tell a fib, say thank you . . .'"

I thought about Ellie. "But you—" Trish said. "Something must have happened. The spell wasn't broken. You pick up our cues."

"A spell," I said. "Is this a curse?"

"No," Trish said. "I hate to sound clichéd, but it's a blessing. You'll see."

"Is John allowed to visit?" I asked. "Does he see me? Does he see his little girl?"

Trish's eyes wandered to a wood-framed photograph of me and John, taken at the beach in front of Casa Del Mar, the grand old hotel. Staying there had made me feel like I was Carole Lombard. John had held out his iPhone to snap our picture. My eyes were squinty, my nose red, my hair whipped into a frenzy. John's mouth was wide and open, as though he'd just been tickled. When I looked at that picture, I could hear him laughing.

For how much longer?

"There's such bureaucracy, sweetheart," Trish said. "It takes years, usually . . . your powers would have to be very keen—"

How much longer could I hear his laughter?

"Tell me about him. Tell me about your husband."

"I wouldn't have picked him out of a Starbucks line in 'Who's Next To Go,' " I said. Trish tilted her head, her eyes questioning me.

"John was tall, good-looking, solid . . . and young . . . too young . . . ," I said. "The first time I saw him, he looked to me like a rib eye."

"Ah! Sex," Trish said. "Mel and I . . . we had wonderful times, even as we got older, and things weren't working as well . . . we had fun figuring it out, best we could."

"I would stare at John while he cooked, or when he played the sax, horribly, I might add, or you know, after we made love, or when he read the Sunday *Times*. I'd pretend I had just spotted him . . . at the airport, on a street corner, on the boardwalk . . . He had the most amazing forearms . . . Can you fall in love with forearms?"

Spice was staring at me, riveted. I choked out my next thought.

"And I'd think, Wow. How did you, Hannah Marsh, land this guy?"

I saw tears in Trish's eyes. Ghosts cry?

"We had priorities. Food, wine, sex, sleep, work. Repeat. Sometimes there'd be more food than sleep, more sleep than wine. Many times there was more sex than sleep, or sex during sleep. Or, we'd play out our pyramid of priorities in bed—sex, then sleep, then wine, food, and work. We'd spend an entire weekend in bed, like the Four Seasons Maui. You don't have to fly. You don't have to tip the concierge . . ."

I paused.

"So often we'd fall asleep wrapped in each other's arms."

She just stared at me, listening.

"Trish." My voice was hoarse. I could barely hear myself above the breeze outside my window. Fall would be over soon. Then there'd be winter, spring, summer . . . and the anniversary of John's death. Time was running over me.

"Time is a heartless bitch," I said.

"You're strong, Hannah," she said. "Time can't take you."

"We were going to grow old together," I whispered.

Trish leaned forward, her arms open. I fell toward her embrace.

* * *

I must've fallen asleep on the living room couch. Spice was curled up next to me, his head resting on my thigh. He seemed exhausted, like me, the mother he never wanted.

My dream, my memory. John and I together, corner table at Portofino, the intimate Italian restaurant on Montana next to the Duckblind liquor store. Early in our relationship, a crisp, cold night. I'm in boots and fishnets, knowing he'll run his fingers along the inside of my thigh during the pasta course. We're arguing about the menu. The squid linguini with duck sausage or the branzino in butter sauce? The arugula salad with lemon-herb dressing or the sautéed octopi? This is important. This determines everything. We hold hands, and it comes to me, vividly.

We would be together, forever.

I looked at the hand that had held his that night. I wondered if anyone would hold it the way he did. Would it feel natural, would I love anyone, or would anyone love me, enough to know it was safe to argue over something as innocuous as, say, garlic? What we knew that night was that neither of us was going anywhere. Until one of us did. Spice shifted, putting his head on my belly. I gazed into his big brown eyes. He yawned. He probably hadn't been sleeping well, either.

"How much do you miss him?" I asked, stroking his ear. The room darkened as clouds moved overhead. Goose bumps appeared on my arms. I felt a chill, as though someone had opened a window. Spice sprang from the couch, wagging his tail and barking. Somewhere, someone was baking cookies. My cellphone alarm rang, reminding me to pick up Ellie. The clouds moved on. The room warmed.

9

Preschool Probation

I turned right onto Sunset off Allenford. Kanye was rap-singing on the radio. I found myself rap-caterwauling along. I took this as a sign that I had, quite possibly, regained my will to live.

"'I love you like a fat kid loves cake,'" I sang. "'Like Cleopatra loved her some snake . . .'" My phone rang, interrupting my brief brush with happiness.

"We're going in Friday afternoon," Jay said. "This is going to fuck up my Halloween. My 'Katy Perry at the 2011 Grammys' is a minimum five-hour commitment."

"The network meeting? Already?"

"They're solidifying their schedule. We need story lines. Unwanted pregnancy, sex video, ex-boyfriend in prison . . . the *Housewife* bitches have raised the bar."

"You say without irony," I said. "I'll come up with ideas. Horrifying ideas."

"Our careers are riding on this, Hannah," Jay said then. "I'll just save time, bring the blue wig and falsies to the meeting."

Guess who'd forgotten about Bunny Hill Preschool's Annual Halloween Fair and Parade? The "normal" moms—"norms"—were dressed in Sexy Nurse or Sexy Witch or Sexy Fairy costumes. Boring wormholes into my brain and depositing droplets of insecurity, they stared as I walked in, in my usual fleece. All conversation stopped.

"You like my 'Frumpy Mom' costume?" I said to Sexy Botoxed Nun. "The five-year-old Uggs are an inspired touch, right?"

Nothing.

I excused myself and checked Ellie's cubby outside her classroom. I came up with a red note. *Dear God, not the red note!*

I avoided Sexy Juvédermed Police Woman's stare, hiding the note in my hoodie pocket before anyone could see. But I knew they had. The wormholes multiplied. The red note was the ultimate preschool humiliation. My child was Bunny Hill Hester Prynne. I turned my back to the norms, and peered at the crumpled paper: *Hannah, please come by my office, regarding Ellie. Rhoda.* There was a happy face stamped next to Rhoda's name.

The new assistant teacher, Laura, walked out of Ellie's classroom. I shanghaied her. "Do you know what this note is about?" Laura had a heart-shaped face and a Wisconsin accent. Around these parts, she's considered plump. Around these parts, Jennifer Aniston could lose a few. The norms swapped Senna laxatives from their porn-addicted Sikh doctor like Chiclets. Within six months, Laura would be twenty pounds lighter and married to a divorced agent dad. My prediction.

"Um . . . no?" she said, in question form. "Um . . . I don't think so?" *Translation: I know but I'm too scared to tell you. You smell of crazy.*

Ellie sat in the corner wearing a ballerina costume that could have jetéd off center stage at Lincoln Center. I kissed her head, careful not to mess up the headpiece Jay had fashioned out of feathers and sequins. I was thankful I remembered to wash her hair the night before, although I'd forgotten (again) to clip her nails. I couldn't use my "she's auditioning for the role of Nosferatu" line again; no one here had understood the joke the first time.

"Mommy, you missed the Halloween Fair," my ballerina said. Jay had dressed her as Gelsey Kirkland. It's sick, but way beyond Ellie's understanding. (On Chloe's website, she suggested making your kids' Halloween costumes out of recycled grocery bags and empty laundry detergent bottles. *And I'm the crazy one.*)

"I know, honey," I said. "I'm so, so sorry."

"You missed the parade, Mama." Oh, sorrow. John would have been there. John would have worn a fireman costume and set up the scary-cookie decorating station. He would have made the cookies himself. Even dead, John was the better parent.

"I have to talk to Miss Rhoda," I said. "Do you want to wait here or in the hall, where I can see you?"

Ellie elected to sit on a bench in her tutu outside Rhoda's office. She put her little hands on her chubby legs, clad in pink tights, watching me behind her glasses. *Cute does not describe. Cute times 800,000, and you're a bit closer.*

I interrupted a conversation Rhoda was having with Faux-Rothchild (missing consonant a dead giveaway) about the spring auction. Faux-Rothchild never failed to introduce herself by her full name. Three times a week.

"How do we fill the cabana gap left by the Tisches?" Rhoda asked. She was dressed as a witch—the hat, the cape; her broom, made of sticks, stood in the corner. Her face was purple, and she'd attached a mole on the tip of her nose.

"I hope they have more kids. They were always good for a cabana or two," Rhoda said. "Does no one do cabanas anymore?"

"Rhoda?" I asked, "did you want to speak to me?" The red note was a throw-down. If this were junior high, I would have tucked my hair into the back of my shirt, and slid my rings to my knuckles.

"Hannah," Rhoda said, "why don't you have a seat?" She gave Faux-R a wave, got up, and closed the door. I saw Ellie's little face disappearing on the other side. I caught her eye before the door closed altogether and my baby winked at me.

Rhoda sat down, her purple face serious and searching. I tried not to focus on the mole. "Hannah," she finally said, "how are you . . . adjusting?"

"Adjusting?"

"To being alone," she said. "Without John? We truly miss him here, at Bunny Hill."

What did this have to do with John?

"I'm fine," I said, shifting in my seat. It's hard being questioned by Margaret Hamilton. I expected to see monkeys flying out of her head.

"Does Ellie talk to you about . . . John?" she asked.

"I've talked to her," I said. "We had a talk. I've tried. I know I have. It's hard."

"She's talking to the other children about her father," Rhoda said.

"Oh," I said, relieved. "Well, that's normal. She misses her daddy." I tried to will my tears back into their ducts.

"Ellie's scaring the other children."

"Scaring them," I said. I grow cold. *This is just the beginning. Our child will be a delinquent because her father is dead. I see tattoos and piercings and discarded e.p.t. tests in her pink wastebasket. I see a terrible garage band. I see Ellie, snarling and hateful and all of fourteen. Good Lord, I see Samantha Ronson.*

"Ellie is telling the children she's having conversations with her daddy," Rhoda said.

I'm shivering. "She's what? Talking to John?"

"She says John reads *Knuffle Bunny* to her at night. She turns the pages, and he reads. And then, she claims . . . they sing together—"

Rhoda sifted through papers on her desk. She picked up a note. Ellie, who'd had trouble being away from me, had been able to sleep in her own bed lately. She cried less. If she needed me, she appeared at my bedside at three in the morning, holding her bear. "Mommy, can I come sleep with you?" she'd ask. Was there ever a question? Ellie used to say she was "nocturnal" and "slept with her eyes open." And now, I was. My sleep was vigilant, watchful, as though if I slept, someone else I cared about would die.

"R. Kelly," Rhoda read from her notes. "I'm a Flirt."

"That was kind of their song. I have no rational explanation for it," I said. I pray that Ellie didn't recite the lyrics to the kids at school. I should have listened to Chloe, who only let her kids listen to Disney soundtracks and, you know, barking dogs.

"She's been talking a lot about death and the spirit world." Rhoda pursed her lips. "Her words, not mine." *Oh, dear. Worse than a Goth, Ellie was going to turn out to be Marianne Williamson.*

"Ellie has always had a great imagination," I say.

"She's so sensitive and there's so much to deal with—much too much for a little girl, I'm afraid. She needs help," Rhoda said.

"I'll get her help."

"It's . . . become something of a problem for us."

"What?"

"Parents have started complaining," Rhoda says.

"Wait. The same parents who'd call John if they needed anything? A snack, a coach, a lifeguard, a handyman, a balloon blower-upper? Those parents?"

"There's no need to get hostile," Rhoda said, smiling. Her teeth look yellow against her purple skin. I focus on the happy face button attached to her black cape at the neck. I want to pierce her with it. "We feel that a change would do Ellie good."

"A change."

"I've got a list of schools here, all very reputable institutions," Rhoda said, handing me a sheet of paper. "I think she'll be quite happy at any of them."

"You're kicking my daughter out of Bunny Hill?"

"We don't like to label this kind of action," Rhoda says. "We don't want to ruin Ellie's chances of getting into a good college."

"Oh my God," I say.

"We're not going to put this down in her permanent record, no worries."

"You're taking her away from her friends. Away from her teachers."

"I knew you would understand—"

"What about the pre-learning track?" I say. "Ellie already knows her alphabet, she can write her name. She knows her numbers—"

"She'll do just fine," Rhoda is saying. The happy face pin is mocking me as she moves toward the door. I see photographs of Rhoda with her husband, with her grandchildren, with all the Bunny Hill kids who aren't on the Dead Daddy Track.

I hate them all.

"What about my tuition?" I said. "We paid through the end of the year."

"Nonrefundable. Check your contract. That's really a shame," she said, distracted, looking for something on her desk. "You take good care, now. Were my keys just here a minute ago?"

"Keys," I said, turning back. Suddenly, there's another woman standing next to the stick broom, shaking her head. She's wearing a housecoat, holding a wooden spoon, her arms crossed at her ample chest. Her brow is shiny with sweat of labor.

"A shand-eh, Rhoda-leh," this ghostly figure says, shaking her head. "A shand-eh."

"Rhoda," I say to her purple face, her yellow teeth.

"Yes?"

"A shand-eh, Rhoda-leh," I said, mimicking the lady in the corner, who's there, tired as the day she passed. I take a guess. "Your grandmother is very disappointed."

Even under the purple makeup, I saw Rhoda turn white.

"Ellie!" I say. She's not outside the office. "Ellie!" Where is she? I want to leave this place as quickly as possible. I run past her cubby, through her classroom, where her drawings are pasted on the wall, and find her twirling in the sandbox for the last time. I see that she's grown so much, just in a month. Time is fluid. Time spills through my fingers. The world keeps spinning, farther from John having stood here, at this spot. At the tree he planted there. At the sandbox he filled. Tulle flies up in the air. Ellie's laughing. The world is cruel beyond measure. Already, at three, she's learned this. Already, she's coping better than I am.

* * *

"Ellie's been kicked out of Bunny Hill," I announce to the Grief Team while attempting to defrost a month-old Chloe vegan meal. "But that's not the bad part."

"What?" Chloe asks. "That's completely unacceptable." She's brought her daughter Lorraine and a sniffing, barking, snarling pack of rescue dogs to the house. Spice is going crazy. Lorraine is on all fours, barking.

"Why is Lorraine barking?" Jay asks. "Should we fetch her a water bowl?"

"She wants attention," Chloe said. "I posted about it on my blog this morning. You wouldn't believe the number of responses I got. At least five or six." Lorraine is in kindergarten at Carlthorpe, what I jokingly refer to as "the missionary school" on 4th and Montana. The children dressed in uniforms, the boys had Brylcreemed hair, the girls wore headbands. When I'd see them lined up on the street for school, they looked like Latter Day Saints dolls.

Aimee walked in, bringing a bad chemical peel with her.

"Did your face get into a fight with a blowtorch?" I asked.

"My agent's about to drop me," she said, opening the freezer and grabbing the ever-diminishing vodka bottle.

"Didn't you defriend Stoli?" Jay said, eyeing the bottle.

"You expect me to quit, now?" Aimee said. "I'm under enormous pressure. You don't just drop old friends like that."

"Aimee, when you were twenty-five, you swore you would never do anything to your face," I said. "Serious actresses have faces that do face things."

"Twenty-five? Oh, right, that was before I got the big role I've always wanted—oh, wait, I never got it, remember?" Aimee said.

"Look at Jodie Foster," Chloe said, "or Annette Bening."

"Jodie has something called a jawline; all the hot lesbians have it," Aimee said. "Bening is beautiful, but she shouldn't go on camera with her real face. It just makes people angry. Besides, my skin's going to look like Drew Barrymore at fourteen in a week."

"Oh, back when she was doing blow," Jay said. "Do they still call it blow? That's why I can't keep a man. I'm so outmoded."

"Let me repeat. Ellie has been kicked out of Bunny Hill," I said.

"Good," Aimee said, "I hate that place. So pretentious. Reminds me of my own childhood, if I'd actually had one."

"They never appreciated her fashion sense," Jay said. "My God, they should give her a medal!"

"I'm calling Rhoda right this minute," Chloe said, punching numbers into her iPhone. "Three years ago, I got them tickets for the *Dancing with the Stars* finale for their spring auction—they'll listen to me—"

"Three years ago, you had money," Aimee said.

"Remember the parties?" Jay said, looking wistful. "Who doesn't love a repressed banker?"

"Guys," I said, "focus. Ellie was kicked out because she's talking to her dad."

"Dad John? Dead John?" Jay asked. "What is going on in this house?!"

"It's not real. She's stressed out," Chloe said. "I saw this coming from a mile away. You know, this would make a really good topic for my blog."

"Now you're just fucking with me, right?" Aimee said to Chloe.

"She's scaring the perfect children who have two living parents," I said.

"Little intact-family punks," Jay said.

"Let's be practical," Chloe said. "Ellie needs help. She's endured a huge loss. Her dad was her anchor. Their worlds revolved around each other."

"And Hannah figures into this situation . . . how?" Aimee said.

"I'm not saying Hannah isn't a great mom," Chloe said, as Lorraine barked. "Down, girl, that's a good girl." Lorraine crept from the room.

"I was a good-enough mom married to Super Dad," I said. "And that was good enough then. But not anymore."

"What do they talk about?" Jay asked. "Has she ever mentioned Uncle Jay?"

"John reads to her at night. And they sing together," I said. "Like before, like always."

"Usher?" Aimee asked.

"Oh, wait. Oh my God, R. Kelly again?" Jay asked. "Not that I'm glad John's dead—I'm not, I adored him, but that I don't miss."

"Bullshit people with their bullshit power trips . . . ," Aimee said, then, "If I adopt a kid and get him in Bunny Hill, do you think I might find a new agent?"

"Where's the cranberry part?" Jay asked, nodding at Aimee's drink.

"Shut it, Mother," Aimee said.

"What should I do?" I asked. "How do I talk to Ellie . . . do I talk to her?"

"Spy on her," Jay said.

Chloe squeezed my hand. "I have three child psychologists on speed dial. I can't use them anymore since the collection calls started—"

"I appreciate it, Chloe," I said, "I really do, but I don't think Ellie needs therapy. She seems . . . happy."

Chloe wasn't giving up. "I'm not saying this is a substitute, but when children lose a loved one, they need something to fill that void. I know you have Spice, but maybe she needs something small and cuddly—"

"Puppy-pusher," Jay said.

"Mommy?" Ellie said from the other room. "Lorraine keeps barking at me."

"She's herding," Chloe said. "It's totally normal. Kids cope with stress in their own ways. It has to do with Billy's unemployment and evolving social conscience."

"And nothing to do with your obsession with strays," Jay said, peering into the living room. "I think Lorraine is shedding."

Aimee laughed, then grimaced, touching her face. "Ow, ow, ow! Don't make me laugh—it burns, it burns!"

I looked at Aimee. *It's bad*, I thought, *when the people who make the most sense in your life are dead.*

* * *

"What are you doing, Mommy?" Ellie asked, as I looked through her book basket for something to read aloud. I picked up *Love You Forever*, then put it down.

Not tonight. That book was too sad, and I didn't want to hurtle into suicidal depression until Ellie was eighteen and out of the house. Spice scratched at the door. He'd been sleeping on the scatter rug in front of Ellie's bed. I would let him out around eleven at night. We behaved like an older couple who have nothing in common after the children leave.

"I want to read a book to you, tonight, El," I said. "I've been such a . . . (neglectful, horrible mother) . . . Mommy's been tired . . . tired and busy . . ."

Busy? Busy doing what? Grieving is a time-suck.

"No, Mommy," Ellie said, her eyes wide. "I'm going to bed, see? I'm soooo sleepy!"

Spice on his belly, his head between his paws. Watching me. Waiting for me to leave. *Even to a dog, I was the third wheel.* Ellie was ensconced in her cocoon, her blanket up to her chin. I bent over her and tucked her in. She was so small.

"Can I read to you tomorrow night?" I asked.

"I'm going to sleep now, Mommy. Go to sleep," Ellie said.

"Okay. I love you." I kissed her cheek, her forehead, her other cheek. I sat down on her bed. "I love you so much, Ellie. You know that, right?"

"Yes, Mommy."

"Is there anything you want to tell me?"

She looked at me with her big, round eyes. "No?"

"I'm here, if you want to talk," I said. "I mean, about anything. You can always tell Mommy anything, you know."

"Good night, Mommy," she said, then rolled over, her back toward me.

"Good night, baby," I said. Knuffle Bunny was tucked in under the sheets. "God bless you." *Do you hear me, God? You kind of owe me, here.*

I patted Spice on the head, then went to the kitchen, poured my second glass of pinot noir (why are we counting?), sat on the floor outside Ellie's bedroom door, and waited. And as I waited, it occurred to me that John might be as consistently late in spirit form as he was in human form. Even in death, he could be insensitive.

I was startled awake by Ellie talking. At first, it sounded like she was having a conversation with her bear. Then I heard questions. "What does it look like there, again?" "Do you have friends?" "Who's your best friend?" "Is Jesus there?" "When are you coming back?" And "Why, Daddy?"

I felt cold fingers dancing down my arm.

I cracked open the door. Ellie's Tinkerbell lamp was on. (Okay, so I'm no Westside faux-decorator mom. Sue me.) She was sitting up, Knuffle Bunny on her lap. She turned the pages, slowly, as though reading them to herself. Spice was up on his hind legs, his paws in the air, dancing. Making happy, grunting sounds.

It was the first time I'd seen Spice smile since John died. *(Yes, dogs smile—you may only know this for sure after seeing them miserable for an extended period of time.)*

I started to shake, gripped by fear. Chloe was right. Ellie needed help. I would call the top child psychiatrist Chloe recommended in the morning—the doctor with the silky voice who was on *Oprah*.

When John died, Ellie's innocence died. He crawled down the rabbit hole and dragged us with him. I gulped down the rest of my wine. John and I needed to have a serious talk.

What's the first thing to do when you want to talk to a dead person? For me, I sat outside for an hour, in the cold, and called John's name.

"John?" I waited.

"John, are you there?" I waited.

"John! I know you're out there! You come down here and talk to me right now!"

Lights went on next door, so I scooted back inside.

I grabbed my laptop and typed in "how to talk to dead" and was promptly confronted with a thousand websites, blogs, and YouTube videos. After scouring through the obvious scams, I found a blog written by a New Orleans medium. She suggested something called "mirror gazing," which sounded cheap and easy.

Perfect.

In our bathroom, I found a smudged hand mirror that John used for shaving. I started to wipe it with my sleeve, then stopped. *John's fingerprints.* There he was. Maybe I could reconstruct his DNA from his prints, build a human Jurassic Park in my backyard. My breath caught in my throat, and I succumbed to the familiar burning sensation, an integral part of my emotional repertoire. Like the second cousin who won't leave after Thanksgiving dinner (and yet, you invite him again next year—*holiday amnesia*).

I went into the living room, holding the mirror with two hands—God forbid, I drop it and get seven years bad luck. Really? *Add it to the pile.* The blog had said I should take off excess jewelry (much like a *Vogue* editor, the dead frown on over-accessorizing), wear loose clothing, and evoke the departed with personal objects.

I took off my wedding ring, and set it next to a picture of John holding Spice. *Light a candle.* I'm not a candle girl. Chloe has candles, for ambience. And to cut down on the electric bill (though she'd never admit it). Aimee has boffing candles; the lighting and music has to be just right. It's like Aimee's doing *Spider-Man the Musical* instead of her trainer. I did have a flashlight. After all, I live in earthquake country. After twenty minutes, I found a penlight running low on battery. Had there been an actual earthquake, my child and I would have perished as I searched for it.

Relax your mind as you gaze through the mirror. My face lit by the flickering penlight, I gazed into the mirror. Okay, get past the circles under my eyes. *Hi.* The worry wrinkles on my forehead. *How are you?* Is my upper lip disappearing? (Under the mustache?)

Wait for mirror to cloud over. Calmly embrace what you find there. My hand reached out to calmly embrace my wineglass. My beloved had died. I was raising a child with emotional problems. I was not paying attention to my work, hair, nails, or eyebrows. I was drinking too much, or as we call it in L.A.: "self-medicating." *No one "medicates" here—they "self-medicate."*

Like Alice, I tried to find John through the looking glass. I stared for what felt like hours. Then, the strangest thing happened. My stomach growled. Suddenly, I was starving. I hadn't been hungry since that fateful September morning. In the mirror, I hallucinated Bay Cities Italian loaves, dolmas, Jon's Pizza, See's candy, langoustines, steak with melted butter and sea salt . . . John's homemade tamales. I found myself sniffing the air, lingering in imaginary aromas. I found myself salivating. What I didn't see was anyone dead. *If you really care, John, you'd appear in your silly apron, and you'd feed me. Just one more time.*

Trish had told me I couldn't rush the dead. She didn't say anything about guilting them.

Jay, Ralph, Spice, and I met for coffee the next morning at the Pirates, a coffee shop that went by an Italian name I never remember. John and I had dubbed it the Pirates after Salvador and Freddy, the baristas, acted like pirates to make Ellie laugh.

We sat outside with our lattes and bran muffins and soaked in the late fall sunshine. "Sixty-seven degrees and clear," I said. "It almost makes me feel like living."

"The meeting's been pushed to Monday, praise Baby Jesus," he said, as he checked his BlackBerry. "Listen, I've been thinking about your situation. If Hidalgo died, I know I would insist on hearing from that bitch. So. Hidalgo has a cousin. Santino. He put the 'eye' in island."

"When did you start talking to Hidalgo again? Isn't he having a baby?"

"His wife is having a baby. I'm helping them out, here and there," Jay said. "And, no, I don't want to hear it. Anyway, Santino . . . he's into Santeria."

"The fruity wine drink or the voodoo?" I asked.

"Please don't call it that," Jay said. "Santino is some sort of high priest. He does these séances . . . they're performance art with animal sacrifice."

"And he gets paid for this?" I asked.

"*Beaucoup*. Tom Cruise flew him out to the set in Germany for that cute Nazi movie he did. Santino has a glass house on Doheny. He works the Girl's Club on Friday nights. He's a 'Lady Impersonator.'"

"He's a drag queen. Why wasn't I born a man who's all woman?" I lamented.

"I'm thinking of making him a reality show," Jay said. "Logo would die. But I'm afraid to get too close."

"Animal sacrifice," I said. "That's the kind of thing the City Council frowns on."

"Pigeons, goats, chickens . . . ," Jay said. "I can tell you Ralph is staying dog years away."

I looked at Spice, who gave me a look that said, "You are evil, get me ham."

"Get me his number," I said to Jay.

Halloween is NoMo's Super Bowl. From 25th to Lincoln and San Vicente to Montana, the streets are filled with costumed revelers spanning all ages and bank accounts. We're not just talking Flash or Shrek or Sleeping Beauty; teenagers show off new cleavage, mothers don Afro wigs and micro-miniskirts, and dads dress up like Johnny Depp in *Pirates of the Caribbean*. Stephen Spielberg and family make an appearance, as do the Schwarzen-Shrivers and the Afflecks. Police cars block off whole streets, and homeowners give away stuffed animals, cash, and giant-sized Snickers. For one night, and one night only, you can feel normal if you're famous, rich if you're poor. It was our first NoMo Halloween without John. Ellie was dressed as Dora the Explorer. Jay's dream of a pint-sized Lady Gaga in a meat dress would have to wait.

Ellie and I met up with Chloe and her charges at the corner of 16th and Georgina, Ground Zero of NoMo Halloween. It was barely dusk, and already there was a 45-minute line at the haunted house on the corner. Jen Garner and her dimpled children were at the front of the line, talking to a comedy director I recognized but couldn't place. The redhead Desperate Housewife was holding the hands of two small children in the middle. We decided to push on.

I was looking for something beyond the earthbound ghosts and goblins. I hadn't heard from Trish, and John had yet to make an appearance except in his Ellie's room. Maybe it was the dark, the shrieks of children, the fog machines, and the flashing lights, but I was overwhelmed. I couldn't tell what was real, what was fake.

We walked crowded blocks to 10th and Georgina, the corner where John was hit. I grabbed Chloe to get my bearings. Somewhere, fireworks started going off.

"Hannah? Are you okay?" Chloe asked.

"I just need to go home. I think Ellie's done, too." Ellie ran off with Lorraine to another house. She was nowhere near done.

"I'll take her," Chloe said. Simon Baker and his brood passed us on the sidewalk. NoMo was a place where even movie stars seemed well-adjusted; it just wasn't fair.

Chloe hugged me, smothering me with her blond wig. I didn't have the heart to tell her that no one knew who Stevie Nicks was anymore.

"We'll be there soon," she said. I watched as she tripped off toward the girls. I turned to head home, but something prevented me from moving. I held my hand out. "Stop," I said. "Stop." I held my hand out to prevent the sudden horrifying image of John's accident before me. In my mind's eye, there was a car, looming large and dark . . .

"Please stop," I said. Strobe lights skipped across my tearstained face. In the celebration, no one noticed.

That morning, at three o'clock, I was a little disturbed to find Marilyn Monroe on my front doorstep. The last of the trick-or-treaters, the kids wearing the cheaper costumes with moms and dads who worked late, had ended hours ago. I had finally just nodded off to sleep. I was in the middle of a drowning dream. I'd jumped off a cruise ship to save Ellie, who'd been swept overboard by a wave. Instead, we were both drowning. *Good times.*

Marilyn was wearing a blond wig, light-up stripper platforms, and a leather bustier. She looked about seven feet tall. I wasn't altogether sure I was not still dreaming.

"So, you've met Santino," Jay said from behind Marilyn. He was dressed as Katy Perry, and was maybe even prettier than her. Next to him, Hidalgo smiled nervously. He looked like he'd just wandered out of an Abercrombie & Fitch ad.

"Where's your outfit?" I asked him.

"I am a male model," Hidalgo said.

"Strike a pose," Jay said. Hidalgo jutted out a hip and his lower lip. "You met Santino, high priest of Santeria, son of Shango," Jay said.

"I'm a fire god." Santino shrugged, tossing it off. I realized, with some alarm, he was carrying two pigeons clasped under his arm. "It's just something I do. I don't ask questions. My card." He fished it from deep inside his bustier. I held it to the light.

SANTINO JAVIER DE LA CRÚZ, FIRE GOD,
WWW.SANTINOFIREGOD.COM
AVAILABLE FOR PARTIES AND HAIR/MAKEUP

"This will be tough to explain to the Santa Monica fire department."

"You have a sharp knife?" Santino asked. "I forgot my double-ax. I am such the idiot."

"I hate when I do that," I said. I walked them into the kitchen. Sharpening knives. Add it to the list, thus far, of things I haven't kept up since John's death: *Walking the dog. Washing hair. Keeping child sane.* Santino started checking out the hardware.

"Nice," he said, admiring the knife John used to cut up whole chickens. "*Vámonos.*"

Jay had brought a bag of votive candles. "I've been meaning to give these to you as a housewarming gift. Four years ago."

The pigeons were still cooing.

"Light the candles," Santino said, as he spread rocks, forming a circle on the ground in the backyard. The air was sweet and moist. Santino started murmuring in Spanish, but a Spanish I didn't fully recognize. It was lilting, melodic, singsong. And scary as fuck. He slowly swirled the pigeons over his head. I felt the pigeons getting worried. *Did they think he was taking them out for a cocktail?*

"Jay," I whispered, tugging at his sequined dress, "I don't feel right about this—"

Santino suddenly thrust the pigeons to the rock circle and brought down the knife. I shut my eyes and screamed, hiding behind Jay.

Then I heard the pigeons cooing. I opened my eyes. The knife had been plunged into the ground. Santino plucked feathers from the birds, then released them. As they flew to the tree (presumably to view the proceedings), he placed the feathers in the shape of a cross inside the circle, sneaked a flask from his bosom, and started drizzling a dark liquid over the rocks and feathers.

"Oh my God, I thought he was going to kill them," I whispered to Jay, as we watched Santino continue to chant and gyrate.

"Not since the goat incident at Paris Hilton's place," Jay said. "He just outsources, now."

Santino finally quieted down and motioned for us to sit. Hidalgo hung on to Jay's arm. I wondered where Spice was hiding—I could use something to hang on to, myself. Santino placed his hands above the feather cross, his eyes blinking rapidly. He flapped his arms and shook his head, his wig falling to the side. Jay giggled nervously. Hidalgo pinched his side.

"I feel him," Santino said. "He is here . . . John . . . John . . ." (Which sounded like "Yawn, Yawn," but I wasn't about to correct his pronunciation. I did yawn, however.)

The wind picked up and flames shot up. We jumped back as the whole circle went ablaze. Santino stammered in Spanish and readjusted his wig.

The breeze ceased. The flames died down.

"Okay, that's it," Santino said, clapping his hands.

"That's it?" I asked. "What's it?"

"That was John," Santino said. "You no feel him? The wind, baby."

"You've got to be kidding me," I said.

"Hannah, Santino is a Son of Shango," Jay pointed out. "If he says John was the wind, then John was the wind."

"Do you have Kool-Aid?" Hidalgo asked. "I'm so thirsty."

"Come on, baby," Jay said. "I'll get you something to drink."

I was left alone with Latin Anna Nicole Smith, who had closed his eyes. I stood, and started cleaning up. I didn't want Ellie to see this mess and start asking questions.

"Stop," Santino said, grabbing my hands. "Don't touch!" His hands were calloused and warm.

"Listen to me, girlfriend," Santino said, his eyes searching my face. "Your husband," he whispered. "He love you very much."

"How do you know?" I whispered back.

"You will see," Santino said. He whipped around, as though someone was shouting behind him. I saw nothing but the tree. My tree.

"Girlfriend, honey, you got lots of action, here, oh my God," he said.

"Not at all," I replied stiffly. "I haven't had sex since John died."

"No, baby," Santino said. "You have the dead." He gazed at me and said nothing, which was more unnerving than "killing" pigeons and lighting my backyard on fire. "Know the Goddess Oya, sweetheart. She runs the show between the dead and the living. The dead, they want to speak to you."

"The dead need someone to talk to? Why? Are they lonely? Seems like there's a lot of them out there . . . I know at least three, not even counting Hervé Villechaize."

"The little man from *Fantasy Island*?"

"Yes."

"He's dead?" Santino said, starting to crumble.

"I'm sorry."

"Are you sure?" Santino asked. I helped him stand on his light-up stripper shoes.

"I'm really so sorry," I said, as I walked him up the stairs into the kitchen.

Like you wouldn't have looked up Oya on Wiki. She's bigger than Oprah—the warrior goddess of lightning, wind, fertility, fire, and magic. Talk about a full-time job. Plus, she guards the underworld and causes hurricanes, tornadoes, and earthquakes. *Do NOT cross her.* Oya is the guardian of the realm between life and death; she can call forth the spirit of death. *So why was John playing hard to get?*

I fell asleep with my laptop on my stomach, waking at the crack of dawn to Spice licking my face, rain pelting the tile roof, and Ellie screaming. Even before my eyes opened, I knew there was a leak in the kitchen, Spice needed to pee (and would refuse to go out in the rain), and Ellie had awakened from a bad dream. I ran into Ellie's room. She was sitting up in bed, crying. My heart broke at the sight of her.

"I had a dream!" she said, shaking in her satin pajamas. "A bad dream!"

"Honey, I'm here," I managed. I put my arms around her and held her tight. "What was it?"

"A scary cow!" she wailed.

I started laughing. Ellie looked at me. "Why are you laughing, Mommy?"

"I'm just so . . . relieved," I said. Spice was whining, so I made him go in the backyard. There'd be no walking couples therapy. I went out back with my hoodie over my pajamas and looked at the mess. Feathers, burned-out candles, scorched circle on the cement. I had to get this shit gone before Ellie started to ask questions. Then

I noticed . . . the feathers had been rearranged into a single word:
BOO.

My back stiffened. "Who did this?"

"What, Mommy?" Ellie ran to the kitchen door.

"Nothing!" I said. "Nothing . . . just someone trying to be funny."
I messed up the feathers, then ran back inside.

10

Social (Paranormal) Networking

Monday morning, and already I was a week behind. I had to check out new schools for Ellie, and I was having my first network meeting, A.D. (After Death). Jay and I had spent the weekend going over fake reality scenarios for Karli and Kevin, including the scenario where we lose our network deal because our scenarios sucked.

I was getting breakfast ready for Ellie, who was taking decades deciding between platform clogs (courtesy of Uncle Jay) or Vans (courtesy of me). Ellie didn't know the meaning of the word "overdress." At times I wondered if Jay hadn't gotten his DNA mixed up with mine.

"I can't go back to my school?" she said, peering up at me. She'd decided on the inappropriate clogs. I'd have to peel them off of her with a paring knife.

"We're just checking out new preschools," I told her. "These ones seem more . . . fun."

Of course, I had no idea whether a new place would be fun or not. I just knew I had to find a school to take Ellie that morning so I could go to my meeting. One of us had to earn a living, and Ellie wasn't old enough unless we moved to a third world country where she'd make Nikes.

I opened the refrigerator to get her milk. Two percent. Was I supposed to force her to drink nonfat milk, like her pediatrician had suggested? No. A dead parent was enough suffering for the time being.

I grabbed the milk, closed the refrigerator door, then opened it again.

Someone had arranged the tiny pickles John kept on hand for emergency charcuterie (yes, you read correctly). And they'd written, in pickle: LOVE.

"Not funny," I said, out loud.

"Mommy?" Ellie asked. "Can I have my milk? I don't like it dry."

She was eating the organic "cheerios"—you know, the kind that cost twenty dollars for a box that lasts two days? I closed the refrigerator. Poured the milk on Ellie's exclusive cheerios. And then, I tiptoed back to the refrigerator and opened it.

Hi.

I slammed the refrigerator door. My knees were shaking. Was my husband flirting with me from The Great Beyond? I needed to ask Trish. I needed to call Santino. But first, I needed to remember how to dress for a network meeting.

Number one on a very short list of schools was a nursery school at Santa Monica Methodist, a neighborhood church just a few blocks west of us. The office manager, a grandmotherly type named Anna, greeted us and led us back into the playground. I heard children's screams and chatter and cries and laughter. The yard was big and messy, with a sand pit, climbing structure, trees and tricycles, lost sneakers and hair bows. Ellie wasn't even enrolled yet, and I was having visions of her tearing up the place, pumping her feet way too fast on that shiny red trike, which I knew would be her favorite. She unscrewed her little hand from mine and made a beeline for it.

Anna looked at me and gave me her toothy smile. "Why don't I take you to meet Stephanie?" she said.

"If I don't get in here, I'll die," I said, though I knew death was not a viable option. Someone had to stay alive for Ellie.

The pressure!

Stephanie Clark, the school director, was chatting with two

smudge-faced boys with white-blond Buster Brown haircuts, about the goldfish in her tank. Pulled back red hair and granny glasses only accentuated her "hot librarian" look. Or maybe hot "Kindle" look. She glanced up and smiled.

"Hi, I'm Stephanie," she said, as she shook my hand.

"Please take Ellie," I said. "Hi, I'm Hannah, I mean. Please take Ellie." Anna scooted out the two boys while we sat. Stephanie looked at me from across her desk.

"Mrs. Bernal, have you seen other nursery schools in the area?"

"No," I said. "I love this place for Ellie. It's messy. It's rough around the edges. It smells like cafeteria food. The moms look like moms and the teachers look like they're tired but having a good time. This is where we want to live out my days—I mean, this is where I want Ellie to go to school."

"Where is Ellie now?" Stephanie asked.

"She's making the Indy 500 rounds with the red tricycle."

"Of course," Stephanie said. "It's the toddler Lamborghini. Can I ask you about . . ."

"My husband. He, ah, died recently. Ellie's been talking to him at night. I'll get help. I mean, that's why we're here. The parents complained at Bunny Hill. They weren't comfortable with their kids hearing about Ellie's dead father. I understand, no one really likes to hear about death, especially from a little girl, who's, you know, grieving . . ."

Stephanie tilted her head, her eyes widened. "I was going to ask about allergies. Does Ellie have any food allergies? Allergic to anything at all?"

Damn my big mouth. "No, no she doesn't." Damn it. Damn it.

"I'm so sorry about your husband," Stephanie said. "It must be so hard for you . . . and Ellie." She gave me a small, sincere smile. I think she might have actually meant it.

"Thank you," I whispered. We sat for a moment as kids' voices punctuated the air. Even in the din, I could hear Ellie's laughter.

"And while those parents should be ashamed of themselves and won't be," Stephanie said, "I blame the school. Shame on them."

I started crying. Stephanie handed me a Kleenex box. I never wanted to leave.

"Would you like Ellie to start today?" Stephanie asked. "We have an opening."

I couldn't get my words out. I just nodded. Maybe there was grace in this world. And maybe there were angels.

I arrived five minutes early for the network meeting and congratulated myself. I still remembered where to go. Greeting the parking attendant at the gate felt natural. I had a moment of panic when I couldn't find my driver's license, but that passed without incident. I had even remembered my notes. Maybe I was getting back to me.

Jay and I met up outside the main building. There was always something thrilling about being on a production lot. I loved the huge billboards on the sides of buildings, the buzzing of golf carts transporting talent, the incessant hubbub of people creating and working and getting things done.

"New York is here, in this meeting. The She-Devil herself," Jay said. "Are you ready?"

"Isn't this more a pro forma thing?" I asked. "What's she doing here?"

She-Devil was the über-chief of the network. She hated Los Angeles. She-Devil despised sunshine.

"I should have picked out your suit," Jay said. "You're too thin for it now, and you need a higher heel. And a haircut. Does my Ellie like her new school?"

"Loves," I said, diving into my bag for a granola bar, fruit snacks, anything. "I'll gain ten pounds right now."

Jay took my face in his hands. It was hard to see his eyes behind the sunglasses.

"No weirdness today, Hannah," Jay said. "I don't care if Ethel Merman appears in a G-string in the middle of the room and starts belting 'There's No Business Like Show Business.' Let's sell the

new season, then go to that Mexican dive across the street. You
need eight gallons of melted cheese. Your 'zaf' has lost its 'tig.' "

She-Devil sat in Todd the Reality King's office. She was dressed in
a power suit so tight she could have used it to scuba dive. She rose,
briefly, as we walked in the room. When she shook my hand and
squeezed, I thought I might need to ice it. Her skirt squeaked when
she backed into her chair. In her late forties, she was 90 percent
muscle, 10 percent balls. She had probably been born in her late
forties.

I started to sweat. I was terrified. *What the hell was she doing
here?*

Kevin and Karli, the half-gay, all-narcissist couple was seated on
the couch, and putting on a sex show. Karli had stuck her tongue in
Kevin's ear and somehow managed to touch his reptile brain. Kevin
was practically stuffing dollars down her miniskirt with his teeth.

Todd the Reality King was rocking in his chair and clapping his
hands like a seal. Did I mention he's pocket-sized? If this were an
earlier era, he'd be dancing (and popping pills backstage) with Judy
Garland.

"Karli, Kevin," Todd said, "good news for us, bad news for our
children's future—your ratings are through the roof." One of the
K's emitted a high-pitched squeal; I wasn't sure which one.

She-Devil observed all with a small, tight smile. I was trying to
recall why or who or how we came up with the nickname, and at
the moment, could not remember her real name.

"But as you know, there's always next season. Let's discuss,"
Todd said. "We really want to ramp this baby up."

"Hannah and I've been brainstorming a number of possibilities,"
Jay said.

"We could get pregnant," Kevin popped off. He's changed from
the Midwestern boy we knew and didn't love. Kevin now sports a
man tan. His eyebrows are threaded. He's wearing a mesh tank top
under his white blazer. If Harvey Fierstein were in the room, they
could have a gay-off.

"Maybe we could have sex," Karli suggested.

"You don't want to ruin your figure," Kevin said. "I hate fat girls."

"Oh, God, you're right!" She giggled. "So do I! Eww!" Her giggle is manic. Mr. Adderall has been paying regular visits to the set, aka rental house in Santa Monica. "And, oh my God, I hate stretch marks." She turned to me. "Did you get stretch marks?"

"Ah . . . no, not really. But I was pretty stretched out to begin with."

"I hear olive oil helps," she said.

She-Devil observes it all, sans expression.

"It does. I like it on pasta," I said. I'm thinking about John. His obsession with finding the perfect olive oil. How many out-of-the-way stores? Sawtelle . . . Abbott Kinney . . . Ocean Park . . . How many restaurants? I'm off on some kind of olive-oil grief tangent.

"A pregnancy would be great," Jay said. "What if we went to a surrogate?"

"Hey, Hannah." Todd turned to me. "What's happening—how you doin'?"

"Well, you know, I'm okay," I said. "I'm getting better. Every day gets a little easier."

She-Devil trained her eyes on me. Jay cleared his throat, signaling "This is not the time." A lightbulb went off in Todd's peahead. It's not pretty, watching stupid people put together thoughts.

"Oh . . . oh, yeah, I heard. Right. The—oh, your husband, right? Ooh. That's a toughie," Todd said. "But don't worry. You'll get over it. Time heals. You know what you should do? Watch *The Secret*—again, I mean."

"Oh my God, I would die without my boo!" Karli said. "Come with me to the Agape. I go every Sunday. It's awesome. Oh my God, we could film it!" The Agape is the Church à la Mode for the "Spiritual Gangsta" crowd—more AA meeting than church. The SMCA love the Agape Church.

I saw Jay blanch beneath his man blush. He knew what was coming.

"Being a widow is not like catching a cold, Todd," I said. "You don't just 'get over it.'"

"Oh, hey, whoa—" Todd held up his palms, gesturing for me to calm down.

"Why is it that no one talks about death in L.A.? I walk into a room and all I get are blank stares. I mean, it's going to happen to all of us, right?"

"Oh, hey, the big D, wow." Todd laughed nervously. "I really— where's my tea?" He called out to his assistant, "Myrna! My Kum-cha Latta!"

"My kitty died last year," Karli said. "I totally get your pain, Han-nah."

"Let's talk more about the surrogate idea," Jay said. "We could get someone really TV great—someone like Snooki, but blond— like an ex–*Hills* girl—"

Cold air rushed at me, as though someone had turned on the air conditioner full blast. *Someone was in the room who wasn't supposed to be.*

A teenager with stringy hair, a sprinkling of acne across his cheeks, a sleeveless Def Leppard T-shirt, and a skateboard under his arm, stood behind Todd. "Dude!" he said, waving at me. "Tell Todd he doesn't need to be so weird about death. It's not his fault. Tell him that."

I shook my head.

"Why are you shaking your head?" Jay asked. "The surrogate idea was yours—"

"C'mon," the teenager said. "Dude! Break it down for the T-ster!"

Everyone in the room was staring at me. She-Devil didn't blink.

"Dude?" I looked at Todd. "Hi. So, Todd. A skater kid, I think you know him, told me you don't need to be so weird about death. It's not your fault."

"Dude, it's me, Teddy, his little bro, and I totally forgive him, it was, like, an accident."

"And, dude, Teddy totally forgives you. It was, like, an accident."

"And, you know, like Megadeth fucking rocks!" And he made the sign of the devil.

"And, you know, like Megadeth fucking rocks!" I repeated.

Todd backed up, as though trying to get away from me, his hands clutching his chair.

"Slap my face and call me Sally," Jay said.

"What kind of shit is this?" Todd demanded. "Why are you doing this to me? My brother died twenty years ago—"

Teddy had disappeared, but the room was still cold. Which explains the priest hovering over Kevin's shoulder.

"Father?" I asked, "can we not do this right now?"

"You tell young Kevin to stop with the pornography," the priest said. "Tell him Father Joe does not approve. He hasn't changed a whit, that boy."

"Kevin," I said, "Father Joe wants you to lay off the porn—"

"Did the Father mention what flavor porn?" Jay asked.

"Get out!" Todd screamed. Myrna came running in with the Kumcha Latta. "Get out!"

An older woman with short gray hair, glasses, and a black dress stood over She-Devil's shoulder. "Tell Debbie Mama loves her," she said, in a loud, Brooklyn accent. "She's working too hard, but I'm very proud of her. But tell her to keep an eye on that middle one. She's hanging out with the wrong crowd, that one."

"Debbie?" I said. "Mama's very proud of you, but keep an eye on that middle one. She's hanging with the wrong crowd."

"And no raspberry at the breakfast table—"

"Raspberry?" I asked. "Oh . . . BlackBerry! No BlackBerry at the breakfast table—"

Debbie the She-Devil blinked. First time.

"You're crazy!" Todd screamed. "That's it! I'm canceling your contract! Myrna, get me the *Housewife* boys! You will never work in this town again!"

I headed for the door, turning back to see She-Devil staring at me, silent as a carb-avoidant Buddha.

We scurried out of the administration building. Jay didn't look at me until we reached the parking lot.

"So . . . people actually say that? 'You'll never work in this town again,'" I said. "Are you still hungry? We could grab a bite."

Jay ripped the sunglasses from his face. He was covering up his lovely gray eyes with green contact lenses.

"I like the lenses," I offered. "You look like Rihanna."

"What is wrong with you?" Jay asked. "I told you not to flip out in there!"

"I'm sorry."

"Do you realize that we've just lost our production deal? Your breakdown has just put us out on the street."

"I'm not having a mental breakdown, Jay. I'm actually seeing dead people. They're talking to me. I opened this portal, somehow—"

"Stop, just stop it," Jay said. "Hannah, I know you've suffered. I know it's hard. But I can't do this anymore. I'm skipping lunch and looking for a job. I suggest you do the same."

11

Arrested Development

I had just lost my best friend. I needed comfort. I needed reassurance. I'm pretty sure I needed Q-tips. I drove to the CVS pharmacy near my house, on Wilshire, a slice of drugstore heaven. It's huge and spotless, bright and well stocked, and I've never seen anyone there that I know. In fact, I don't know if I've actually seen anyone inside the store. I just love browsing rows of lip gloss and hair color and pregnancy tests and notebooks and cold medicines and highlight markers. And bags and bags of candy corn.

I had my little red basket on my arm, wandering up one aisle, down another, ignoring my vibrating BlackBerry. Probably Jay screaming at me, or my long-lost agent telling me to get long-lost. I wanted to feel like a normal human being who just needed ultra-moisturizing hair conditioner. I felt that could solve everything, if only I could mend my split ends.

My phone wouldn't stop. I didn't recognize the number, the area code was a 310—I was sure I'd forgotten to return a library book to the small Montana branch. But as it had only been a couple of months, and my husband had died, I let it go. I had the Dead Husband Card and was not afraid to use it, even for overdue books.

It kept buzzing. Finally, I answered.

It was Stephanie, the nursery school director. "Are you okay?"

she asked. I pictured her freckles and red hair and sincere concern.

"It's almost five. You never picked up Ellie," Stephanie said. "I'm just checking to see if you're all right."

I ran out of the store, clutching my basket with life-saving shampoo, conditioner, and conditioning rinse. I even had John's favorite razors, I don't know why. I ran to my car.

Someone was yelling "Stop!" Someone in a red vest, with a CVS nametag pinned on his chest. I was already starting up the car. Who was this vested man yelling at?

Ellie had been waiting for me. For hours.

Her father leaves her. Her mother abandons her.

I put my car in reverse and drove over the store manager's foot.

One thing I can say for the Santa Monica Police: They are extraordinarily polite. "May I cuff you, now, ma'am?" . . . "Are you comfortable in the backseat?" . . . "The temperature okay for you?" In fact, they are more like waiters than policemen. I remember screaming as they approached me, "I need to pick up my daughter!" as though Ellie had been marooned wearing only floaties in shark-infested waters, not rolled up in a comfy blanket, being fed Goldfish by a sweet, young nursery school director. The Youth of Today, Officers Campos and Johnson, sat me down at the curb and had me breathe into a paper bag. *This is not my bright, shining moment,* I thought, as I stared out at the rush-hour traffic on Wilshire Boulevard with a lunch bag on my face.

These cops were Justin-Timberlake-in-uniform cute. Campos had a baby face, abs of steel, oh, and a halo.

"You have a halo," I gasped into the paper bag.

"A halo?" Campos asked. "No one's ever told me that before."

"Maybe you're an angel," I said.

"That's not what my girlfriend says, but thanks," Campos replied. First, there were the voices. Then, apparitions. Then messages. So why not auras?

Officer Johnson was six-feet-something of burliness—I'd peg

him as Mr. July in the 2011 Santa Monica Police Department Calendar. His aura was purple.

"Does Johnson, here, have a halo?" Campos asked.

"Of sorts," I said. "Does purple count?"

"I love purple," Johnson said.

"It's a beautiful aura," I had to agree.

I was taken to the Santa Monica Jail, which should be rechristened the Frank Gehry Jail, because of its modern, angular architecture. I spent an hour and a half in an immaculate cell with bored teenaged gang members from SaMo High, picked up for fighting over sexting, and a Persian woman who'd ripped off twelve pairs of jeans at Diesel on the Promenade.

"How many jeans do you need?" I asked. The woman was highlighted, French-manicured, very 1995. She probably drove a wine-colored Bentley.

"They are very good jeans," she said. "But too expensive. Is ridiculous!"

I had called Jay, but he didn't answer. He was probably wearing his best women's Levi's, downing margaritas with Hidalgo at The Hideout on Entrada. I couldn't blame him. Aimee roused herself out of bed and picked Ellie up from school immediately after I called. Chloe barely reacted when I told her I'd been arrested, like she'd been expecting it all along. The new NoMoMama.com topic practically wrote itself: *What to wear to pick your best friend up from jail.*

"Assault with a deadly weapon?" Chloe asked, after posting bail. "Theft? You stole Caviar for Blondes shampoo? Hannah, you're not even a blonde."

Campos, who'd been talking to a short, bald, serious-looking man in a crumpled suit, approached as we were leaving. He looked out of place here at the art gallery/jail.

"Did you want a copy of the police report?" Campos asked. "My supervisor was asking." His halo was still glimmering.

"No," I said. "I was there, I don't need to see it."

"You were there?" he asked. "When your husband was killed?"

"Oh," I said. Oh my God, no. "No, no, I wasn't talking about John."

"We will find the guy," he said. "The man driving the gardening truck that hit your husband. We've got good leads."

"Oh," I said, "thank you." My knees buckled, and he caught me. "I'm sorry," I said. "I'm so sorry."

After I recovered, Chloe walked me out of the station, into the night. The moon was high in the deep purple sky. The chill was telling me that Thanksgiving and Christmas were around the corner. The holiday season. Food, gifts, celebration.

I wasn't ready. I doubt I'd ever be ready again.

Aimee had bought Ellie dinner, tucked her into bed, and then, as she was feeling ill, tucked herself into a vodka and Emergen-C. As Aimee and Chloe chatted over the demise of my character, I dragged myself into Ellie's room and lay down next to her.

"I owe you better, Ellie," I said to my sleeping girl. "I should just give you to someone who could raise you right. Like Jennifer Aniston or Courteney Cox. They seem nice . . . and they have excellent hair."

Later, I crawled into my bed and stayed there for the next week, with one thought keeping me company: *My baby deserves better than me.*

I woke up early a few mornings later to find Trish standing over my bed.

"What are you doing here?" I asked, gasping for air. I rolled over. "You're not supposed to come into my room."

"You're making the rules now?" Trish said. "Get up. This behavior is a bit dramatic, even for me. And I was an actress—back when it mattered."

"I'm being berated by a dead person," I said, catching my breath. My chest felt sore. "What's with my breathing?"

"You're giving yourself pneumonia," Trish said. "It happens to a lot of widows. That's why you need to get up and about."

"Good morning, sunshine," Jay said, appearing at my doorway. I hadn't heard from him since we parted ways in the network parking lot. He walked right through Trish.

"Ooh," Trish said. "I hate when that happens. It's demeaning."

"I'm sorry," I said. "He doesn't look where he's going."

"Please, please stop doing that," Jay said. "It's bad enough that we've now been blackballed at every network. Even the yet-works have heard about it."

"My first husband was a poof," Trish said. "We were kids, only married a year. God, did I love that man."

I put my pillow over my head.

"I'm done with the pity party," Jay said, grabbing the pillow. "Done. You've been in bed a week. You are getting up and taking Ellie to school."

"He's right, you know," Trish said. "What's that scent? It's musky . . ."

"Aramis," I said to her. "He's trying to bring back 1985."

"Who are you talking to?" Jay asked. "Please, Hannah. Please stop."

"Tell Ellie I'm sick. Every part of me is sick. Even my fingernails. I can't breathe, but I don't care. I want to die. The hairs on my arms have lost the will to live."

"Such drama," Trish said, looking at her nails. "Suddenly, she's Theda Bara."

"Sweetheart, I'm not going to placate you anymore," Jay said, pulling the covers back. I caught a whiff of his cologne. Jay was always ready, just in case sex broke out on the street somewhere. "Two words: Alexander McQueen. He stayed in bed ten days after his mother died, then got up and hung himself. You're on day seven."

"That's a rare thing, that kind of love," Trish said. "I hope you appreciate this fella."

"Why can't you both just leave me alone?" I said. "Just let me go."

"Honey, I got news for you. You're not a diva, you're no Marilyn

Monroe. You're not even Alec Baldwin. You're a mom who's had horrible shit happen, who has to man up and raise a daughter. Because if you die and I have to raise Ellie, which I'm happy to do, she's going to end up looking like Cher."

"Indian Cher?" I asked, wheezing. "Just a suggestion."

"Nineties Cher," Jay threatened.

"He wouldn't dare," Trish said.

Jay pulled the curtains open. Light flooded the room.

I sighed and swung my legs over the side of my bed. When I looked back, Trish had disappeared.

Jay reached out and took my hand. "Come back to the living."

"What are the benefits?" I asked him.

"Love," he answered.

Jay ran water into my bathtub, felt the water with his hand, then turned to me. "Take it all off," he said, rolling up his sleeves. "I'm not looking."

I disrobed, slipped off the socks I'd been wearing for a week, and sank into the warm water. I was naked in so many ways, I didn't care anymore.

"Tilt your head back," he said. When Jay was young and Sylvester ruled the airwaves, he'd cut hair in a shop in West Hollywood.

"I haven't had my hair done in . . ."

"I'll be your hairipist." He poured shampoo into his palm, rubbed his hands together, and massaged it into my scalp. "Now, breathe, baby. I'm not leaving you." Tears spilled down my cheeks. There was so much love in this house, in this tiny bathroom, in the hands of a gay man who wanted nothing more than to settle down with one person for the rest of his life. And that person would probably be me.

The doorbell rang. Ellie's little feet scampered toward the door.

"Hi hi!" I heard Dee Dee Pickler call out. "Is your mommy here?"

I wrapped a towel around my body and headed to the living room. *(Spice cowered before my nakedness. I tried not to take it personally. It's not like we're dating.)*

Dee Dee wore a tennis skirt that showed cheek when she turned, and pink wristbands. "Honey, I heard all about your arrest. Don't worry, I haven't told a soul."

"You play tennis?" I asked, ignoring her. Already, my chest was starting to feel better.

"Never. I wrangled an invite to the Riv, the Riviera. Do you know how many seventy-year-old widowers play tennis?"

"So you came by to . . ."

"I don't want other Realtors getting wind of your meltdown," Dee Dee said. "I'm trying to keep it out of *The Mirror.*" *The Santa Monica Mirror* was the local paper that wrote up every local petty crime with a humorous slant. *Shit.*

"It's all a misunderstanding," I said.

"We have to find you something really cute."

"I'm never selling Casa Sugar," I insisted.

"Who's selling what?" Jay asked, emerging from the kitchen into the living room.

"Oh, Jay," Dee Dee said. "My new business card . . ." She handed Jay a pink card.

Jay took a look at it, reading, "Dee Dee Pickler, Realtor-Life Couch."

"Life Couch?" Jay asked.

"It's a misprint. So . . . what happened with the job?" Dee Dee asked me.

"How do you know about that?"

"Everyone knows. That homeless guy, Bob, who panhandles at the Starbucks on 15th and looks like Bob Dylan but definitely isn't, because I made out with him and he tasted like goat ass?" Dee Dee said. "*He's* concerned! You know Santa Monica. There's no privacy. It's Wisteria Lane with Priuses. If you want privacy, move to Beijing."

"I'm on temporary leave," I said.

"That's why you're bathing after noon," Dee Dee said. "Look, honey, I grieve for your situation. I do. It must be horrible, losing a husband. I'm trying to learn, what's the word? Em . . . em . . ."

"Empathy," Jay said. "Do you mind if I sit down for this? I wish I had popcorn and a Red Bull."

"I want to be there for you," Dee Dee said. "The market is dropping off like Zsa Zsa's limbs. I can get you the best price. I already have a buyer—deep pockets, short escrow, don't ask me how I do it. Okay, go ahead and ask."

"This house is all I have left of John," I said.

"Exactly," Dee Dee said. "You need a fresh start. Honey, in six months, who knows where the market will be?"

"I'm not worried." But I was worried. I lived in Worry, USA. Not even a nice place to visit.

"We're all worried. Why do you think I give seminars on the side? I mean, besides the fact that I'm learning that it's good to help others. Really, I'm just covering the Tijuana Botox at this point." She flashed Jay her horse veneers.

"Listen, honey. You're how old? Fifty?" Dee Dee asked me. "I'm forty-five. I've blown every Persian surgeon—I love how that rhymes—and I still only landed one whale. Well, he wasn't a whale, more like a guppy, the loser. You're competing against twenty-year-olds and rich divorcées. You have to take care of yourself, sister."

"I don't want a man," I said. "Especially not a sperm whale."

She checked her fake Rolex. "Gotta run. I'm taking my baby daddy back to court. Meghan wants to jump and she's my only way to get in with the Spielbergs. Don't wait to call me—you could be looking at Jasmine Gardens. And I want to see you at R+D on Thursdays or the Huntley any night. Luke Wilson hangs out there, you know."

She waved and was out the door.

"Isn't Jasmine Gardens the trailer park under the 10?" Jay asked. "You and Ellie are moving in with me before you move to that freeway exit, my dear."

"Just the other morning, I saw a flyer . . ." I said. "Coyotes, in big letters, with a picture of a small dog, *Oliver RIP* . . ."

"I see that every week in this neighborhood," Jay said.

"It read, *If you run into a coyote, wave your hands, stomp your feet, and yell,*" I said. "Next time, I'm going to try that with Dee Dee."

Later that night, Trish informed me she'd almost been arrested for shoplifting three weeks after her husband, Mel, died. They'd been married forty-seven years. His death wasn't unexpected. He was old, she was old. He'd had bypass surgery. They lived each day to the fullest, meaning they watched Bob Barker on *The Price Is Right*, Mel tended their rose garden, which swallowed up the front lawn, they shared evening walks, classic movies at the Aero, meals at Izzy's Deli.

So, Mel passes away one quiet morning in their bed. The night before, he asked that she open a window for his spirit to pass. They have the burial service, an intimate, austere ceremony. Trish was ready for this, she told herself. She cried, she missed him, but she knew, above all, she had been one of the lucky ones. She plays mah-jongg with the girls. She takes the trash cans out to the curb herself. She drives. She shops for groceries and cooks for one.

Trish was caught shoplifting at Pavilions. She'd left the store with her grocery cart to get the Pavilions card from Mel, who used to always wait in their Charger, listening to Vin Scully do the Dodger play-by-play as she did the shopping. The store manager knew Trish. He understood and let the incident go. But afterward, Trish was too embarrassed to return to the store. For years, she'd drive to the Pavilions miles away, on Lincoln. "My shame was greater than my sadness, Hannah," Trish told me. "Don't let that happen to you."

12

Manny 911

School Director Stephanie leaned over her desk in her office at Santa Monica Methodist, swallowed up by stuffed animals, Play-Doh sculptures, pillows and quilts, and an aquarium with a hermit crab named Frieda, who had a peace sign painted on her shell. Her small hands were folded. She wore a thumb ring, the kind of thing that looks good only on her and Nicole Richie.

"You need help during this transition," she said.

"Transition?" I asked. "Being widowed is not a career move."

"Hannah, I'm sorry," Stephanie said. "Let me be real with you. I don't want you cracking up. Ellie needs you to be a whole mother to her."

"A whole mother and a whole father," I said. "I'm doing everything I can." I brushed away a tear. I looked through the windows to the hallway. Normal moms walked by. Normal moms with their long-ago highlighted hair in a ponytail. Normal moms wearing Juicy velour sweats, brought out again after the second baby. Normal moms pushing strollers and murmuring about lack of sleep and what to make for dinner that doesn't include the word "fingers." Normal moms keeping their complaints to themselves as their marriages become confusing, their trust wavers, their idealism is bombarded by transgressions as major as another woman, and as minor as a baby's spit-up. What I wouldn't give for their happiness and misery, their smiles and secrets.

"Ellie needs you to be healthy. Are you seeing anyone?"

"Dating? Am I dating?" *What was worse? The thought of another man touching me or the thought of me wanting to touch another man?*

"Oh, no, no, nothing like that—"

"Right, because, you know, I can't even think—"

"I know. For a long time."

"Centuries," I said. I pictured my future. Black shoes with heavy soles, black stockings, wool dress, and, yes, a rocking chair. And the remote. Because even when I'm in my eighties, *American Idol* better still be on. Good news: If I still looked forward to *Idol*, maybe I had not lost the will to live.

Bad news: If I didn't have Ellie, I would have already shot myself. Who am I kidding, I wouldn't have shot myself; I'm a total wimp. I would have asked one of the Grief Team to shoot me. They owe me that much. Jay wouldn't need much prompting.

"I meant, are you seeing a therapist?" Stephanie asked.

"I have my friends," I said. "Frankly, among them, the pharmaceutical industry is having its best year ever. But they saved me and Ellie, and they don't cost two twenty-five an hour."

"Sounds like they're good friends, but you might want to try a professional group setting," Stephanie said. "My aunt joined a group after my uncle passed away. She found it very helpful. Do you have someone to help you with Ellie?"

Ellie. John was the house-spouse. For all intents and purposes, he was both Mom and Dad. There's one in every school. You know the type. He looks younger than the other dads because he's always smiling and never wears a suit. He's always got one kid hanging over his shoulder, even while he's hammering together the May Day set. He looks abnormal not toting a skateboard. The teachers sigh when they speak of him. The mommies gape at his calves when he runs past, pushing an empty jogging stroller. He annoys the other dads—"*I would be in great shape, too, if I didn't have to earn a living!*"—but he's so good-natured, he wears them down, and then they, too, become members of the Favorite Dad Fan Club.

And when he leaves, the world stops spinning.

"Like a nanny?"

"If you don't mind . . . I was going to make a suggestion—"

"I'm afraid I couldn't afford it," I said. I was worried. The property tax bill hadn't come, but neither had John's life insurance check. We'd used up a lot of our savings for the planned trip to Greece. Before our little family was run over by the Grief Train.

"It wouldn't cost you a thing," Stephanie said. "Brandon, our intern, he's a UCLA MBA—he went back to school to get his teaching credentials. We've been friends since freshman year. He dated my roommate."

"He wants to teach little kids?"

"He loves kids. And he lost his job last year. Brandon was a trainee at Morgan Stanley. He's looking for room and board. He just started working with the kids in the older group, and he's gentle and sweet, but firm. He could help you out, maybe he could use a small stipend."

"Does he eat?"

"I don't think he ever stops eating. He was on the varsity volleyball team. But he cooks. And he can help out with laundry." She looked at me. "I don't know, it just feels like a good fit. I think Ellie would absolutely love having him around."

"He's in good health?" I had to ask. You never know.

"He's only twenty-four."

"Testicular cancer is a young man's disease," I said, before admitting, "I'm spending way too much time on the Internet. Still can't take someone else dying on me. Death is unfuckingacceptable."

"I can almost guarantee it." Stephanie smiled. "At least for the next year or so."

"I'll meet him," I said. "Even though I don't need any help. I've got everything completely under control."

Stephanie sized me up. "Is your shirt on backward?"

"It's a look," I replied. "Just—have him call me." I walked out. A *manny*, I thought. How pathetic that someone would think I would need a manny.

"I love a manny!" Jay said. "Hey, why don't you try Hidalgo? He's looking for another job, besides male modeling."

"I need someone who wears something other than Speedos."

"Whatever, don't be mean. He's trying. And I love him."

"He's not trying. He's taking you to the cleaners. He flirts with other men in front of you. And his wife is pregnant."

"Relationships are complicated," Jay said. "So, when do I meet our manny?"

The next day, "our" manny was scheduled for an interview. I managed to get out of my pajamas, my second skin, and run a comb through my hair, i.e. dreadlocks.

"You know," Jay said, fingering my split ends, "losing the will to condition is a sign of mental illness." Jay had arrived drenched in Tom Ford Black Orchid cologne, wearing skinny jeans.

"You look like Fergie," I said.

"I've prepared a list of questions. I knew you couldn't handle this yourself. Ellie needs to be protected. She has a dead father and a mother who doesn't tweeze."

I was about to read the list when the doorbell rang. I beat Jay to the door, and thanked God that I had put on eyeliner. Or maybe I hadn't. No, I don't think I had. But Jay had, at least. So we were good there.

"Hi," Brandon said. "You must be Hannah." Brandon was well over six feet tall, and that was the least of his physical attributes.

"It's that obvious," I said. "Raccoon eyes, rat's-nest hair. I just look like a widow, is that it?"

"I thought it was you," he said, "because you answered the door?"

Jay intervened. "Hi, I'm Jay. Why don't you come on in and sit on my fa—"

"Couch," I said. "Please, sit."

Brandon looked from me to Jay.

"It's safe," I lied. "I'll be with you throughout the entire interview."

He laughed, exposing perfect teeth. I liked him, despite this.

Jay sat down across from Brandon, whose knees, when he sat, were almost to his chest. "Now . . . Brandon," Jay said, "are you comfortable? Would you like some water? Something stronger, perhaps?"

"I'm fine." Brandon smiled. *God had touched every part of him with the Pretty Stick.*

Jay perused his list. "Okay. Here we go. Ellie cuts her finger while cutting a lime for her favorite uncle's margarita. Do you get a bandage? Call nine-one-one? Show her how to properly cut the lime, then continue making the margarita?"

"You guys are screwing with me, right?"

"I'm dead serious," Jay said.

"A three-year-old shouldn't be handling knives at all," Brandon said.

"Very good," Jay said. "It was a trick question. Now—Ellie wants to wear checkered tights to school with a vintage rabbit coat, courtesy of her favorite uncle, of course. How do you react?"

"I think children should be able to express themselves with their clothing choices—to a limit."

"You would mix patterns and textures? At such a young age? You would allow that?"

"Jay, that's enough," I said.

"I believe you should encourage children to express themselves as freely as possible, within reasonable limits," Brandon said.

"Fine, let's just agree to disagree," Jay said. "I'm glad we got our first fight out of the way."

"Brandon," I said. "I'm sorry. I just can't hire you."

"She doesn't mean it," Jay said. "You don't mean that, do you, Hannah?"

"Fair enough," Brandon said. "May I ask why?"

"You're the best-looking man we have ever seen—and we've seen a lot. You're Calvin Klein billboard material. It would distract me from my worries—and I'd feel pressure to put on makeup and comb my hair. I'm not ready yet."

"I'm more Old Navy," Brandon said. "Trust me. Look, Hannah, I want to get my life back on track. I thought I would have it all together by now. I don't. The world changed on me . . ." He faltered.

"I understand," I said. "What was promised, was taken."

Brandon nodded, his eyes big and sad. I felt like punching myself in the head.

"I need a place to stay where I can get my work done," Brandon said. "My roommate's blood count is Four Loko. I can't do it anymore. He's a trust fund baby. He may not have to grow up—but I do."

"May I make a suggestion, Hannah?" Jay asked.

"Not if I'm reading your mind, you can't," I said.

"Kitchen. Now," Jay said. He dragged me into the kitchen, closing the swinging door behind us.

"You need this boy," Jay said. "Can't you see? I don't want you to turn out to be a character in a bad Bruce Willis movie, which is redundant in itself, and I can't believe I've sunk so low. Hannah, Brandon has been sent by God. Ask him if he's into the Daddy thing."

"Okay, I'll hire him. But nobody here can touch him. Except maybe furtively, like on the elbow. On odd-numbered days."

Jay hugged me. We went back into the living room to tell Brandon the good news.

I picked Ellie up from school, and brought her home to meet Brandon. Within moments, Brandon was on his hands and knees, Ellie riding his back as though he were a large, frisky dog.

"She never laughs that way with me," I said.

"She doesn't laugh that way with me, either," Jay said. "And I'm funny. Or maybe I'm more wry than funny. Do you think he's ever tried a man?"

Ellie jumped off Brandon's back and landed on the floor, then gave him a big hug around his neck. My chest ached. What had I done?

"She never laughs that way with me," I repeated.

* * *

Word of Manny spread more quickly than Dee Dee Pickler's legs at a yoga retreat. Aimee dropped by, in full hair and makeup.

"Look at what Hannah brought us. It's not even Christnukkah," Jay said, indicating Brandon outside pushing Ellie on the swing hanging from the avocado tree.

"Just like John used to push, only taller," I said, as I watched Brandon.

"He's okay," Aimee said, viewing him from the kitchen window. "Beachy, common. I prefer older, more distinguished—"

"Grateful, pay for dinner, don't care if you haven't waxed in six months, and the Alzheimer's guarantees they'll forget your phone number. Am I close?" Jay asked.

"How'd the audition go?" I asked.

"Terrible," Aimee said. "I'm too old. Why doesn't someone just take me out in a pasture and shoot me?"

"Because they don't waste bullets on old cows?" Jay suggested.

"I have a theater degree from Yale," Aimee said. "I could have been Meryl Streep, and instead I'm begging for Papa John commercials."

"You'll get more work when you're menopausal," Jay said. "All those osteoperosis commercials."

"Don't talk to me about Sally Field," Aimee grumbled. "Between her and Jamie Lee Curtis, they've got the old-broad market cornered."

Brandon strode in, carrying Ellie under his arm like a giggling loaf of bread.

"Hi," Brandon said, noticing Aimee.

"Hi," Aimee said, her face turning red.

"Are you blushing, Aimee?" Jay asked.

"No," Aimee said. "Of course not. It's called 'flushing'—from my new cream."

"You know, Branny, men don't age like women do," Jay said. "Look at the back of my hand—it's like an infant's."

"Once you get past the granny knuckles," Aimee said.

"I'm sorry, but are you the woman in the shampoo commercial?" Brandon asked.

"Pantene?" Aimee said. "I've done a few hair commercials . . . Well, more than a few."

"She's the Greer Garson of shampoo ads," Jay said.

"Oh my God," Brandon said. "I remember you! You washed your hair in the horse stall. I had such a crush on you. I told my buddies at school, they all made fun of me."

"Really?" Aimee asked.

"You know how cruel third-graders can be," Brandon said. The silence was deafening. I lived eight lifetimes in that silence.

"I'd better go," Aimee said.

"Nice meeting you," Brandon called after Aimee's hastily retreating, aged figure. "Wow. She's even hotter now."

"Third grade?" I asked. "You had to say third grade?"

"Did I say 'third grade'?" Brandon said. "Man, I'm such an idiot!"

There was a knock at the front door, followed by the sound of small feet skittering across the wood floor and the inevitable barking.

"Angel, don't touch that; Bakasana, come to Mommy. Be good, no peeing, Mulabanda! Mulabanda! Bad dog!"

Chloe, wearing a low-cut cocktail dress from a charity event she'd hosted in better times, hurried into the kitchen, dragged by dogs and children. Bakasana, the Rescue Pom and Mulabanda the (terrifying) Rescue Pit had anointed the area rug in my living room before. The third was a skinny, gray shepherd mix.

"Angel's my new rescue," Chloe said, looking at the mangy beast while straightening out her dress. Two of her kids, Penelope and Joshua, on all fours, barked and lifted their legs at the center island, but Chloe only had eyes for Angel. "She just showed up at my house one evening. She was so hungry. Isn't she beautiful?"

"She looks strung-out," Jay said. "Is she a Promises Rescue?"

"How's my best girl?" Chloe asked me.

Spice was having none of the new dog. He paced behind my legs, growling, head down.

"I'm Chloe," Chloe introduced herself to Brandon. "Hannah, you didn't tell me you had company. I would have tried to look nice."

"Chloe, you look like you're a ten-thirty invite to the *Vanity Fair* party," I said.

"He's mine," Jay said. "I mean, Chloe, meet Brandon, our new manny. He's mine."

"Ellie's new manny," I corrected. "Don't listen to Jay the Manny Poacher."

"Do you like dogs?" Chloe asked Brandon.

"I love all animals," Brandon said. "I'm kind of indiscriminate that way."

"Me, too, I love all animals, too," Chloe said, flustered. "They're so much nicer than human beings, don't you think?" This was probably the closest Chloe had come to flirting since college, when she had first met Wasband Billy passed out on the bathroom floor of his fraternity house.

Jay, the kids, and the dogs followed Brandon, a Pied Piper in board shorts and leather flip-flops, into the backyard. "It's fifty-eight degrees," Chloe said. "Does he ever wear clothes?"

"Never," I said. "I'm not sure Jay would let him, anyway."

"Hannah, I need to talk to you," she said. "Billy's taken up competitive bike racing."

"Competitive hand standing wasn't enough?" I asked. "He spends an inordinate amount of time in Lycra."

"You know what this means?" Chloe said. "My Billy is having an affair."

"First of all, you two are separated, even though I don't buy it. Second, your Billy has never even looked at another woman."

"Yes, he has. His yoga instructor," she said.

Billy had many annoying traits: Republican, BMW driver, Giants fan—but he wasn't a player. Or *was he?* The truth about men in L.A. is that any of them can get a hot, young girlfriend. All any L.A. man needs is a decent leased car, that's it. You don't even have to own. Billy doesn't have a job, but he does have a BMW that hasn't run out its lease.

"I feel like my whole world's coming apart at the seams," Chloe said.

"You two are having problems—that's normal, given the circumstances—but he loves you. He would never, ever even look at another woman. He would only look at her really solid IRA."

"Tatiana can put her legs behind her head."

"Okay, so he's probably thought about it," I said.

"Billy's job was his life. He loved shorting mortgages. Now, everything's changed. He's so confused. The other day, he said something positive about universal health care. I'm afraid I've lost him forever."

Jay walked in from the backyard. "Well, if Billy goes for same-sex marriage, I'm not speaking to him again."

"You never did," I said. "Jay, by the way, not to change the subject, but that wasn't a very funny joke you pulled on me the other night. When Santino was here."

"Santino is no joke, sister."

"Not Santino," I said. "You rearranged the feathers. I went out there in the morning, they spelled out the word 'boo.' "

"I did no such thing," Jay said. "I mean, I was high as a schoolgirl at a Justin Bieber concert, but I would remember."

"Are you sure?"

Jay just gave me a look. "I don't know who's rearranging your feathers, sweetheart, but it ain't me. Although it does sound like something you could use, if you know what I mean."

13

Thanks but No Thanks

Thanksgiving hit with the fury of a thousand dried-out turkey breasts. Jay was bringing yams and Hidalgo; Aimee was bringing green beans and three bottles of wine—two for her, one for us; Chloe was bringing a Tofurky, her children, her dogs, and a very limber Billy. Brandon was spending Thanksgiving with Stephanie and her attorney fiancé. I had been assigned the turkey, stuffing, and pies.

I took out a bank loan and purchased an organic, free-range turkey and all the fixings from Whole Foods. I walked the aisles with purpose and direction. I no longer questioned every item, comparing it to what John would have purchased. Whole pecans or crushed? Cornmeal or mix? I was on my way to mastering groceries.

In my kitchen, I handled the turkey like a baby, buttering the skin gently, cooing to it as I slipped it onto the rack. Five hours later, my turkey was done. Casa Sugar smelled like the start of a perfect Thanksgiving.

Even Ellie was impressed. "You made Daddy's turkey?" she asked.

"I sure tried," I said, admiring the golden, roasted skin of my bird. I got dressed and ran my fingers through my hair, put on a coat of mascara. I was ready to pull this off.

My guests, however, hadn't gotten the memo.

Jay was first to arrive, without the yams and without his date.

"Where's Hidalgo?" I asked.

"Don't ask," he said. "I need a drink."

"Where are my yams?"

"On the floor of my car," Jay said. "I'll get you a spoon. This entire day is killing me softly."

Chloe came up behind Jay, with her brood. Her face was red and puffy.

"What's wrong?" I said. Her kids ran past me, in search of Ellie.

"Nothing, why?" she sniffed. "Here," she handed me a Tofurky, still in its plastic wrapping. As though I, in a million years, would know what to do with a Tofurky. Except laugh at it.

"You sure everything's okay?" I asked.

"Couldn't be better," she said, her chipper meter spinning. "Billy's joining the Israeli Army. He won't be able to make it for dinner."

We were seated around my dining room table, covered in an orange and brown paper tablecloth from Target.

"Is this something the pilgrims ordered? The only time orange and brown works is never," Jay grumbled.

"Shut up and count your blessings," I said.

"Mommy," Ellie said. She was wearing leopard tights, a tutu, and a purple velvet T-shirt. "We have to say grace. Like at school."

She grabbed my hand, then Jay's, closed her eyes, and bowed her head. Jay and I smiled at each other. Chloe's kids quieted down and followed suit.

"Hi, God," Ellie said. "How are you? Thank you for our food. Thank you for Thanksgiving. Thank you for Uncle Jay and Brandon and Auntie Chloe and all my friends and mostly thank you for Mommy. And please, God, take care of all the rescue dogs, and tell Daddy we love him very much and wish he could be here and we will never forget him, especially on Thanksgiving. And that's why we like Thanksgiving. Thank you. Amen."

"Amen," I said. Ellie remembered that this was John's holiday. How? She was so little.

I heard murmurs of "Amens" around the table. Among the adults, there was not a dry eye in Casa Sugar.

"I'm really sorry about the yams, God," Jay said.

"Does everyone want to say what they're grateful about?" Chloe asked.

"Ask me in a couple years," I said.

Aimee never showed up, with or without the green beans, but my turkey and cornbread stuffing were a smash hit. John would have been proud. Halfway through the meal, we finally got to the topic of Billy's enlistment.

"Not to be insensitive, Chloe, but Billy's not Jewish," I said. "He is aware it's the *Israeli* Army?"

"I know, I told him," Chloe said.

"So . . . the handstand career didn't work out for him?" Jay asked. "I'm sorry . . . but where did this come from?"

"He's looking for a purpose," Chloe said.

"Like everyone else running down San Vicente?" Jay asked.

"At least Billy's still breathing." I sighed. "Tonight I feel like I keep looking over my shoulder, for John to open up another bottle of wine." Seeing the kids' attention diverted, I said quietly, "I keep listening for his laugh. Or his swearing, if he burned his finger on the pie. Every year, he did that."

"Well, if my love life were any more tragic, I'd be Vivien Leigh," said Jay. "It's not easy being the Sugar Daddy to a married Catholic Latino model who's hung like a paint can."

"He has a wife," Chloe and I said, at once.

"He doesn't love her. He loves me. She knows it. I know it. *Manfinders.com* knows it."

"Love doesn't conquer all, Jay," I said, putting my hand on his. "I wish it did."

Jay gave me a small smile. "I don't believe that, Hannah," he said, "and neither do you."

* * *

Chloe left with her kids and dogs after maniacally cleaning up the kitchen. Every pot and pan had been scrubbed, the dishes had been properly placed inside the dishwasher. (Note to self: *Never have a falling-out with Chloe during the holidays.*)

"I can't believe Aimee didn't show," I said. "Is she avoiding me? Lately, I call her, she doesn't call back. She's barely even responding to my texts."

"Honey, maybe she just needs a break from all the emotional stuff," he said. "She's not strong like me."

"Strong? Muffin tops on chubby girls make you sob," I said. "Wait. You don't think something's happened to her? Do you think she's . . . dead?"

"Hannah, no," Jay said. "She's not dead, just selfish."

"Ever since John . . . ," I said. "I assume people are dead if they don't call me back. Jay, Aimee could be hurt, lying in that apartment, and we would never know it. She's never given me the key."

"Wait," Jay said, "I know I'm in a tryptophan-and-alcohol haze, but remember when Aimee went missing two years ago? She was holed up in a post-op in Brentwood." Jay grabbed the phone. "She's not dead—she's hiding out somewhere and watching Sandra Bullock movies on Starz." Jay made all of three calls before tracking her down at the Beverly West Recovery Retreat on Rodeo Drive. Brandon had just walked in my front door.

"We'll be back," I told him, as I grabbed my jacket. "Aimee's gone post-op."

Twenty minutes later, we were at the Beverly West reception. Jay held a bouquet of peonies that he insisted we buy at the flower shop on Doheny, where the clerks look like boy band meat. The receptionist stared impassively. Impassive was the new shock, disgust, sadness, anger, glee, and mirth. L.A.'s west side was expression-free.

"Room Twenty-three," she said. "Three doors down, on your left." Her voice was also impassive. Perhaps there was personality Botox? If there were, I could use some.

* * *

Aimee was on a huge bed, propped up on pillows, her eyes and cheeks swollen, and a (yes, indeed!) Sandra Bullock movie playing on HDTV.

"It's like Ash Wednesday," Jay whispered.

"I heard that," Aimee said.

"Aimee," I said, "you are not allowed to have surgery without us. We thought you were dead."

"Is Chloe here?" Aimee looked around. "I don't want to be blog-bushed."

"Ambushed? No. Boob job, mid-face-lift?" Jay squinted, trying to assess the damage.

"No," Aimee said, wincing as she moved to her side.

"Lipo and a side of pinned ears?" Jay asked.

"Jay," I said, "this is serious."

Stone Cold Aimee started to cry.

"Aimee, please, please don't cry," Jay said. "If you cry, I cry and I look like Carol Channing when I cry."

"I had something . . . in my breast," Aimee said. "I had to have it removed."

"Dear God, don't take the hair," Jay said, clasping his hands together.

"Jay, you handled death better than this," I said.

"Hair is what's important," Jay said.

"The hair stays," Aimee said. "I'm just doing radiation treatment."

"Oh," Jay said, "so it's the fun cancer."

Aimee managed to smile.

"What's with the puffiness?" I asked. Aimee touched her cheek.

"Sweet Jesus, it looks like you swallowed a cat," Jay said, peering even closer.

"Just a little filler," Aimee said. "The doctor put it in after my breast procedure."

"They can do that?" I said. "They can put filler in and take cancer out?"

"You can have a heart transplant and lipo," Jay said.

"This is L.A.," Aimee said. "Anything is possible."

"Except a normal life," I said.

* * *

It was midnight by the time I got home, but I actually had the energy to clean my house. Don't get crazy, I don't mean dust or vacuum. I mean, throw out old copies of O. *You have your standards, I have mine.*

But first, I tucked in Ellie, who'd surprised me by lying awake when I went in to check on her.

"Can you read *I Love You Forever?*" she asked.

I'd read that book to her when she was two. It had taken me hundreds of butterscotch chips to help me recover.

"Are you sure? It's sort of pathologically sad, you know," I said.

"It's funny."

"Funny?"

"The baby's so cute!" she said. "And the kitty. And Daddy knows all the words." Ellie looked at me with wide eyes.

"You know you can tell Mommy anything, right?" I said.

Ellie nodded. Her lips sealed shut. I hugged her to my chest, sank my face into her hair, and inhaled. I had given her a bath earlier. In my world, bathing my child was victory. The clean watermelon scent in her hair was my Olympic Gold Medal.

Later, after tossing out grapes that had been in the refrigerator so long they were turning into Chianti, I went into the backyard and lit up a cigarette. Aimee had left a pack of old Marlboros in a kitchen drawer with a lighter that looked like a stack of poker chips. I wondered when she had been in Vegas.

No one smokes in California. Maybe there are a few loggers up north, or the desert people on the Arizona border, living in trailers. But no one smokes in Santa Monica. Months ago, Ellie burst into tears upon seeing a woman lighting up in front of Fromin's Deli on Wilshire.

"She's going to die!" Ellie wailed from her car seat.

I slammed on the brakes. "Who, Ellie, who?" I asked, whipping my head around.

"That lady!" Ellie continued to wail. "She's smoking!"

She was pointing at a waitress with hair dyed blond ages ago, casually smoking a cigarette. Here in Santa Monica, the woman would die of loneliness or ostracism long before she died of lung cancer.

"Did Daddy smoke cigarettes?" Ellie had asked me, one damp morning, as I watched her dress for school. It was like watching Kate Moss getting ready to go clubbing. They probably wore the same size.

"No, honey, why?" I asked.

"Because he died, Mommy," Ellie said.

I wasn't even sure it was legal to smoke in my own backyard. Santa Monica loves its city ordinances. They have more city ordinances than homeless people, and we adore our homeless. Spice sat next to me on the cement steps. I lit up, drew in. And coughed.

"Who am I trying to be, Spice?" I asked. "Anouk Aimée?"

I tossed the cigarette. Screw it. Stick to what you're good at. Me, I'm good at wine. My nightly glass of wine had become a goblet. I still had my Dead Husband Card. *There are some things money can't buy, and for those, there's widowhood.* The breeze picked up. Spice started barking.

"Hannah . . . ," the wind said. "Hannah . . ."

I jumped up, knocking over my wineglass on the step. The moon lit up the night. Clouds moved across the sky. I took a deep breath.

"John?" I asked. "John, is that you? Where are you?" Leaves swirled around me. The clouds dispersed.

"I'm at Trader Joe's, picking up those spicy Spanish olives," the wind said. "Can you open the Montepulciano for me? I'm in a Mediterranean frame of mind."

The wind was very lucid tonight. I sat down, hand on my pounding heart.

"Not funny, John," I said. "Dead people shouldn't be cracking jokes."

"I thought it would be a nice icebreaker," John said. I still couldn't see him. "You used to like my sense of humor."

"When you were alive!" I was trying to find him. "Where are you? I want to see you."

"Happy Thanksgiving, baby," he said. "I wish I could have made the turkey for my little family."

I wanted to kiss him, to have him hold me and say that we would grow old together. That we would make love again. That he would never leave. Just like he promised. Lovers make many promises in the heat of passion. *I will love you forever. You're the only one. I've never tried anal before.* Our promises were more like: (Breathless) *I promise I will clean up after the dog.* (Gasping) *I promise to make you fat.* (Panting) *I promise my parents won't visit for more than six days.*

I had loved our life. I ached for him to still be my messy John. I'm still picking up his notes, his papers, but they're dwindling. Soon there will be no detritus at all. Soon I won't be picking up after him at all.

I couldn't take it anymore. "I didn't want to be this Oya person. I just wanted to be Hannah!" I said. I got up and went toward the screen door.

"Who? Hello?" John the Dead said. "Where're you going?"

"I can't do this. I feel like I'm having a nervous breakdown. We had a nice Thanksgiving and I don't want to ruin it by being crazy."

"Well, that's pretty cold. After what I've been through."

"After what *you've* been through?" I found myself staring at the avocado tree. "How about after what we've been through? How about Ellie? What about Jay and Chloe and Aimee? The UPS guy? I've had to comfort the entire city of Santa Monica—I don't dare set foot in Venice. Were you at your memorial service? Your ex-girlfriends were all there, thank you very much!"

"Of course, I was there," John said. "It was kind of thrilling, actually."

"You left us," I said.

"I'm sorry I died," John said. "What do you want from me?"

"I want you to be *not dead*. I want you to be breathing. I want to hold your hand and kiss your cheek. I want to hear you sing R. Kelly

off-key. I want to trip over your tennis shoes that procreate every
ten days. Damn it, I want you to be alive so I can kill you with my
bare hands for dying on us!"

"I made a mistake," John said. "Anyone can make a mistake."

"A mistake?" I said. If we were going to argue like this, I needed
a marriage counselor.

"I'm only human—I was only human. Now, I'm more like a floating particle . . . You won't be able to see me until everything's been
formalized. Talk about bureaucracy. These people make the DMV
look like they're NASA."

"You weren't wearing a bike helmet. You weren't thinking."

"I'm so sorry, baby," John said. "It was a beautiful morning—the
light filtering through the sweet gum trees and tall pines on
Carlyle—it's, well, it's like up here, actually. You see that light here
all the time."

"That gardening truck . . ." In my mind, I suddenly had a vision
of his black Nikes on someone's manicured hedges. *Who had picked
them up? The paramedics? The cops?* I saw his watch. I had given
him that watch. He'd loved that watch.

"Gardening truck?"

"Yes, the gardening truck," I said. "The one that hit you? Come
on, you were there."

"I wasn't hit by a truck."

"Yes, you were," I said. "Look, I don't want to argue with you.
The police report said it was a gardening truck. The guy driving was
an illegal—he took off."

"Hannah, listen to me. I am telling you, it wasn't a truck. I was
there. I'm kind of a key witness. The person who hit me was driving
a Range Rover."

"What the hell?" I said. "You know how I feel about those mon-
sters. I knew that one of those things would kill someone on these
streets. I just didn't think it'd be you—"

"The driver was one of those 'crazy, busy' mom-types, looking
down at her phone. I remember thinking—wow, texting while driving, not smart—"

"Texting," I said. "I didn't think this could get worse."

"I was on the side, but she swerved, hit me, and took off. It was so quick. The guy in the gardener's truck actually stopped to help. He held my head, Hannah. He said the most beautiful prayer in Spanish . . . '*Dios te salve Maria . . .*'" John paused. "I forget the rest, I was kind of busy dying at the time."

My breath caught in my throat.

"Hannah?" John asked. "Baby, what is it?"

Some things shouldn't be known, I thought. *Some things we cannot live with*.

"Please, John, tell me there wasn't any pain." Tears ran down my face.

"No, honey," John said, "there wasn't any pain. I was in shock."

"Thank God, thank God," I sobbed, holding my sides, rocking.

"I'm so sorry," he said, his voice getting weaker. "Hannah, find the gardener. You need to help him out. He was an angel."

"I love you so much. I wish you were alive."

"I love you, too. I wish I were alive," John said. "Help out that gardener. That'll give me some peace. And then you can find the Range Rover."

"Range Rovers are like holistic life coaches in Santa Monica," I said. "You know six out of ten people claim that on their W-9s."

"I have to go . . ."

"Don't leave."

"I love you."

"Don't leave," I screamed. "Don't leave!" Spice started barking again.

"Mommy?" Ellie called from inside. My eyes held on to the dark. The wind had ceased. It was time for the living to get on with it.

Jay was right, though, about love.

Love isn't buried with the dead.

14

Grief Spreads Like Butter

After dropping off Ellie at school, I made a trip back to the Santa Monica Police Station. Once again, I admired its modern, pristine architecture. It looked like it should house Warhols, Pollocks, and Johnses (*Jasper Johns, people!*).

I asked the policewoman at the front desk for the detective who was working the Bernal hit-and-run case. If you're old enough to remember *Barney Miller* (*if you're not, be happy, work hard, and don't let bad boyfriends get you down*), you think of a jail as a run-down, dusty old place filled with characters. This place was like a futuristic movie set with gorgeous extras.

"May I say who's asking?" the policewoman asked.

"Hannah Bernal," I said. "My husband was the . . . victim." I felt like human buzz-kill.

"Oh . . . yes," she said. "Hold on." She scurried past a group of police officers huddled around Starbucks lattes and cranberry scones.

"Mrs. Bernal?" someone said, a moment later. I turned and was eye-to-eye with a stocky bald man sporting a thick black mustache. His gaze was so intense, it felt like he was getting into the ring, despite the suit and tie. *This is exactly the kind of person*, I thought, *who brings out my Tourette's.*

"I'm Detective Ramirez." He held out his hand. It felt like I was shaking a tree stump.

"Hi, Hannah Bernal," I said. "I have some information on my husband's death."

"Odd," Detective Ramirez said. "I was just about to call you."

Five minutes later, Detective Ramirez clasped his hands as he peered at me over his cluttered desk. "Mrs. Bernal, we've just found the hit-and-run driver responsible for the death of your husband."

"You found the woman driving the Range Rover?" I asked.

"Range Rover?" Detective Ramirez said. "The suspect was driving a gardening truck."

"Oh, see," I said, "I'm sorry. You have the wrong guy. My husband was run down by a woman driving a Range Rover."

"Mrs. Bernal, the driver is a Hispanic illegal who was driving a gardening truck."

"It's not him," I said. "He didn't kill my husband."

"Mrs. Bernal, this is the man who was running away from the scene."

"Of course he ran. He was probably scared out of his mind."

"Mrs. Bernal, are you interested in attending the court hearing?"

No wedding ring on Detective Ramirez's thick fingers. *What a surprise*, I thought.

"I'm interested in attending the hearing for the woman who hit my husband, then left him in the street for dead. I am not interested in convicting the man who comforted my husband as he lay dying."

Detective Ramirez leaned back. "You know, Mrs. Bernal, usually people are grateful when we have news concerning their loved ones, no matter how painful it may be."

"Detective," I said calmly, recalling the Om at the end of yoga class, "I am grateful for all your hard work, but as difficult as this must be for you to hear, you have the wrong guy."

"If he's the wrong guy, why did he run off the minute he heard sirens? My mother had a saying. *Cuando el rio suena, agua lleva.*"

"My mother had a saying, too," I said. "Although . . . it's really not pertinent to this situation. May I see him?"

"See the perp?" he asked.

"Yes," I said.

"I don't think that's a good idea," he said. "Look, I know this is hard for you. Trust me. But the sooner you accept this, the better off you and your little girl will be."

"Please." I put my hand on his forearm. It felt like he ate pit bulls for breakfast.

Detective Ramirez walked me down a stark white hallway with polished cement floors.

"You could eat sushi off this floor," I said. We walked past cell after cell, one cleaner than the next. "I love what you've done with the place," I joked.

We stopped at the cell on the end. There was a lean, dark-haired man in ill-fitting jeans staring out into the silver-white sky.

"Del Toro!" Detective Ramirez barked.

Ramirez took a step back, motioning me to move forward. "Are you going to stay here?" I asked.

"Oh, yeah," he said, smiling. His teeth were white and even.

"You have nothing else to do?" I asked.

"I have thirty cases on my desk. Murders, arson, rapists, kidnapping. Cases dating back decades . . . but yes, I'm staying here."

"Well, perhaps you can interpret then?" I asked.

"I don't speak Spanish."

"Oh."

"Disappointed?" Detective Ramirez said. *Was he teasing me?*

The prisoner called Del Toro stared at me through the bars. He wore tennis shoes, loose jeans, and a crumpled T-shirt. He was young, maybe twenty-two, twenty-three, but he looked like he had the weight of the world on his skinny shoulders. I wanted to hug him.

"Can I go inside?" I asked Detective Ramirez. He snorted.

"*Señor Del Toro*," I said, "*Me llamo Hannah Bernal, yo estoy*—oh, God, what's the name for widow? Um. I'm the widow of the man . . . *hombre* . . . you're accused of hitting with your gardening truck."

"That morning haunts me still," Del Toro answered in perfect, poetic English. "I've been wanting to meet you ever since I held your husband in my arms."

"You speak English?" I asked. *Estupida.*

"I was raised just on the other side of the Texas border. Near Nogales," he said. "I picked it up on television game shows. In particular, *Wheel of Fortune* was very helpful. Do you know Miss Vanna White?"

Ramirez was suppressing a laugh.

"You could have told me," I said, turning to him.

"Not really," Ramirez said. "I needed this—it's been a rough morning."

I focused on Del Toro. "You comforted John, *mi esposo*, my husband . . . you gave him solace. I'm grateful you were there for him."

A tear ran down Del Toro's cheek. He wiped it away.

"I didn't want to leave him, but I don't have papers."

"You said a prayer."

"A prayer for the dying . . ."

I felt Ramirez watching every facial tic, listening to every syllable.

"Did you kill John?"

"No, oh, *dios mio*, no. I saw . . . he was on his bike. And there was this big black car—"

"A Range Rover?"

"*Sí*, yes, a Range Rover—"

"Okay, that's enough," Detective Ramirez said. "Mrs. Bernal, I'm going to have to ask you to leave."

Detective Ramirez escorted me out the front doors. Sun hit my eyes. The fog had lifted. "Range Rover," Ramirez said, in a flat tone.

"A black Range Rover," I confirmed, as though that were more specific.

"I suppose you have the license number?"

"No."

"You've just described sixty percent of the cars driven in Santa Monica."

"Isn't that annoying? What are all these people doing with Range Rovers? There are no bogs to drive over here. I've never even seen a bog. What is a bog?"

"Mrs. Bernal, how did you come to this conclusion, as unlikely as it is?"

The sun was shining into Ramirez's eyes. He squinted and looked like an angry grapefruit. He flipped on a pair of Ray-Bans.

"John told me," I said with conviction.

"Your dead husband John?" His eyebrows shot up over his sunglasses.

"I only have one. That I know of." *Hi, inappropriate joking.*

"Mrs. Bernal, have you had a psych eval?" Ramirez asked. "You were arrested a couple weeks ago. The death of a loved one can affect one's mental state."

"I am not crazy, Detective. John told me about the Range Rover just the other night. We were reminiscing about Thanksgiving and then . . ." I shut my mouth. *Hi, Crazy!*

"You know what I think?" Ramirez said, taking off his Ray-Bans and looking into my eyes. "It's one of two things. You're having a nervous breakdown—that's best case. Or you had something to do with his death. That's why you're trying to get this guy off the hook. You feel guilty. Did you want your husband dead? Was it his life insurance?"

"How dare—" I didn't finish my thought as a cloud passed overhead and a church bell rang. A robust African-American man in an L.A.P.D. uniform appeared over Ramirez's shoulder. He was young (although most people seem young at my age), maybe late twenties, early thirties. His badge read JACKSON. He must have been dead at least ten years—he was dimensional, opaque; he'd done his time.

"Tell Nacho to stop picking on widows," Jackson said. He laughed, his chest heaving.

"Stop picking on widows, Nacho," I said, gazing back into Ramirez's eyes, my reflection stern in his Ray-Bans lenses.

"What did you just—"

"Ask him when he got so fat," Jackson said. "In '89, he was a skinny little thing. Shit, he jumped fences like a junkyard dog."

"This person . . . Jackson . . . would also like to know when you got so fat," I said. "Not my words. I would never say you're fat—stocky, more like."

"What did you say?" Ramirez asked. "Why did you say Jackson?"

"That's what it says on his nametag."

"Where?" He whipped around.

"Right behind you, but you can't see him."

"You're giving me the creeps, lady," Ramirez said. "You need to stop this—now."

"Or what? You'll arrest me? Put me in Prada Jail?" I asked. "He's in uniform. L.A.P.D. Big smile, big laugh."

Ramirez said something in Spanish, rubbing his shiny head with his thick fingers.

"He better remember me!" Jackson said. "I saved that fat man's life!"

"Don't forget. He saved your life, Detective Ramirez."

"Oh my God," Ramirez said. "Where is he?"

"You can't see him, I'm sorry."

Ramirez glanced nervously over his shoulder, then turned back to me.

"My partner . . . I was a rookie. We rode in the South West division. Eighteenth Street territory. Back when I thought I could, you know, make a difference. It was just a traffic stop. A parolee. I should have known, I should have called for backup—"

Jackson was still standing over his shoulder, his hands on his hips, listening.

"Your partner looks happy," I said. "I wish you could hear him laugh."

"He's laughing?" Ramirez looked up. "Oh, man, that laugh—"

Jackson started to fade.

"It's so crazy," Ramirez said. "What you miss—and then, what you forget you miss."

We stood there as people walked by, as the sun found its way to us.

"Find the Range Rover," I said.

"Dead people or no dead people, we got our guy," he said. "But I'll put some calls out. On one condition—you get professional help. There are groups who can help you. I don't know you but I know enough about your situation. And I know it could go either way. Mrs. Bernal, you owe it to your daughter."

He trucked back into the station. I angled my face to the sun, letting the warmth and essential vitamin D sink in (encouraging freckles, age spots, melanoma—can't I just have a moment?). I heard a noise, opened my eyes to see a homeless woman pushing a baby stroller filled with bottles and cans. I can't tell you how disturbing it is to see baby strollers filled with things that aren't babies. The homeless woman suddenly pointed her finger at me. And laughed.

Because I wasn't wearing sunscreen? Maybe she recognized me as the person she was twenty years ago. We weren't so far apart, she and I; my hair was dreading up like hers. My skin would thicken and wrinkle. Probably within the next ten minutes. I hadn't paid that much attention to my teeth lately, and who knows if my dental insurance was good anymore. I doubt it. I was gawking at my future—typical Santa Monica homeless woman—and she was mocking her past—typical Santa Monica latte-slinging, hand-wringing, hybrid-driving, liberal-voting, yoga mat–toting bourgeoise. The flip side of the coin was not so flippin' far.

Meanwhile, I was still in love with my dead, though conversational, husband. How would I recover from my grief if we never stopped dating? Detective Ramirez was right. It was time to call in the professionals.

"I'm getting help," I said to the laughing homeless woman. "Okay? I'm getting help."

Widows and Widowers of Santa Monica met at a stately Tudor built over two lots on Georgina, just west of Casa Sugar. I parked in front, admiring the huge lawn, manicured coral trees, and ocean

views, and navigated the brick walkway. I heard soft voices, silver-
ware tapping good china, classical music playing in the background.

I rapped the antique knocker on the large wooden door, waited,
then pushed it open. There was a sea of gray heads, bobbing up and
down in conversation. Everyone wore a nametag. Women were
walking in behind me with Pyrex dishes, heavy with casseroles. I
was empty-handed.

An elegant woman in her sixties, with a silver bob, wearing a suit
and a silk scarf, waved to me from the other side of the room, then
weaved through the crowd, and took me by the arm. "You must be
Hannah," she said, smiling, "I'm Amelia. Welcome. Let me introduce you around—"

"I forgot a casserole," I said. "Should I go out and get one?"

"Oh, don't worry." She laughed. "Only the gals who've been here
awhile know to bring food."

"They all look so happy," I said, focusing on the crowd's smiles
and laughter. No frowns or sad faces; I would have settled for a
yawn. "Are you sure they're widows?"

"Time heals all things, dear."

"Oh. They must have been widowed a long time ago, then."

"No," Amelia said. "The more time you're married, the less healing you need. Come on, let's get this party started. Every Tuesday,
we have a Zumba class . . ."

A few minutes later, I was having a conversation with Lilith (who
wore a tennis skirt cut short above her wrinkled knees) about her
dear, departed husband, Millford.

"You were married how long?" I asked.

"Forty-two years," Lilith said, tearing up. *The widow I was looking for.* "Wonderful years."

"You're so lucky." I sighed. "I wish I had even ten years with
John. I'd settle for ten."

An eerie quiet descended over the room. A tall gentleman with
thick silver hair, still wearing his confident handsomeness from de-

cades past, was making his way to the buffet table. Just as he reached the deviled eggs, he was widow-rushed.

"Horace," I heard. "Horace, over here . . ."

"Lilith," I said, "who's that?"

"Why? Are you interested?" she asked, her gaze narrowing.

"Not at all," I said, "I'm just curious."

"You get near him, missy," she hissed, lipstick marking her teeth, "and I'll cut you."

Lilith ran off toward Widower Number One. "Horace! Horace, dear! I made your favorite! Lemon meringue pie!"

Time to go, but I wasn't leaving empty-handed. I fought my way through the granny rave, snatched a few homemade oatmeal raisin cookies, and made my escape.

Widowed Partners in Transition's homepage described themselves as a healing group for women under forty-five who'd recently lost a loved one. *Hello, target audience.* I headed to the Urth Café on Main on a bright, crisp winter morning that Packers fans would kill for. While Urth Café was hardly the ideal setting to grieve (surrounded by lululemon asses and Gaiam yoga mats) I liked their quart-sized lattes and their street parking.

(L.A. sidenote: There's a lot you can overcome in your search for the perfect mate in L.A.—including a rap sheet or pan-sexuality—but if you can't find a parking spot on a Tuesday afternoon, you'll be single the rest of your life.)

I stood in line, waited for my two-ton latte, and looked for the group on the back patio. There were several women and one guy crowded around a small circular table. They looked worried. They looked depressed. They looked like they'd forgotten to brush their hair. *My people.*

I caught the eye of the woman leading the group. She was wearing a stretchy top, had wiry black hair, and a prominent nose with a diamond piercing. "Hi . . . you joining the group?" she asked.

"Is this the . . . for widows?" I asked.

"You could say that. Have a seat," she said, smiling. "Welcome."

Yoga Instructor-Grief Counselor, I guessed. L.A. was the Hyphenate Capital of the world.

"I'm not much of a joiner," I said. I squeezed between an Asian lady with a boy cut, and a large-boned Scandinavian woman, and placed my latte on the tiled table. "But I figure, hey, I qualify."

"I'm sorry to hear that," the leader said. "I'm Shalimar. We're all . . . dealing with our special form of grief."

The All-American brown-haired girl was crying into her napkin. A guy with a crew cut, wearing a down vest that made him seem even more bulky, pulled her in for a hug, muting her sobs.

"What's your name?" Shalimar asked, snapping me out of my trance.

"Hannah Marsh . . . Bernal."

"How long ago did you lose your partner?" Shalimar asked.

"September. It feels like this morning, and like . . . years . . ."

Their sad, knowing eyes were upon me. Maybe this would work, after all. Shalimar put her hand on mine as a lone tear drifted down the side of my nose.

"I cry at the weirdest times," I said.

They nodded.

"In line at Whole Foods," I continued. "Ron Artest was there, in his Laker uniform, ordering vegan food—and I lost it. I think he felt bad."

More nodding.

"Santa Monica Seafood. The pesto shrimp sent me into heaving sobs. It's not just the prices. My baby would have never let me buy that," I said. "Ordering a latte at the Pirates, not ordering the Americano, too . . . that took weeks."

All-American whimpered.

"I have to physically stop myself from saying the words 'Americano, bone dry.' "

More weeping.

"Mail makes me cry. Mail. Looking at the name on the envelope . . . T-shirts. Clogs. The soles—the way they're worn down on the side."

More tears.

"The outgoing message on my phone machine. I can't change it. I can't. Stray hair from the brush. I kept all of those. I collected them for our daughter. Is that weird?"

Six sad heads swayed side to side.

"I miss John so much," I said. "No one has ever had a better husband."

The swaying stopped. The weeping came to a halt. There was silence.

"*Husband?*" Shalimar asked.

"Yeah . . . ," I said, looking at her. "John, my husband—"

I looked at the group. Nose rings. Butch haircut. A wife-beater. The crew-cutted guy was no guy. But really, nothing had been a dead giveaway that this was a lesbian grief circle.

"Did I say husband?" I said. They just stared at me.

"John . . . ," Shalimar said.

Widowed Partners. You idiot, I thought.

"I meant . . . John . . . anna . . . ," I said. "Johnanna?"

"Nice try," Shalimar said.

"So he had a penis," I said. "What difference does it make? Grief doesn't discriminate."

"I'm so sorry, Hannah," Shalimar said. "But this group is only for gays and lesbians."

"I voted against Prop 8," I pleaded. "I made out with a girl my freshman year in college—I kind of enjoyed it?"

"I'm sure you'll find the right fit, honey," Shalimar said. "There're plenty of other groups out there."

I gathered my pride and my latte and walked out. Again, I belonged but didn't belong. I had loss, yes, but not the right kind.

I wrapped my scarf around my neck, and turned down Barnard, then toward the Venice Pier. The last time I'd been to Venice Beach, on a foggy June morning, John and I had rented bikes and strapped Ellie on a seat in the back.

"She's going to fall," I'd said.

"She's not going to fall." John laughed. "Bad things don't always happen . . . Don't always expect the worst, Hannah Banana."

He secured Ellie's baby seat, put a yellow bike helmet on her head, smushing her curls, and took off down the bike path, with me following, my eye never wavering, willing our precious cargo to stay, stay, stay . . .

A young family now whizzed past me on bikes. I woke from the past and found myself standing in front of Hairy Eddie's Tattoo Shoppe. *(Yes, shoppe spelled just like that—this was the "classy" area of the boardwalk; it didn't reek of week-old vomit.)*

"Walk in," I heard myself say.

Inside the shop, myself said, "Have you lost your damn mind?" Tattoos and I have an understanding—we stay away from each other. Even during the Westside Mom Yin-Yang/Celtic Cross/Child's-Name-Inside-Your-Wrist trends. During these and most other trends, I lie down until the trend is over. Also, I hate needles.

"Are you asking me?" An African-American man who must have stood 6' 8", over three hundred pounds, with a clean-shaven head, addressed me in a soft voice.

"Sorry, did I say that out loud?"

"You did," he said. I stared at the walls covered in tattoo designs, from dragons to naked women to Snoop Dogg, and signed photographs of rap artists, actors, and, well, strippers.

"Is Hairy Eddie here?" I asked.

"You're looking at him."

"Forgive me. You're not hairy."

"I forgive you," he said. "I'm not even Eddie. I just thought the name combo sounded cool. You looking for something special?"

"It's like this—" I started. I glanced at his handiwork. There was a photo of a man covered in tattoos, including his head. It was hard to tell what race he'd been born to. It was indeterminate, like so many things in L.A.—"of indeterminate sexuality" being number one on our indeterminate list.

"My husband died," I said. Hairy Eddie nodded. "And I . . . I want to get something to remember him by. He was a chef, so . . . we could be creative, here . . . like a chicken? Or maybe some cookware?"

Hairy Eddie rubbed his chin with his hand. He wore a thick gold wedding band. He seemed accustomed to women who talked on and on.

"Don't do it," he said, shaking his head.

"What do you mean?" I said. "You're Hairy Eddie—tattoo artist to the stars and their cars. Look at the *Venice Magazine* piece over there—you're supposed to be selling—"

"There are four stages in life when you should get a tattoo. When you're in high school, when you join the military, when you get your first recording contract, or when you're so drunk you can sing the lyrics to 'Oye Como Va.'"

"How are you going to make a living if you don't pander to middle-aged white women going through life crises? You're eliminating half your customer base."

"Young lady, all I know is, it never comes out right with dead people. You will regret it," Hairy Eddie said. "Maybe not today, but someday, for sure. When you have more happy days than sad. You will regret it. And so will your lover."

The word "lover" made my stomach turn.

"Hairy Eddie, who's neither," I said, "you're not the first person who thinks I've lost my mind. But despite the fact that I'm deathly afraid of needles and will probably faint during this whole operation, I'm here. I am here. And I need this. I can live with the regret of doing it. But maybe, maybe . . . I can't live with the regret of not doing it."

Hairy Eddie peered down at me. "Le Creuset or All-Clad?"

Dizziness, fat tears, heaving—five minutes into my tattoo, I was Heather Locklear in a Lifetime movie. Finally, Hairy Eddie, sweating bullets from his brown eggshell head, finished after what seemed like days, washed down my shoulder blade with hydrogen peroxide, and stared long and hard at the tattoo.

"What?" I asked. "What is it?"

"Truly, I'm an artist, but I wish I hadn't done it."

He handed me a mirror. On my shoulder, in shades of green, blue, and gray, was a frying pan, expertly crafted. John's name hugged the curve of the pan, along with his birthday and the date of his death. I started to cry. Again. *If I had a dime for every time I broke down . . . I'd have decent plumbing.*

"You hate it," Hairy Eddie said.

"I don't hate it. Everyone will know, now. I could have just taped the *Santa Monica Mirror* clipping to my forehead," I said. "You see, now? You see? That's why I'm forgetting things. That's why I ran over the CVS clerk's foot."

"Here," he said, taking a bottle of Silver Patron from a shelf behind him. He grabbed a couple of shot glasses advertising casinos and poured two fingers in each.

"To life," he said, handing me a glass. Warm tears made tracks down my cheeks. I wondered how bad I looked. I still had the capacity for misplaced vanity.

"C'mon," he said. "You can do it. Say it."

"To life," I said. I kicked back the whole shot. "Exactly how pathetic is my tattoo?"

"This is nothing. I've done faces, bodies . . . Someone brings in a picture, their wife, girlfriend, boyfriend, husband . . . I can make 'em twenty-five forever, on your skin. But then, you have to live with it. Then, the tattoo, in effect, prevents you from what you have to do. Which is to heal. To go on. To live."

He took another shot. Filled my glass.

"You have a chance, you know," he said. "You're hot."

"Shut up. You say that to all the girls with frying pan tattoos."

"I'm serious," he said. "You'll know. Someday. Then you come back here, we'll get married. My wife won't mind."

"Even with the tattoo?"

"Not a thing, little darling. Some girls, I have to cover three, four dudes' names. I had to make a penis into a flamingo. Don't tell me that's not a hard day. I did a tattoo for this dude, businessman. Dead wife. You know what he wanted? Broke my heart."

"What?"

"Her Amex card. On his biceps."

"Wow," I said. "That almost makes me feel normal. So . . . another round?"

"Easy, sister," Eddie said. "You're not as big as you used to be. You'll fill out. Don't worry. You'll start eating again. Someone will feed you."

I felt lighter as I walked out of Hairy Eddie's, even carrying the weight of my dead husband's frying pan on my shoulder.

15

You're Dead to Me

I opened my front door to find Dee Dee Pickler sitting on my couch in a Santa's Promiscuous Little Helper costume, chatting up Brandon.

"Hi, Dee Dee. Nothing says Christmas like silicone," I said.

"Thanks, sweetie. Listen, I was on my way to a party, just wanted to see how you're holding up." Dee Dee popped up from the couch, adding furtively, "Man-oh-manny . . ." I heard a tinny version of *"Guan TONAMARA . . . Guajila . . ."*

"Oops, *excusez-moi*," Dee Dee said, then answered her phone with the pink Swarovski crystal cover. I scooped up Ellie and ushered Brandon into the kitchen, out of Elf Tart's hearing range.

"Stranger danger, Brandon," I said. "Never let Dee Dee in the house when you're alone."

"She said she was a friend of yours," Brandon said.

"Frenemy. Dee Dee is a frenemy, without the 'fre,'" I said. "That's not fair. She means well, she does . . . but to you, she means business."

"Hannah," Dee Dee called, as she traipsed into the kitchen. "There you are, you two."

"Brandon," I said, "why don't you take Ellie somewhere safer, like . . . the Tijuana border?"

Brandon carried Ellie into the backyard.

"Wowser, hope the parts I don't see aren't built like Ken," Dee Dee said, staring after Brandon. "You don't waste much time, do you, Miss Merry Widow?"

"Brandon's just helping me out with Ellie."

"Sure. So. How's the job search going?" she asked. "No worries, I'm sure you can find something else. I'm going to help Brandon get into real estate. So . . . you're not sleeping with him?"

"He's a baby."

"Perfect. The girls and I are going to Vegas for the weekend." Dee Dee smiled. "We're looking for a mascot."

"Over my dead body," I said.

"Ooh, I thought so," Dee Dee said. "That boy would kill in real estate. With those shoulders, forget it. When the market recovers, he could be a top seller."

"Brandon wants to teach," I said. "He loves children."

"Yeah . . . what's that like?" Dee Dee said, then, "Oh, hey, I came here to tell you. Have you heard about the Widower? The ultimate single, and he's perfect for you."

"No, thank you. And, anyway, what would I say? Hi there, I hear your wife died. Guess what, my husband died, too. We have so much in common."

"Have you ever dealt with an ex-wife? I'll take six-feet-under any day," Dee Dee said. "Recon tells me he hangs out at Caffe Luxxe. Double espresso, extra foam. No sugar. Croissant on the side."

"Does he wear a sign that says 'Yes, I am the Widower'?"

"In this town?" Dee Dee said. "He's lucky he survived the memorial service. I heard he got a tattoo with his wife's name on it. Have you ever heard anything so pathetic?"

I rubbed the pain in my shoulder from my new frying pan.

"Hannah," Dee Dee said, attempting a concerned expression; South-of-the-Border Botox rendered her a Popsicle Face. "I'm worried about you. I don't think you realize what could happen. People are going into foreclosure all around us—writers, lawyers . . . Two houses down your street are bank-owned. You don't even know."

"Dee Dee, your sincerity frightens me," I said. "Don't worry—Jay and I will start working soon. He's been all over town, trying to find the right fit."

"Jay's working on a deal. *Solamente*. But I'm sure you knew that."

I felt queasy. Was Jay job-cheating on me?

"I'm sure he was planning on telling you," Dee Dee said. "Enjoy your funemployment with your new manny. But keep this in mind. My developer—he's called the Turk. He's buying up teardowns. That man loves him some columns. What does he love more than columns? Marble driveways. What does he love more than marble driveways? Nothing. Not even his family."

"My home is not a teardown. It's on a historical registry."

"It's a teardown when the bills come due," Dee Dee said. "And the city wants as many tax dollars as possible—which means, registry, shmegistry. You give me a call when you feel up to it. But don't wait too long—the housing market is soft and getting softer. It's like the coke years."

She looked out the window at Brandon and Ellie.

"I don't know where this is all going to end, frankly." She sighed. "I'd be hanging by a short hair, if I had any left."

I put Ellie to bed, after reading *Knuffle Bunny Too*. Brandon had gone out for the night, dressed in faded jeans, flip-flops, and a perma-tan. December was Santa Monica's coldest on record, but the sun still shined on our manny.

"Have a nice night," I said. "Don't come home too late. Call your surrogate mother if you need a ride." I thought about my financial situation, about a possible move, about what I would do without him. Ellie would be heartbroken, again.

I called Jay. "Hi, I'd like to report a friendship violation," I said, into his voice mail. "Dee Dee told me about your new deal. Call me before the homeless guy in the argyle sweater throws it in my face."

* * *

I fell asleep on the couch and had a nightmare. Dee Dee and the SMCA dressed as Elf Hookers hoisting lit torches and banging at my front door.

"Stand aside!" Nightmare Dee Dee said. "We're coming for your manny!"

I blocked the doorway, but the ladies of the SMCA stormed through. I awakened in a cold sweat to coyotes yelping. As I listened in horror, they snacked on something small, furry . . . and bedazzled. I listened until there was nothing, no sound at all.

I checked my phone. Two A.M. I looked in on Ellie, then wandered into the kitchen where my mail was stacked on the counter. Brandon's handiwork. I wasn't up to stacking yet. I grabbed graham crackers and milk, sat down, and sorted through it.

There was an invitation for Ellie to a four-year-old's birthday party. *Good*, I thought, *I'm doing something right. She's making new friends.*

A coupon booklet for things I didn't need but was dying to save money on.

A letter from the State of California. I ripped it open.

Our property tax bill. We were behind on our second payment. And by "we," I meant "me." I was behind. I would spend the rest of my life trying to catch up. I checked the date. Four weeks before it went to collections. *Merry Fucking Christmas.*

Finally, there was a letter from our insurance company. A policy check!

I ripped it open. Instead of a check, there was a letter, folded in three.

> *Dear Policy Holder,*
>
> *We regret to inform you that your life insurance policy claim is no longer valid. Payments were not made to your account in the last three quarters. Your policy has lapsed and we will not be making a payment on this account.*
>
> *If you have any questions, please call customer service*

*Monday through Friday between the hours of 8:00 A.M. PST
and 3:00 P.M. PST.*

Thank you for your business.
Howard P. Morgan
Claim Specialist

My knees were shaking. All that was not lost, was lost.

"Oh my God," I said. "This can't be happening." I ran into the backyard, clutching the letter.

"John!" I yelled. "Get over here this minute!"

Dogs barking. An old Lab, a shih tzu. Lights turning on, bedrooms, bathrooms. I didn't care. In a few months, the neighbors would miss me yelling at my dead husband at 2:00 A.M. Wait until the Shah of Iran's palace started going up.

"John," I said. "I know you're out there!" *Can one argue with a dead person? Yes, you can, but you have to be motivated.*

"Hannah?" John said. "What's wrong? Why are you so upset? Is it Ellie?"

"Ellie? No, God, no, it's not Ellie."

"What is it?" John said. "I'm sorry, I was distracted. I was just getting into it with Julia Child. She's really stuck on how to boil an egg. I say, drop it in when the water's boiling—and salt the water. She says—"

"John, your life insurance policy expired." I said, "You didn't keep up with the payments. How could you do that to us?"

"Oh my God," John said. "I didn't?"

"No! Yes. You didn't. We are screwed!" I was pacing, frantic.

"Now, don't overreact, Hannah. We can figure this out—"

"You died and left us . . . with nothing . . ."

"Hannah, you had a job when I died. And you have my books—"

"We spent the rest of your advance on our Greece trip, remember? I'd have to sell a million to see royalties. You know how it works!"

"Oh, right," John said. "We made that deposit . . . How much was that?"

"Eight thousand," I said. The amount sounded enormous, wasteful. Silly.

"Shit. You should just go to Greece," John said. "Go, and finish my cookbook."

"What's it going to be called, *Cooking for Destitute Widows*?"

"Hannah, I'm sorry. You didn't marry an accountant. You married a guy who wears Crocs to work."

"I should have known—I've never trusted Crocs," I said. "They're not shoes, they're not sandals—why can't they make up their minds?"

"You're insulting my shoe choices? That's just going too far."

"I'll show you too far," I said, pulling my shirt off my shoulder, revealing the frying pan tattoo. "Look what I did for you!"

"Wow," he said. "Is that Le Creuset?"

"Hairy Eddie insisted on going high-end."

"It's sweet," John said. "It makes me wish I were still alive. I could have prevented you from putting a permanent frying pan on your body."

"Even my dead husband can't appreciate the gesture." I sighed. "John, unless I figure something out, I'm going to have to sell the only home Ellie's ever known. It's just too much for her. It's not fair, John. It's not fucking fair."

"Hannah, listen to me," John said. "You are the most resourceful person I know. I mean, short of Jesse James. He's taken me at poker like eight times."

"The outlaw? Shouldn't he be somewhere south of here, like hell? Or Orange County?"

"The guys running the show are big on second chances," John said. "Also, let's face it, how fun would it be if only the righteous made it up here? We've been to those dinner parties, remember—you leave at nine thirty."

"John, I forgot to tell you. I found the man. Del Toro. Who stopped to comfort you."

"You forgot to tell me?"

"I'm sorry, I have a lot going on. It's not like I can just call you up. I can't just call you up at any time, right?"

"One of the things I like about this place," John said. "No cell-phones. Although the reception would be excellent. Is he okay? Did he remember?"

"Of course he remembered," I said. "He was sad that he couldn't do more to help. But he's not okay. He's in jail, John. They're going to try to convict him of manslaughter. Maybe worse, because he fled the scene."

"Baby, you can't let that happen. Look, this financial stuff, I know you're going to pull through," John said. "You're going to catch a break. But you need to find that Princess of Darkness in her Range Rover. I have a bad feeling things could turn very ugly for poor Del Toro."

John was right. I didn't trust Detective Ramirez to follow up, even with the show I'd put on for him. After John faded on me, I walked into my kitchen to discover Jay, in a scarf and cap, shaking his head. Jay had his own key to Casa Sugar, and was welcome to come and go as he pleased. Sometimes he just didn't want to sleep alone.

"How long have you been standing there?" I asked.

"Long enough," Jay said, "to see you having an argument with a hundred-year-old avocado tree. I mean, it can't even defend itself."

"I wasn't arguing with the tree," I said. "I was arguing with John. Well, not arguing. More like a fervent discussion."

"Hannah, you have to stop this, I beg you," Jay said, then, "And what, pray tell, did you do to your shoulder?"

"You have more to answer to than I do," I said. "Someone here is making a deal at a network. Someone who is supposed to be my partner."

"Hannah, I was going to tell you," Jay said, "when the time was right. I'm working on an HGTV show—it's just something to tide me over."

"And me? What about me?" I couldn't have sounded more pathetic.

"I tried, Hannah," Jay said. He sat down at the chopping block. "I really tried. Honey, people think that you've completely lost it."

"You don't believe me," I said.

"I think you need to take a year off, get some help, then come back stronger than ever."

"I'm going to lose my home," I said.

"Hannah, you could lose more than that," Jay said. "You could lose Ellie—"

The thought had never occurred to me. *Could they take away my daughter? My baby?*

"You think I'm lying?" I asked, voice breaking.

"I think you're in pain. So much pain that you're manifesting . . . illusions."

"How would I know about Todd's brother, or . . . or Trish . . . ?"

"I don't know. You could have known these things. They could have been in the recesses of your mind—"

"The police detective's dead partner?"

"Babydoll, I'm closer to you than anyone, but you haven't seen any dead person around me."

"Has anyone close to you died? Someone you really loved."

"No," Jay said, after a moment.

"Well, maybe that's the reason," I said with a sigh. "Consider yourself lucky. In the meantime, I'm so over dead people. I have live people problems to deal with. Dead people don't pay the rent."

16

Coffee-Mates

I was sitting at my kitchen table, assessing my financial future.

On one side of the ledger was Casa Sugar. On the other side, economic financial ruin. I had two options: I could rob a bank or get one of those easy-to-find high-paid television jobs. I made some calls.

"Sony Pictures Television Studios, how may I direct your call?"

"Hi, is Phil Henry in for Hannah Bernal?"

"Who?"

"Phil Henry. He's president of the TV studio—"

"Oh. Um. Hold on." (Muffled voices in the background.)

"Hi, are you still there?"

"I'm here," I said.

"Yeah, he left a while ago."

"Oh," I said, "do you know where he went?"

"Home," the operator said. "Yeah. I'm pretty sure. Home."

This scenario repeated until my ear went numb. Brandon watched patiently as I crossed out names and phone numbers on my Rolodex.

"What is that?" he asked, pointing to my Rolodex.

"It's a . . . Rolodex?"

"Oh."

"It has phone numbers in it."

"Really?" He picked it up and examined it as though it were a dinosaur bone. I snatched it back.

"Listen, can you take Ellie to school?" I asked. "I have to make a trip to the bank. Mama has to put on her begging shoes."

"Sure," Brandon said. "I want to talk to you, though."

"Are you quitting?"

"No."

"Do you want to get paid?" My jaw started to ache.

"No. I'm good. For now."

"Do you have a substance abuse problem?"

"No!" Brandon laughed.

"Then please, don't tell me anything right now. I can't handle any more news, okay?"

"I just want advice. I'm thinking about what that lady, your kind-of-friend, said to me—you know, about real estate. I'm thinking about going to one of her seminars."

"Brandon, you'll be great at anything you choose to do," I said. "You are a hard worker and a good person. Just like me. Wait. No. Things are going to turn out great for you. Not like me. But what you don't want to do is go to any kind of seminar run by Dee Dee. It could only end in the *Santa Monica Mirror*. Trust me on this. Just . . . stay in school. I'll keep you fed. Just . . . do that for me." I gave him a kiss on the cheek, and geared myself up to get ready.

Humiliation required the proper wardrobe.

I assessed myself in the mirror of my neglected closet, dressed in my best hat-in-hand outfit, then headed out to Bank of the West. I would need a lot of luck.

Would luck even recognize me, at this point? Maybe if I wore a carnation in my lapel or a funny hat.

But first, coffee.

* * *

Lunch is easy. Coffee is hard. Allow me to paraphrase: There are eight million coffee shops in the big city. And by big city, I mean Montana Avenue. I passed three Starbucks in six blocks, then drove slowly past Caffe Luxxe. Was I brave enough to enter? Was I cool enough to order? A slim brunette sipping a latte, her baby in a sling on her chest, was chatting outside with a lean, bearded man in a porkpie hat. Let's call them Angie and Brad, because that's probably what they call themselves in the privacy of their eco-friendly pressed-bamboo NoMo dwelling. Even from my car, with the windows rolled up, their unctuousness seeped through the cracks. I just knew that baby was wearing cloth diapers. Luxxe was the kind of place where people got tired patting themselves on the back.

I drove a few blocks to Peet's, land of a thousand waxed cyclists and, I hear from Dee Dee (Montana Avenue's Perez Hilton), married swingers. All that was missing from Peet's was a disco ball. The line was nine deep in Lycra and biking caps. (There're many things I'm not good at: *When to stop eating See's Bordeaux chocolates, guessing women's ages at the Brentwood Country Mart, and standing in line.*)

It would take me twenty minutes to get to the counter but I had snagged a prime parking spot right in front on Montana, and everyone in L.A. knows: You don't give up a prime parking spot. *Ever.* I don't care if your hair's on fire or Robert Pattinson is beckoning you from an oceanfront room at Casa Del Mar. A good parking space is like finding a twelve-carat diamond in your dog's morning pile.

What I didn't know was that the Lance Armstrong monkfish in front of me was utterly devoid of decision-making powers. I stood behind his stretch-polyurethane-covered behind (which was not unpleasant to look at, had I been a woman of normal needs, and not a dried-up grieving relic). I still appreciated such wonders, but at a distance. Like the Santa Monica Mountains on a clear day or the blue Pacific. Or Taylor Lautner.

I waited.

"Um, let's see, an Americano to go, one sugar, no make it Splenda, is Splenda okay? Which is the one that makes your heart race?"

And I waited.

The biker was tall, over six feet in his cleats. He wore a cap over thick, dark-blond hair that poked out from the sides. I could see a few grays.

"No, you know what? I'm going to have a vanilla latte." (BEAT) "Hold on, too sweet? What about this almond bar?" He turned so I could glance at his profile. He was lightly tan, hadn't shaved that morning, handsome enough to momentarily distract me from my annoyance.

Still, I waited.

"I changed my mind. I changed my mind. I'm so sorry. Really. How's your tea? Will that wake me up? What do you think?"

The counter girl had a blank stare, as though her bodily functions had shut down one by one. I was waiting for someone to stick a feeding tube down her throat.

"But . . . you know, I don't really like tea . . . I never did. I don't think . . ."

"Lance Armstrong is going to have coffee," I interrupted. "Straight up, on me."

The barista woke from her coma and smiled. I felt like I'd saved a life.

"I'm not sure I want—," Lance started saying to me.

"I know. You're not sure what you want. But I know what I want. I want to order and get out of here."

"I'm sorry, I didn't mean to hold you up."

"I hope you're faster at biking than you are at ordering."

"Let me pay for this," he said. "Let me pay for your drink. What are you having?"

I hadn't thought of what I wanted. I wasn't ready. I looked at the board. Names jumped out at me—latte this, mocha that—I had no idea. What do you want, Hannah?

"I want to save my house," I said. "I want a bailout. But I'm not rich enough to get one."

Lance's eyes were surrounded by lines, and he had bags underneath them. He was probably a couple years younger than he looked. I wondered why he wasn't sleeping.

"My friend in need here is going to have a medium vanilla latte," Lance said.

"Two percent," I chirped. I didn't want him to think I was a complete pig. Why? I don't know. Lance was the first man who'd noticed me in months, I guess.

I grabbed my latte as soon as it hit the counter and sprinted (walked rather quickly) out of there. I didn't look to see if Lance was hanging around outside in the bright and perfect sun, deep in the tight groups of bikers sitting at tiny round tables. My self-loathing was enough to keep me company.

Minutes later, I found myself in front of a loan officer's desk at Bank of the West, the one bank on Montana that hadn't been shut down. I thought of the banks and lending institutions that no longer existed in this neighborhood; at least, I thought, I wouldn't be alone if I, too, vanished.

Sort of like John, I guess. One minute, my one love is rushing out the door to the Farmer's Market. The next, I'm getting the nightmare phone call.

"Are you currently employed, Mrs. . . . Miss . . . ?" the banker asked politely. His nametag said Joon Kim.

"Miss?" I wasn't married . . . or was I? If I had to choose, I was definitely amiss. Even remiss.

"I'm a total miss," I said. "A miss-hap, if you will." *I was joking. Truly.*

"Miss Bernal," Kim continued expeditiously. I had a feeling he'd been through a lot of these uncomfortable-as-an-underwire-bra conversations. As he painstakingly revealed valid reasons the bank could not possibly approve a second mortgage, I pictured him doing something fun, like . . . karaoke. *Mr. Kim, drunk on cold sake on Monday eighties night, belting out Culture Club's "Do You Really Want to Hurt Me?"*

I started humming.

"Though we value your patronage," he said, pushing a brochure across his neat, disturbingly empty desk. I glanced at the title: "Life on a Budget." "The Bank of the West unfortunately cannot restructure your home loan at this time. Do you have any questions?"

"No," I said, then, "Yes, I do. You seem nice. Can my daughter and I come and live with you?"

"I'm sorry, Miss Bernal, but you're in a better position than many. You can sell—"

"For what? For barely more than I paid. Maybe not even that."

"You can take that money, put it away, rent an apartment—I have a card," he said. "Someone who can help you. She's very good—"

He opened his drawer, took a business card from a stack, and slid it across the desk.

I took a look. "Dee Dee Pickler?"

"Yes? You know her?" he asked. Did I detect color rising in his cheeks? Is this how Dee Dee secured her loans?

"I'm familiar with the way she works," I said. Kim was full-on blushing. *Wow.* Mustang Dee Dee sure did get around.

"She's very good," he repeated. "She'll help you—"

"No, thanks," I said. "I'll figure something else out. I'll just . . . squat. I think I'd be good at that. Thanks for your help."

I stood, turned, and bumped straight into Lance Armstrong. He was still holding the coffee that I'd made him order.

"Oh . . . hi," I stammered. "I was just leaving . . ."

"Hey, Joon," Lance said. "I hope you helped out our customer here. Did you tell her about our newest homeowner policy?"

Kim looked puzzled. "No," he said. "I didn't know—"

"Why don't you step over here . . . I'm sorry, I didn't catch your name," Lance said.

"I never threw it at you," I said. "It's Hannah. Hannah Bernal."

"Hannah," he said, "you have a nice smile—that is, when you smile. Follow me."

I'm smiling? I asked myself, as I followed Lance. He was still in his biking gear. If he looked ridiculous at Peet's, he looked like ridiculous times a hundred in a bank, even in Santa Monica. I felt my face as I entered the office, a nameplate on the door—Tom DeCiccio. *Yes, I was smiling.*

* * *

I am excellent at apologizing—like most women, I've been doing it all my life. I'm pretty sure "I'm sorry" were my first words. Examples: "I'm sorry I made you cheat on me." "I'm sorry I bumped you while you were stealing my purse." "I'm sorry my breathing annoys you." So, I just dove right in: "I'm really sorry about my Lance Armstrong comment." I thought about using my widow card.

He waved. "No worries. I look ridiculous in my biking gear."

"You're in incredible shape," I blurted out. "Oh, God. I'm sorry for that comment, as well. And I'm sorry for anything else that embarrasses me or you, or the both of us."

Tom slipped off his cap and sat down behind his desk. "Now what can I do to help you?"

"What can you do to help?" I asked. "Are you ready?"

"I'm sure I can handle it," Tom said. "It's been a tough couple years for a lot of people."

"Okay," I said, then, "I lost my husband. I lost my job. I'm going to lose my home." I bit my lip to keep from crying. Please, please don't cry in front of cute Tom, I implored myself. Too late. At this point, I could cry at a *Jersey Shore* rerun. I was as sensitive as a blister, a human blister on the bottom of the foot of humanity.

"Oh, I'm sorry," Tom said. He did look genuinely sorry, not just "I'm sorry I opened my office to this batty woman with the half-combed hair" sorry.

He handed me a Kleenex box. I pulled out a tissue, then another. I couldn't keep my tears from running. Nothing worked. Not images of silly dog tricks or fat baby elbows or Dwight Howard's foot-wide grin.

"Did he . . . leave you?" Tom asked.

"Did who leave me?" I asked, through the sheet of salty, snot membrane covering my mouth. What's more attractive than a sniveling widow? Try *everything*.

"Your husband?" he asked. "Did he leave you?"

"No. I mean, yes. My husband died. One bright morning, he's

healthy, happy, not a care in the world—so carefree that he forgot to pay off his quarterly life insurance bill—the next minute, he's dead. And no one wants to talk about it. I mean, grief meetings—they don't even want me—how many husbands have to die before I qualify?"

"My wife died," Tom said. He flipped through his calendar while I composed myself. *Did I hear correctly?*

"Let's see, just passed the five-month anniversary not long ago, that would be the twenty-eighth . . ." He looked at me. "Yes, so, Patchett left us on August 28 . . ."

"Patchett?" I said, before I could stop myself.

"It was a family name. Her great-grandmother's last name."

"I'm so sorry," I whispered. Patchett? I found myself wondering what she looked like: A Patchett would be tall, blond, jumping horses before noon . . . everything I found hard to relate to in one name. *Why was I hating on a dead woman?*

"Cancer . . . her brain. There was nothing we could do. She was very brave."

She was brave. Of course. Everything I wasn't. I suppose she was a doctor, as well.

"She was a pediatrician."

Who went to Harvard.

"She graduated from Yale."

I had to chuckle, "I called Harvard."

"How'd you know?" Tom asked. "She went to Harvard under-grad."

I was going to walk out of the bank with no bank loan, no second mortgage, and no self-esteem. At least it hadn't taken longer than thirty minutes.

I focused on the silver-framed photographs on the chest behind him. Exquisite blond girls, hair bands, green eyes, one with braces.

"Your children?"

"Three. Three daughters," he said. "You?"

"One daughter. She's three . . ." My voice caught in my throat. "Oh my God. Her birthday is coming up." I was crying again.

"I'm sorry," Tom said. We sat there for a few moments. My sobs were like the drunk party guest who wouldn't shut up.

"I feel like I'm going crazy sometimes," I finally managed. "I just . . . you're really going to think I've lost it . . . I just got this tattoo . . ."

I pulled my sweater off my shoulder, exposing the frying pan that would live in infamy.

"Wow," he said. "A frying pan."

"Yeah, right?"

"That's pretty terrible." Tom nodded. "But I think I win." He pulled up the tight, short sleeve on his biking shirt, exposing a bleached shoulder. And a tattoo. A Gold Amex card. The name PATCHETT MILLER DECICCIO, complete with credit card number and that guy's head.

"Oh my God. Truly, truly . . . awful," I said. Was I flirting? *Put the flirt away. Put it away, now!*

"No one understands," he said. "Not even Hairy Eddie."

"Who's not even hairy," I said. "What's that about?" I was in the presence of the Widower. Dee Dee had gotten her recognizance wrong: He was supposed to hang out at Caffe Luxxe, not Peet's. And fuck it if he didn't look like George Clooney, you know, pre-Darfur. Before he was Dar-furrowed.

"Would you like to have coffee sometime?" Tom asked.

"I . . . I don't know. I mean, I should probably drink less coffee because you know, heart palpitations, but what's one latte—"

"It's just coffee, Hannah," Tom said, using my first name. "I just don't meet many people in the same . . . situation."

"It's not like I'm cheating—you can't cheat on a dead man." Even if you are still talking to him. "I can do coffee. I mean, why not, right? As long as I do the ordering . . ." I gathered up my purse, and my used Kleenex. "Oh . . . but what about my . . . housing situation?"

"Let me crunch the numbers. I think we can work something out," Tom said. "At least for the time being, until you get your feet on the ground. I don't want you to worry. By the way, that's a truly awful tattoo."

"Thanks. And yours makes mine look like the ceiling of the Sistine Chapel."

The Hannah Bernal who walked out of the bank was a different person than the one who'd walked in. For one thing, this new Hannah Bernal felt a tingle she hadn't felt in . . . since John.

"I wonder if the tingle police will get me," I said, as I walked past the window of a real estate office. Dee Dee Pickler's face was plastered on flyers featuring "awesome condo's (sic)" in Santa Monica. I saw my reflection in the glass. I barely recognized this girl—smiling eyes, hair blowing in the breeze. My shoulders weren't pressed against my earlobes. Could bad luck have skipped off to warmer climes? Taken a break poolside in South Beach? I crossed my fingers and headed to my car.

Tom called two days later, and we set a coffee date. It seemed to take hours to decide which coffee shop; the wrong place could set off a whole ugly chain of events.

"What will you be wearing?" I joked. "So that I'll recognize you."

"Um, a gray suit, light blue shirt, maybe not the light blue shirt— maybe white—"

"Tom?"

"Yes?"

"I'm kidding."

"Sorry. Right." We decided on the Pirates, my hometown favorite; I'd yet to see a set of hemp-wearing triplets in line.

"The Jurassic?" Salvador, one of the baristas, asked, as we got to the front of the line. He was built like a Mayan runner, short and compact, with a black braid to his waist.

"No." I couldn't order my usual bran muffin with Tom next to me. I had dubbed it "The Jurassic" because it looked like something dinosaurs left behind after breakfast.

"Just a vanilla latte." Salvador smiled. I had a flashback of Salvador's face when I told him John had died. Why had I come here with Tom? I went to pay for my latte.

"Not going to happen," Tom said. "Let me get that."

"I barely know him," I said to Salvador, my upper lip sweating like a bribe-taking senator on *60 Minutes*. "He's my banker. We just both like coffee, as it turns out."

Salvador watched as Tom helped me to an outside table and pulled my chair out, angling it so the sun wouldn't be in my face. We sat and talked about our lives, pre- and postapocalypse. We laughed. We paused. Salvador came out several times to check on us.

"Is he giving me a dirty look?" Tom asked. "I think he just tried to kick me."

"He loved my husband."

"Ah, I understand," Tom said, checking his watch. "Oh, hey, look at the time. Do you realize we've been here almost two hours?"

"Oh, I'm sorry," I said, apologizing, for what, I didn't know.

"No, no," Tom said. "I just . . . I usually don't talk this much."

"Misery loves coffee," I said. He laughed. I liked the wrinkles around his eyes, the hair that was too gray for his age. The polished outside and damaged interior. An interior that I was particularly qualified to understand.

"Will you do this again?" he asked.

"Of course," I said. "It was fun . . . I mean, not fun, like the eighties—you know what I mean."

As he left, a black Range Rover turned the corner and raced past, just missing a pedestrian in the crosswalk. Reminding me that I needed to call Detective Ramirez. Reminding me that I was still in a relationship, albeit a complicated one. My cellphone rang.

"Are you dating the Widower?" Dee Dee Pickler asked.

"No," I said. I turned to see if she was following me.

"Two-hour coffee date?" Dee Dee said. "I call that an engagement party."

"Bye, Dee Dee."

"The Turk is all fired up and ready to go," she was saying, as I hung up.

* * *

Aimee was undergoing radiation treatment, and had moved in. She didn't ask, of course. I insisted, of course. I wasn't sure how I was going to make it work, as Aimee couldn't be in the same vicinity as Brandon.

"Are you ashamed you have cancer?" I asked. "Is that why you don't speak to him?"

"No," she said, "I'm just a snob." I didn't buy it. I was feeding Ellie toast points dipped in over-easy egg yolks when Brandon walked in and handed Aimee *The New York Times*. (Yes, she is the one person still reading newspapers.)

"Hey, all," he said, as he poured orange juice. Brandon had the sleepy look that a five-year-old gets when he first wakes up. I guess it's the look we all have, but Brandon's is missing wrinkles and folds.

"Hey, B," I said.

He smiled and shuffled out. I looked at Aimee. She hadn't even raised her head. I was getting a little fed up; like my widow card, her cancer card was almost expired.

"Why didn't you thank him for bringing you the paper?"

"Didn't I?" she said.

"C'mon," I said, as Ellie slurped on her sippy cup. (I know; she should be drinking from a regular cup by now—I know I know— sippy cup = bad bite = lisp = braces = low self-esteem = blow jobs at twelve = pregnant at sixteen = trailer park in Riverside. Every decision I make for this child has her ending up in a trailer park where the trailers are held together with duct tape and child molesters are at the top of the food chain. It's a wonder any single mother bothers to wake up in the morning—you can't win.)

"You treat him like he's invisible. He's over six feet of visibility."

Aimee shrugged. "I don't know why you all think he's so cute."

My front door opened. I heard Chloe, followed by her . . .

"Don't bring those things in here," Aimee said, "I have cancer!"

"What's cancer?" Ellie asked. I wiped the yolk from her chin.

"Something Auntie Aimee is getting a lot of mileage out of," I said sweetly.

"Dogs give you cancer?" Chloe asked. "I've been taking mine to St. John's for years—they're therapy dogs."

"Therapy dogs," Aimee said, as they started barking wildly. "For them or you?"

I was helping Ellie down from her seat when I turned to see an elegant gentleman with slicked-back snowy hair, wearing a dark, old-fashioned three-piece suit, seated next to Aimee. His long body was squeezed into the chair and he was holding a pocket watch. I recognized him from my steamed vagina interlude. I almost dropped Ellie.

"Mommy!" she said, looking up at me.

"Are you cold, Ellie?" I asked, shivering. Chloe rushed her barking dogs outside and tried to collar Spice, but he wouldn't leave. He was circling the man, his head low . . .

"Why's Spice acting so strange?" Aimee said. "I wonder if we're going to have an earthquake."

"Why are you here?" I said to the man. "You scared me—I almost dropped my kid."

"Hannah, are you all right?" Chloe asked.

"Quick, hand her a therapy dog," Aimee said.

"Chloe, take Ellie outside," I said. "Now."

"C'mon, El," Chloe said. "Come on, let's go play with the puppies—"

Aimee shifted to stand. "Stay there," I told her. "He's sitting right next to you. I remember him from the spa."

"Who?" she asked. "Hannah, please stop this—"

"He's . . . related to you." The fine facial features. The long limbs. He was calmly waiting. Waiting for what?

"What would you like me to say to your granddaughter?" I asked.

Aimee jumped up. Orange juice hit the floor.

"Stay!" I ordered. Her grandfather started fiddling with his pocket watch.

"Okay, come on," I said, "I have to get Ellie to school." I was losing my patience with the dead. The living have to get on with it, you know? The dead, what, do they have business meetings? Nail appointments? Looming bankruptcy? No.

"What-what's he doing?" Aimee asked. I could feel her body shaking from across the table. "Why's he here? Is he here? Hannah, please, I can't take this."

I held my hand up to quiet her as he opened the watch to show me a picture of a young girl, maybe Ellie's age. She had black bangs, a round face, green eyes with dark lashes. Little Aimee was delighted with the person taking the picture.

"He's showing me a picture, Aimee. Inside a pocket watch . . ."

"A pocket watch . . ."

"A green-eyed little girl with black bangs and the biggest smile I've ever seen."

Aimee gasped. "I'm wearing a white dress with a sailor collar," she said, starting to cry. "Poppy."

"You look so happy, Aimee." *I'd never seen her look so happy. Or even, rather happy. Maybe not even mildly satisfied.*

"My grandfather took that picture," Aimee said. "A year later, he was dead of a stroke. My family fought over his money. Nothing was ever the same. Ever."

"What's his name?" I asked Aimee.

"George," she said. "George Cannon. I knew him as Poppy. Tell him I miss him. I can't see him, but I can feel him. I swear I can."

"Mr. Cannon," I said, watching him. He'd heard her.

"I'm sorry," he said, mouthing the words. "I'm sorry."

"Aimee, your grandfather . . . he's sorry."

There was more. It was difficult for him to get the words out, difficult for me to understand. Aimee reached her hand out to where her grandfather was sitting. He reached back, their fingers interlocking. He was fading quickly. "He wished he could have protected you . . . ," I told her. "Aimee? He wants you to know that. I'm not sure I understand—"

"My stepfather, Hannah," Aimee whispered. "He said he'd hurt my mother . . ."

My hand went to my mouth, as I watched his face. I reached out and touched her. "You were born happy, Aimee." I repeated his words. "Aimee, you were his little girl, his ray of sunshine. He's worried that you will never know, never believe . . . never be happy again."

He was gone. Spice started barking, as though beckoning him back. Aimee rolled onto the floor and curled up, her shoulders shaking as she sobbed. I sank to the ground and held her.

"I didn't know, honey," I said. "I'm so sorry."

I stared up toward the ceiling, as I rocked Aimee back and forth. *Was I helping people with this "gift"? Or hurting them?*

Over the next few weeks, Tom and I set more coffee dates, entirely by text. I felt very modern, and slightly confused.

"Does this say 'I don't care if you ever ask me out on a proper date but I want to look hot anyway'?" I asked Jay and Aimee, as I modeled my wares in my kitchen, black tights and a snug white v-neck T-shirt, showing the bit of skin that hadn't been hit by the blotchy, crepey, saggy trifecta.

"Foresooth, describeth yonder knave." Jay was feeding Ralph, whose coat had been tie-dyed to resemble a mating seahorse. Jay usually slips into Olde English after attending the Renaissance Faire, but that was months away. Some costume designer's birthday party at the Shangri-La Hotel rooftop on Ocean over the weekend had affected the knave's braineth. He was doing everything humanly possible, including speaking dialect that sounded idiotic, to forget Hidalgo.

"Really nice. Single dad. Three daughters, one more beautiful than the next. Banker, frat boy, recovered Republican. He says words like 'gosh.' And, he's sporty." I grabbed an apple from the fruit bowl on my chopping block. "In other words, if our spouses hadn't died, we wouldn't have looked twice at each other."

"Sounds romantic," Aimee said as she ate breakfast, appearing quasi-Parisian in a silk robe, her hair in a loose bun.

"Prithee, m'lady, whither thine coffee-mate moveth from our regal Starbucketh to handjobeth in backseat of chariot?" Jay asked.

"We're coffee-mates," I said, as Aimee daintily ate a piece of toast. Her skin looked translucent. "Radiation is so working for you."

"Hi, kids," Chloe said, as she joined us, wearing white cotton yoga pants and top. "Do you really think you should be drinking so much coffee? It's bad for your prostate."

"Please tell me you put that on your blog," Aimee said, without looking up. "How's Sergeant Billy?"

Should I break it to her? "I think my prostate's just fine, Chloe."

"Sergeant Billy is fine. He's off the Israeli Army kick for now," Chloe said. "Hannah, make sure the coffee's organic. And fair-trade."

"That stuff tastes like melted wax," Aimee said.

"Everything tastes like melted wax to you, Aimee," I said. "It's the aftereffects of the radiation and Russian vodka."

"Not true," Brandon said, as he walked in. "Aimee loved my banana oatmeal muffins this morning. She needs the potassium. My mom underwent radiation treatment a few years ago, so I'm up on this stuff. Plus, she hasn't had a drink in two weeks."

Aimee turned a deep purple-red found only in sea urchins.

"Maybe I'll just have green tea," I said.

"Good choice!" Chloe clapped her hands together. Things like this excited her.

"Have whatever you want," Aimee said. "It'll end badly, but you might as well have fun, no matter how brief." Apparently, the visit from Poppy hadn't improved her outlook on life.

"Whatsoevereth is your problem, fair maiden?" Jay asked.

"My problem?" Aimee asked, her hair falling around her face. "Besides cancer?"

"Boringeth!" Jay said, waving his hand.

Aimee took another bite of toast. "Well, maybe I'm just an old has-been," she finally said. "Actually old, never-was, has-been."

We all stared at her. No one moved a muscle.

"Quit begging," Brandon said. Instead of cracking Brandon upside the head, Aimee started laughing. The rest of us felt safe enough to follow suit.

"Funny *and* hot," a delighted Jay commented. "Who knew our little Branny had it in him?"

* * *

Days later, Aimee and Brandon were in my cramped living room putting up a Christmas tree that had gone missing from Rockefeller Center.

"Stop. No. To the left." Aimee waved her hands from where she was laid out on the couch as poor Brandon maneuvered the tree around. "No . . . no . . . not right. Put it back where it was, I think—"

"The White House called," I said, leaning against the wall. "They want their tree back."

"That's perfect," Aimee said, ignoring me. "That's good. Wait. To the right, now. Branford, come on."

"Branford?"

"I just call him that," Aimee said.

"Can you tell she's feeling better?" I said to Brandon.

Brandon groaned and moved the tree. "I think I liked it better when she wasn't talking to me."

Ellie had awakened me at six in the morning with the exciting news (according to her advent calendar) that "Turtle Dove Day" was upon us. Meanwhile, Aimee had overdosed on the Christmas decorations. She'd bought nativity crèches, wreaths, tablecloths, indoor/outdoor lights, ornaments, and centerpieces at Michael's, the crafts store, and nailed seven Christmas stockings to the mantel.

"I don't know if I even like Noble Fir," she was saying to Brandon, as my phone started vibrating. "I might prefer the Scotch Pine." Brandon collapsed on the floor.

I stepped over him, and took the call. It was Tom.

"Want to see the crèches on Ocean Avenue?" he asked. "I take my girls every year. Christmas was Patchett's favorite holiday."

"Sure," I said. I was not surprised that Patchett loved Christmas. So did John, especially after Ellie was born. Every overly decorated, pine-scented year with him, I was reminded of what Carrie Fisher once said: "No one loves Christmas like the Jews."

* * *

"Mixing families already? Too soon," Chloe clucked, as she watched me getting ready to witness Jesus's Birth. "My readers would have a definite problem with this."

"She would?" Aimee asked sweetly.

"Are jeans Baby Jesus–appropriate wear?" I asked, as I slipped on my trusty bootcuts, a jacket, and tennies. "Look, I don't know if it means he's serious or not serious at all. Probably the latter. He hasn't even kissed my cheek yet."

"Just go," Aimee said. "Enjoy yourself."

"It's a bad idea," Chloe said, "to expose your children to the idea of you two living happily ever after."

"Like your marriage?" Aimee pointed out. "Or do we call that Happily Never After?"

I parked on Georgina, and Ellie and I walked toward the Palisades, where the birth of Jesus was set up in wooden booths using neat and tidy, easy-to-remember steps.

Tom was already there with his three tow-headed girls. The first was tall, with braces and pin-straight hair. She was the strong, serious one. The middle girl had curls, her father's dimples. And the mischief in her mother's eyes. The baby was seven, all jutting elbows and knees, her hair in a ponytail, her mouth pulled tight, holding on to her father's hand. This one was fragile. Ellie, whom Jay had dressed in a newsboy cap and riding boots, ran up and showed off her Spanish to the girls, counting backward from *diez*.

Together, we navigated the stretch of the nativity scene, crowded with people taking pictures, and cars cruising slowly past along Ocean Avenue, where passengers could view Jesus and Friends from the comfort of their hybrid SUVs.

Twilight drifted toward the cliffs above the Pacific. Palm trees swayed in shadow against the sky as the wind picked up. Tom and I watched the girls play tag in ragged silhouettes. I felt content, yet sad. My emotions were schizophrenic. The girls wheeled and danced while I smiled, held back tears, and shivered. Because of the cold. And because I knew we were being watched. I was learning.

Nothing gets past the dead.

John the Departed noticed that I was starting to wear makeup.

"You're wearing lip gloss," he had said one night, the week before. "And you colored your hair."

I touched my hair, then wiped the back of my hand against my mouth. "I just wanted to feel . . . normal."

"It's that kid, the manny, isn't it?" John said.

"Brandon? Oh, honey, I heat soup for him, I don't sleep with him. He's like the Teutonic deity I never had."

"I watch them play," John said. "I watch him swing Ellie . . . I listen to her laugh and talk . . . and it kills me. I mean, if I weren't already dead enough. I die all over again."

"I understand, John. I do."

"Hannah . . . her memories of me will be replaced by him."

"Never, honey. That'll never happen."

"It's true." John sighed. "Ellie doesn't even want me to read to her anymore. Sometimes he reads to her. And he's good at it. He cares. I feel it. Like his Knuffle Bunny—he acts out all the parts. It's disgusting."

"Honey, I know," I said. "It's unfair beyond all comprehension."

I didn't tell him about Tom yet. I couldn't.

"I miss you so much sometimes that I stop breathing," I said, instead. And it was true, too. "It's as though my body shuts down for a moment so I can die, too. And I wanted to die so badly when you left. But I can't die. I don't have that choice. Ellie took that away from me the moment she was born. Sucks to be me, having to be alive and all."

I'd noticed that just lately, John was becoming more visible. I could see his outline and occasional glimpses of his hands, his shoulders, his hair . . . just enough to torture me with the memory of his body. It'd been months since we'd made love that last time, the last morning, his last morning.

"John . . . do spirits have . . . you know . . . do they do it?"

"What do you mean?" *Dead husbands, just as obtuse as live ones?*
Yes.

"Do they . . . you know . . . have sex?"

"Well . . . I haven't."

"What do you mean, you haven't?"

"I mean, I haven't. I'm pretty sure some of the others have."

"But you don't have bodies—"

"It's more of a mental thing."

"Okay . . . so have you mentally fucked anyone lately?"

"Were you always this crazy?"

"No. I'm definitely crazier now. I talk to dead people."

"I loved you in life and I love you in the afterlife. What more do
you want from me?"

I watched his outline, swaying in and out of focus with the breeze.

"I don't know, honey," I said. "I'm going to bed . . . I'm kind of
tired."

"Have you been looking for it, Hannah?"

"Looking for what?" *What did he mean? Sex?*

"The Range Rover."

"I'll call Ramirez," I said, "first thing tomorrow morning." I threw
a kiss to the breeze, but John was already gone. I turned toward the
kitchen, my guilty soul knowing I couldn't wait a lifetime for a bout
of lovemaking, mental or otherwise.

Dead people pop up out of nowhere. Talk about distracting. Cold
bursts of air, chimes that only I hear, lost keys, windows slamming,
birds suddenly taking off in flight. Try keeping a line of thought
when there's always someone trying to get your attention. I felt like
a mother of twelve, except I couldn't even lock myself in the bathroom to get away. I tried iPods and headsets that are used on air-
craft carriers. I tried mantras. I tried running to get away from
them. Running! It turns out there are ghosts who used to run
marathons—a skinny guy in his late forties, had a heart attack at the

last L.A. marathon right before the finish line at the beach—talk about bitter, that one.

I had opened a portal to the other side, but was not fully equipped to handle the logistics. It's not like I can hire an assistant, even if I had the money. I can't handle my own living logistics, much less the needs of the dearly departed. It's all I can do to get my kid to school on time.

"Play it again, Mommy," Ellie—dressed for her nursery school's Christmas Pageant wearing a thin hairband and a red velvet dress with a wide sash—requested from her car seat. John's R. Kelly CD. How many times can I hear "I'm a Flirt" before someone gets hurt? Apparently, millions.

"You don't want to rehearse 'Away in a Manger'?"

Ellie shook her head. "I know that, cold."

"Fine," I said to Ellie before turning the woman sitting next to me. "Can you get that?"

Hold up, I thought. Who's this lady in the passenger seat? She looked in her fifties, wearing a green smock and wide-brimmed hat, with faded red hair. She was holding gardening shears. I slammed on the brakes just in time to avoid a Latino woman pushing a baby stroller across Wilshire.

"Mommy?" Ellie said. "Play it again!"

"Hold on, Ellie," I said. "Let me just . . . pull over."

The woman smiled and peered back at Ellie. Ellie smiled at her and waved. Ellie could see her. I pulled the car over to the curb.

"Ellie, do you know this lady?"

Ellie shook her head.

"Hi," I said to the woman, who smiled pleasantly at me. "Do you mind . . ."

I reached over and touched the gardening shears. My hand went through them. You have no idea the relief.

"Just checking," I said.

The woman had a distinguished bone structure, silvery blue eyes, and freckles dotting her face and her hands. She wore bright red lipstick on a pert mouth. She reminded me of someone.

"Do you need to tell me something? I have to get Ellie to school, running late as usual."

"Stephanie," she whispered, with a soft Southern accent. "Tell her it will only get worse. She needs to get out. Now." And just like that, she vaporized. I was starting to get used to the now-you-see-it-now-you-don't sensation. I wish I could learn it myself, without, you know, having to make the ultimate sacrifice.

"Did you hear that?" I asked Ellie, looking into the rearview mirror.

"The lady?" she said. "She's worried about Miss Stephanie."

I pulled into traffic and thought about our girl Stephanie. She'd been quieter than usual, but I was so wrapped up in my own myriad problems that I hadn't thought to inquire. But who was I to question the dead?

The school was abuzz with excitement over the Christmas Pageant. I dropped Ellie off in her classroom and headed for Stephanie's office. Anna, the office manager, told me she was already in the auditorium. I found her getting the costumes ready for Baby Jesus, Mary, and Joseph.

"Steph, you have a minute?"

"Ooh, can it wait?" she said, turning to me. "Is it Ellie? Everything okay?"

"No, Ellie's good," I said, reading the new lines in her face. She'd gotten thinner. Or was I looking for something?

"Can we talk later?" Stephanie said. "The first show comes on in an hour."

I took her hand. Her mother's message was urgent.

"No, I'm sorry, this is going to sound weird," I said. "Stephanie, I need to know if you're okay." I decided to be blunt.

She flinched, so slightly that no one except for the person who'd been visited by her dead mother would notice.

"I had a visit from your mother this morning."

"My mother?" Stephanie motioned for Mary and Joseph to wait for her.

"She was in my car. Wearing a smock. She'd been gardening—"

"My mother gardens . . . ," Stephanie said. "Hannah, are you okay?"

"She had a message for you—" I wanted to repeat it word for word. I didn't want to get anything wrong. "She was wearing a wide-brimmed sun hat—she had shears with bright green handles. When did she pass . . . ?"

"My mother is alive, Hannah, alive and well—I mean, she had a scare a few years back . . . her heart," Stephanie said. "But she's perfectly fine now. You're freaking me out. I can't deal with this right now—"

Who the hell was that, with the red hair and freckles and gardening shears?

"I'm so sorry," I said. "I don't know—I should go—"

Anna came running backstage, holding a cordless phone in her hand. Her face was pale. "Stephanie, it's for you," she said, holding the phone out. "It's *your father*."

Stephanie and I looked at each other.

"Answer it," I said. "Please." I was trying to ignore that the temperature in backstage had dropped; I was the only one who'd noticed.

"Daddy?" she said, into the phone. She closed her eyes. "No . . . not Mommy . . . no . . ." Her skin turned alabaster. "When did this happen?" Her eyes were on me, now, tears spilling onto her cheeks. All movement backstage had ceased. "Are you sure? No, no. Let me just . . . get myself together here. Can I call you back, Daddy? I'm sorry—I love you, Daddy."

She handed Anna, who was also crying, the phone.

"She was in her garden," Stephanie said, shocked. "She collapsed in her garden . . ."

"I'm sorry," I said, reaching out to her. "I'm so sorry."

Stephanie looked at me. "What did she say to you, Hannah?"

"Maybe it's nothing." I knew it wasn't nothing.

"What did she say?" she asked again as Anna started herding the children and actors away from where we were standing.

"She said to get out. Now. It's only going to get worse."

Stephanie just sat there, twisting her engagement ring.

"Is he hurting you?" I asked.

She didn't answer.

"Do you need help?" I asked. "Let me help you. I can get Brandon—"

"I'll call my girlfriends," Stephanie said, sounding exhausted. "I'm moving out today." She exhaled like she hadn't breathed in months. I grabbed her hand and held on.

"I'm going to stay until I see you make those phone calls," I said. "Your mother's depending on me."

We went to the office, and I sat with her while she made her escape plans. It wasn't until I checked my phone later that I realized I'd missed a coffee date with Tom. He'd left several messages; I could tell he was not used to being stood up.

I called him as I headed back to my car. He answered his phone with an officious "Tom DeCiccio," though I knew he could see my number on the telephone pad. "Tom!" I said, "I'm sorry—I got caught up in something."

"It's okay," he said. His tone made it obvious that it wasn't okay.

"How was your skinny vanilla?" I asked. "I have to know. The world has to know."

"Fine."

"Are you mad at me?"

"No," Tom said, then, "Maybe we should go to a movie or something."

I froze. "You mean, like a non-caffeinated date?"

"Yeah. Like dinner and a movie," Tom said. "If you don't want to, that's fine. I understand."

"No, it's not—"

"But I'd like to take you out."

"Out, sure, okay," I said. How would I explain this one to John?

"Friday night. I'll pick you up at seven."

"Sure. Really?" I was saying when he hung up.

That night, I put Ellie to bed, poured myself a glass of pinot, and headed outside, under the cover of my dear avocado tree. Even though I could speak to Jay (once he kicked the Olde English habit), or Aimee, or Chloe—or even Brandon—there was one person who could truly relate to my pain. My anguish. My suffering. My thoughts of getting laid.

It didn't take long for Trish to appear. Except for the dark hair, she reminded me of photographs I'd seen of Georgia O'Keeffe. Long braid wrapped around her shoulder, those deep-set eyes, sharp cheekbones. Wearing loose white pants with a drawstring and a caftan top. Basically, she was a dead woman who was much cooler than I.

"Damn, damn, damn. I wish I could have a sip . . . or three," Trish said. "What is that? Italian?"

"Yes . . . pinot grigio. It's light—so if you finish the bottle, you don't feel so bad."

"I still prefer bourbon," Trish said. "Would it kill you to buy a bottle of Chivas and set it on the table out here? No, don't—it would kill me!"

She laughed. Dead people make a lot of dead people jokes. It's funny the first hundred times.

"So what's happening in our little suburban enclave?" Trish asked, floating sideways with the breeze.

"I'm starting to have feelings for . . ." I started to speak, then hesitated. "Can John hear this?"

"Oh, I forget," Trish said. "The rules haven't been explained to you. We can only visit one at a time. It avoids complications. And fights. As you can imagine."

I couldn't imagine. Ghostly brawls?

"I'm feeling guilty," I finally said. "I think I like someone. A man someone. Well, maybe that's not even true—he's nice and attractive. I just agreed to go on a date with him."

"Oh," Trish said. I couldn't tell if she was grimacing, because the breeze had picked up again and knocked her torso back.

"What do I do? I can't imagine kissing someone else—but I look at his mouth, and I kind of wish I could touch it. I know it's wrong—I'm so afraid the minute I kiss someone else, John will fade. That our time together will . . . wilt. Right now, I can still feel him—I still feel our moments, our lovemaking, our Christmases, our baby's birth, our mornings alone, together. But if someone else enters the picture, if I let them—those new moments will take over . . ."

I was starting to cry. Again. If crying were an Olympic sport— and don't think I won't petition for it—I would be taking home the gold. Unless, say, Brett Favre showed up.

"I had sex a few weeks after I was widowed," Trish said.

"What?!"

"I mean, that's what we're talking about, here, with the holidays and births and mornings. We're talking about you having sex."

My tears dried up immediately.

"You had sex right after you were widowed?" I asked. I mean, Trish was what, in her seventies, then.

"Oh, yes. You know Mr. Reindorp, down the street?" Trish said.

"That old guy?" I asked. On a good day, Mr. Reindorp looked like he voted for Lincoln.

"Ah, Jerome. He was something." Trish sighed. "He couldn't stand up without a floor jack, but he was the high school quarter-back when he was lying down."

"Wow, I'm so not there yet," I said.

"Sex is normal. And grief sex is even more normal. Honey, there were widows and widowers banging each other all over this neigh-borhood. We blew the roof off the place."

"You know, Trish? This 'talking to dead people' gift thing should be returnable."

"I miss those days," Trish said wistfully. "Do you ever see Mr. Reindorp? Who's he doing? Not that old witch across the street—"

"Mrs. Graff?" I said. "She uses a walker!"

"Don't be swayed. She's a dirty bird, that one."

"Thanks for your help," I said.

"There's no right time," Trish told me. "You're allowed to enjoy another man. You might find it . . . a relief." She was fading. I was beginning to feel that ghosts were like people—any conversation with me that lasted more than five minutes bored them.

"Hannah . . . John died," Trish said. "You didn't."

17

Sex, Warts and All

Wednesday morning, and the Grief Team was huddled sullenly around my kitchen table. There was an air of ennui that reminded me of a Jean-Paul Belmondo movie, but with kale juice. Jay's iPod was playing sorrowful German techno-disco; I was sure crows would soon be falling out of the sky. Chloe was feeding string cheese to her dogs out of my refrigerator. Aimee was reading the paper and complaining about the political climate in Jakarta. Meanwhile, I felt giddy, like I was living the final act of a romantic comedy, but hadn't told anyone about my—

"Hannah. You have a date," Jay said, his eyes narrowed to slits.

"She's turning bright red," Chloe said, looking at me, "like a farmer's market tomato."

"It's so SaMo to draw delineations between farmer's market tomatoes and evil grocery store chain tomatoes," Aimee said.

"How could you hold out on us?" Jay said. "We're your best friends."

"Who are, you know, still breathing," Aimee added.

"Okay," I said. "So . . . yes, I have a date. This Friday night. With Tom." Jay hugged me. You would have thought I'd just announced I was giving birth to Gerard Butler's baby.

"It's nothing, just dinner and a movie, a French film."

"The one with the two hot, young, smooth-skinned French-

Algerian actors who get naked twenty-three minutes and twelve seconds in, or the one with the tits?" Jay asked.

"It's too soon for anything French," Chloe said. "Why not the Reese Witherspoon movie? I love everything she does. Did you know she picks up her kids from school every single day?"

"Hannah," Jay said, "your chances of getting some just multiplied."

"I'm not sleeping with him," I said.

"Of course not," Chloe said.

"Of course, yes," Jay said.

"De rigueur," Aimee said. *"D'accord."*

"Exactly," said Jay. "You know what this means, kids? It means . . . we have a project."

"A raison d'être!" Aimee said.

"Something to do," Chloe asked, "besides sit with our feelings?"

"I appreciate your concern, I do," I said, "but I can handle this on my own. I've been on a date before."

"When was your last first date?" Jay asked.

"Ah . . . over four years ago."

"Before Twitter, before Facebook, before sexting . . . ," Jay said.

"Before papers," Aimee said.

"Papers?"

"Call your gyno right now," Jay said. "You need to get in before Friday. Girl, you need your papers!"

I hung up the phone. My gynecologist had a cancellation that morning—I'd be able to see her before my date with Tom. Not that we were going to go all the way (oh, dear God—my thighs were not ready for prime time) but the big show could happen someday, and apparently I needed to have my papers ready.

"My people always have their papers on them," Jay said, fiddling with his iPod.

"They actually bring signed notes from their doctors?" Chloe said. "I'm so glad I'm not single."

"But you are single," we all said at once.

"No, I'm not," Chloe said. "We're separated but living together."

"What do you call that," Aimee asked, "besides a recipe for murder-suicide?"

Chloe turned to Aimee. "I bet you don't have papers. Because then you'd have to tell the truth."

"I don't have any diseases," Aimee said. "I've never even been pregnant. I can't."

"Pregnancy is not a disease," Chloe said. "It's a gift."

"Snore," Jay said.

"If it's a gift, I'd return it," Aimee said. "There's no way I would raise a child in this world."

Chloe clucked her tongue. "All that sex, and no baby."

"No, but she almost killed a man once," Jay pointed out. "That counts for something."

Brandon looked up from buttering his toast. "What happened?"

"Darling, Aimee gave a man a brain aneurysm during sex," Jay said. "He came within seconds of dying. And came within seconds of dying."

"He said he was fine," Aimee said. "It was a headache. Sometimes that happens after sex. Look it up. It's called 'coital cephalgia.'"

"She's a loaded weapon, Brandon," I told him.

"Aimee should come with a warning, 'Do not ride if you have a heart condition,'" Jay said. Aimee threw an orange at Jay, who caught it and smiled. Brandon walked out, his toast left on the plate, half buttered.

"I feel like I'm debuting at the Met," I said.

"Don't think of it like the Met," Jay said. "Think of it like dinner theater at Fort Lauderdale."

"Thanks," I said.

"Now," said Jay, "we have two days to get our girl in dating shape. On the third day, we pray. I'm sick of dying Ralph's hair over and over and sewing him little outfits—I need this. Girls—wardrobe, plucking, waxing . . . then we start on Hannah!"

* * *

I sat in Dr. Batra's waiting room, wondering how my hip, young Indian-American gynecologist could afford French *Vogue* and Italian *Elle*. I was old enough to remember when gynecologist's offices only had *Parenting* magazine and the *Free Press*. Now there were the stand-up advertisements for Botox and Juvéderm and vaginal rejuvenation. Remember when vaginas were nobody's business?

I was moved to a pastel green room with a pastel green reclining table, where I heard water gurgling through the walls.

"What's that?" I asked the cherub-faced medical assistant, pointing to where the water sounds were coming from. "Broken pipe?"

She frowned. "It's our sanskrit meditation series."

"Oh," I said. "I'm used to other sounds for my medical and dental needs—when I think dentist, I think Celine Dion and Bryan Adams. My gyno mix tape would be more like Tina Turner and early Madonna."

She just stared at me.

"I forgot—mix tapes—they're from the late eighties. You were probably just a kid."

"I was born in '91."

Now it was time for me to stare. *People born in the nineties should not even be talking yet. Or driving. Or feeding themselves. Enough!*

"Please take off all your clothes and put on this robe." She patted a pink, fluffy robe folded up on the examination table, and walked out.

Dr. Batra was my new doctor—she'd taken over Dr. Kelso's practice. Dr. Kelso was old school. Dr. Kelso's robes were made of paper. And music? Forget it. I undressed, first stop on the journey toward Grief Sex. I waited in my fluffy pink robe and read the latest *Harper's Bazaar* with SJP on the cover. I was not at all comforted by her muscular arms, happy marriage, and twin babies.

Dr. Batra, all five feet of golden-skinned mellifluence, slipped into the room. She lowered her head, her shiny black hair combed back into a bun, gave me a warm smile, and took a seat on the short swivel chair that added an element of fun to a gynecological exam.

"So, Hannah," she said, her voice like honey on bread, "how have you been? How long has it been since I've seen you?"

"A year," I said. I'd only seen her once, one year ago. When everything was normal. I had a child, a husband, and a career. Now I was batting one out of three. I sighed.

"That bad, huh?" Dr. Batra asked. "Do you have any questions? Concerns?"

"I have many, many concerns. Only a hundred of which have to do with my nether regions."

She smiled. Warmly. Again. It was hard to hate her, despite her youth, unblemished skin, and Harvard medical degree.

"Are you and your husband sexually active?" she asked. Her eyes flickered toward my ring finger, ever so briefly.

"Not exactly," I said. "That'd be a neat trick. Not that I haven't thought of it."

I looked at her puzzled expression.

"He died. My husband died. This past September. I . . . I can't take the ring off."

Her big dark eyes turned sad, her warm smile vanished. "I'm so sorry," she said, involuntarily rubbing her rounded belly.

"You're pregnant," I said. "Congratulations."

"Thank you," Dr. Batra said softly.

Uncomfortable silence made a guest appearance. Neither of us knew what to say.

"Shall we start?" Dr. Batra said. I put my feet in the stirrups, and Dr. Batra inserted a speculum inside me—a warm speculum. I flinched.

"Is it cold?" she asked.

"No, it's warm—when did that start happening?"

"Oh, we warm them up here. It's much more pleasant."

I lay there with the warm speculum inside me—not as sexy as it sounds.

"Forgive me for asking, I have to ask, are you ready to become sexually active again?" Dr. Batra said.

I snorted. Not smart when your legs are wide open, in stirrups, with a microwaved speculum inside you.

"Well, yes, when I walked in here, I was becoming open to the idea of having sex," I said. "I probably won't, though. I mean, I might someday. And if that happens, I should be prepared. You know, have my arsenal ready. My papers. I hear you have to have papers now, to have sex?"

"Some people are cautious that way," Dr. Batra said.

"Where would you carry that? In your wallet?"

"There's probably a special pocket in your purse," Dr. Batra said. "I hear Prada's started putting them in." Of course, she'd know about Prada.

I looked at her closely. "Do you love your husband?"

"Oh, yes," Dr. Batra told me, "I do. Very much."

"I'm happy for you," I said. "Truly."

"Thank you," Dr. Batra said, then, "You're going to need to get vaccinated for vaginal warts."

"That's not the segue I would have selected," I said. "Isn't this what you give twelve-year-old girls?"

"Usually around fourteen. Before girls are sexually active."

"Fourteen? Where have you been, Doctor?" I said. "Do you see what fifth graders wear around here? Nothing, but shorter than that."

"You need this shot, Hannah."

"Oh, dear God. I'm not sure I can even make out. And now, I have to worry about warts?"

It was all too much. I started to cry. I've never felt so helpless and alone before. Even though I've been both, I hadn't been smart enough or experienced enough to feel alone and helpless. Now I was old enough to know.

"What kind of baby are you having?" I asked, changing the topic.

"A boy baby," she said, smiling.

"Oh, nice. Enjoy," I said. "Enjoy everything. With your husband, with your baby. Every sleepless night, every spit-up. Every discussion that turns into an argument. Can you promise me that?"

"You sound like my grandmother. She was married to the same man for over fifty years," Dr. Batra said.

I sniffed the air. Someone was baking cookies. "Do you smell that?" I asked. "Vanilla?"

Dr. Batra peered up at me from between my legs, confused. Behind her, a dark-skinned man with a full head of jet-black hair and the doctor's same almond eyes appeared. He also wore a doctor's coat and a tie.

I jumped. "Ouch!" I said, as she poked me by accident.

"Whoa," Dr. Batra said. "What's going on here?"

"Do you have to show up now? Really?" I wanted to slam my legs shut, but there was the matter of the speculum.

"Hannah," Dr. Batra said, "who are you talking to?" She rolled back on her chair.

Meanwhile, the man was trying to tell me something.

"I'm sorry, I—"

"Do you need . . . help?" Dr. Batra asked. Two sets of the same beautiful eyes staring at me, expressing concern. *The baby*.

"You want your daughter to get checked?" I asked the spirit hovering over Dr. Batra's shoulder. Dr. Batra turned and then looked back at me, alarmed.

"Hannah, who are you—"

"Dr. Batra—Saria—you need to check your baby. The baby's not getting enough oxygen—"

Tears were coming to Dr. Batra's eyes. "Why are you saying this, Hannah? Why would you say—"

"Your father is very concerned. Please go today. Please. He loves you and the baby—"

"Hannah!"

"And would it kill you to call the baby Rajnan?"

Dr. Batra went white. She was about to faint. I grabbed her wrists as she went down. I was still in the chair, in the stirrups, with that medieval instrument inside me.

"Help!" I yelled. "Help!"

The medical assistant/toddler rushed in. "We need an ambulance for the doctor," I told her. "And I need to get this thing out of me . . . Oh, and my papers?"

I glanced back up. The spirit was gone.

* * *

"The baby's going to be fine," I said, hanging up the phone in my bedroom. "I may have to find another gyno, however. Dr. Batra is completely weirded out."

"This dead people thing is too much," Jay said, from my closet. "Your schedule is filling up. You should be getting paid already. Now, get in here."

Jay insisted on dressing me for my first official date of the post-widowhood millennia. Meanwhile, I was trying to ignore the dead girl with the black fingernails and frosted eye shadow trying to get my attention.

"Seriously, they are a pain in the ass," I said as I went to the closet. "They're used to rules—maybe I can set up my own rules. I mean, you're right, it's not like I'm getting paid for this."

I held my arms out as he slipped a dress with a tag still on over my head. I squeezed into it and looked in the mirror.

"Hi, old hooker," I said.

"Don't," he said. "My touchstone is Jane Fonda in *Barbarella*."

I grabbed jeans and a pair of boots I hadn't worn in a year. I hesitated for a moment—John loved me in those blue suede boots.

"Should I?" I asked, out loud.

"What is it your old friend Sylvia Sidney said?" Jay asked, already bored of dressing me.

"I'm not dead." I repeated Trish's words.

"I'd love to meet her, by the way," Jay said.

"Trish's more Georgia O'Keeffe than Sidney."

I slipped on the jeans. They fit, though not as snug as they were a few months ago. I'd found the only way to lose weight and keep it off: widowhood.

Fuck off, Master Cleanse. We got this.

"Well, I'm not mad at Georgia," Jay said, "but I adore me some Sylvia."

I pulled the boots over the jeans. I was wearing a flesh-toned, stay-away-from-my-boobies bra. I opened my underwear drawer and pulled out the big guns—a black lace number I'd bought in a moment of insanity at La Perla. I'd worn it once. Frankly, I wasn't the type of girl who was built for speed, if you know what I mean. I was built for comfort.

"Now, I know you want some," Jay said. He put his fist to his mouth. "I think I'm going to cry." I took off my granny bra. I never thought twice about undressing in front of Jay. We were like an old, married couple, down to the not-having-sex part.

"You know what I'm ready for?" I assessed myself. "I'm ready for mascara."

"Oh, that reminds me," he said, "I have a little gift for you. It's nothing." He handed me a silk pouch.

"You shouldn't have," I said. I opened the pouch. Inside were condoms and a small tube of K-Y Jelly.

"K-Y comes in convenient travel size?" I asked. "And Magnum condoms?"

"A boy can dream," Jay said.

I left the house, waving goodbye to Jay, Brandon, and Ellie. "I'm proud of you!" Jay screamed, as I drove away. Two women walking Labrador retrievers, the NoMo drug of choice, paused and watched as I drove off.

Our French film (with tits) was showing at the Aero Theater on Montana, but first I was meeting Tom for dinner across the street at R+D Kitchen, an aggressively singles place. The bobble-headed norms were squeezed around tiny tables sipping mojitos and eating fourteen-dollar guacamole and chips. Why did other people look like they belonged no matter what? I felt like an outcast everywhere except my living room.

Tom was nowhere in sight. I sat at the one empty seat at the bar, made myself as small as possible, and tried not to throw up; I was suffering dating performance anxiety. I ordered a chardonnay (which rhymes with outré for a reason) from the pretty bartender, and listened to conversations around me. The tennis-y blonde to my left, wearing chandelier earrings and a white halter top, complained that her JDate profile needed upgrading—the men she attracted were too Jewish-looking. The three men to my right, dressed as though they walked off a Duran Duran video, drank European beers and talked about the economy and Jennifer Aniston's tits. I felt like I'd taken a barstool in the Village of the Damned.

The world had gone on. Like it had a right to. Before I fell into a black pit of depression and despair, without the poetry, I heard a familiar voice behind me.

"Hannah, I'm so sorry," Tom said. He'd breezed in wearing a polo shirt and khakis, the Goyishe Uniform. "Have you been waiting long? My babysitter didn't show up until late—I love her, but she's not what you call punctual."

I was so relieved to see him, I couldn't speak. He kissed me on the cheek. His lips felt like cushions. I wanted more. I wondered what hell felt like this time of year.

"What are you having?" Tom asked. His thick, wavy hair was combed back, his light tan accentuating his perfect teeth. The blonde on my left had taken note, enough notes to form a book. She couldn't have noticed more if he was carrying a midget on his shoulders. I felt her faux-purple-eyed laser-gaze on me. She took in my hair, my nondescript watch, the lack of fast-twitch muscles. I knew what she was thinking—What's Mr. Hot, Eligible, Non-Jewishy Guy doing with that frizzy-haired monster who couldn't manage a pull-up? Tom put his arm around my chair and I mustered a smug glance at the blonde. Smug is harder than you think; it took muscles I haven't used in years.

A few minutes later, Tom and I were seated across from each other at a booth.

One and a half glasses of chardonnay (which, incidentally, was the exact quotient to get into my pants, circa '87) and halfway into my cheeseburger, I realized I was surviving my first postwidowhood date. I pushed down that familiar feeling of guilt and self-loathing in my stomach (easy to do when you've got a quarter pound of beef and a slab of cheddar coming its way) and focused on Tom.

Anyone looking at us would have seen a regular couple sharing a conversation over food and wine, not two people who'd been abandoned by the normal world. He was the Widower, and I the Widow. This was our first real date. We were ocean explorers, charting the Strait of Magellan, we were Sacajawea and Lewis and Clark.

We were middle-aged white people living and suffering in the suburbs.

"I kind of have to avoid hanging out at the riding ring, though," Tom was saying.

"What do you mean?" I asked. I was sipping my chardonnay and dreaming of waking up in his arms. Skipping the sex, just getting to the snuggling part.

"Well, there's a divorced mom there," he said. "A wacky stage mom. I made the mistake of going on a date with her. I thought that was her real hair. Silly me."

I must have grimaced, because Tom said, "Just one date."

"Oh . . . you're dating?" I asked. Inside, I screamed: *When? How? Why? Who? Where? What?*

"She took the whole thing way too seriously," Tom said, while I quietly experienced sensory overload. "It was probably my fault. I should have been upfront with her."

I looked at my plate. The leftover meat was congealing beneath a blob of cheese. "Oh," I said. "So you slept with her." You would have been proud of how casually I said this. I thought about how I'd gotten waxed down there, how I'd had my eyebrows plucked . . . how Jay had gone with me and now looked like a baby with a man's penis. *Sacrifices were made.*

"Just once," Tom said. "She's crazy."

"You're sleeping with women," I said. "I mean, of course you're sleeping with women—it's not like you're sleeping with men, right?" I looked at him. "Right?"

"Of course not. I've, ah, seen a few . . . women. No men." He smiled. "I know that seems suspect, here on the Westside—"

He'd been seeing normals, all along. Tons of normals. Thousands.

"When did you start seeing . . . non-survivors?" I asked.

"I've been dating for a couple months, Hannah," Tom said.

"How is that possible?" I asked. "I can't even imagine."

"I got lonely," Tom said. "I did therapy. It's only natural that I'd want to go out."

"Therapy?" I asked. "That's healthy."

"My therapist was very helpful," Tom said. "She was very understanding. I had to stop seeing her."

"Tom," I said, "you dated your therapist?"

"Not exactly. We didn't . . . go out."

"Oh my God," I said. "Wow . . . wow . . . wow . . . I haven't even . . . kissed anybody, much less screwed my therapist."

"I waited over two months," Tom said. "I wanted to be respectful."

"So, like, weeks," I said. I was trying to joke—really. Meanwhile, the rickety wheels in my head started turning. "Wait—you were at Peet's the morning I met you. You're a Caffe Luxxe guy, right? The Coyotes told me—they had you pegged the day of the memorial service."

Tom looked down at his plate. "I . . . kind of have to avoid Caffe Luxxe."

"Oh God. Don't say it."

"I slept with a barista," Tom says.

"Not the one with the—" I pointed to my nostril. "And the . . ." I pointed to my eyebrow.

He bit his lip and nodded, silent.

"Oh, dear," I said. "Oh, left-nostril, right-eyebrow-pierced dear—"

"And her—" He pointed to his tongue.

"Why?" I asked. "What was the attraction?"

"Like I said, I was lonely . . ."

"So am I," I said. "I mean, if I were ever alone, I'd be lonely. If my friends would leave me alone for twenty minutes."

"I'd heard stories . . . about tongue piercings," Tom said. "It turned out to be scary. I almost got injured."

"Who are you?" I asked. "Whoever you are, you shouldn't drink. You're in full reveal mode."

"I just feel comfortable telling you things," Tom said. "Hannah, you have to understand. Men are different from women."

"I'm aware of the differences—it hasn't been that long."

"I know," Tom said, "but it has been a while . . . right?"

I pondered my options. I decided I wanted nothing more than to sit in my Christmas pajama bottoms and watch *The Office* on DVR. *Is that so wrong?*

"I'd better go," I said, trying not to betray my hurt feelings. My quivering lower lip was not cooperating with my brain's directive.

"But we didn't even go to the movie," Tom said.

"I can look at my own boobs," I said. "They're not French but they'll do."

"Hannah, I don't want to lose our friendship," Tom said, as I slid out of the booth, walked past the crowded bar with fashion-forward normals, and into the night.

"Friendship," I repeated to Jay, as I took my shoes off, sank into my couch, and began to navigate 543 HBO channels.

"It's your last month of cable," Jay said. "It's important to bid *adieu* to each one of the HBOs."

"Friendship," I muttered, while I spilled a box of Junior Mints into my mouth. "I'd been agonizing over whether to let him stick his tongue in my mouth."

"Can I have the condoms back?" Jay asked, as I put my head on his shoulder.

"All yours," I said. We watched *Valentine's Day* until our eyes bled—which took about, oh, three minutes.

"What genius made Jessica Biel the girl who can't get a date?" Jay said. "And what's Jennifer Garner grinning about? Enough already!"

I was falling asleep in his arms.

Suddenly, Spice started barking at the screen.

I opened my eyes and tried to focus on the TV. Bakasana, Chloe's Rescue Pom, was on TV, lounging on a mink doggy bed, being fed grapes by a female Pom. I heard Frank Sinatra in the background. Spice started scratching at the television set.

"Oh, shit. Jay," I said, "do you see what I'm seeing?"

"Yes," Jay said, "the end of Julie Roberts's career." He pointed the remote at Bakasana and turned the television off. Blocks away, I heard the familiar howl of a coyote.

"Jay," I said, "do all dogs go to heaven?"

"Of course," he said.

"Even Pomeranians?" I asked.

Jay looked at me. "Do we have a problem?"

18

Bottoms Up

"Have you seen Bakasana?" Chloe asked, shoving a flyer of the Pomeranian's peculiar mug into a guppie's face as he ate strawberry layer cake for breakfast at a sidewalk table outside Sweet Lady Jane's, the new go-to spot on Montana. *Go-to spots are my run-from spots, just fyi.*

"Chloe," I said, "don't disturb people while they're pretending to eat." Eight A.M., and already Chloe had printed up flyers with Bakasana's distinctive face plastered on them.

Jay, tugging an insouciant Ralph wearing a tennis visor, took me aside. "You have to tell her about your vision of Bakasana in Doggie Heaven," he said. "She's making a fool out of herself in front of my people. Unattractive dogs offend them. It's good you left Spice at home. By the way, when did NoMo become WeHo? We should call it Sweet Gay-dy Jane's."

"What if I'm wrong about Bakasana?" I said, watching as Chloe approached a pair of women wearing tennis togs. "She'll never forgive me."

"What if you're right? She'll never forgive you," Jay said. "Besides, do you really have time to track down what now may very well be coyote scat? You've got issues of your own, my dear. How are you feeling this morning?"

"A little older, a little wiser, a little sadder. I don't know what I was hoping for with Tom, but it wasn't that he was a slut. And meanwhile, on the work front, I can't even get a meeting with a network parking guard."

"You tried the Yet-Works?" Jay said. "Bravo, Logo, Own, anything with an O?"

"Of course," I said, with a sigh. We watched as Chloe pressed a flyer into the hands of a reluctant young mother pushing a baby stroller, then handed another to the baby.

"Stop the madness," Jay said, as Chloe showed a flyer to a poodle tied to a mailbox.

"Hannah!" someone yelled. "Jay!" We turned to see Aimee waving from her convertible.

"Look who's happy," I said, returning the wave.

"Put another poor soul in the ICU, no doubt," Jay said.

Aimee double-parked then sprinted across the street as cars braked and honked.

"Guess what?" she said as she ran up, breathless. "Oh my God, did you see my knees when I was running? Remember when our skin fit?"

"You found Bakasana?" Chloe asked, handing Aimee a flyer.

"Who?" she asked, appraising the flyer. "What an ugly monkey."

"I'm guessing you just got a clean bill of health," I said.

"No, no, this is important," Aimee said. "I have an audition for Mamet's new Lifetime show. Do you know what this means?"

"Confusion," Jay said.

"Scale," I offered.

"Who's Mamet?" Chloe asked. "Oh, the one with all the toilet words."

"And yet, it still breathes," Aimee said, addressing Chloe. "Kids, Mamet saw my Chico's ad and tracked me down. I've trained my whole life for this moment. Strasberg, Stanislavsky, Katselas . . ."

"Scientology Celebrity Center," Jay said.

"I was trying to get close to Bodhi Elfman," Aimee said. "Oh, no—I only have a week to get my colon cleansed."

"That was my next thought," I said. "Mamet requires a spotless colon. Isn't it easier just to get a mani-pedi? There are eighteen thousand nail places on Montana."

Aimee was already scrolling through her BlackBerry. "Let's see who's available . . ."

"You're the only person who has high colonics on speed dial," I said.

"Not in L.A., sadly. Wait a minute," Aimee said. "Let's make a weekend out of it, the four of us on a cleansing vacation. There's a spa I heard about in Palm Desert."

"I can't enjoy a cleanse while Bakasana and Angel are missing," Chloe said. "That would be insensitive."

"Angel's missing, too?" I asked. "That skinny one with the nutty Sharon Stone eyes?" A disturbing thought entered my head. I tried to catch Jay's eye, but he was busy adjusting Ralph's visor.

"Yes, but I didn't have a single picture of her for a flyer," Chloe said. "We never had time for a photo shoot. I feel just terrible about that. Do you think that's why she left?"

Jay cleared his throat. I got the message.

"Chloe, there's something I need to tell you about Bakasana," I said, "and maybe about Angel, too—"

"Can we get back to my offer?" Aimee said, interrupting. "I need to make reservations immediately. They get totally booked up for New Year's. Who's up for an intestinal scrubbing?"

"*Moi*," Jay said. "I could lose a few. And maybe a twelve-pack will lure Hidalgo back."

"He's already married," I said. "You're acting like a sorority girl."

"So?" Jay said. "Your point being?"

"Well, I can't go," I said. "I'm not ready to have fun that doesn't sound fun, and I couldn't leave Ellie. Not in the year of the dead father."

"Oh, please. Ellie would love to have Brandon all to herself," Aimee said. "Chloe, pretend we're at the West L.A. Animal Shelter for two nights. C'mon. Let's start this year off with a bang. So to speak."

Chloe sort of blinked, then turned to me. "What did you need to tell me, Hannah?"

I looked in her wide, trusting eyes and swallowed hard.

"That we're on a boat to Palm Desert!" Jay interjected, then pursed his lips. "I've never been out there with a group of girls. I usually go with hairless boys wearing cheap sunglasses. Am I losing my edge?"

"Never. Think of it as an embarrassment of riches," I said, as Chloe took off toward an old lady attempting to enter the Pirates coffee shop and Aimee started speed-dialing.

"Embarrassment of bitches, you mean," Jay replied, with a wink.

I rehearsed my conversation with Ellie about our mini-vacation. "Mommy is going on a very, very short trip with Auntie Jay, I mean, Uncle Jay and Auntie Aimee and Auntie Chloe. Brandon is staying here with you. I'll be gone for only two nights."

This is what I actually said: "Ellie, Mommy loves you so, so, so much. I'm so sorry, I'm going away. You know what, I don't need to go—I'll never leave you—" while tears streamed down my face. Ellie stared at me as though she were looking at a snail; sort of interested, mildly disgusted.

Brandon gently interrupted my snotfest. "Ellie, your mom is going to Palm Desert, which is a really nice place—and you and I get to have fun here, together, for two whole nights. How does that sound?"

"Yay!" yelled my daughter, sticking the knife in my back. She hugged Brandon, around his knees.

He put his arms around her, and looked at me. "Sorry," he said.

"No, don't be sorry," I said. "I'm glad she loves you so much."

"I love her, too," Brandon said. "Don't I, El?" He swooped her up and lifted her to the ceiling.

"Yes!" she said. "Yes!"

I watched them, lost in their happiness. I didn't feel sorry for myself. I was thinking of John. My husband, Ellie's father, had been replaced.

I hate you, death.

* * *

I can't remember the last time I took a vacation.

Oh, wait. There it is.

John was writing *Spanish for Bachelors*. I was a few months pregnant. We landed in Barcelona. August, ninety degrees in the shade. Our small hotel was in the Gothic Quarter, overlooking a *placa*, near a huge cathedral where geese honked at all hours. I was so sick, nauseous, vomiting all day. Even with severe jet lag, there was no sleeping in this ancient Spanish city that awakens at midnight. The air was dense and my clothes clung to my damp skin. The smell wafting up to our hotel window of *paella* and *sarsuela* in crowded, thick-walled restaurants with low-slung ceilings sent me running to the nearest *baño*. The only thing I remember digesting there is warm flat bread our hotel served in the mornings.

It was the most romantic trip of my life.

John never left my side. He held my hair back as I crouched before toilets on tile floors that had probably been around since Queen Isabella sent Columbus on an extended cruise. He'd stroked my growing belly, my swelling breasts, pressed cool, moist hand towels to my forehead, and threw coins at the guitarist strumming outside our hotel window, requesting anything by Barry White.

I came out of my reverie in our home, in my own sun-dappled bedroom, an overnight bag open on the bed, packed for our two-night expulsion-excursion. I thought about Greece. Three non-refundable coach tickets to Athens, and I still hadn't canceled the hotel. I could post them on Craigslist. Maybe I'd be the lucky on-line seller who wasn't sliced into a million pieces and dumped in Barstow.

To a single mother, nothing is scarier than Craigslist.

A car honked outside. I heard Tony Bennett singing, and Jay yelling my name. Time to go.

Two hours out of L.A., and the farther we drove, the more I began to suspect that Lite Glow Spa was not in the Palm Desert of my Frank-Sinatra-wooing-Ava-Gardner dreams. Wearing a straw fedora with a pack of Salems tucked into his Dacron shirt pocket, Jay drove our rented convertible Cadillac and played Bobby Darin and Dean Martin on his iPod until I felt like choking on a string of cocktail pearls. Chloe was silent most of the way, except to request that we post Bakasana flyers at rest stops.

"Do you think Billy will remember to give Mulabanda his diabetes shot?" Chloe asked.

"No," Jay said, rubbing out his cigarette in the car's ashtray. He couldn't have looked happier if Ricky Martin, or Ricki Lake, for that matter, were seated next to him. "I just love an ashtray."

"They paved paradise and got rid of ashtrays," I said.

"What a gorgeous day," Aimee said, leaning back and gazing up at the cloudless blue sky from the backseat. "It couldn't be more beautiful."

Chloe stared out the side window, sinking low in the backseat.

Meanwhile, Aimee continued to be uncharacteristically chatty and upbeat. "I love this weather," she blabbered. "I love dry heat."

I realized I might actually prefer the Lost Brontë Sister Aimee.

"You hate weather of any kind," I said, turning around in my seat. "Since I've known you, there is no weather you will not complain about."

"Nonsense," Aimee said. "Smell that clean desert air. I feel healthier already. Hey, there's a McDonald's at the next off-ramp—"

We passed a road sign emblazoned with the big red M.

"Chicken McNuggets on me," Jay said. "This McFag is McHard as a rock just thinking about 'em."

"Hi, McCancer," Chloe said. "You obviously haven't been reading my blog. My kids have never touched a french fry."

"Good luck with that," Aimee said.

McDonald's drive-thru turned us into animals. We amassed five Big Macs, family-size fries, two McNuggets, three vanilla shakes, and a jumbo Dr Pepper for Jay. Chloe ordered oatmeal.

"Doesn't this kinda sorta negate the whole 'cleansing' objective?" I asked, as we gathered up the greasy wrappers.

"*Au contraire,*" Aimee said. "We need something to be cleansed."

Twenty minutes later, we took an off-ramp in the middle of nowhere and hung a right on a side street, where tract houses were huddled together behind concrete walls swathed in graffiti.

"Where are we?" Jay asked. "My Palm Desert doesn't do 'Clownie Was Here.' "

"Stop being such a cultural elitist," Cultural Elitist Numero Uno Aimee said. "Stretch your world a little."

"I like NoMo. I don't want a stretched-out world," Chloe said, sulking.

We located Lite Glow Spa at the end of a dirt road where several low, reddish buildings hunkered together. Tumbleweeds blew past our Caddie.

"Does anyone else hear the twangy rhythms of Ennio Morricone?" I asked, as we parked next to a Bentley in a dirt lot just outside the "spa."

"I'm not getting out," Chloe said. "This place is tacky, and I'm too upset to get an enema."

"C'mon, Chloe," Jay said. "I just sucked down eight thousand McNuggets and a Dr Pepper—I need some cleaning up in here, yo!"

"Chloe," I said, "have you not seen the Bentley? It can't be all bad."

Chloe just sighed and got out of the car, grabbing her overnight bag, a Vuitton from better days.

"Why don't you eBay that thing?" I asked. "You could get a fortune for it."

"Better yet, give it to your friend who's recovering from illness," Aimee said, as the four of us walked to the red clay building with a sign that read LITE GLOW SPA, then through a large doorway to the front desk.

Tiffany, the receptionist—sporting five earrings in her left ear—checked us in. "We have a menu of services here at Lite Glow Spa," she said, flashing meth teeth.

"Listen, Princess," Jay said, "I want two things—a massage by a guy with hands that could tear apart a sink, and a colonic that ends with my liver in a jar."

A tall, lean, über-tanned man wearing doctor's scrubs appeared at Tiffany's side.

"Happy New Year and welcome to Lite Glow Spa," he said with a European accent. He sounded Austrian, like a member of the von Trapp family. "I am Dr. Manheim, the resident doctor here."

"Do you hear angels singing?" Jay asked, shaking Dr. Manheim's hand.

"I'm so glad you've arrived," Dr. Manheim said, seducing us with his pearly teeth.

"I'm so glad you're glad," I said, losing that last tasty morsel of my dignity.

"Are you a medical doctor?" Aimee asked.

"I am," Dr. Manheim said. "I can assure you."

"I'm assured," Chloe said.

"Me too," I piped up.

"Why don't they have you on the website?" Aimee asked.

"Oh, I don't want the attention," Dr. Manheim said. "I like keeping my operation small and manageable. Now who's going to be first for their colonic?"

We all raised our hands at once.

Good news. Dennis Quaid was staying at Lite Glow Spa. Thus, the Bentley. During our tour of the facilities, we spied him eagerly supping on broth in the dining room. I half expected him to be hooked up to IVs.

"What's he doing here?" Aimee asked. "And when did I start outweighing Dennis Quaid?"

"Same thing you're doing here," I said. "He must be manoerexic."

"Some guys have all the luck," Jay said, sniffing.

We were taken to our rooms by a bellman/massage therapist, Jacques, who lovingly described the décor as Santa Fe meets St. Tropez.

"Santa Fe meets homeless shelter," I said, to myself. After I cleaned the drawers out (small black pellets = rat poop), Jay and Aimee appeared at the door, dressed for dinner. Jay wore crisp white linen and lace-up loafers with red soles.

"Colon cleanings are black tie?" I asked. Aimee was wearing a turban and a floor-length sundress. "Very Sex and the Desert," I said. My wardrobe choices? Loose-fitting jeans, a long-sleeved T-shirt. Flip-flops.

"Someone has their Forever Single look on," Jay said to me, pity in his beautiful gray eyes.

"I checked," Chloe said, as she walked in the room. "I don't think that Dr. Manheim character is a real doctor."

"He could play a doctor on *All My Children*," Aimee said.

"That's canceled, you know." Jay paused thoughtfully. "Do I miss me some Wings Hauser. Dr. Manheim seemed to like you, Hannah. God, I hate the straights."

In the spa's dining room, four long wooden tables packed with colonic-seekers lined the room, cafeteria-style. Shoved against the far wall was a small refrigerator, the kind you'd find in a frat house hallway. Next to it were three large metal canisters, each with its own label. On the labels was handwritten scrawl: TEA, BROTH, JUICE.

We squeezed into a table and enjoyed paper cups filled to the brim with broth. Okay, we didn't actually enjoy the broth; we tolerated the broth. I looked around at the clientele—mostly WIBYs—Women of Indeterminate Birth Year. I sat next to a very blond woman with lips bigger than her hips.

"Wow, you have great meridians," Mega-Lips said. "Is that your real hair?"

"Thank you," I said, trying not to stare. Now I know what Medusa's victims felt like. "And yes, I made this hair myself. I'm to blame."

Meanwhile, Jay was casting his eyes about for boy candy. "Do I look thinner?" he asked. "I feel like Gisele three weeks after the Brady baby."

"Mr. Bundchen, you are still up to your hips in Chicken McNuggets," I said.

"If anything, you look a little puffy," Aimee said.

"Hey," Chloe said, elbowing me in the side, "Manheim is staring at you."

"What?" Aimee said. "Staring at Hannah? Why the hell did I bother wearing a turban, for God's sake? Whatever. Go for it. You deserve some happiness."

"Something to bring home as a souvenir," Jay said, as I glanced over at Dr. Manheim.

His gaze was undeniable; I had caught the good doctor's attention. My stomach growled.

"Hold his gaze for two seconds," Aimee said.

"I can't," I said.

"You must," Jay said. "Take one for the team."

"You can do it, Hannah," Chloe said. "Get back on that horse."

"I hate horses," I said.

"It's a metaphor," Aimee said. "You have to learn to flirt again."

"I'm not sure I knew how to do it the first time."

"That's true," Jay said. "I remember. It looked like Regis doing the Dougie."

"Now that's just mean," I said. "Watch me. Watch me gaze." I turned in time to be eye-to-crotch with Dr. Manheim.

"Have you ever seen the desert sky at night?" his crotch asked.

With no response coming from my frozen vocal cords, Jay piped up. "Hi, I'm Jay and I'll be your interpreter tonight. The last time Hannah saw the desert sky, she was a chubby fifteen-year-old wasted on Annie Green Springs."

"What he said," I croaked.

"Come," Dr. Manheim said. "I'll show you." He pulled out my chair for me.

We strolled past the spa, past the little bungalows where the colon assaults took place, past the sputtering tile fountain, to a spot where two beach chairs were set up in the red sand, surrounded by cacti aplenty. Between the chairs was an ice chest, with plastic champagne glasses set on top.

"Please," Dr. Manheim said, his hand on a chair. I pushed away the thought that this wasn't the first, second, or hundredth time he'd brought a "client" outside to look at the stars. Dr. Manheim handed me a champagne glass and opened up the ice chest.

"Would you care for some champagne?" Dr. Manheim asked. "It is New Year's."

"Is it on the spa menu?" I asked. Wind chimes softly serenaded us.

"Only for my favorite patients," Dr. Manheim said as he popped open the bottle and poured.

We clicked our glasses and I took a sip. Then another.

"So, Dr. Manheim," I said.

"Call me Karl."

"You can call me Karl, too," I said. Was it possible to be drunk off two sips? My last meal was hours ago.

The linty Swedish Fish at the bottom of my purse taunted me.

Karl's clear blue eyes registered confusion.

"So, where did you go to medical school?" I asked.

"Universidad de Ara Macao. It's the Harvard Medical School of Northern Honduras."

"Isn't the Macao a bird? The University of the Red Macaw . . ." I stared at his hands, his forearms, the creases between his eyes. "Karl, you're not an actual medical doctor, right? I'm cool with that, it's not like you're taking out my spleen."

"Well, it's like the Harvard Medical School of Chiropractic."

"You're not from Austria."

"I'm a Texan."

"You were a drug dealer?" I speculated. "No. Wait. Hiding from a former life . . . which is why you can't put yourself on the website." A breeze picked up, along with the wind chimes.

"I like you," Karl said, at last dropping the fake Austrian accent. "You're funny."

I tilted my head back. Karl the All-American was on point about one thing: These stars were must-see TV. Swarovski crystals twinkling against black velvet beckoned. A crystal dropped out of the sky, falling between distant mountains.

"A shooting star!" I said, pointing at the mountains.

"Did you make a wish?" Karl asked.

My first thought was for John to be here with me. Then, my true wish, deep in my heart, was for me to find happiness again.

Karl reached over and kissed me.

"That wasn't my wish," I said.

His response reeked of unleashed testosterone. "You may not have been asking for it, but I think you needed it."

"Really?"

"I've learned a lot from my exile in the desert," he said. "There's so much mental anguish out there. For some reason, people want to believe the solution is in their lower intestine. That's where I come in. With my equipment, of course."

"You know, you're not bad for a fake doctor."

"Thank you," he said, carressing my hand. "So you want to make out?"

"Maybe just one more kiss, nothing consequential," I said. "I just need to prove something."

Leaning toward me, he put his hand on my cheek and pressed his lips against mine. He held the kiss . . .

"I can help you prove other things," he said, sliding his finger down my neck. I shivered. All over my body, things were waking up.

"I'm good," I said. "I'm good, for now. Thank you." Even if I had wanted s-e-x, my body was too weak for anything but the missionary position minus the missionary. Three hours into our spa excavation/vacation and girlfriend here needed an IV, stat.

I could tell by his silence that Karl was disappointed. Should I sleep with him to assuage his bruised male ego? *Maybe he had been a fat teenager. What if he'd had a mean stepdad? Or maybe his basketball coach had made him run hundreds of extra laps? Should I make the poor guy feel better by giving him a naked hug?*

"Hey, you know that blonde . . ." I said, mentioning the woman I had briefly talked to in the dining room. Blondie had lips for miles, like so many Westside she-wolves (where you're only as old as your plastic surgeon's datebook). "Age is just a state of blind in L.A. I can't tell if she's retired or a runaway."

"Her meridians have serious issues," he said.

"She was very complimentary of mine. And she thought I had

hair extensions. Like someone would do this"—I grabbed my hair—
"on purpose."

"You do have efficient meridians," Karl said, "and great hair. Or
at least, lots of it."

"Thank you. She's in room seven."

"Nine."

"Go get 'er," I said. "But don't light any candles—she could
melt."

Karl fled for greener, lasered pastures, leaving behind the champagne and plastic flutes.

I poured myself another glass of Brut, vintage Tuesday. Kissing
another man, a perfect, or highly imperfect stranger on New Year's
Eve hadn't sickened me—just the opposite. Karl's kiss had awakened me, cheered me up, made me think about possibilities. Trish
was right: I wasn't dead.

"Can you cheat on a dead man?" I asked. Did John sense my
betrayal? He wasn't there, not in the black sky nor the shadows.
Stars bobbed and weaved around me and I slipped into a half-asleep,
half-awake state, a similar feeling to when I watch Ben Affleck in a
romantic comedy. The wind chimes serenaded me.

"That was cute," someone said.

"John?" I opened my eyes.

"Who was that clown?"

"You followed me here?" I asked.

"That's exactly the thing a guilty person would say," John said.

"Peevish ghost," I said. "I'm sorry. Nothing happened. I mean,
not really."

"What does 'not really' mean? Like, I not really-ed made out
with him?"

"I kissed him."

"Aaaagh!" John yelled.

"What do you want me to do?" I asked. "It is New Year's. You
would have been married by now."

"I definitely wouldn't have been married," he said.

"Why? You hate marriage?" I said. "What are you saying? Our
marriage was so bad?"

"No, crazy lunatic person," he said. "I loved being married to you. I just might want to *not* be married for a while."

"Oh, I see. You would have screwed everything within a five-mile radius." I thought about Tom, the Widower ManWhore. *Maybe I'd been too hard on him.*

"Not a five-mile radius," John said. "That only gets me to Robertson. Everyone knows the cute girls are in Koreatown."

"Shut up," I said, suspecting he was right. "I hate you."

"I hate you, too," John said. "I hate that you're moving on. I feel it in my bones. Well, not bones . . . Anyway, I guess you're supposed to move on. You must."

"I don't want to move on. I want to stay where I'm comfortable. Miserable, USA."

"If you don't move on, Hannah," John said, "think about how unhappy Ellie will be. She needs her mommy to be happy."

I thought about Ellie. I remembered kids growing up, kids whose mothers never got out of their terry-cloth robes, or who dropped their children off at school wearing pajamas under their raincoats. I felt sorrier for them than for myself, the orphan.

"So who was Doctor Feelgood?" John asked. "The poster boy for suspended medical license?"

"Karl's a doctor of chiropractic-ish from the Red Bird University. It's one of the finest in Northern Central America." I giggled, and John laughed. A warm breeze wrapped itself around my body; it felt almost human. I relaxed and closed my eyes as the stars wrote bedtime stories in the sky.

John had been waiting for me at home, wearing his daytime uniform: baggy shorts and a T-shirt with the arms cut off, just in case a pickup basketball game materialized out of thin air. He had lunch ready. "I sliced the leftover steak from last night, and some arugula and wild greens, peppercorns, sea salt—I put my mustard dressing on it."

I had barely tossed my keys on the couch when he rushed over, his hand under a forkful of arugula topped with a sliver of steak, drenched in a mustard vinaigrette.

He shoved it in my mouth, his eyes lighting up as he watched me eat.

"Honey," I said, between chews, "I don't have much time— I have to get back to work."

"Thank God, you come fast," John said, as he pushed me toward our bedroom. I protested as he slipped off my heels, my skirt, my panties. I covered my pussy with my hands.

"I didn't have time to shower this morning," I objected.

"Shut up," he said. "Why are you talking?" He pushed away my hands and dove in, his head between my legs, making quick work of me with his tongue. He loved my body, every part. Parts I had never seen and didn't really care to. I was helpless. I came. John had my clit on a hair trigger.

"The romance is gone," John panted. "I'm sorry." He mouthed my neck, like a mother lion with her cub.

Someone shined a flashlight in my eyes. I shielded my face. When I was able to focus, I realized where I was: sitting on a beach chair in the desert, a bottle of champagne at my feet.

Jay was squatting down next to me. He brushed my hair from my eyes.

"You slept here all night. Happy New Year's Day."

"You looked so peaceful," Chloe said, standing just behind him with Aimee. "You had a smile on your face."

"I had a dream about John," I said. "One of our lunches."

"Lunches? You mean afternoon sessions. I remember those," Jay said. "You always came back a little late and a little flustered and a lot fucked out."

"I'm starved for my man," I said. "God, I used to tell him I'd cut him up in little pieces and make a stew out of him."

"That's love?" Aimee asked, lifting the champagne bottle and pouring the rest, a few warm drops, into her mouth.

"Of course. I've loved that much," Jay said. "It's never been taken from me, though. It just walks away . . . or, you know, makes out with some other guy in my Jacuzzi."

"I hate you," Chloe said, turning to me with tears in her eyes.

"What did you just say?" I squinted at Chloe.

Aimee and Jay just stared at her.

"I'm jealous of you and your dead husband," she said, pouting. "Maybe I'm just tired of hearing how great everything was."

"Oh?" I said. "Oh, I see. We've gotten our roles mixed up. You were the happily married, well-connected rich girl, I was the harmless chunky girl whose shoulder everyone cried on, Aimee's the beautiful and ultimately tragic single girl."

"Wait," Jay said, "I want to be the ultimately tragic single girl."

"Jay, you're the sweet, funny, lovelorn girl. You're tragic, but not ultimately tragic."

"Now I'm the nutcase whose husband is probably screwing the yoga instructor," Chloe said. "I'm just not 'intellectually challenging.'"

"A yogini who does 'life work' on the side is intellectually challenging?" Aimee said.

"Even by L.A. standards, that's bad," I said.

"Stupid is in the water," Jay said. "My New York friends are the worst. All they do is talk about books. Everyone knows books are obsolete. It's like Buddhism. It's done. Next!"

"I could have done more," Chloe lamented. "Billy wanted me to stay home. He insisted that I put aside my career."

"You were a salesgirl at Alaia," I said. "That's not exactly a vocation."

"I was good, though. I had passion," Chloe said. "I had choices and I gave them up for him."

"Nice try," Aimee said after a moment. "I almost believed you."

"I'm pretty sure I meant it," Chloe said, shrugging. A nurse, or a young man dressed to look like a nurse, came out and regarded our little group. "I'm looking for Jay Oleson—are you ready for your procedure?"

"I'm first," Jay said and clapped his hands together. "Could you die?"

"We might," I said. "The day is young, and so aren't we."

Soon after, Martha, a soft-spoken Ecuadorian lady with small hands, was poking a tube up my butt.

"Let me know if you find anything up there, like the keys to my '85 Scirocco or those white Gucci sunglasses I bought on a whim, before the crash."

"The tip of the hose is now entering your rectum," she said.

("Wrecked 'em?" the voice in my head said, "I nearly killed 'em!")

"But we've just met, Martha," I said. "Shouldn't you at least buy me coffee?"

Martha smiled as she worked in the hose. I tried to remain calm as she turned on the water, which fed into the coiled hose. "When the water moves up into your colon, it may cramp a little," she warned, sounding like Latina GPS—soothing and efficient. I was not soothed, gentle reader.

"Cramp!" I yelled. "Holy Mother of God Cramp!"

"But . . . the water has not even moved inside yet," Martha said.

"I'm practicing," I said sheepishly. Our Palm Desert vacation was making me sheepish. I had sheepishly made out with a quack doctor, I had sheepishly disrobed. I had sheepishly consented to a hose being stuck up my butt.

I was living my entire life sheepishly. What was I afraid of? *What wasn't I afraid of?*

Water splashed my colon.

"I'm drowning from the wrong end!" I said.

"Relax for a moment. Let the water flush out your toxins and impurities."

"But there'll be nothing left," I said. "That's all I've got. My toxins keep me alive."

Twenty minutes later, I was limping back to my room.

"Chloe," I said. "Chloe!" I heard water running. She was taking a shower.

"I just pooped myself!" Chloe shouted from the bathroom.

"Oh my God," I said. I grabbed my belly. I had an urge . . . I ran for the bathroom, flipped up the toilet seat, and expelled an organ. "I think I just lost a kidney," I said. Chloe jumped out of the shower.

The doorbell rang. "Hey, kids," Jay said, in a singsong voice.

"My body is folding in on itself," I shouted from the bathroom. Pulling up my sweats, I shuffled ever so gingerly into the bedroom.

Aimee, in her robe, was seated on the edge of the bed, rocking back and forth and mumbling. "I'd love a cigarette," she said. "I feel like toxing all over again."

"Girls, I had the most amazing experience," Jay said, sitting on the bed. "I know this year is going to be different. I had a vision of love. Not the Mariah Carey version—this one doesn't shatter glass. Hidalgo is THE ONE. All caps."

"Not the Next One?" I managed. "Or the One Before That? Or the One That Will Do In a Pinch?"

"I had a vision, too," Aimee said. "That I would get the role of a lifetime. It's the Mamet role, I know it."

"I had a vision," I said. "A vision of . . . a sausage and egg McMuffin."

Jay smiled. "Last one to the Caddie's a rotten piece of last season's gladiator look."

We passed the reception desk, where Dr. Manheim was bidding *adieu* to Joker Lips. He caught my eye as he patted her old-man ass. As I waved goodbye, the temperature in the lobby dropped. Wind chimes sang. I stopped in my tracks.

"Hannah," Aimee said, turning around. "Come on. Our final drive-thru awaits."

Jay regarded me. "Oh no. Don't tell me."

"What's going on?" Chloe asked.

"The cold. Wind chimes. There are no wind chimes here. I don't see wind chimes." I looked up and saw a slim, blond teenaged girl, her hand on her hip, watching Dr. Manheim and Jack(ie) Nicholson with obvious disdain.

"That is so frikkin' gross," the girl said to me. "Like, what's wrong with her face?"

"It's a cultural thing," I responded. "I'm really sorry, but I must run. My friends and I, we're kind of in a hurry."

"Ooh, well, so sorry to hold you up," she said. "I'm only, like, dead. *God*."

"I know. You have my sympathy. Truly. Did you want me to convey something?"

"Hannah," Jay said, checking his watch. "How long is this going to take? Should we wait in the car?"

"Yeah, I totally want you to say something," the girl said, agitated. "Tell that asshole that he can run but he can't, like, hide. Tell him Courtney Eubanks is not amused."

"Tell Dr. Manheim? Karl?"

"Manheim? Excuse me? The last time I saw him, he was Jimmy from Dallas and he was my boyfriend and he was giving me mouth-to-mouth while my car blew the fuck up."

"Oh, no. You died in a car crash? That's terrible."

"Yeah. We hit this stupid old pine tree. Oh my God, my dad had just bought me that BMW. Orange-red 325i convertible for my Sweet Sixteen. It was to die for. And I did!"

"I'm sorry," I said. "You're so young."

"Well, yeah. Hi. Look at me. How are you? Living? I'm dead. I had everything. The hair, the nails . . . the shoes." She let out a loud sigh that only I could hear. I shivered. ". . . the boyfriend. Everything."

"Dr. Manheim, Jimmy, I mean—was he driving?"

"Yeah. We were fighting over some girl, and you know, we had a few drinks. Whatevs."

"Is Dr. Manheim a fugitive?"

"Well, duh. He freaked and fled to Mexico like the next day." She rolled her big eyes. "My sister wore my Calvin Klein slip dress to the funeral. I was so pissed. I lost Jimmy, my Beemer, and my favorite dress."

"You loved him."

"Well, of course," she said. "He was the nicest, cutest boy in school. Everybody loved Jimmy."

Dr. Manheim was about to greet new recruits. I had to grab him, quickly.

"Karl," I said.

He turned and smiled. *Oh, those blue eyes. Oh, the secret behind them.*

"Jimmy, Courtney Eubanks is not a happy girl," I said. "It's time to get your meridians in order."

He stood there, his eyes registering panic. "Jimmy . . . Did you say Courtney . . . Eubanks?" he asked.

I put my hand on his shoulder. I could tell he was in shock.

"It's time for you to go home, Jimmy," I said. "You need to face up to the past. You can't run anymore."

He looked at me, suddenly small and vulnerable. "Who are you?" he asked, his voice barely above a whisper.

As I looked at him, I thought about his question.

"I'm a hyphenate. I'm a mom, a widow," I said, "and . . . a medium. Take care."

I grabbed my bag and walked out.

19

Growing Pains

After John died, I had put my sex drive in the drawer with all those business cards I can't seem to throw out. Like, someday I'll need a cab ride in Phoenix with Mazur. Or a haircut in Brooklyn by a woman I met on a plane five years ago.

I remember liking men, vaguely, like the Italian waiter at Toscana who treated me like a queen in the days when I had an expense account. Someday we will look back at expense accounts as we do dinosaurs. We'll stroll through museums, like the Credit Card Museum, where we'll visit rainbow-colored cards with unlimited balances. At the What We Used to Care About Wing (adjacent to the What Were We Thinking? Wing), we'll don headphones and listen to Anna Wintour describing "seasons," when socialites would buy designer clothes that would be deigned obsolete months later. And we'll sit there, on those hard benches in the middle of the "Never Wear White After Labor Day" room and laugh our food-stamps-and-unemployment-just-ran-out asses off.

I'm digressing. I'm uncomfortable with the idea of sex. I'm uncomfortable with the idea that I miss it. I'm uncomfortable that my friends are fucking like rabbits on Viagra and Red Bull.

Enter, Jay. In the last week, Hidalgo had been kicked out by his long-suffering wife, had moved in with Jay, and had tearfully accepted Jay's proposal. His vision had come true.

"The date's set. June 20th," Jay announced, using his manic bridal energy to slice peppers on my chopping block. He'd brought over enough groceries to feed the Westside (which doesn't require much, granted) and set about making a mess of my kitchen, jostling my vague plans for Poquito Mas takeout.

"That's when my parents got married," he continued.

Ellie and Brandon had headed over to Douglas Park to hit the monkey bars before dinnertime. I knew my only job was to listen and be supportive, but I had already failed. *You've heard of a Bridezilla? How about a Gay Groomosaurus?*

"How romantic is that?" I asked. "Your parents haven't spoken to each other in thirty years."

"The ceremony will be on the Vineyard," he said, sliding the peppers into a pan before drizzling olive oil on them.

"Why the Vineyard?" I said.

"There's a delightful bed-and-breakfast."

"You don't eat breakfast."

"You've got to help me with the rehearsal dinner choreography," Jay said.

"*Choreography?* Jay, you make fun of people like you."

"Why can't you just be happy for me?" Jay turned, waving a kitchen knife.

"Because you're making a huge mistake?"

"You used to be nicer," Jay said, "when John was alive."

"Death is a downer. Try walking in my shoes sometime."

"First of all, I'd never walk in Uggs, hello. Second, you need to stop feeling sorry for yourself."

"I'm not feeling sorry for myself," I said, feeling sorry for myself. Someone knocked at the front door, then let themselves in. "Hello?" I called out.

"Hey, peeps," Chloe said, sauntering into the kitchen, then opening my candy drawer. "I'm starving. Chocolate, come to Mommy." Chloe grabbed the two-pound See's box. See's is a staple in my house. *Take my TV, take my car, take my grandmother's earrings—but do NOT take my See's.*

Chloe tore through the box and shoved a chocolate into her mouth.

"My last Bordeaux? You know that's not organic," I said.

"Oh my God," she said. "That's so fucking good."

"Why are you swearing?" I asked. "What's going on?"

"I had a heart attack last night," Chloe said, her mouth full. Yet she was smiling.

"What?" I said. "Are you kidding? I mean, are you okay?"

"Billy's on his way to Camp Pendleton. He left me alone."

"Camp Pendleton?" I asked. "What are you talking about?"

"He joined the Marines?" Jay asked. "He's going to be all brave and few?"

"Yesterday, Billy went to the recruitment center on Wilshire," Chloe said, as she disemboweled my See's box. "You know him—he talked his way in. Billy can talk his way into anything."

"I can't believe I'm hearing this," I said. "A forty-year-old man joining the Marines."

"Yeah. So I'm alone with the kids—I've never been alone," Chloe said. "I can't do it. I'm in constant fear that someone's going to knock on my door and ask me to balance a checkbook. Anyway, something amazing happened."

"Get to the good part," Jay said. "We're planning a wedding on a time crunch."

"It was dinnertime," she began, way too slowly. "I was just taking my tempeh casserole out of the oven. My heart started racing. You know I don't do caffeine. Ever. Long story short, I fainted."

"My God, Chloe. Why didn't you call me?" I asked.

"Tyler, my big boy," Chloe said. "He's really sweet. He's like, almost grown up . . ."

"Sweet Jesus," Jay said. "Can we scroll down to the bottom?"

"He's kind of small for his age, no?" Chloe asked, concerned.

"You feed him twigs and berries," I said. "Has he ever had a glass of milk?"

"Milk causes diarrhea and mood swings," Chloe said. "Do you have any? It'd go perfectly with the chocolate."

"Can we skip to the punch line?" Jay pleaded.

Chloe opened the refrigerator. "Tyler called the paramedics while I lay passed out on the cold red Spanish tile."

"Now you're Steinbeck?" Jay said.

"When I awoke—" Chloe paused to chug milk right from the carton. She put it down and burped. "—there was a beautiful angel bent over me."

"An angel?" I asked. I had yet to see a real angel, only dead people with issues.

"His name was Cody," Chloe said.

"Angels have biblical names—there's no Book of Cody," Jay said.

"He held me in his arms and kissed me," Chloe said. "I mean, gave me mouth-to-mouth."

Jay rested his chin on his hands. He read homo-romos—homosexual romances—in his spare time. He had a library full of titles like *Land of the Forbidden Men*.

"I'm in love," Chloe said. "I haven't felt this way . . . I don't re-member if I ever felt this way."

"Does Cody know?" I asked, hearing the front door open again.

"Is someone talking about Cody the Paramedic?" Aimee asked as she walked in. "He's famous in these parts. Or should I say, *infa-mous*. NoMo moms love him."

"Him, I've never met," Jay said. "How is this possible?"

"Cody feels the same way I do," Chloe continued, unperturbed by Jay's and Aimee's commentary. "I could tell by the way he checked my pupils, and took my blood pressure. And when he asked me what day it was, he was so gentle. Do you have Ben and Jerry's?" She opened the freezer.

"Wait. What am I missing about the Santa Monica paramedics?" I asked.

"They're aggressively gorgeous," Aimee said. "There's a lot of pressure to look pretty when you're trying to recover from an audition-induced panic attack."

"Hannah, they recruit them," Jay said. "Surfers, skateboarders, beach volleyball players. Not that I've done my research, not that I've called nine-one-one when I overcooked my broccoli rabe."

"I need to see Cody again," Chloe said. "Is that so wrong? I am still a married woman."

"Well, that's true," I said, my tone deliberately even, "but you are separated from a middle-aged ex-banker on his way to Marine boot camp."

"That sounds crazy," Chloe said, "when you put it like that."

"Call him," Aimee said. "Call Cody. Why not? What do you have to lose?"

"Why, thank you, Aimee," Chloe said. "Okay. I'll put meat loaf in the oven at seven—I've decided to start eating meat again—I'll check my hair, get dizzy around 7:45, Tyler calls the paramedics. By the time the meat loaf is done, Cody is giving me mouth-to-mouth."

"It's not like a radio station," Jay said. "You can't request your favorite paramedic."

"Honestly, Chloe," I said. "Who cares which one you get? They sound like they're all the same."

"Wait a minute. What if it's true love?" Aimee said, looking at us. "Love is the only thing that really matters, right?"

"Hi, my name's Hannah," I said, holding out my hand. "I don't believe we've met."

"Stop kidding around," Aimee said, before glancing at her phone. "Ooh, I've got to run. We'll continue this conversation another time."

We stared as Aimee waved and glided out of the kitchen.

Jay waited until we heard the door slam. "We have to call someone right away," he said. "How about that MoonGlow place on Wilshire?"

"The psychiatric facility in Santa Monica backed by a reclusive billionaire?" asked Chloe.

"What about straight-up, no-frills?" I said. "UCLA Psych Ward might be perfect."

"God, Aimee seemed so . . . sweet," Chloe said. "She's really not well, is she?"

"Maybe she's overdoing the self-love again," Jay said. "Remember when she landed at the emergency room on 15th? I love that place—it's like a Williams-Sonoma. She put her shoulder out."

I thought about the look on Aimee's face: She'd been bitten by the love bug. Hopefully the love bug that doesn't carry Hep C. *Damn it, I was jealous*.

I wondered if Tom thought about me at all. I missed our friendship, or relationship, or . . . coffeeship. Whatever ship it was, I wanted to be sailing on it.

Ellie, Uncle Jay, and I strolled the Promenade on a bright Saturday afternoon, killing time before heading over to the latest Pixar movie. Ellie walked between us, holding our hands, skipping and jumping and pretty much guaranteeing a shoulder injury. Third Street was filled with teenagers on the prowl, German tourists, homeless men with cardboard signs stating varying and creative infirmities and needs. At Ellie's insistence, we stopped to watch a family of sinewy adolescent boys performing frightening gymnastic feats. We slipped through the necklace of people surrounding them, Ellie pulling us through to the front.

We watched for a few minutes, and Ellie pointed at the pile of dollar bills peeking out of an open box placed in front of the boys. Jay slipped a five into her hands, and she held it high as she walked over, and dropped it in the box. One of the boys, shirtless and sinuous, made a big show of Ellie's generosity.

I was thinking about that box of money. And all the boxes up and down the Third Street Promenade—the guitar cases, shoeboxes, cartons—all filled with dollar bills.

"I want that cash," I said to Jay. "What could I sell on the Promenade?"

"Grains of rice with someone's name on them?" Jay suggested. "Because there's not enough of that in the world."

"I have to find a job, Jay," I said. "When the going's tough . . ."

"It's time for the tough to get cash," Jay said. "I'd heard that from an auntie who lived through the Great Depression."

"And all we get is Double-Dip Recession," I said, "which sounds like dessert."

"The 'Super-Fucked Recession' rolls right off the tongue," Jay said, out of Ellie's hearing range. He grabbed my hand. He'd gotten a new tattoo of a pair of lips on his forearm. "Come on, movie's about to start—little purple aliens will help you forget your troubles."

The next morning, I drove my car down Montana and spotted a sign in the window at Caffe Luxxe (slightly concealed by the beautiful people and their shimmery auras): NOW HIRING BARISTI

I could baristi, I thought. I pulled over, nose-checked myself in the rearview mirror, then went inside, where I spotted Mr. Scary Redhead, the tatted guy behind the counter.

"Hi," I said, quavering before his freckles and piercings. "Who do I talk to about the baristi job?"

"You mean barista," Evil Redheaded Monster said. "Baristi is plural." *Are all redheads evil?* Think about it. Hitler was a redhead. Stalin. Dahmer. John Wayne Gacy. Yes, they were all redheads. Don't argue with me right now.

"You mean like octopi?" I asked.

"Talk to Melissa," he said, nodding in the direction of an average-looking girl, but for the giant nose hoop piercing the space between her nostrils, like a bull. *A nose hoop. For when a nose ring isn't enough.*

I walked over to where Melissa was seated. "I was told by—" *Evil Redhead*—"the man behind the counter . . . I'm looking for a barista job."

"Good timing," she said. "We're in a lull right now. Have a seat."

I looked around as I sat. Usually, the place was packed, with a line that stretched from Ed O'Neill to a Desperate Housewife. Whenever I stood in that morning lineup, I was the only person I didn't recognize.

I played a game with myself. If I were able to get through the interview without staring at Melissa's nose hoop, I would later give myself a Drumstick as a reward.

"Foam art is really important," she said. "I can't stress that enough. We take our foam very seriously."

"Of course, you do," I said. "Um. Exactly what is foam art?"

Melissa pointed at a lovingly framed coffee portrait hanging on the far wall. "The espresso designs in the foam," she said, in a somber tone.

"Oh," I said. "Yes. Wow. How do you even do that?"

"We have a rigorous training program," she said, lowering her voice. "I mastered the leaf and heart quickly, but I was unusually dedicated."

"Does one get paid during training?"

"Tips. In this location, that's plenty."

"I'm in."

"I have to warn you," she said, "Santa Monica Caffe Luxxe is supercompetitive with the Brentwood Caffe Luxxe. We don't even talk to each other. And we would never set foot in their shop. We are only looking for the most loyal baristi."

"I understand," I said, taking a deep breath. "I'm ready to face my foam."

A week or so later, Melissa had a sour expression on her face. The source of her unhappiness? You're looking at her. I had just put the finishing touches on a latte. "Give me another chance," I said. "I can foam better. I know I can." I'd been having trouble focusing—the spirit world hearts a good coffee place. Every other customer seemed to have a grandparent, parent, family pet, sister . . . something or someone who absolutely needed to communicate to them that very second. I felt like AT&T but with better service. I did my best to ignore the spirits, or reassure them without frightening my customers, but as a result I was not the Michelangelo of foam art. *What could a budding barista do when distracted by celestial beings?*

"I had such high hopes," Melissa said, muttering something else under her breath.

"What is that?" Mean Horrible Evil Redhead asked, staring at my latest creation. "It looks pornographic."

I ignored him and told the customer, "It's a leaf." This clean-cut lawyer came in every morning precisely at 8:35, bringing with him his dead grandmother who desperately wanted him to get married and settle down. "With seductive undertones," I admitted. My foam art looked like a vagina.

The lawyer left, shaking his head.

"Ooh, look who's foaming," Dee Dee Pickler said, as she breezed to the front of the line, packed in lululemon tights, a yoga mat tucked under her arm. Her breasts looked like a butt. *Butt-boobs*.

"Look who's . . . cutting the line," I said. You should see me play tennis—Just. As. Good.

"You work here? That's so . . . what's the word . . . open-minded."

"Hi. Two words. I'm not working. I'm researching."

"Well, how about researching my next cappuccino?" Dee Dee ordered.

Melissa had a sharp eye on me. Her nostrils were flaring; the nose hoop vibrated.

I felt like a matador. And now, I was trying to ignore an old chestnut mare that had wandered into the shop, dropping the temperature around me by about a hundred degrees. Melissa had already asked me not to wear a wool hat and scarf to work; as a result, I was freezing all the time.

"Absolutely," I said, shivering as I turned to the espresso machine.

"Think leaf, be leaf," Melissa hissed.

The old horse rubbed her nose up against Melissa's sleeve.

"I got this," I said, motioning for her to back off. I expelled a shot of espresso from the machine, poured steamed milk over it, manipulating the foam into my leaf. I presented my cappuccino, placing it on the counter next to the tip jar.

Dee Dee and Melissa bent over the counter to study my foam as Evil Redhead stood behind us, arms crossed. Finally, I had perfected the leaf. I could feel it in my soul. Evil Redhead returned to his station.

"It looks . . . ," Dee Dee said, then tilted her head. "Wait . . ."

"It's changing," Melissa said, as Evil Redhead turned back. I gazed at the foam. She was right. My leaf was shifting into a . . .

"Penis?" Evil Horrible Redhead said.

"I'll take it," Dee Dee said, dropping a dollar into the tip jar, and grabbing the drink. "Ring me, Hannah," she said, before sauntering outside.

"I'm sorry, Hannah." Melissa sighed. "You're just not barista material."

"I was distracted. I can do better," I insisted. Melissa just shook her head. Evil Redhead fluttered his fingers at me as I took off my apron and handed it to her. The old mare shimmied and neighed.

"Do you miss your horse?" I finally asked Melissa. "She misses you."

Melissa eyed me warily. "What horse?"

"You must have had a horse—maybe when you were a child?"

"I never had a horse," she insisted.

"A chestnut mare. There's some sort of connection . . ." I knew, by now, that I couldn't be mistaken. It was odd for me to discover this talent at this stage of my life—but I knew enough to believe in it.

Melissa's hand suddenly went to her mouth. "So long ago," she said, barely above a whisper. "My dad started drinking, my parents divorced, we lost our farm. But it was ages ago . . . I was five or six, I would ride with my mom. What was her name?"

Melissa looked away, then grabbed my arm. "Nutmeg," she said. A lone tear appeared, making a trail down the side of her cheek. Now I understood . . . the nose hoop, the attitude, everything.

"Nutmeg still thinks about those rides," I said. "You made her very happy." I gave Melissa a long hug, and walked out with my head held high, past Dee Dee and her ass-boobs. She followed me to my car, sipping her latte. "This 'dirty latte' is delicious, by the way."

"I just got fired," I said.

"Hannah, you don't have to do this," Dee Dee said. "You know the Turk has a firm offer on the table." I listened and watched the perfect young mothers and the perfect babies and the perfect sitcom star drinking the perfect cappuccino with the perfect espresso leaf drawn into the perfect head of foam.

This was never my reality, I thought. *This is their show. This always belonged to them. I was just a tourist here.*

"Hannah? Are you okay?"

"Goodbye, NoMo," I whispered. I had to let go.

After sitting down and sorting out the gory details with Dee Dee at her office on Montana, and starting to make my peace with downsizing, I came home to find Aimee weeping on my front door step.

"What happened?" I asked. "I haven't seen you in forever." I was exhausted. I'd walked home, passing every useless jewelry, clothing, and sustainable furniture shop on Montana. They seemed foreign, as though I'd never noticed them before. *What had I been holding on to?*

"I lost the role," Aimee said, through her tears. I sat down and put my arm around her, staring up the street that I would no longer call my own. The palm trees that looked like dignified old women. The new marble mansions and old plaster bungalows. The shiny cars, the French racing bikes.

"Let's go inside," I said.

We sat in my kitchen and I ran my fingers along the chopping block. Our home was going to be lost to me and Ellie. Another death in a family so small.

"I had the Mamet role, Hannah," she said. "I got the call on Thursday."

"Wait—you had it, then you lost it? Why didn't you tell us when you got the role?" I asked. "We could have celebrated, at least for a couple days."

"I don't know," she said. "I wanted this role for so long. My entire life, really. Then I got it—and it was like—is this it? Is this the feeling?"

I nodded, listening.

"I thought about what I'd given up to get this part. I'd given up my life, Hannah. I've given up chances for love, for true happiness. I felt so sick, I couldn't get out of bed."

"So what happened?" I asked.

"I didn't pass my physical," Aimee said. "I had even showed up to the set."

"Are you okay?" I asked. "Was it the radiation? How could you not pass a physical?"

"It's all a mistake, but they've already hired someone else," Aimee said.

"They went younger?" Jay asked, holding Ralph and wearing huge sunglasses, as he came into the kitchen. Chloe tagged along behind him, with a couple of dogs in her wake, of course.

"Bigger," Aimee said. "They went with Kirstie Alley. My manager said they wanted 'real.' Real? This is not a world I want to live in. All I'll ever be is the shampoo girl."

"Well, my crisis trumps your crisis," Jay said, sniffling. He took off his sunglasses. His eyes were red. "After all the excitement, Hidalgo went back to his wife. All he left me with was an Indian headdress."

"I'm sorry, honey, but you knew he was married," I said.

"She trapped him," Jay said. "Women are so lucky." All you have to do is get knocked up. I wish I had a uterus."

Chloe looked up. "Billy told me I had purposefully trapped him," she confessed. "But it was an accident. I got married in my fourth month. I was one big breast."

"I thought you were a nun, Chloe," Aimee said. "You act like one. Except around paramedics."

"Aimee, that is so mean," Chloe said. "You know, bitterness causes wrinkles."

"Everyone else in this kitchen is allowed to get married," Jay said. "How does that work?"

"It's not that simple, Jay," Aimee said. "Put yourself in Hidalgo's wife's place."

"You're telling me this? You, who has a heart of stone."

"I'm an actress. I empathize for a living."

"No, you don't," Jay said. "You wash your hair for a living."

Aimee just looked at Jay, her mouth open. Then, she slowly stood and walked out. I heard the front door slam.

"Hi, Andy DICK," I said to Jay.

"Well, she said it first." Jay sulked.

"I'm leaving," Chloe said. "Dogs don't care if I have a harmless flirtation with nine-one-one. Or premarital sex. They don't judge."

"All I want is marital sex," Jay said, to her retreating figure, "but people like you won't let me!" Jay sprang from his barstool and I listened to the *bang, bang, bang* of Louboutin loafers and the jingling of his squirrel tail keychain as he slammed the front door.

I was left alone.

"I'm selling Casa Sugar," I said to no one. "Hannah doesn't live here anymore."

Brandon, Ellie, and I ate takeout from A Votre Sante on San Vicente. Ellie had her usual tempeh and grilled vegetables (no, I'm not kidding), I had a thin Margherita pizza. Yes, I ate the whole thing, but I've mentioned it's thin, have I not? Brandon ate a turkey burger.

(Perhaps you have to live in L.A. to understand the prior paragraph. I apologize.)

Neither Brandon nor I were in a talkative mood. He'd become quieter in the last week or so. I'd find him at the kitchen table, staring off into space, looking very *Men's Vogue* layout, like something Tom Ford might order for breakfast, lunch, and dinner.

I sat at my center island, seeing everything through new, sad eyes; the way the light falls on the kitchen table in the evening, it was so . . . Ansel Adams.

Those old shelves were small, the doors don't close and never will, but boy, are they solid. My avocado tree was perfectly framed in my French windows.

I inhaled that pizza and sighed it out.

Ellie bounced in and talked schoolyard politics, a new girl named

Chase (really? Chase?), and why caterpillars are so delightful. Meanwhile, I saw all that would no longer exist for us. In our bleak future, Brandon, I imagined, would also be gone.

I should be used to this, I reasoned to myself. *"Come on, Hannah—things disappear—you know that—keys, sunglasses, jobs, financial security, husbands . . ."*

Brandon and I continued to eat in silence as the little girl with the glasses sat up on her stool, oblivious to our mood, feeding our souls with her voice. It seems that Ellie is here to save me. I know it's unfair to put the onus on someone who's not tall enough to ride roller-coaster rides at Universal Studios, but it's the truth.

Later, Brandon and I, in our nightly ritual, took turns saying good night to Ellie—first I say good night, and read a book, then Brandon comes in to say good night and tell her a story about his brothers and sister growing up. Tonight, we'd grunted good night to each other and went our separate ways—not far in a 900-square-foot house.

Then I did what I normally do under these or any other circumstances. I cracked open the Russian River pinot I'd found for $7.99 (Von's Card), poured a glass, poured a little more, and headed outside to sit under my avocado tree. I wanted to soak in the night and the next thirty-to-sixty days or however long escrow lasted.

The back door swung open, and Brandon emerged.

"Can I talk to you?"

"As long as I don't have to respond," I said. "One of those days."

"Raise a finger," he said. "One is yes, two is no."

"You've been dealing with three-year-olds for too long," I said.

He smiled, and raised a finger. Under the veil of our kitchen lights, he was backlit like a six-foot-six angel.

"You're quitting," I said.

"No," Brandon said. A small thought wiggled its way into my aged cerebellum.

Brandon was in love with moi. The signs were everywhere. More than once, I caught Brandon staring as I unpacked groceries. He couldn't be that crazy about Granny Smith apples. The poor boy was head-over-heels in love with his grandmother.

"Brandon," I said, "I don't know how to say this . . . I'll just come out and say it. My parts are over forty years old. You and I could never work out."

Brandon looked at me.

"We're too different. For one thing, you're tall and blond. That's a combination I've never understood."

Were his eyes welling up?

"You're upset," I said. "I'm so sorry."

Brandon broke out laughing, then leaned over and gave me a bear hug, which lasted long enough to make me miss John's bear hugs more than I would miss oxygen or chocolate or the grape. Hardly an embrace of the romantic kind—I guess the kid wasn't madly in love with me—but nevertheless, welcome.

An avocado fell from the top of the tree, hitting Brandon on the head.

"Ow!" Brandon said, rubbing the top of his head. He looked up.

"John!" I said.

"What?" Brandon asked.

"What?" I said.

"You just said 'John,'" Brandon said, his gray-blue eyes of youth clear as HDX.

Another avocado fell from the top of the tree.

"Why don't we go inside?" I said, escorting Brandon into the kitchen. "That wind is really picking up!"

We stepped inside the kitchen. "Hannah," Brandon said, "I do love you. I love the way you stay so strong even when you're so lost. I love the way you listen to people, and how everything is funny to you, even death. I love the way you've survived. I've learned so much about how to live from you."

"Stop, I feel like Oprah—without the money and the Gayle."

"You have your Gayle. You've got Chloe, Jay, and Aimee."

"Not anymore. We broke up. It was like *Friends* when they ran out of story lines. You know, Phoebe got pregnant with twins and Monica got jealous."

"What's *Friends*?" Brandon asked.

"Wow," I said. "You're younger than my Paxil prescription."

"Aimee's mad at you?"

"Aimee's mad at everyone," I said, "but now even more so than usual. Just when I sensed her bright and sunny side."

Brandon looked down at his feet. I guess a size fourteen and a half can be pretty interesting.

"You okay?" I asked. "Can I get you anything? Drumstick, no nuts?"

"Hannah," he said, "I need to find a real job."

"I knew it. I knew it." I felt like I'd been punched in the stomach.

"I won't leave right away. Something's changed. I'm . . . involved with someone, Hannah. It's pretty serious."

"So, you're getting married?"

"Well, not yet. But I like her a lot. She's good for me. She's not like anyone I've ever met before." Color flooded his cheeks.

"You're beaming," I said. "That's just . . . gross. I'm kidding. It's so nice. Keep that look. I miss it. I really miss it."

"Thank you for being so supportive," Brandon said. "It's time to go out and earn a living. I just wanted you to know I'd be looking for something else."

"Life goes on, my boy," I said, and gave him a hug. He kissed my forehead, then shuffled out of the kitchen, leaving me alone with a box of Drumsticks.

Dangerous times at Casa Sugar.

"Life goes on," I said, ripping open the box. "How incredibly annoying."

I went outside. I had a bone to pick with my dead husband. (Trust me, you get used to this kind of thing.)

"John!" I yelled. "JOHN!"

"What?" he replied. He sat on top of the tree, looking ever so nonchalant.

"Get down here this instant," I said.

"I didn't mean to hit him," he said.

"Oh, but you did," I said. "You hit him right in the head with an avocado."

"It was ripe," he pointed out.

"I don't care. You don't hit people in the head with vegetables—that's terrible. You're not a poltergeist."

"How many times have I told you, Hannah?" John said. "An avocado is a fruit."

"How many times have I told you I don't care?"

"Did you ever care?" John asked.

"What do you mean by that?"

"What are you doing, flirting with the manny?"

"I wasn't flirting. I was . . . mentoring."

"Any more mentoring and you'd be picking out baby names. And, by the way, no one that tall is smart."

"That's enough. He's a sweet boy and I need him. Ellie needs him."

"Great. Hurt me some more. It's not like I'm dead or something."

"I'm sorry," I said. "I really am."

I listened to the breeze, and the sound of a neighbor's son's garage band eviscerating "My Sharona."

"John? Is it quiet in . . . where you are?"

"In heaven?"

"I didn't want to ask. I don't want to believe in heaven because then I have to believe in hell."

"Well, we don't actually call it heaven," he said. "It's called Philadelphia."

"What?"

"I'm kidding. Ben likes to say that."

"Ben . . ."

"Franklin. You know he died of syphilis?"

"He told you that?"

"You should see all the women this guy had—they are still all over him."

"Is it better up there?"

"Never. My family is down there," John said. "But I don't want you to be up here with me. It's not your time. So I have to sit here and wait, still madly, deeply in love."

I sniffed, and wiped a tear from the end of my nose.

"Also, I miss my pans." He sighed.

"Don't be mean," I said, "although, they miss you, too."

"Hey, did you track down the Range Rover?"

"Honey, I'm sorry, I haven't."

I waited. No response.

"John?"

I wondered why I hadn't told him about Casa Sugar, about selling our home. Perhaps the pain would be too much to process. The dead grieve, too, you know.

I sat back in my chair, drank the rest of my wine . . . and sleep made its move.

20

It's About Fucking Time

Six forty-five in the morning and someone was pounding on my front door. I had awakened moments before, and was busy negotiating with the coffeemaker when the banging started. "Death" was my immediate thought, followed by "impending nuclear holocaust." No one bangs on doors in NoMo.

I ran to the door and opened it. A man stood there, all gut, full facial hair, wearing mirrored sunglasses. They're expensive.

I'm wondering what the Mafia wants with me. And what kind of Mafia. The Italian Mob is old school. There's the Mexican Mafia, the Gay Mafia (they specialize in media, fashion, and bitchy asides), the Armenian Mafia, the Hungarian Mafia, the Russian Mafia . . .

"I have appointment. You are Hannah?" the man said, with an unfamiliar foreign accent. I started to close the door. He stuck his foot in it.

"Dee Dee made the appointment," he said. "I need to see house."

"Dee Dee?" I said. "Dee Dee Pickler? Oh, are you the Turk?"

"My name is Jerry," he said.

"Well, you're not the new owner yet," I said, calmly as I could. "Dee Dee did not contact me. And . . . Jerry's a Turkish name?"

"You need to sell house to me, yes?" he said. I nodded. "I need to see house first."

"Can you . . . just come back? My daughter doesn't know." Poor

Ellie. How could I lose the only home she'd ever known? I'd lost everything—our tree, our swing, our backyard, our bathtub, our memories. My guilt receptacle overfloweth.

"I don't have time. I need to see house now."

"Please, she's not awake yet. I don't want to scare her."

"Hey, buddy." A sleepy-eyed Brandon padded up behind me, wearing shorts and a rumpled T-shirt. "Is there a problem?"

The Turk looked up, *way up*, at Brandon. "No, no," the Turk said, smiling. "Not at all. I thought I had appointment."

"Apparently, you didn't," Brandon said, smiling back. "Maybe you'd like to make one."

"Yes. Good idea," the Turk said. "I go to make appointment." The Turk scampered away to the black Hummer blocking my driveway.

"You're selling Casa Sugar?" Brandon asked. "Why?"

"You make it sound like I want to. I don't want to. I have to."

"I see," he said. "Does Ellie know?"

I shook my head, afraid I was going to cry as Ellie walked in, her morning face bright with curiosity.

"Hi, baby!" I said to Ellie, then turned to Brandon. "Keep an eye on her while I jump in front of a Santa Monica blue line."

"At least those buses are electric," Brandon said, teasing me, as he grabbed Ellie and carried her off toward the kitchen.

An hour later, Detective Ramirez was on my front steps. I had already dropped Ellie off at school, and Brandon had donned his best (and only) suit for a job interview. I'd tied his tie for him like a proud mother. John never wore ties. Not even to our wedding.

Standing behind Detective Ramirez on my steps was the Turk.

"Is your boyfriend here?" Ramirez asked.

"My boyfriend," I said, thinking. "Do you mean my manny?"

"He's not your boyfriend?" Ramirez asked.

"No, but why are you asking me that?" I said. "I don't feel like sharing my personal life with either of you, especially when it comes to boyfriends or lack thereof."

"Your manny allegedly threatened Mr. Mansour," Ramirez stated.

"Threatened him how?"

"Called him a name," Ramirez said, then looked at his notepad. "Did your manny call Mr. Mansour a 'titty baby'?"

It took me a while to stop laughing. "He said nothing of the sort. If there was threatening going on, it was a one-way street from . . . Jerry." I pointed at the Turk. "He banged on my door at six forty-five in the morning."

"I have appointment," the Turk said. "I have rights."

"Is he buying the house?" Detective Ramirez asked. "Mrs. Bernal, is Mr. Mansour buying your house?"

Dee Dee had explained to me that it was too late to sell it through proper channels. I'd have to make a direct sale or risk being foreclosed on. The price she quoted to me had been fair. In the short term, I would have enough to tide me over.

"We're in a negotiation phase," I said. "I haven't signed any papers yet."

"So that's almost a yes, but he hasn't been able to look at the property," Detective Ramirez said. "Would you mind if he took a look around?"

"No," I said, finally. "Please. Don't touch anything."

"He won't," Detective Ramirez said. "Hear that? Don't touch anything."

I stepped aside and watched as the Turk strode through Casa Sugar. I felt as though he were walking on my heart.

"Titty baby is what passes for crime in Santa Monica? I feel infinitely safer," I said to Ramirez. "Isn't this the kind of thing a patrolman checks into?"

"I wanted to see you," he said, then retreated. "I mean, I've been checking up on Range Rovers."

"You found it?" I said, my heart skipping a beat.

"No. The D.A. wants to proceed with a trial. We're interviewing possible witnesses."

"You're trying an innocent man," I said. "How do you sleep at night?"

Detective Ramirez changed the subject. "Have you seen him lately—my partner?"

"No," I said. "The dead usually accompany someone they were connected to in life."

Detective Ramirez glanced over his shoulder, and I followed his gaze. All I saw was the neighbor's wisteria, draped over the lattice divider like a purple shawl; a sight I passed every day with nary a thought, yet appeared more beautiful than anything Monet could come up with on a very good day.

"If you see him, can you tell him something for me?" he asked.

"Of course," I said.

"Tell him . . . I'm sorry," he said, sucking in his breath.

"He knows," I said. Ramirez wiped his nose with the back of his hand. I felt like hugging him, but that could be seen as an attempt to grab his gun from his holster. Did I feel like getting shot? No. *Maybe.*

The Turk reappeared, grinning. "I'm done," he said. "This is good-size lot. Maybe two days to take down house. Easy."

"You're just going to take down the house? Isn't Casa Sugar on the Historical Registry?"

The Turk looked at me. "Historical? I pay the city, no more historical! But first, I have to take out tree."

"You have to . . . what?"

"Thanks," he said to Detective Ramirez, then walked off to his Hummer.

"He can't murder my tree! Can he?"

"If he's buying the place," Ramirez said, "he can do what he wants with it. Unless it's a California Oak. Those are protected."

"Oh my God," I said. "This can't be . . ."

"I'm sorry, Mrs. Bernal," Detective Ramirez said. "I'm sorry."

I closed the door as he stood there, then slid to the floor, grabbed my sides, and wept.

* * *

In the back of my brain, I remembered the girl with the frilly name who tied herself to an ancient redwood in Northern California to prevent loggers from chopping it down. I was going to be that girl, sans youthful glow. As I scoured the house looking for rope, I thought about how she'd sat in that tree for a year. I was going for a week.

Or until I got really hungry.

I found a long piece of rope in a forgotten drawer, climbed up the avocado tree, tied the rope around my waist to the trunk, and waited for news crews. (Wait! Did I call them?)

Five minutes passed. I heard someone yelling my name.

"That was quick," I said. "I'm back here!" I wasn't afraid. I'd faced death, taxes, unemployment, a floundering real estate market. What else could they do to me?

Tom DeCiccio came into view, decked out head-to-toe in biking gear. He made ridiculous look delicious.

"Hey," I said. "How've you been?" I gripped the branch I was sitting on. I hadn't eaten breakfast so I was woozy. I'd forgotten to bring up a pillow to sit on. I'd forgotten to pee. *Hi, bright, shining moment.*

"Hannah," Tom said, "what are you doing?"

"I've tied myself to my tree. I don't care what happens. I don't care if the police or the fire department come. I'm not coming down."

"But you're only a few feet off the ground," he helpfully pointed out.

"Did you want something? Besides mocking my foray into environmental justice?"

"I know you're selling your house," he said. "We're starting the paperwork on it."

"So?"

"So, I wanted to check up on you. I figured you'd be upset. But all in all, it's the right move."

"I'm not upset," I said, trying to be strong.

"Then . . . what are you doing in that tree?"

He had me there. Tom was brighter than he looked, despite the beanie.

"The Turk's taking the tree down," I said, choking up. "It's just too much for me. It's all just too much."

"Please, can you come down here?" Tom said. "Please?"

"Why?" I said. "What do you care?"

"Hannah, I care about you. I'd like to comfort you."

"No," I said, "I'm fine." My chest heaved. "I'm really fine. Just go away."

"Hannah," he said, "I've missed you."

"The Happy Widower missed me?" I said. "Between assignations? When would you have time?"

"Hannah . . . come on," Tom said. "I have a right to date."

"I know, I know," I said. "I just thought . . . I don't know what I thought. What does it matter?"

"Will you please come down?"

"No," I said. "I have my convictions . . . plus, I'm afraid to come down."

Tom stepped over, stood beneath me, and held his hands out for me to jump.

I untied the rope and leapt into his arms. He fell back onto the ground. I thought I heard his spine crack. *I leap into a man's arms and paralyze him for life.*

"Oh God, are you okay?" I asked, as I heard him groan beneath me. "I can't believe I did that."

Tom opened his eyes, pulled my face toward his, and kissed me. My head started spinning as his tongue pushed its way into my mouth. All over my body, switches turned on; the entire rusty machine was whirring to life. Even with him wearing Lycra bike shorts, I was a goner. But then, so was he.

Wow. So. Grief Sex. How to describe? You know, different types of sex match different emotional states.

There's Make-up Sex. Or Sad Sex. There's Sex just to get it over with Sex. There's Guilt Sex. Anger Sex. Happy Sex. Embarrassed Sex. Anxiety Sex. Bliss Sex. There's I'd Rather Be Doing Anyone Else, but You're Here Sex.

Those are all Grief Sex's bitches. Yep, that's right. Those sexes couldn't hold Grief Sex's jockey strap.

Grief Sex with Tom may have been the best sex I've ever had. And no, haters, it wasn't because I hadn't had sex in forever. Okay, maybe it was. I'm not going to get into details. But when we emerged, our legs and arms wrapped around each other, we were laughing and crying.

"That's not normal," I said.

Tom shook his head. "I know," he said.

"It's my first time," I said.

"Really?"

"Well, I mean, not my first, first time. I am a mother."

He pulled me closer, and held me tight in his arms, as I cried. I cried because I had sex, I cried because I missed sex. I cried because I was grateful and because I was guilty. I cried because I was happy (which made me feel shitty). I cried because I was lonely, and maybe, just maybe, I wouldn't be lonely anymore.

That's a lot of crying, let's face it.

After Tom left for work, I stared at myself long and hard in my bathroom mirror. I had to see if this experience, making love for the first time since John's death, had changed me. Was I in love? I don't think so. But I was definitely, solidly, in interest. The truth was, my heart had been so damaged, so traumatized by John's death, that maybe from here on in, love would feel different, unrecognizable in its new, subdued form.

All of a sudden, I felt old beyond my years. Too wise, even for my forties. In the quiet, bells started going off around me, the air cooled, and the toilet seat suddenly dropped.

"Not now!" I said. "Can't you see I'm having a moment?"

Surrounded as I was by death, I decided that life was too short and precious (even if it weren't short enough in some cases) and I needed my disgruntled, estranged, and strange best friends in the world now more than ever.

Also, I needed to brag.

* * *

Jay's small, tidy craftsman house, in a row of other small, tidy craftsman houses, was situated on a small, tidy street west of Main, just off Santa Monica beach. I overpaid for beach parking and headed to his home, organic dog biscuits in hand. I knew my audience.

I heard the music a half block before I reached Jay's home. *George Michael*, the lean years. Which predates George Michael, the surgery years. Whatever was happening with Jay required immediate attention.

I rang, and after a drawn-out moment, Jay opened his front door, clutching Ralph to his chest.

"Hi," I said. "I brought you a present, and I just had amazing sex."

"Well, hello, Merry Widow," he said, looking at his watch. "That was quick."

"No, it wasn't," I said, feeling defensive. "It's been months."

"In my grandmother's day, if a woman were widowed, she'd never have sex again."

"Do you want the biscuits or not?" I asked, waving the bag in his face.

Jay grabbed the biscuits and motioned me in. "Details" was all he said, as he sank down on the couch.

I sat facing him, our knees touching, mirroring each other's posture. "Okay, I was tied to my tree and then I fell on top of him, and then we kissed."

"Wait," Jay said, "who are we talking about, here?"

"Tom the banker."

"Nice. Waxed?"

"No!"

"Trimmed?"

I had to think. "I guess so."

"Circumcised?"

"Yes," I said, sitting on his living room couch. "Who isn't circumcised these days?"

"Dominicans," Jay said. "We call those 'hooded anteaters.'"

"Enough. Why are you listening to George Michael, circa mid-eighties?" I asked.

"Any of his other circas worth listening to?"

"'Cowboys and Angels,'" I said, "you're playing it over and over, aren't you?"

"No," Jay said, sitting next to me. "Of course not. I intersperse it with 'I Can't Make You Love Me' . . . I just can't get Hidalgo out of my head."

"So when are you killing yourself?"

"About an hour. I have to highlight my hair first. I'm a hot mess. Sweet Baby Jesus, save me."

My BlackBerry started buzzing.

"Please get an iPhone. BlackBerrys are uncivilized," he said.

"You're pretty judgmental for a potential suicide," I said, then answered. "Hello?"

"Emergency," Aimee said.

"Are you okay? I'm with Jay—"

"Oh, that," she said. "Promise me you won't tell him anything."

"But you haven't told me anything."

"The reason I didn't pass the physical?" she said. "I'm pregnant."

I straightened up and looked at Jay.

"What?" Jay said.

"You're joking," I said.

"Why would I joke about something as horrible as that?" Aimee said.

"How do you know?"

"Holy Mother of Oh My God," Jay said. "That old witch is pregnant?"

"Don't tell him!" Aimee screeched.

"He knows," I said, as Jay tried to wrestle the phone from me, settling for listening in by pressing his head against mine.

"I can't tell you who the father is," she said.

"Translation: The girl doesn't know," Jay said. "Are we keeping it?"

"No," Aimee said. "Where would I put it?"

I was gripped by maternal longing. "You must keep this baby."

"Hannah, I kill everything I touch, you know that."

"Have you told the father?"

"He wants to get married," Aimee said.

"My God, what a scumbag," Jay said facetiously.

"That's sweet," I said. "Do I know him?"

"I've lived alone for twenty-five years. Do you know what that does to a person?"

"It makes them a selfish bitch?" Jay offered. "I don't believe this. I can't get married, and she won't get married."

"Hannah, Jay, please, I need your support," Aimee said.

"We can raise the baby. Together," I said.

"I'm a selfish bitch. Even Jay said so."

"Full disclosure," Jay said. "I may have been talking about myself."

"Where are you right now?" I asked Aimee.

"I can't be a mother," Aimee said, pacing my kitchen. "Mothers have to do things, like take care of a child."

The four of us, including Chloe, who'd brought over pastries and was serving them with tea for our baby-or-no-baby discussion, had gathered around my kitchen table. Ellie would dance through every so often, as a gentle, extremely cute reminder of what could be.

"You take care of Ellie when I need you," I said. "You've taught her things."

"Like what?"

"Like . . ." I looked around for help.

"Always put vodka in the freezer?" Chloe said.

"You do know you can't do Botox during the pregnancy?" Jay said.

Aimee looked as though someone had punched her in the mouth.

"Why would you say that to her?" I asked, grabbing Aimee's hand.

"I can't have this baby," Aimee said. "I need to schedule an appointment right now. Today."

"Not being able to get Botox injections is hardly an acceptable reason to have an abortion," Chloe said.

"Okay, then. What about fillers?" Aimee asked, sounding like a wounded child.

"Jury's out," Jay said.

"How do you know all this stuff?" I asked.

"At one point, I was looking for a surrogate to carry Hidalgo's and my child," Jay said. "I looked through a million pictures. One came close, until I noticed the cankles. Ankles are so important in life, don't you think?"

"I'm about to break up with you again," I said.

"Please don't. Those were the worst three days in my history."

"I can't do this," Aimee said. "I was supposed to get the biggest role of my life."

The four of us sat in silence. You've gotten to know us—you know what it must take for us to sit in silence.

"Has it ever occurred to you," I finally said, "that there is no bigger role than being a mother?"

Aimee shut her eyes. I wanted to take her uterus from her, put it into a uterus-holder inside a terrarium, and feed the baby until he, or she, was ready to be born. It sounded like a story line out of *Nip/ Tuck: The Later Years*.

"Just yesterday, my sweet little Lorraine told me that God doesn't make mistakes," Chloe said. "If you believe in God, or fate, or universal energy . . . Aimee, this pregnancy, this baby, is meant to be."

Chloe to the rescue.

"God picked a selfish, middle-aged actress for this role?" Aimee said. "He really has a problem casting parts."

Jay kneeled down before Aimee and took her hands in his. "Nonsense, honey. I was a selfish bitch until I had Ralph, and then Ellie. You're going to be a great mom."

The light in my kitchen dimmed as clouds moved across the sun. Construction noise outside had ceased. All was silent, but for the light touch of a wind chime.

Aimee started to cry.

I watched as Jay wiped her tears, as Chloe hugged her and kissed her cheek. I watched as Aimee's grandfather flickered in and out, the grief that had been etched on his face replaced by something greater: *hope*.

To recover from his breakup with Hidalgo, Jay had taken on a new workout routine. The old workout routines of the eighties (coke), nineties (Ecstasy), the new millennium (HGH and 5-hour Energy Drink) wouldn't work anymore. I needed his advice, but the only way I could catch him was to pin him down at "the Stairs."

Starting before six A.M, dozens of scantily clad pros and non-pros (celebs and civilians), hot and wannabe-hot, singles and swingers, trudge up over 180 concrete stairs off 4th Street down to Entrada and up again for their daily workout, sweating, heaving, grunting, and smirking all the way. The bluffside views from the top of the stairs are breathtaking—you can see the wide Pacific, the Santa Monica Mountains, and the sumptuous homes of rich folk who have to contend with boot camps taking place on their front lawns.

I feel about these stairs the same way I feel about brussels sprouts; namely, they shouldn't exist.

"I have to have the talk with John," I said, my chest heaving as I climbed the narrow stairway, hoping one of these Stair Maniacs knew CPR, and would be willing to administer it on a person with a BMI of more than 2. Jay's perky ass served as my tracking device— as long as I kept it in view, I would live.

"How do you tell a dead husband you've slept with someone else?" Jay said, as he skipped a step. "It's just going to hurt his feelings."

"I'd feel dishonest if I don't," I said.

"So you're going to rub it in his face," Jay said, between deep breaths. "Wait. Does he have a face?"

"Yes. I can see his features. He's matured, now," I wheezed. "Is there an end to these stairs? Where's civilization?"

A shirtless Stair Master in running shorts came up behind me, breathing down my neck. He finally ran past me, spraying me with his bodily fluids. I prayed I wouldn't get sick.

"Like, only thirty more . . . This is so *Ghost and Mrs. Muir*. Remember the movie? I had such a crush on Rex Harrison. I've spent decades looking for my Henry Higgins."

I stopped, catching my breath, as a tight sixty-year-old woman skipped past me.

"What are you doing?" Jay said. "There's no stopping on the stairs! You can't hold up the line. It's like a Liverpool soccer match—you'll get trampled."

"Can we get back to me breaking up with my dead husband, please?" After glancing at my phone, I resumed my snail's pace. Tom had texted me, checking in, ending in a smiley face emoticon. Why did that make me feel giddy instead of creeped out?

"Don't tell John," Jay said. "It will only upset him. And who wants an angry ghost?"

"We still love each other," I said. "I wouldn't want him to find out some other way."

"You mean, like from another ghost?"

"Dead people love gossip," I sputtered. I saw daylight. We were almost at the top. I felt a kinship with the Chilean miners.

"Oh my God. What do you do if you're banging Tom and some dead person pops up?"

I took three more steps.

"I haven't gotten there yet." I shuddered. Was it possible? "I have to come up with a set of rules. Dead people are like toddlers—always testing the boundaries. They need discipline and structure."

We reached the top. I felt like vomiting. At least thirty people were standing around, stretching, waiting their turns. Both private expansive lawns and the grassy meridian on 4th were filled with people working out with weights, doing sit-ups, push-ups, and most of all, pick-ups.

"Let's go over there," Jay said, regarding the grassy area. "That's where all the mancandies are handing out their headshots."

As he kept talking, I followed him as best I could, on legs that felt like Jell-O.

"Hey, you could write your own line of books: *Raising Your Dead Person; All the Best People Are Dead; The Dead, They're Just Like Us, Only, You Know, Dead.*"

We crossed to where the Young and Sweaty were stretching their quads, and sat down in the grass. Jay started doing sit-ups, while I watched.

"Hold my ankles," Jay said. I complied. "Now. Words, please? What do you say to your dearly departed?"

He sat up, touched his elbows to his knees, and went back down again.

"Honey, I love you, but I'm only human—the live version," I said. "And I slept with someone else."

"Good luck with that," Jay said, as he repeated the sequence. "That certainly never worked for me."

"So, what do you say, instead?"

"Nothing," Jay said, lying back. "Sometimes, dishonesty is the best policy."

Brandon had asked to take a couple days off. He looked so distracted, I could hardly say no. What's harder than being a forty-something? How about being a twenty-something? Meanwhile, I was feeling more grounded, no longer convinced that anyone I loved might die at any minute. Ellie would keep breathing, even without me hovering over her. Jay could cross the street alone. Chloe might survive her husband, her kids, her paramedics, and her dogs. Aimee, well, Aimee, I wasn't so sure of. Was it time or Grief Sex that was calming me down?

I put Ellie to bed, poured a glass of pinot, and went outside, savoring the clean air, the darkening sky shadowed by clouds.

"Star light, star bright," I said. "The first star I see tonight . . ." I took a deep breath. "I wish I may, I wish I might . . ."

"Your wish is my command, fair lady," John said.

"I missed you." Because I did, I always would. People always talk about closure in death, in tragedy, in disappointment. Instead of closure, all I had was lingering.

"I was just thinking about the first meal I ever cooked for you," John said.

"Lemon chicken," I said.

"Lemon chicken?"

"Yeah . . . it was lemon chicken," I said. "Remember? Olive oil and lemon juice—"

"That wasn't our first meal."

"It was the first meal you cooked for me," I said.

"Was it?" he said. "I was thinking it was the turkey lasagna—"

"No, no, that came later."

"I think you're wrong, I have to say."

"You dipped that Bay Cities bread in the sauce, and shoved it in my mouth. Then we fucked for hours."

"Days."

"Weeks."

"Years."

"Years," I said quietly. Tell him, I thought, *tell him tell him tell him.*

"I wish I could hold you," he said.

"Oh, John."

"What do you want to tell me?" John asked. "There's something wrong. I mean, it's all wrong, but there's another layer of wrong."

"John, I did something . . ."

"Hannah? Are you breaking up with me?"

"No," I said. "But hey, you're dead. You're not exactly a great catch."

"I figured," John said. "Oh God. I knew this would happen eventually—"

"Do you want to know about it?"

"Not really," John said. "Was he any good?"

"John—"

"C'mon, tell me," John said. "I've got to know."

"Jesus," I grumbled.

"I met him, you know—Jesus, I mean," John said. "Not shy that one. You know what? I don't want to hear the details about your liaison—about his penis size, or anything."

Beat.

"I said, please don't tell me the size of his penis," John said.

"I'm not discussing penises with you," I said.

"Are you in love?" John asked.

"No." I wasn't in love. Not yet. I could see the possibility, though, shimmering like a coin at the bottom of a fountain.

"Good. That I got over him. I can't still make you come eight times a night, I mean, with Isaac Hayes's help, but I still have your heart."

"John," I said, "someday you're going to have to share it."

"But I can keep a piece of it. Forever."

"Yes."

"Like if your heart's a pie, I get a nice big piece, right?"

"The biggest piece, next to Ellie's."

"Hannah?" John said.

"Average. He was average-sized, okay?"

"Ha! I knew it!"

"For God's sake," I said. "You'd think dying would make you a bit more mature!"

"He's average he's average he's average!" John said, and laughed. I laughed with him.

21

Valentime's Day

As Mr. Barry White once said, "Happy Valentime's, my dear." I woke up, remembering how John loved saying that to me, in his best (which was *the* worst) Mr. White timbre.

Tom had asked me to go to dinner at that new Italian restaurant on 26th. Even though we'd slept together a few times since that fateful tree-hugging morning, I was still surprised that he'd asked me out for Valentine's.

"You do know that Tuesday night is Valentine's," I'd said to him.

"Hannah, I know," he'd answered. "I'll pick you up at eight."

The phone in my bedroom rang, just as I was thinking about what dress to wear that night (with Jay's approval), and I picked up.

"Happy Valentine's Day!" Jay said, too eagerly. This could only mean trouble. Jay hated to be alone on Valentine's Day.

"Happy V-Day," I said. "Don't make me do brunch."

"Never," he said, "we're going Rollerblading. It's the perfect day for it."

"Rollerblading?" I asked. "Should I bring my leg warmers and tube top?"

"Chloe's in, since Billy's still away at boot camp. She'll celebrate Valentine's later, with a nine-one-one call. Anyway, she promised not to bring the dogs. See you at Ray's on the boardwalk in an hour."

An hour later, there was Jay, Chloe, the dogs she promised not to bring, and me, looking like a Heffalump on wheels. Dozens of happy couples had the same idea as us, judging from the crowded bike path. I had rolled, stopped, rolled, stopped about five feet when Dee Dee Pickler, holding hands with a much older man, hurtled toward us on Rollerblades, heading north toward Malibu. Or the nearest Houston's.

"Hi, kids!" Dee Dee said, as she rolled past us, then stopped.

"Wow," I said to Jay. "He's old."

"Which side was he on in the Spanish Civil War?" Jay said.

"I'm so glad I ran into you," Dee Dee said.

"Who's that?" I asked. The man had let go of her hand, and was on his knees, wheezing.

"He's cute, right?" Dee Dee said. "I thought I'd try something different."

"Where'd you find him?" Jay asked. "The cemetery?"

"Aren't you a clever boy?" Dee Dee asked. "How did you know?"

"You found him where?" Chloe asked, rolling up on the conversation. Chloe had been a champion ice skater in junior high. She can do tricks on skates. I don't hate her for this, but sometimes I do pray to the God of Tripping and Falling on Your Ass.

"I'm not telling you," Dee Dee said. "You're single-adjacent. You'll try to horn in on my action, you little minx."

"I must hear this," I said. *"Please."*

"Okay. You know who the wealthiest five percent of the country are?" Dee Dee asked, beaming. "I can't believe no one's ever figured this out!"

"Who?"

"Widowers," she said. "And widows—though I'm not prepared to go there. I hung out at the cemetery near some fresh grave sites, and *voilà,*" Dee Dee said. "I got myself a prize. Goodbye SoMo, hello Bel Air Country Club! He's a lifetime member, holla!"

"I'm not sure what I'm most offended by," Jay said, "the grave-robbing thing or the fact that you just said 'holla' without irony."

"Irony would have changed everything," I agreed.

"Who cares?" Dee Dee said. "I'm going to be spending the rest of my life drowning in Arnold Palmers and tennis pro cock."

"I never thought I'd say this," Jay muttered, "but I could have done without that cock visual."

"Oh, Hannah, I forgot to tell you," Dee Dee said. "The Turk is out of the picture."

"What do you mean?"

"I had an outside offer. Someone outbid him," she said. "I found the Turk a lovingly restored Spanish Colonial built in the twenties. He's tearing it down next week."

"Who outbid him?" I asked.

"I can't tell you," Dee Dee said. "He made me promise to keep it a secret. NoMo Widower must really like you. People are so nutty, huh?"

Dee Dee's paramour keeled forward and collapsed onto the boardwalk. Bicyclists and Rollerbladers gathered around him. Someone shouted for a lifeguard.

"Let me take care of this—we'll talk later. Remember, don't say a word," Dee Dee said, then turned to the crowd. "Move over! If he's alive, he's mine!"

I was stunned. "Tom is buying my house? What am I supposed to think?"

"How do you feel?" Jay asked.

"Weird," I said.

"Look," Jay said, "maybe Tom's helping out, in his own awkward heterosexual way. Let's not jump to conclusions."

"Ask him, Hannah," Chloe said. "Maybe there's an explanation. It is Valentine's Day."

I rushed into the bank still wearing my biker's helmet, making a bee-line for Tom's office. He was in a suit at his desk, a pile of papers in front of him. A middle-aged woman (my age minus self-absorption) was seated to the side, taking notes.

"Hannah?" Tom said. "What's up?" He looked happy, although surprised, to see me.

"Why did you make an offer on my house?" I asked.

"Hi . . . Elsie, can you leave me and Mrs. Bernal alone for a moment?" Tom asked.

Elsie sized me up, probably to see how dangerous I was.

"Don't worry," I told her. "I'm not packing heat, just self-righteous indignation."

Elsie took her notepad and left. Tom turned to me. "It's not what you think," he said.

"What am I thinking?" I asked. I wanted to believe him. After all, he did cut a dashing figure in his suit. I suppressed the urge to pull him closer by his tie.

"I was going to tell you tonight, at dinner," Tom said. "It was supposed to be a surprise. I did make an offer on your house. I outbid the Turk—now you have me saying 'the Turk'—Mr. Mansour, so that you could keep your house. I know how much you love it, Hannah. You tied yourself to a tree, for God's sake."

"You made an offer so I could stay at Casa Sugar?"

"Yes," Tom said, sitting back in his chair, clasping his hands behind his head.

"How exactly does this work?" I asked. "You're not just . . . giving me my house. I mean, I would never expect that . . . I didn't expect any of this, anything that's happened in the last six months—"

"I buy your house, and you pay me rent."

"I pay you rent," I said, repeating. "Oh. So you're my landlord?"

"You can stay as long as you like," Tom said. "I get the tax benefits of ownership, and you don't have to move. I see it as a win-win for both of us."

"I don't know what to say," I said.

"I really wanted to do you this favor," Tom said.

"Thanks for the favor," I said. "Now, can you take the favor knife out of my back? I'm sorry, but this just feels so weird to me, Tom. What if you decide one day that you don't like me?"

"Wait. You're not . . . turning me down? You want to lose your house?" Tom said, bristling. "Because that's what's going to happen."

"I know what's going to happen. The cardboard boxes scattered around my house remind me every minute of every hour of every day," I said. "What I needed was to refinance."

"I'm sorry," he said, "you're too much of a risk."

I felt like I'd been slapped.

"You are, too," I said. "Happy Valentine's Day."

I walked out, my dignity and bike helmet still intact.

Well, my dignity not so much.

When apartment-hunting in SaMo, there's only one place to go: Westside Rentals. This business has the scariest mascot since the San Diego Chicken. Rental Man is an oiled-up, shirtless muscle-head who dances and preens on the sidewalk outside their Wilshire offices. He gives Rip Torn's mug shot a run for its peanuttiness.

In my former life, when I had a job, a husband with a job, and dropped a mint at Whole Foods for veggie sushi, I'd drive past Rental Man and thank God I'd never have to use Westside Rentals; Dancing Bluto scared the bejesus out of me.

Hi, hubris! Here I was, with Aimee, as Dancing Bluto crazily grinned at me and reached out . . . opening the door to the offices.

"Thank you, spray-tanned, Axe-wearing gentleman," I said. He nodded and grinned maniacally as I scooted past.

I stood in line with the rest of rent-paying humanity, and paid for my list of rentals. Basically, I was searching for the same apartment I had when I was just out of college.

"You're an idiot," Aimee said, back in the kitchen at Casa Sugar, as I went over the rental list. She was drinking chamomile tea, with not a splash of vodka. This was news, among my friends. "Did you even find out what the Biking Banker was going to charge you?"

"No."

"You should have found out before you turned him down," Aimee said.

"I don't want to talk about it," I said. "What about a shared studio with a nightclub entertainer?"

"Stripper."

" 'Must have compatible work hours,' it says," I said. "And must be open to visitors."

"Hooker."

"Yes, indeedy," I said. "How much do you think she makes?"

"No, Hannah," Aimee said, "you cannot 'hook.' "

"Does it say 'she'?" Jay walked in, carrying a bag of groceries from Trader Joe's. "Let's not jump to conclusions." My BlackBerry buzzed. I looked at the tiny screen: Dee Dee Pickler. It could only be bad news—so, why not? I answered.

"Hannah?" Dee Dee said. "I have bad news and good news."

"I'll take the good news," I said.

"The good news is, you still have a buyer. Thank God, because I already spent my commission. Hey, ever have plastic surgery in Uruguay?"

"Not lately. Don't you go to Brazil for that kind of thing?"

"Not since Tameka almost died, girrrrrrl . . ."

"What are you calling about, Dee Dee?"

"The Turk is back on, and he's not even mad," Dee Dee said. "Of course, I had to work my magic. Hey, what'd you say to the Widower? He was pretty shaken up."

"Nothing," I said. "It's not important."

"He's cute and has a job—I wouldn't look that gift WWB in the mouth, if I were you."

"WWB?"

"Widower With Benefits. Or, you know, FLF. Father I'd like to Fu—"

"Bye, Dee Dee—"

"Escrow's moving fast. Do you need help packing?"

"No, thanks."

"Thank God. I don't even help my kid pack for camp. I have no interest, sorry. That's Dee Dee Time."

I hung up on her. This was Hannah Time.

22

Saving Manny's Privates

"Why are there so many boxes, Mommy?" Ellie asked one night. I'd unfortunately missed my "bad news window" before we bought out Box Brothers.

"You know what, honey? We're going to be moving soon. Isn't that exciting?"

"No."

"Mommy has to sell the house. We're going to find someplace really cozy."

"But we're not going to live here?"

"No, we're not."

"Who's going to live here?"

"That's hard to say, honey. There might not even be a Casa Sugar after we move out."

"Where's she going?"

Casa Sugar was a she. A living being that held all of my happiest memories. *Can I cry Uncle now, God?*

"We're moving to a very nice place."

"Uncle Jay's house?"

"No, not Uncle Jay's house."

"Aunt Chloe's house?"

"No, not Aunt Chloe's house." If my life were a Lifetime movie, right now, at rock bottom, a miracle would occur. This is assuming

I'm being played by the incomparable Heather Locklear. But, assuming I'm not Heather Locklear, I won't be swept off my feet by a Doctors Without Borders surgeon/fighter pilot/media heir. It's unlikely I'll discover a dear departed aunt owned Walmart. I don't anticipate a tax break. Or even coupons I can use.

I put a distressed Ellie to bed. I ached with exhaustion.

"Hannah."

The sight of Brandon, dressed in a suit jacket and jeans, made me jump.

"You're going out?" I asked. "You look nice." I wondered about his girlfriend and his sudden desire to become an adult. He was so young, yet so serious.

"I'm heading to the Huntley," he said, "for that real estate networking conference."

"Oh, okay," I said, "I understand. Have a good time . . . networking."

"Hannah?" Brandon said. "You need me tonight?"

"Forgive me, I'm tired," I said. "Go, have fun."

I waved him off. I had a full night of packing boxes and pinot ahead of me.

Jay called a few minutes after Brandon left. "What are you doing?"

"Packing."

"Move in with me."

"I keep telling you no."

"And I keep asking you why not."

"You'd lose your mind in approximately eight minutes."

"Not if you didn't touch anything, ever. What about moving in with Chloe?"

"Too busy with stray dogs and stray kids, a crazy husband, and hot paramedics."

"Right," Jay said. "I won't even suggest—"

"Not Aimee, please," I said. "You know better. I'm going, baby. I'm tired."

"Love you," Jay said.

"Love you, more," I said. Twenty minutes later, Jay and Chloe appeared at my front door, holding a bottle of wine and a grocery bag from Bay Cities.

"What are you doing? What's this?" I asked, as they invaded my living room.

"Packing-slash-Pity Party!" Jay said. "You really think we'd leave you alone to pack?"

"Bay Cities," I said. "You shouldn't have. I don't mean that. Of course you should."

I used to worry about eating their Italian loaves. Overdoing the carbs; once, long ago, I had considered that a problem. *Oh, Pre-Widowhood Hannah! You're so naïve! I loves ya!*

"The bread, the cheese, the butter, the wine," Jay said. "The gay. What more could you possibly need?"

"And me, the packing nazi," Chloe said.

"I love you guys," I said, hugging and kissing them with wet, wine-soaked kisses.

"Mother's been at the spigot," Jay said, as we walked into the kitchen. "Where's Manny?"

"Brandon's at a real estate networking thingie," I said, as I tore into the warm bread, "at the Huntley."

"At the where?" Jay asked, looking greatly alarmed.

"The Huntley."

"And who do you think is running a real estate conference," Jay asked, "at nine o'clock on a Thursday night at the Huntley?"

"I don't know," I said, feeling stupid. "I didn't think about it."

"You know what they call the Huntley on a Thursday night, do you not?" Jay asked.

"The Cuntley," I said, realizing. "Oh my God."

"It's the SMCA," Jay said. "It's a Coyote Den!"

"What should we do?" Chloe asked. "Should I get my shotgun? It's out in the car."

"Wait. Get your what?" I froze.

"Billy gave me the shotgun before he left. For protection."

"Against what?" I asked. "Fog? Yoga mats? Pressed juice?"

"After Bakasana disappeared, I got paranoid about coyotes,"

Chloe said. "I'm so scared that one of them is going to come after my other dogs. I would just shoot it in the air, of course, to scare them off."

Jay and I exchanged a look. I had never told her about my Bakasana vision. And my feeling about who I believed was responsible for his demise. But now was not the time.

"Chloe, whatever you do," I said, "do not even think of using that gun. You're the NoMoMama—it's the number one rule of parenting—no guns. We'll get rid of it tomorrow."

"We're wasting precious time, people," Jay said.

"Right," I said. "We have to go. Chloe, will you stay here? Ellie's asleep."

"I'll be locked and loaded," Chloe said with a wink.

Jay and I jumped in his MINI Cooper and careened down Montana Avenue. When I say "careen," I mean, we stood in traffic behind NoMoMorons who couldn't decide whether they should park, walk, whine, or go home.

"The SMCA knows every inch of the Huntley," Jay said, as he honked. "Those bitches know every corridor, suite, back room, bed post, bathroom floor tile. God, they're glorious."

"I can't believe I just let him go," I said. "He's like my son, and I watched him march straight into the lions' den."

"Be prepared," Jay said. "There may be nothing left of him, except maybe a dimple. We must stay strong. If we do save him, he may be a shadow of the Brandon we know and love and want to sleep with."

Jay slammed on the gas pedal and we sped around a BMW.

"Go, boy," I said, holding on to the dashboard.

"We've got to save our child," Jay said. "And this may be my only chance to see Luke Wilson naked, while it's still worth it."

We parked in front of the Huntley, sneaked past valet, and took the elevators up to the penthouse. We exited into a large, white, brightly lit nightclub with a long Plexiglas bar in the middle. The place was crammed full of people, but all I saw were teeth, hair, and boobs—and that was just the men. Loud, electronic music smuggled in from the Eastern Bloc in the early eighties assaulted our tender ears.

"I thought this music went down with the Berlin Wall," I said. I hadn't changed my daytime depression outfit, which hardly went unnoticed by the bust-by-Monsanto hostess.

"We're looking for a boy," Jay said breathlessly to the bosomy hostess. "He was here for a real estate conference."

"At this hour? Who does real estate conferences?" she said, making me feel old and unhip. I think that covers the insecurity bases. Wait, wait—I forgot poor. I felt poor, too.

"He's very tall, very handsome," I said. "Like a son to me, I feel terrible."

"Straight as six o'clock. Sadly," Jay added.

"That guy—the giant blonde?" she said. "He left."

"Did he leave with anyone?" Jay asked.

"I'm not supposed to tell you that but since she's such a bitch— he was with Dee Dee Pickler."

"Where'd they go?" Jay said.

"That's none of my business," she said, suddenly prim.

Jay snapped his fingers. "It just came to me. Who you look like," he said to the hostess. "Did anyone ever tell you you're the spitting image of a Kardashian sister?"

"Seriously?" she asked, her face lighting up.

"The pretty one," I added, "not the manly one, the Mandashian."

"Do you have a card?" Jay asked. "You know, you could make big money being a Fauxdashian."

"Take my number," she said. "I'd die to do that!"

Jay whipped out his iPhone, and the girl gave him her number . . . then added on three more.

"That's too many," he said.

"That's the room," the Fauxdashian said with a wink.

"Fabulous," Jay said. "Who does your cheeks, by the way?"

* * *

We came off the elevators and hit the fifth floor running—in the wrong direction.

"Turn it around," Jay yelled.

Finally, we found 526.

"Times are tough," Jay said. "I expected a higher floor."

"What do we do now?" I said. "We can't just knock."

Jay pressed his ear to the door.

"Do you hear anything?" I asked. "Don't answer that."

"Muffled sound, murmuring. Now a humming sound. A click. More murmuring." Jay knocked on the door. "Room service," he announced.

"I feel like we're in a Martin Lawrence movie," I said.

"Room service," Jay repeated, then whispered, "I'm Martin and you're the lame white guy."

The door opened. Dee Dee was standing there, in lingerie. "You've got the limes and the ice cubes?" she said, and then, "You can't have him."

"Step aside, Dee Dee," I said.

"He's mine. He's mine and I want to keep him."

Jay pushed the door open and we slipped in. Brandon was tied to the bed wearing boxer shorts. He giggled.

"Brandon," I said, bending over him. "Are you okay?"

He snorted.

"Oh, snap," Jay said. "Why's he still in his shorts?"

"I like to use my teeth," Dee Dee said. "It's why humans have incisors."

"I never thought of that," Jay said. "Talk about taking care of all your real estate needs."

"You should be ashamed of yourself, Dee Dee," I said. "I think he's drugged or something. How could you do this to this sweet, innocent boy?"

"Oh, please." Dee Dee rolled her eyes. "You're such a Girl Scout." She looked at Jay. "Don't you ever get bored of this one?"

"Hannah?" Jay asked. "Do you mean Hannah?" I felt like he was stalling for time.

"You should roll with my girls," Dee Dee told him. "We know

how to have a good time. Tijuana Cipro is so cheap nowadays. Plus, we have our own bail bondsman."

"Tempting," Jay said, "but I'll stick with the Girl Scout."

"Jay," I said, "undo him, please."

"Girl, you know your way around a slipknot," Jay said to Dee Dee, staring at Brandon.

"Jay! Get going! What are you doing?" I said.

"Debating," Jay said, before he finally started in on the knots. "Is this the same room you took Luke Wilson's manhood in?"

"Well." Dee Dee tilted her head. "Maybe it was the Unknown Wilson . . . It was a Wilson, for sure. He wore Birkenstocks and had breath like damp tree bark."

"That's a Wilson," Jay said.

"You know what?" Dee Dee said, as she went for the hotel phone. "Wait just a hairy minute. You can't just barge in here and take my party favor. Hello, security?"

Jay rushed at the phone, slapping the receiver to the floor.

"Guess who I saw at the bar?" Jay said. "Wait. Maybe I shouldn't tell you. You're not ready for this. You're too . . . young and inexperienced."

Dee Dee's face brightened. "Who?"

"The big 'O,'" Jay said. "Owen."

"Oh my God," she said, checking her phone. "But I haven't even gotten a text. How is that possible?"

"No one else recognized him. He was in the corner. Wearing a baseball cap and Ray-Bans, the official celeb uniform. Guess who he was talking to?"

"I can't! Who?" Dee Dee said.

"John Mayer."

"Sexual Napalm John Mayer?" Dee Dee asked. She sat back on the bed and started hyperventilating.

Brandon giggled. I was afraid he might throw up on me.

"I'm not up for this," Dee Dee said, through short breaths. "I'm not ready. I talk a good game and all, but I'm just a sexy, middle-class white lady trying to get her piece of the American Dream."

She lay back on the bed, and put her hand on her stomach. "I'm feeling very *Eat, Pray, Love* right now," she said.

"I just can't be a party to that," I said.

"We're leaving," Jay said. "I'll send the *Real Housewives* crew up to tape this for a future episode."

"Send up a bottle," Dee Dee said. "I don't care what kind. I need to curl up with something."

Hurrying, Jay and I got Brandon halfway dressed and quickly out of that depraved den of real estate iniquity before Dee Dee could change her mind.

By the time we reached the car, Jay and I were both sweating from carrying a big load of man between us.

Stuffed in the MINI Cooper's backseat, Brandon said, "Dee Dee was supposed to give me advice. She didn't give me advice."

"She was going to give you a lot more than that, my young friend," Jay said. "We're a good ten years away from a cure for that kind of advice."

"My head hurts," Brandon said. "It's ouchie."

We sped toward Casa Sugar. Chloe greeted us at the door as we dragged Brandon up the steps.

"Oh, poor Brandon," Chloe said. "Aimee's here. I'll get my tree tea oil. That'll wake him up."

"Brandy!" Aimee said, as she emerged from the bathroom. She threw her arms around him.

"Brandy?" Jay asked. "Isn't she a fine girl?"

"Are you okay, baby boo?" Aimee said, showering Brandon with kisses. "I was so worried."

"Baby boo's okay, baby loo," Brandon said.

"Oh my God," I said. "Is this really happening?"

"Baby talk," Jay said. "Endearing or repulsive? I can't decide."

"I was going to tell you," Chloe said, as Aimee wrapped herself around Brandon, kissing his ear.

"I thought I was going to lose you," Aimee cooed in the woozy young man's ear.

"I'd never let you lose me," he slurred, manfully—or, boyishly.

"I'll never let you go," she gasped as she maneuvered him to the couch.

"I'll never let you let me go," he said as they sat down, and then lay his head in Aimee's lap.

"That's it," Jay said, grabbing Brandon's hand. "He's going back to Dee Dee."

"Brandon is the father of my baby," Aimee said, rubbing his golden-haired head.

"What? Our little Brandon?" Jay asked. "They grow up so fast!"

"When?" I asked. "How? I mean . . . Wait, don't tell me."

"Christmastime," Aimee said, rubbing Brandon's head. "He was like a gift, just waiting to be unwrapped."

"And I'm the incurable romantic?" Jay asked.

"I've never seen you look so happy, Aimee," I said. "It's sweet, in a somewhat alarming way."

"Thank you," Aimee said. "You know, Hannah, if you'd never talked to my grandfather, I don't think I would ever have been open to love. But I'm ready now."

Jay put his arm around me. We all had tears in our eyes.

Brandon burped, then fell back asleep.

There was a knock at the front door.

"Dee Dee," Jay whispered, in fear.

"Don't they know NoMo is closed?" I looked at Aimee. "Take the boy in the back." I felt like a frontier mother.

"Should I get my gun?" Chloe asked, too eagerly.

"No!" Jay and I said at once.

I opened the door, as Aimee shuffled Brandon back into his room. A woman with gray hair and glasses—who couldn't seem more innocuous if she had taken Method classes—was standing there, wearing black flats, khaki pants, and a white blouse.

"Are you Hannah Marsh?" the woman asked. She had a soft voice, like someone who'd spent a lot of time at the library. Or who'd had their vocal cords cut because they barked too much.

"Yes. The house has been sold. And, it's late—"

"I need to talk to you," she said, her voice rising. "It's about my mother."

"Do I know you?" I asked.

"No. We've never met."

"Then what is it about your mother?"

"She's dead," the woman said.

"Aren't we all, honey?" Jay said, escorting her inside. "I've never been so tired in my life."

23

Raising the Dead

(It Helps if You Are a Good Listener.)

The woman looked around the living room. "I heard you talk to dead people," she said. "Is that true?"

"No," I said.

"Yes," Jay said, "constantly. It's like a dead people *telenovela* in here."

"They talk to me," I said. "It's nothing I have control over. Trust me."

"I need to contact my mother," she said, her voice cracking. "She died a few months ago but it feels like yesterday. I know it might sound strange, but I wake up and I listen for her shuffling around in her slippers on the kitchen floor. And the cats don't know what to do with themselves. They just look at me with their big kitty eyes, wondering when Nana's coming home. Wondering what I did with her. They were her babies, you know. She loved them so . . ."

She started crying. Any other house, people would look at her like she's insane. In this house, she was family.

"My dogs would be lost without me," Chloe said, now on the verge of tears, herself. "They'd be running around, 'Where's Mama? Where's Mama Chloe?' I can just see their little faces . . ."

I wondered how long I would be listening for John's footsteps, his soft thud on the wood floors. His humming. Then, I realized . . . did I listen anymore?

Time heals all wounds, even the ones that seem like they will bleed forever. How screwed up is that?

"What's your name, sweetheart?" Jay asked.

"Rachel," she said, turning to me. "I heard about you. I was at the coffee shop on 17th. Some women in tennis skirts were talking about you. They said your house was for sale. That you had a little girl. And that you were . . . um . . . not well."

"Not well, or batshit crazy?" Jay asked.

"The second one," Rachel admitted.

"NoMo is like *Gossip Girls* for the perimenopausal," I said.

"Is it true? Can you contact my mother?" Rachel asked. "Please?"

I hesitated. First of all, I wasn't sure I could do it. Second, I wasn't sure I wanted to.

"I just want to be normal," I said. I'd felt abnormal long enough. Ellie and I needed normalcy more than we needed money, more than we needed Casa Sugar. We could do normal in an apartment next to the Santa Monica Freeway. *Fuck it.*

"I'm begging you," Rachel said.

"I don't conjure up people," I said. "They appear. Or they don't."

"Usually at inopportune moments," Chloe said, then whispered, "like in the bathroom."

"Or the gyno's office," Jay said.

"Or the V-Steam," I said.

"Please, Hannah," Rachel said.

"I'm not good with begging," Jay said. "I cave every time. *Every. Time.* Hannah?"

"I'll try," I said.

"She's no Jennifer Love Hewitt," Jay cautioned, putting his hand on Rachel's shoulder, "but then, who is?"

"Lend an ear, Hannah," Chloe said, turning to Rachel. "Your mother sounds wonderful. Why are all the best people dead?"

* * *

The sky was darkening as Rachel and I sat in my chairs under the avocado tree. I fully immersed myself in the moment, willing the memories to sink into my marrow, so that someday, when I looked out from my new apartment window and saw, say, a Dumpster . . . I'd remember, at my deepest core, this avocado tree in the moonlight. The stars above its branches.

I took a deep breath.

"What's your mother's name, Rachel?" I asked, closing my eyes.

"Beatrice," she said.

"Beatrice," I repeated her name, like a mantra. I hoped I could help Rachel contact her mother. Wouldn't that be a mitzvah? "Beatrice," I called.

I heard Rachel sigh. That sigh sounded like it had taken years to come out.

Remember to breathe, I said to myself. Breathing is as important as red velvet cream cheese cupcake icing. *Maybe. Close.* "Beatrice," I repeated. I felt nervous. I wanted to help. And if I managed to contact Rachel's sweet old cat-loving mom, I would no longer be the neighborhood crazy; the mad movers could take back their mantle.

I was looking to dead people for validation. *How's that for a therapy topic?*

"Bea—"

"What? What do you want?" an annoyed voice said. Like I had awakened her from a nap . . . the big nap, I guess.

I opened my eyes.

"Did you hear that?" I asked. I looked to the sky. That voice didn't sound like it belonged to anyone's mother.

"I think I got the wrong Beatrice," I said to Rachel.

"What is it?" the gravelly voice asked. "Why are you bugging me?"

Rachel stared up at the sky, eyes anxious, wanting.

"Are you Beatrice Richards?"

"Yes, what?" I couldn't see her—her demise was too fresh.

"The Beatrice Richards whose daughter is Rachel?"

"Oy. Yes. What do you want?"

"Can you just confirm that with me? I'm sorry, I've got to get this right." I was still worried I had the wrong person—or spirit.

"What're you, Citibank? I don't need to prove anything to you. I'm dead!"

"Please. Just. Something?"

"Okay." I heard Dead Beatrice sigh. "Rachel has an extra toe on her left foot."

"Whoa—a what?" I asked.

"It's not my fault. Her father was a genetic freak."

"Rachel," I said, as gently as I could. "Do you have an extra toe on your left foot?"

Even in the moonlight, I saw her face pale.

"No one knows," Rachel whispered. "I've never been able to wear flip-flops—or walk barefoot in the sand—or do sports in high school. I was too ashamed."

"It could come in handy for rock climbing," I said, trying to help.

"I died so I could get away from her," Beatrice said. "Let me tell you—Rachel's a whiner, always has been. And look at her. I would die if I had those thighs. I did die! She'd be pretty without the bulk. I told her all the time, did she listen to me . . . no one would look at her—"

I couldn't shut Beatrice up. Meanwhile, Rachel was waiting, delicate hands trembling in her lap. I wondered if she'd ever had a boyfriend, ever had someone other than her mother show her what love is. *And what it's not.*

"Is she talking?" Rachel whispered.

"Yes," I said, as Beatrice continued her dead mom diatribe. "She wants you to know . . ."

"From the time she was born, she was nothing but a burden— a burden, I tell you! She cried day and night, night and day, that's why her father left—"

"Shush!" I said out loud.

"What?" Rachel asked. "What's wrong?"

"Did you just shush me, young lady? A dead woman? Is there no respect at all?"

"Your mothe"—I looked into Rachel's eyes— "Your mom . . ."

"Yes?" Rachel asked.

"Her hairstyle makes her look like a diner waitress, I tell her constantly—"

"Misses you terribly," I lied.

"She does?" Rachel asked. Her face opened up. Tears streamed down her cheeks.

"Your mother loves you," I said. "Her greatest wish is that she could have had one more day with her daughter."

"Really?" Rachel asked, brow wrinkling.

"She says you look pretty, Rachel," I said. *I was on a roll.* "But you could put on a little weight."

Rachel stopped crying. "That's not my mom. You're lying to me."

"Death changes a person," I said, perhaps unconvincingly.

"Not that much," Rachel said. "Tell me the truth. What did she say?"

I took a deep breath. "She says you're a whiner, you have a weight problem, and bad hair."

Rachel started crying again. "Oh, Mommy," she said to the sky, "I miss you so much!"

I walked Rachel through the house to the front door.

"So how'd our little reunion go?" Jay asked from the living room couch. He was thumbing through an old copy of *Martha Stewart Living*. The house was silent. "Chloe had to get back home—she has a homestead to protect."

"Our session was incredible," Rachel said. "I feel so much better. How much do I owe you?"

"Owe me?" I asked.

"What's your fee?" She reached into her fanny pack and took three hundred-dollar bills from her wallet. She pushed them into my hand.

"I can't accept this," I said.

"Okay, okay. I'll give you five," Rachel said. "Five hundred must be the going rate." She reached back into her fanny pack, with its endless amounts of hundred-dollar bills.

"Please, I don't want your money," I said.

"Yes, she does," Jay said, snapping the bills out of my hand. "And more than that, I want her to have the money."

"You're a good friend," Rachel said.

"The best. Tell all your friends about NoMo's own Miss Cleo, here," Jay said. Rachel looked confused. "I mean, when you get some friends. And take care of your pussies."

We watched Rachel get into her 1970s Mercedes convertible. I'd see those old cars parked outside aging, run-down houses in NoMo, and always wonder about who lived inside. Someone who liked nice things, once upon a time.

"Mother, we've just found you a new gig," Jay said to me, as she drove off. "I have the business card in my head. Ready?"

I looked up into his eyes.

"The Happy Medium," Jay said.

"There are crazier ways to make money, I suppose."

"Not really," he said, putting his long, muscular arm around me, "but who gives a frock, sweetheart?"

That night, under the avocado tree, I consulted with Trish. I call her O.G., for Original Ghost. We hadn't spoken for a while, but like old friends, we fell right back into a rhythm.

"Trish, what do you think? Am I disrespecting the dead by charging for hookups?"

"We're dead, who cares? I don't hear AT&T asking that question."

"I want a real answer, before I turn this place into the Starbucks of the Netherworld."

"*Zeiguseunt,*" she said. "It is what it is. Don't you worry your pretty little head. It's meant to be. You worry too much, you know that?"

I smiled. "I have plenty of reasons to worry."

She laughed, then waved and drifted away. For the first time in months, I felt something bubbling up inside me. Happiness. *Or perhaps acid reflux.*

* * *

Jay and I went to a stationery store with a sweet, sticky name in the Brentwood Country Mart to select business cards. I almost needed a stretcher to carry me out.

"Eight hundred dollars for fifty," said the clerk with the shiny ponytail and private school education. "They're two-ply," she added, with a wink.

"Two-ply?" I asked. "Like toilet paper?"

"It's the weight," Jay whispered. "Feel the weight," he said, as though handling a Ming vase.

"No, thanks," I said. "I fly one-ply."

A week later, Aimee, Chloe, and Jay presented me with a small, chocolate-colored box, tied with a light blue ribbon.

"Open it," Jay said.

I held it in my hand. "Is it a very, very small man?"

"Open it," Chloe said. I untied the ribbon, and lifted the top of the box. Inside were perfectly embossed business cards on the best stock.

The Happy Medium, 310/555-2354

They had a drawing of a tree on the side. My avocado tree.

"Is this . . . This isn't two-ply, is it?" I asked, looking into their eager little faces.

"We just couldn't do the one-ply," Jay said, beaming.

"One-ply is for amateurs," Aimee said. "You're a professional."

"One client does not a professional make," I said. "I love it. Aimee, you drew the tree? It's . . . breathtaking."

"That old shrub? It's nothing," Aimee said. "It's just simple, elegant, and timeless. Like us."

"I'm elegant, Aimee's timeless, by design, and our little Chloe is simple," Jay said.

Spring arrived, and business was booming. Lines formed outside Casa Sugar's front door. NoMos would try cutting to the front by offering more cash or by displaying a sudden interest in me as a human being. However, the khaki-shorted SoMos held their ground.

"Holy dead people mother lode," Jay said, as he'd escort a lulu-lemon-wearing, Brazilian-blow-dried, Vuitton-and-Vicodin-addicted NoMo to the back of the line. "Dead is the new black."

Everyone had issues with the dead—and I mean everyone.

"I have to speak to my brother. He knows where my mom has her safe-deposit box."

"My sixth-grade teacher. She believed I could be anything. I never said goodbye to her."

"I'll never forget Oscar," said a man with gray hair and a sad smile.

Because he was attractive, had a penis, and wore Italian shoes, Jay paid more attention to him than the NoMo and SoMo momsters.

"Oscar?" Jay asked.

"My childhood dog," the man said. While waiting politely in line, he showed Jay a picture in his wallet of a Scottie.

"Do you want to get married?" Jay asked.

"Jay," Aimee said, making her way down the line, clipboard in her hand, jotting down names, "this is not a groom pool. Keep this line moving." She'd started waddling just recently, even though she was only about four months pregnant. I call it Method Waddling.

"This medium stuff is wiping me out," I told Chloe, when she came out back with a glass of iced tea and lemon cookies. "I'm exhausted."

"You have to pace yourself," she said.

"I miss funemployment," I said.

"Lilo just called," Jay said, heading outside, phone in hand. "She'll be here any minute. The place is crawling with paparazzi. If you channel Brittany Murphy, you better tell me what the hell happened to my girl. *Love her.*"

Jay had taken control of our burgeoning business, herding the grieving masses into my tiny living room and soothing their spirits with madeleines, peppermint tea, and fashion tips.

"You'll have to start booking appointments in advance," he said. "And by you, I mean, me. And by me, I mean commission."

"You've already helped me so much," I said. "I can't ask you to do more."

"You can if you're paying me," Jay said, "which you're going to start doing after you pay off your taxes and mortgage payments. Which, at this point, is about a week away."

I'd been doing so many readings, all paid in cash or check. I hadn't kept track of the total. That was Jay's job. All he said to me after a few days was that we were in "Kenneth Cole territory."

We had moved up, apparently, to "Louboutin studded moccasin territory."

"What time is it?" I asked.

Jay checked his watch, which he wore solely for fashion reasons.

"I think it's two—"

"Is it two, or not?"

"Well, my watch is always fast. I think."

"Didn't that watch cost—"

"Yes," he said. "But the more expensive the watch, the worse it tells time. Everyone knows that."

"I'd better pick up Ellie."

"Brandon's got her—he's taking her for a haircut afterward."

"A haircut?" I asked. "But I just took her a week ago, to Super-cuts."

"Yeah," Jay said, shaking his head. "No. That didn't work for me. I called Andy LeCompte. He made Nicole Richie into a movie star without a movie, that's how good he is. She's going in at three o'clock. And we're going to pretend that Orphan Annie bob thingie never happened."

I shrugged my shoulders. If it takes a village, our village chief was Tim Gunn.

"Who's next on the docket?" I asked. I put down my iced tea and rubbed my palms together. "Mama needs a new pair of Havaianas."

Jay and Chloe exchanged a look. I knew better than to ask Jay what that meant. Chloe, on the other hand, was incapable of lying. She'd crack like a spoiled egg.

"Chloe, spill," I said.

"That nice man Tom is here, and he wants to talk to you," she said. "I don't know what to tell him."

"Nice work, Chloe," Jay said. "Good job keeping it all together."

"Tom's here?" I asked. "What does he want?" I sucked in my stomach.

"He wouldn't say," Jay said.

"He wants to talk to his wife," Chloe said.

"Dear God," Jay said.

"Go get him," I told them. "This should be interesting."

Jay took a long look at me, appraising his subject. "No, I don't think so. I'm going to tell him to come back another night when the light's better. You're a little sallow right now, I hate to tell you."

"Jay, the man wants to speak to his dead wife," I said. "This isn't speed-dating."

"Honey," Jay said, "on the Westside, even marriage is speed-dating."

Tom returned to Casa Sugar the next night at around 7:00. By that time, Jay had had his way with me. I was moisturized, manicured, and made-up. I looked perilously close to desirable. Jay had even managed to defrizz my hair, with product found only in *Jet* magazine ads.

"Hi," I said to Tom, who wore a lightweight sweater and jeans. He looked handsome as ever. As I came in for a hug, I sniffed his cologne. I felt wistful. Without even realizing, I had missed him.

"You look radiant," Tom said, then shook his head. "I'm sorry, I shouldn't say that."

"If you mean it, you have to say it," I joked. "It's a sin, otherwise. Come on in."

Tom entered the living room, and I took his hand and walked him through the house into my backyard. I motioned for him to sit across from me.

"Are you okay?" I said. "I don't want you to be nervous."

"I'm nervous, and frankly, you look great," he said. "Oh, is she going to hear that?"

"Who?"

"My wife."

I smiled. "No, don't worry," I said. "Give me a second. I'm getting pretty good at this, I have to say. Close your eyes, okay?"

He did. I pretended I was closing mine, too, but left one eye open. Tom looked as edible as ever. The perfect amount of scruff, and just the right dose of grief.

He was pretty much irresistible. I sighed and closed my eyes. "Patchett, right?"

"Who? Oh, yes, Patchett. I'm sorry," he said. "I'm afraid she'll be angry with me."

"For what?" I opened my eyes. I wanted to hear it from him. *For your penis being the boss of you?*

"Hair. I can't do hair," he said, opening his eyes. "I'm really trying to do my daughter Livia's hair the way Patchett did. It never works."

His lip trembled. He started to cry.

Of course, I did, too.

"Patchett used to comb it, braid it," he said. "It never tangled. Never. And I can't seem to . . ." He held up his hands, staring at his fingers, those instruments of betrayal.

I grabbed his hands. "I'm sure you're doing fine, Tom," I said. "She's not going to be mad at you. She'll understand. Maybe she'll even have a tip. Something she didn't think of telling you, before she passed."

"Maybe?" he said plaintively.

"Hey, if anything," I said, "*I'm* mad at John—*he's* the one who died, right?"

Tom smiled. "Yeah, that's right. Why'd Patchett have to do that to me? Why?"

Why not? Trish's voice echoed in my head.

"There are no reasons," I said. "There's just right now. Do I sound like a very special guest on *Oprah*?"

Tom looked at me. "I think I like it."

I smiled. "Ready to start?"

He nodded. "Yeah, I'm ready. Do you think she misses me?"

"She misses you, Tom," I said. Of that, I was sure.

I closed my eyes.

Patchett is, in a word, lovely. I smelled her before I even saw her. Her scent was like Downy fabric softener mixed with baby powder, of everything that is fresh and clean. I didn't get that "dead" feeling from her, like I get with most of my "clientele."

Patchett was surprised to hear from Tom. "You know," she told me, "he's not really one to ask for help. He keeps it all bottled up inside. I'm not even sure he cried at my funeral."

"Oh, I'm sure he did," I said.

"It's okay," she said. "I've known Tom since college—I know he loved me. He's just . . . well, he's a banker. Does he miss me?"

"With everything he is . . . ," I said. "He misses you in ways he can't even articulate. Do you miss him?"

"Oh, yes . . . oh, yes . . . ," Patchett said. "Please . . . my babies . . ."

"Tom," I said, "Patchett wants to know how the babies are doing . . ."

Tom sat up straight, as though he was about to give a presentation.

"They're great," he said. "Livia just turned five; I mean, Patchett knows her birthday, of course. I had a party, a Dora the Explorer party—"

"He's doing this all himself?" Patchett asked.

"All by himself," I said, choking back more tears.

"You know what the worst part of being dead is?" Patchett asked me. "It isn't missing my girls' weddings or graduations. It's the walks home from school, the car rides, looking in the rearview mirror and seeing my sleeping baby, rushing to soccer practice . . . having my first disagreement with Chelsea, my oldest, over something stupid, and realizing that she's no longer my little girl . . ."

I thought of Ellie, who wouldn't be little forever. *How can that be?*

"Someday, someday soon . . . she's going to step outside into the bigger world. The worst part is that . . . I'm not a part of that world. I'm not even on the sidelines. I'm so pissed at fate."

"I thought being dead meant being free from regret," I said. "I was so wrong."

"Can we keep in touch?" Patchett asked. "I'm afraid it's the only way he'll communicate with me."

"Of course," I said. "I wish I could give you my card."

"Listen," Patchett said, "I know we just met—and you have no reason to trust me. But Tom's a good man. He really is. I'm not saying he's perfect. He's a neat freak, and he says the wrong thing trying to do the right thing, but he's willing to learn."

"Wait—are you trying to . . . ?"

"Set you up with my husband?" she asked. "Well . . . I've seen the women in this town. My best friend was after him two seconds after I was buried. I don't think she even waited for the service to be over before she asked him to feel her new boobs."

"This is a first for me, Patchett," I said, "and thank you. I appreciate the gesture. As a mother, I know how much that means, coming from you."

"What gesture?" Tom asked.

"Oh," I said to her, "you might look up John Bernal. He's my . . . he was my . . . husband. He's the reason for my . . . gift, I guess."

"Thanks," Patchett said, "but you know, we don't date here. It kinda sucks, because there's a lot of really interesting dead men."

"All the best ones are dead, huh?" I said.

I heard her warm laugh . . . and then, she was gone.

Tom and I sat in the backyard as Patchett faded away. I could hear his sniffling, felt his hands move over his face. NoMo was pitch-black at night—the streetlights came on only intermittently, but his emotional state was undeniable.

"Come on," I said, my hand finding his knee, "I'll walk you out."

I shivered as we made our way to the front door. SaMo nights were cold, even in spring.

"Does it always have to be so cold here?" I asked. "What does Santa Monica think it is, Chicago?"

". . . hates California," Tom said, "it's cold and it's damp."

"That's why the lady is a tramp . . . ," I said, trying to rub the cold from my arms.

Tom put his arm around my shoulders, and hugged me on my doorstep. I hugged him back. When he kissed me, I pushed him away, gently.

"Too soon," I said. "I feel like I'm betraying Patchett. I liked her. I didn't know I could like a perfect person."

"I'm sorry," Tom said. "I don't know, I'm just confused. The whole thing's overwhelming. I'm just very grateful to you."

"So that was a gratitude kiss? With tongue?" I said, teasing him. "Just . . . give me another hug. I miss hugs."

He opened his arms and grabbed me, pulling me to his chest. I inhaled, deeply. Why do men smell so much like . . . men? I loved that. I missed that. *Why can't they smell like . . . paper?*

"Oh," I said, "I have something to show you."

I went back inside, and came out with a ledger.

"I was going to come in Monday. Take a look," I said, as I handed Tom the ledger. He ran his eyes over it. I saw his expression change.

"You're paying off the note," he said. "Hannah, I'm so happy for you."

"I'll be all paid up, at least through this month, and then we'll take it a month at a time—"

"That's fantastic," Tom said. "Well done, Hannah."

We hesitated, our bodies inches apart, our minds hovering around what damage we could inflict upon each other and the furniture— at least, that's what I was thinking. Financial security is my aphrodisiac.

"You should go," I said.

"Right," Tom said. "I'll call you. Tomorrow morning. We'll start with coffee."

I waved as every NoMo mom's wet dream got into his silver BMW and drove away.

Seven A.M. The doorbell was ringing. Casa Sugar was crawling with ghosts. I stepped around the pill-popping producer who'd been watching me sleep, the Hollywood wife complaining in my hallway, and the character with the beer gut lying on my couch with a re- mote in his hand.

I looked out the peephole. Detective Ramirez held up his badge. *What the neighbors must think! I had more police cars outside my house than the SMPD parking lot.*

I sighed and opened the door.

"Good morning, Rude Awakening," I said. I was barefoot, wear- ing my favorite robe, which is a mess, as all favorite robes are. Ellie and Brandon were still asleep.

"Ms. Bernal," he said. Under his arm was a stack of files.

"I'm about to make coffee. Do you want any?"

"No," Detective Ramirez said.

"You turn down coffee? Is coffee so hard? Is everything about you gruff?" *Why was I suddenly thinking about his kissing skills?*

"What do you mean by that?" he said, sounding hurt. "I'm here on official business."

"You found the Range Rover?" My heart nearly leapt out of my chest.

"No. Ms. Bernal, are you running a business out of your home?"

"A business?" I asked, stalling.

"Yes, a business," he said. "Are you being paid in cash?"

"I'm not running that kind of business."

"That's not what I'm asking."

"But I could if I wanted to," I said. "Someone would surely pay for my services after seeing me in this ten-year-old fleece robe with the coffee and formula stains."

He didn't respond. Instead, he just stared at me.

"You're here to harass a middle-aged working girl?" I asked. "Really?"

"I'm not harassing you," Ramirez said. "The Santa Monica Police Department does not harass. We encourage."

"You nudge."

"Yes. That's right. And I'm asking a simple question. Maybe you'll give me a simple answer. Are you running a business out of your home?"

"No. Well. Maybe." I was never a good liar. "Detective, I'm trying to pay off my mortgage. I was on the verge of losing my house."

He handed me a card. It was my business card. The Happy Medium was suddenly less happy.

"What you're doing is illegal," he said. "You need a business license."

"Did someone complain?"

"We've had complaints."

"Complaints plural? Or complaint singular?"

"You're too much, you know that?"

"Who was it? Tell me or I'll just keep asking."

"I can't tell you that, Ms. Bernal," Ramirez said. "I don't care how many times you ask me, there's no magic number."

"Was it Dee Dee Pickler?" It had to be Dee Dee. Who else? She'd lost her commission. Labial bling doesn't come cheap.

"I'm prepared to make a deal," he said.

"Oh, great," I said. "I hate deals. Anytime anyone wants to make a deal, I get dealt." I knew I wasn't going to like whatever he was going to sell me. But I also knew I had to buy.

"You help me, I help you," he said, handing over the files.

"I've watched enough TV, I know how this goes," I said. "I'm the plain housewife with the special gift, and you're the detective who needs my help."

"That's right," Detective Ramirez said, "we need each other, but can't stand each other, but want each other. In the TV version, of course."

"At the very least, I want Benjamin Bratt to play the detective."

"And I get Elizabeth Montgomery," he said.

"She's dead."

"I don't care," he said. "She was the best."

"She was." I had to agree. I found myself getting jealous over a forty-year-old character from *Bewitched*.

"Cold cases," he said, regarding the files. "Maybe you have a gift. Maybe not. But if you do, the City of Santa Monica needs your help."

"What do you mean, maybe?" I asked. "People are paying good money for my services."

"Great. Be sure to let the IRS know," he said. "Take a look. See what you see. Or hear, or whatever you do."

"How many unsolved mysteries do you have in here?" I asked. "Santa Monica's a vast, crime-ridden metropolis? Since when?"

"You'd be surprised. We have an unsolved murder just a few blocks west of here."

"I feel like Angela Lansbury, only older," I said.

"I loved that show," Ramirez said. "I think she's a very good-looking woman; I'm not ashamed."

"Ever thought of getting a life?"

"Never. What would I do with it?"

Ellie ambled into the living room, took one look at Detective Ramirez, and went for my leg, clinging to me, thumb in her mouth.

"Hi, there," he said, taking off his sunglasses.

"Can I touch your head?" she asked.

"Ellie," I said, "that's inappropriate."

Ramirez smiled and knelt to her level, so that they were looking at each other, eye-to-eye. He bent his bald head down. "Give it a try," he said.

She rubbed his head ever so lightly with her chubby little fingers.

"Good?" he asked.

"Good," she said, giggling. Ellie was flirting with Detective Ramirez. Ramirez looked up at me and smiled. Is this the first time I'd seen his teeth? *Without me being afraid of getting bit?*

"I wanted to let you know," Detective Ramirez said, looking at me. "We're going to trial next week. On, you know"—he hesitated—"the hit-and-run."

"Mr. Del Toro didn't do it," I said. Ramirez stood and wiped imaginary creases from the front of his pants. He was buying time.

"Please," I said, grabbing his hand. "You believe in me now, and I'm telling you. That guy is innocent."

"I'm sorry, Hannah." He turned, waving at Ellie as he left. He walked like an English bulldog, side to side.

I shook my head, and found myself wondering if he'd ever ask me to dinner. I liked the way my name sounded, coming out of his mouth. I squeezed my hands around the stack of files. My workload had just doubled.

I had dropped Ellie off at school, and was meeting Jay and Aimee for coffee at the Pirates before medium hours. Ramirez's files were in my Whole Foods "Yes, This Is My Bag" bag. I took out the pile and placed them on the table in front of me.

I sipped my vanilla soy latte and opened up the first file.

A little girl. Pigtails. Freckles. 1978.

Oh my God. I closed my eyes, just briefly. Immediately, I saw a man's hands. Rough. Carpenter? *Someone who'd been working on the roof.* I put that one aside, for now. I needed a moment.

Next one. A grandmother, killed in her bed. No sign of forced entry. I looked at the date. August 2, 1987.

Okay, this one, I could handle. I closed my eyes, then opened them again. The woman was sitting across from me.

"My grandson," she said, her voice low and sad. "He'd been doing drugs. He was stealing from me. He's dead now, too."

I nodded. I heard dogs barking. I looked up and saw Chloe tying her dog menagerie to the lone newspaper vending machine outside the coffee joint. Waving a copy of the *Santa Monica Mirror*, she rushed inside and sat across from me. She was breathing hard and her eyes were spinning.

"Chloe, do you have rabies?" I asked.

"Bakasana . . . I want to talk to Bakasana," Chloe said, as Jay and Aimee walked in, Aimee waddling and Jay prancing like a Lipizzaner stallion.

"Bakasana?" I asked, acting dumb. "What do you mean?"

"Angel killed him," Chloe said. "I know it. She came back last night and tried to snatch my Jack Russell mix, Mulabunda."

"Angel?" Aimee asked. "That weird dog?"

"Angel isn't a dog," Chloe whispered, slapping the newspaper against the table.

"What do you think she is?" Jay asked, although he already knew the answer. "A unicorn?"

"She's a coyote," Chloe said. "Look at this. Look at the picture. I had a coyote living in my home, eating my gluten-free food." She pointed to the newspaper. On the front page was a picture of a coyote, wandering 16th Street, a small animal in its jaws. The by-line read: COYOTE TERRORIZES NORTH OF MONTANA.

"And your dogs, apparently," Aimee said, looking at the photograph. She read the first few lines of the article. ". . . female coyote responsible for latest spate of pet killings in exclusive North of Montana neighborhood . . . Oliver, Beckett, Zoe, Miles . . . Keats." Aimee looked up. "Someone named their dog Keats? Really?"

"That's her. That's the hemp collar I bought online," Chloe said. "It's from a Peruvian transgender co-op, took me forever to find it."

"So . . . Bakasana's a dog chew . . . ," Jay said, glancing at the article.

"Chloe, I saw Bakasana . . . in a vision," I confessed, putting my hand on hers. "The good news is, he looked happy. For a Pomeranian."

"Chloe, is Angel loose?" Aimee asked.

"Well, she's had a couple litters, I think," Chloe said. Jay and I looked at each other, suppressing an urge to laugh. "I have to stop Angel's killing spree, and I'm going to take care of this. My way."

"Meditation and thistle tea?" Jay asked.

"How can you guys joke about this when I'm hurting?" Chloe said.

"Nobody likes Pomeranians, Chloe," Aimee said. "They never have. It's all a lie."

"Whatever. I'm going to find that bitch," Chloe said. She stood up, and shook the newspaper. "In the name of every Fluffy, Scooter,

Lucky, Keats, and Bakasana, I'm putting an end to her reign of terror."

She strode out, untied her dog from the vending machine, and rushed down the street.

"Wow," Jay said, "she's very Joan of Arc this morning. Or should I say, Joan of Bark."

I thought for a moment. Something nagged at me.

"Guys," I said, setting my latte down, "does Chloe still have that gun?"

We ran up 17th after Chloe. At her house, we were surprised to find Billy, dressed in tight yoga shorts and a *Spiritual Gangsta* tank top, answering the door. An Om meditation tape played loudly in the background.

"Billy, didn't you join the Marines?" I asked, surprised.

"Well, those mini-shorts are very *all that you can be*," Jay said.

"I tried," Billy said. "Boot camp is hard. I was competing against eighteen-year-olds. Plus, I couldn't use my smartphone. I got an honorable discharge, though." He looked shorter when not dressed to invest. I hadn't seen him in months. "I'm sorry about your husband, Hannah," Billy said. "I don't think I ever got the chance to say that. I liked John a lot."

John thought Billy was a blowhard. Billy thought John was a sandal-wearing omelet maker. Either times had changed drastically or death brings out the dishonest in people. I let it go.

"Thank you, Billy," I said. "Is Chloe home? We're looking for her. It's important."

"She dropped off the dogs a few minutes ago," he said. "I don't know where she went. Try the co-op. Or wait, Whole Foods?"

Whole Foods was the Santa Monica fallback location. If you were searching for a spouse, boyfriend, dog, child, Jimmy Hoffa, the first place you look was the deli counter at Whole Foods.

"Billy," I said, "did she take that shotgun with her?"

He looked at me, alarmed. "Let me check." Billy left the room, then walked back a minute later. "It's not here," he said. "Hannah—is Chloe okay?"

"Fuming in silence tires me out, especially in my condition," Aimee said. "Your wife is crying out for help. You left her alone with I don't know how many kids and dogs, and what about this yogini girlfriend?"

"Tatiana?" Billy said. "She wasn't my girlfriend."

"Tatianas are always girlfriends," Aimee said. "Have you ever heard of a wife named Tatiana?"

"Whatever it was . . . it's over," Billy said. "I love my wife. My kids. And my practice. *Namaste.*"

"Billy," I said, "this isn't about you. Chloe needs our help. Now."

"I'll use my Marine training," he said. "We'll find her. Let me get my gear on." He hurried to get dressed.

"I hear you rolling your eyes, Jay," I said, as I watched Billy bolt the stairs in his teeny-tiny shorts.

Marine training only works on water, apparently; it was for shit on land. We spent hours driving from 26th to Ocean, from San Vicente to Montana, and back again. We didn't bother with SoMo. Angel knew her neighborhoods: NoMo meant steak from The Farms, and a higher ratio of pets to clueless owner.

Chloe wasn't answering her phone. As we sat at the curb on Alta and 20th, I remembered my conversation with the coyote lady, months ago.

"Coyotes hang out in abandoned houses and empty lots," I said.

"There's a ton of those in NoMo," Jay said.

He was right. Older homes were being bought up like gold bars and demolished overnight, so fast that you couldn't remember if they'd really been there, or if they were part of a dream.

"There's an abandoned lot down the street from our house," Billy said.

* * *

We reached the empty double lot just as the fog rolled in.

"Remember John Carpenter?" Jay asked. "This fog is creeping me out."

"Is that the dude who sang background on 'We've Only Just Begun'?" Billy asked. "That was our wedding song."

The fog surrounded the palm trees, choking them as they swayed, tentative in the gray. A chill set in. A house on one side of the lot, a single-story wood-frame, had a FOR SALE sign planted in its front yard. Dee Dee Pickler's Photoshopped face smiled out from the clapboard as it rocked on its hinges. The retouching on her pic was so extreme, she looked like Carrot Top. We peered through the wire fencing surrounding the huge lot. A really rich person, not just vanilla rich, was going to build here; double lots were rare and coveted.

"See anything?" I asked Jay. Aimee came up behind us.

Just then, I saw movement in the corner, behind the single California Oak that had been left behind. The tree had a mournful cant, as though saying, "What happened? Where's my home? Where are those kids who used to climb me?" and . . . "When are they coming for me next?"

I spotted Chloe beside the tree, on her knees. A shotgun lay in the weeds in front of her.

Billy saw her, too.

"Chloe!" he said, making a run for the fence, attempting to hop over. And another. And . . . one more.

"Chloe!" I called. Jay and Aimee shouted, "Chloe!"

Jay knitted his hands together to give Billy a boost over the fence. I went next. "Stay here," I said, turning to Aimee, "you're being sane for two." I hopped the fence (pulling a muscle I didn't even know I had) and stumbled over to Chloe and Billy.

Under the brush, Angel was nursing her pups in a makeshift den. Chloe put her hand out to ward me off.

"She has pups," I said, hushed. "They're still called pups, right?"

"Coyote infants?" Jay said, jogging up from behind me. "I can't look it up, I'm Google-handicapped. No service in Santa Monica."

"I couldn't do it," Chloe whispered.

Jay and I knelt down beside her.

"Oh, my Lanvin tennis shoes," Jay lamented. "I'm not an empty lot person."

"Of course you couldn't do it, Chloe," I said. "You're not like the rest of us. You can't just randomly shoot things."

"Don't get too close," Chloe said, her eyes never wavering from Angel. "She doesn't want anyone else near her."

As if on cue, Angel growled.

"She trusts me," Chloe said. "Someone trusts me. My friends don't trust me. My kids don't trust me. My husband thinks I'm an idiot."

"Chloe, baby," Billy said, "don't say that."

"Don't you *baby* me," Chloe said. "How did my life come to this? Everything was so perfect. I had erected a careful construct of cooler-than-thou domestic bliss, from our half-Asian children who were supposed to be highly gifted and musically inclined, to my sniveling liberalism and your snarling conservatism. And then, I'd take pictures and blog about it and eventually appear on *Good Morning America*."

"This all sounds like torture," Jay said.

"Billy, our kids aren't even smart, let's face it."

"They're smart enough."

"They don't play piano or violin. They're tone-deaf."

"But they are photogenic," I said. "And who always has the best Christmas cards? Who?"

"Hand me the gun, Chloe," Billy said.

Gaping NoMos were starting to gather outside the fence. They were the usual suspects: dog people, stroller people, dog-and-stroller people, bicyclists, serious bicyclists, skateboarders (these are adults), runners, joggers, walkers, serious walkers . . . all of them enjoying an after-dinner Pinkberry.

"I don't even know you anymore, Billy. And I'm not sure I even like you," Chloe said, sighing. "I wish I could just start my life all over."

Billy stepped toward Chloe, and Angel growled. Billy backed up.

"Honey, you do like me," he told her. "You like me despite everything, and I like you despite everything. We're stuck with each other. It's a life sentence. Besides, we can't afford a divorce. That option closed in 2008. So please, hand me the gun. Carefully."

"Promise you won't run off and join another militant group."

"Not even the Boy Scouts. Now, come on, baby, let's go home before someone actually gets shot."

Chloe handed me the shotgun, and fell into Billy's arms.

Now, you know how guns go off accidentally in movies, in nightclubs (if you're a professional athlete), or anywhere in Florida, and you wonder how people could possibly be that stupid?

Well, judge not lest ye be judged.

As I took the shotgun from Chloe, the damn thing kicked and went off, blasting a hole into the side of the empty old house next door. I screamed, dropping the weapon. I didn't hear anything else until after everyone around me stopped screaming. Only then did I hear it.

Someone else was screaming, from inside the house.

"Oh my God," I said, "I just killed someone."

The Turk ran out of the old house, tripping over his pants, which were around his ankles, and clasping his shirt to his chest. The Turk's chest hair skipped his bald head and continued down his back. His ample stomach, adorned with a bunny trail, hung over his shorts.

"Bear sighting!" Jay shouted.

There was more screaming, then Dee Dee emerged from the house, her hands clutching her ass.

"Call a doctor," she yelled, "and a plastic surgeon! This is going to leave a scar!"

From out of the crowd, a woman who gave every appearance of being the Turk's wife grabbed him, yelling at him in a foreign language that required no translation.

"I'm still getting commission!" Dee Dee bellowed. "I've got a signed contract!"

"Dee Dee," I said, "an ambulance is on its way. Are you okay?"

"My butt is bleeding," Dee Dee said, as she looked over at me. "I just got shot in the ass. Why haven't you returned my calls?" Ever the businesswoman. I had to give her respect, however grudgingly.

"Dee Dee, here, let me help you," I said, taking my sweater off. "Calm down and press this against your bottom."

"I can't calm down, I'm in pain," Dee Dee said. "You want to upgrade?"

Meanwhile, the Turk's wife slapped him across the face, and was dragging him off by his ear.

I hooked my arm around Dee Dee and was holding her up when a middle-aged woman appeared at Dee Dee's side, hovering just above the ground. She looked like Dee Dee but with original parts.

"Tell this bitch I know what she did at my funeral," the apparition said.

"Oh, no," I said. "What happened?"

Dee Dee looked at me, confused. "What do you mean what happened?" she asked. "I just took a bullet in the ass."

"My own sister tries to give my husband a blow job at my funeral!" the apparition complained. "Tell her Janie says hello. Then tell her to go fuck herself." She turned to Dee Dee, who was staring at me. "You'll always be the fat little sister—all the lipo in the world won't fix your personality! I hope you get nose herpes!"

"Dee Dee," I said. "Janie says hello . . ."

"Janie who, for God's sake?"

"Janie, your sister." Dee Dee's eyes widened as a police car drove up, sirens blasting. Detective Ramirez got out of the car and rushed over.

"Are you the only cop in this city?" I asked. "This is getting ridiculous."

Ramirez flipped off his Ray-Bans and grumbled. "Can't you stay out of trouble?"

"It was an accident," I said, as the paramedics placed Dee Dee facedown on a stretcher. "Hold on," I said.

I turned back to Dee Dee, and bent down close to her. "Like I said, your sister, Janie, says hello," I said. "And she hopes you get nose herpes."

Dee Dee screamed as the paramedics maneuvered her into the ambulance. I watched it drive away.

Finding your friend before she commits coyote-cide? Fifty bucks.

Watching your friend's marriage being saved? A thousand dollars.

Hitting Dee Dee Pickler in the ass with a shotgun pellet? Priceless.

I put my hands up for Detective Ramirez.

"Go ahead," I said, "cuff me. I could use a vacation."

"If you served mai tais, Santa Monica jail would be the Kahala Hilton, Detective," Jay said. "Cuff me. I'm ready and curious. I was holding the gun."

Aimee stepped forward. "I don't need you to take the fall for me, Jay." She looked at Ramirez and swung her hair around. "I'm guilty, Detective. Guilty as hell."

She was milking it. This was Aimee's Glenn Close moment. Screw David Mamet.

"Oh, great," Ramirez said. "This is cute. Your friends are really cute."

"They kind of are, aren't they?" I said.

"It's my gun, Detective," Chloe said. "I'm responsible."

"Honey, no," Billy said. "Detective Ramirez, my name is Billy, Marine Corps Infantry. Well, I would have been, except for the climbing wall." He shook Detective Ramirez's hand. "Sir, this gun belongs to me. I'm the guilty party. And I'm a former banker, I probably deserve some jail time, anyway. If you'll have me."

Detective Ramirez contemplated our motley crew. He gazed at me with those dark, piercing eyes. I don't know why, but I heard a Julio Iglesias song in my head—and you know how it is, once Iglesias happens, it's impossible to get rid of. *There's no cure for Iglesias.*

"No more guns," he said. "You people shouldn't be anywhere near guns. May I ask what happened?"

"Well," Chloe said. "See, I adopt dogs."

"She adopted a coyote," I said.

"Which ate her Pomeranian," Jay said.

"Ate her what?" Ramirez asked.

"The coyote just had pups," Chloe said. "You want one?"

Detective Ramirez widened his eyes. "White people really are crazy."

"They really are," I said.

"How you coming on those files?" he asked me.

"I just started this morning."

"Maybe you'd get more work done downtown."

"This is Santa Monica," I said. "There is no downtown."

He sighed. In this light, I thought, Detective Ramirez looked a bit like a Latino Bob Hoskins.

Something you don't know about me?

I've always had a secret crush on Bob Hoskins.

24

The Happy Medium

After the shooting incident, life began to settle down. Ellie is happy in school, and has grown about three inches. Her legs remind me of her father's. Her laugh, I recognize as mine. Recently, she and I witnessed a "NoMo mad mover" crossing San Vicente, a skinny middle-aged woman covered head-to-toe in white, from her visor and face shield, to her tennis shoes, pumping her arms like there was money in it. The two of us burst out laughing; I looked in the rearview mirror and caught my daughter's eye. An appreciation of the absurd? That, she got from me. Brandon, meanwhile, is close to getting his degree, and already has a job lined up, working with Special Ed kids at the local public school. Aimee is on self-inflicted bedrest; Greta Garbo's fatal illness in *Camille* has nothing on her pregnancy. Chloe and Billy are adopting a baby from the Congo, which seems like a bad idea because they're just getting to know their own children all over again. The good news is, Chloe is no longer adopting dogs. Since she integrated a coyote into a new feeding ground, i.e. NoMo, she's on the pet adoption shit list. Meanwhile, Billy found a job he loves: teaching both high school math and yoga classes at a Venice charter school. Chloe and Billy are selling their home through Dee Dee, and are moving into a condo in SoMo. They're putting the kids in public school and are weirdly happy and in love. Dee Dee's recovered from her ass-hap (mishap), and is in a serious relationship with the ER doctor who patched her glute.

Early this evening, Jay and I had a meeting at Casa Sugar with She-Devil. Remember her? Turns out, she'd been thinking about how to market me since that disastrous network meeting. She couldn't get me out of her mind—which is both flattering and disturbing. She had Todd the Reality King make the call a couple days ago. (He also made an appointment later this week to communicate with his dead brother, the teenaged skateboarder with the Mega-Death fixation.)

This afternoon, I threw in a little session with She-Devil's dead grandmother; yes, I can be a show-off. Anyway, She-Devil wants *moi* to host a show—a lifestyle/communicating-with-the-dead hybrid. She loves Casa Sugar, and thinks we should tape in the house. The network likes that I am "real." In other words, I'm chubby, at least in the opinion of a TV camera and media execs. Oh, Jay and I are producing.

"I've finally gotten over Hidalgo," Jay said, as we skewered chicken kabobs in the kitchen after our successful meeting. We had planned our first summer barbecue that night. Tom and his daughters were coming over, along with Chloe and her brood, and of course, Aimee and Brandon. I'd even sent along an invite to Detective Ramirez.

"You've given up on love completely," I said, ignoring the gray-haired Malibu stoner sitting on my stool who was trying to get me to light a bud. He died snowboarding, forgetting that it was July.

"Never," Jay said.

"You've fallen in love again?" I asked, repressing a sigh.

"Just wait until you meet Vladimir," Jay said. "I've already proposed. How does Iowa in June sound?"

"It sounds like when Ellie and I are scheduled to go to Greece, remember? For our 'girls only' trip?"

"Don't remind me," Jay said, pouty. Our conversation was interrupted by pounding.

"Someone's knocking at my front door, or that's an especially annoying poltergeist."

"Door," Jay clarified.

"Love the wedding idea. It's good to know bad ideas never get better," I called out, as I opened the door. A woman, a NoMo Momster, stood there, tiny phone to her ear. "What? You're kidding me," she said. "Of course they're not invited—their kids aren't even in private school—"

She looked me up and down, then said into the phone, "Hold on a minute—"

"Hi?" she said to me. "I need to speak to the Happy Medium?" Chiseled and hyper, she carried a big Louis Vuitton bag over one sunbaked shoulder. She strode past me and looked around, sort of sniffing the air before turning to stare. "Can you go . . . get her, please? Does she live here? Am I in the right place?"

I didn't respond. My breath had caught in my throat.

"Hold on a sec," she said to her phone, "I'm trying to get an answer here."

"I don't do readings after six," I said, finding my words.

"That's okay, we'll make it a short one; I've been crazy busy," she said. "Maria insisted. She said Oprah's crazy about you. And I said, why not, right? Is there a clean restroom somewhere?"

I pointed down the hallway as Jay came in from the kitchen.

"Who is it?" he asked, as she walked out of view. I went to the window. Parked in my driveway was a black Range Rover.

"No," I said. "Oh, no."

"What's wrong?" Jay asked.

"Jay," I said. "I need to do this reading. Get her name, please. Just write it down. And then call Detective Ramirez. He should be here in about ten minutes."

The NoMo Momster came out of the bathroom, wiping her manicured hands. "So. Where is it that you do your little thing?"

The woman who'd killed my husband sat across from me. I didn't know how I was going to get through this without strangling her.

"Cute backyard," she said, looking around. "Sweet."

"Close your eyes," I said. "Just . . . give me a moment."

"Sure," she said, and closed her eyes. Her wedding ring with its huge rock sickened me. I looked at her fingernails, metallic polish, the perfect length. Her beaded prayer bracelets probably cost a fortune.

John, are you there? Can you see her? Is this the one?

"Is there someone you want to talk to? Someone you feel . . . I don't know . . . guilty about?"

"I'm sorry?" she asked.

"Is there someone specific you want to talk to?" I said. "I mean, talk, I don't mean, you know, text, while you're driving, or anything."

She tilted her head. "What?"

"You know, one of the first dead people I saw was my husband. He's dead. He died. *Recently.* Wait. Last year. In September. It was a beautiful morning."

She listened.

"He was forty-two years old. We have a daughter. She's four now. She misses her daddy."

"That's sad," the woman said. "How did he die?"

"He was on a bike," I said.

She opened her eyes.

"Just down the street," I said. "It was early one Saturday."

"You know what? I have to go," she said, gathering her purse and sunglasses.

"I talk to him, my dead husband, John," I said. "I talk to him, all the time."

She stopped packing.

"Do you know what he told me?"

"No. Why would I?"

"He told me who ran him down and left him for dead. He told me who did it," I said. "You know what the best news is? We have a witness."

She made a break for the kitchen door. I followed her to the front of the house, catching up just in time to see Detective Ramirez outside, checking out the grille on NoMo's Range Rover. Jay stood next to him, his arms crossed.

I waited at my front door.

"I'd like to take you down to the Santa Monica Police Station for questioning," Detective Ramirez told Mrs. NoMo, who glanced nervously back at me.

"I'm crazy busy," she said. "My charity event, Mothers Against Plastics, starts in an hour. There's no way."

"I recommend you call your attorney first," Detective Ramirez said.

Minutes later, Ramirez escorted the woman from my property, and another officer came and impounded the Range Rover. Jay stood close to me, his arm tight around my shoulders. I was reminded of how he held me up the morning of John's death.

Jay held out his hand. "Detective Ramirez gave me something for you," he said. On his palm was a circle of red yarn strung with colorful beads. I recognized the bracelet. I picked it up.

The beads had letters on them, spelling out . . . D-A-D-D-Y.

I looked up at Jay, who was crying. "It's over now, darling," he said.

I grabbed him and sobbed into his chest. I would never let him go. I cried and cried until I could not cry anymore.

The fog was rolling in.

A coyote yelped.

Wind chimes played a soothing melody.

Somehow, we still managed that night's barbecue. The kabobs came out perfectly cooked, the breast meat still, miraculously, juicy. Jay had made a deep, citrusy sangria that tasted of sunshine mixed with alcohol, and poured it liberally into jelly jar glasses. We arranged bright flowers throughout the house, and in a vase outside on my new picnic table. Tom had arrived, bearing lemon bars. His three girls played hide-and-seek with Ellie, delighting in her every movement, every word. Spice's whole body shook with joy as the girls surrounded him, taking turns rubbing his stomach and scratching his back.

For a brief moment, the dead left the living in peace.

Acknowledgments

Thank you to my agent, Jennifer Rudolph Walsh. Thank you to Linda Marrow, my editor, and Libby McGuire, my publisher. I'd also like to thank Kim Hovey, my associate publisher, Susan Corcoran, my publicity director, and Paolo Pepe, my art director. I also very much appreciate the hard work of Dana Isaacson. Thank you to my manager, Stephanie Davis. Thank you to my sisters, Suzanne "Suzy" Levangie Kurtz, Marianne "Mimi" Levangie, and Julianne "Julie" Levangie Purcell. Thank you to my mom and dad, Phillipa Costa Brown and Frank Levangie. Thank you to my nephews and niece, John Henry Kurtz, Jack Grazer, and Frankie, Jonathan, and Angelina Levangie. Thank you to Mark Kriegel. Thank you to my good friends Julie Jaffe, Mimi James (queen of the one-liners), and Yahfatyah Reed. Thank you to my friends on Facebook and Twitter; though I may never meet them, they brighten my days. Thank you to all the mothers, sisters, daughters and grandmothers I've met on book tours, in nail salons, on line at the movies, and at my sons' games for their insights, wisdom, and laughter. And finally, thank you to the widows who've been gracious enough to take me on their own journeys of love, loss, and life.

Thank you all.

PHOTO: © DAVID HUME KENNERLY

GIGI LEVANGIE GRAZER is the bestselling author of four previous novels, including *The Starter Wife*, first a miniseries and then a series on the USA Network, and *Maneater*, now a Lifetime miniseries. Her most recent book, *Queen Takes King*, is currently under option at Lifetime. Grazer has also written the screenplay for *Stepmom*, starring Julia Roberts and Susan Sarandon, and articles for *Vogue*, *Harper's Bazaar*, and *Glamour*. She lives in Los Angeles with her two children and one miniature dachshund.

www.gigigrazer.com

About the Type

This book was set in Berling. Designed in 1951 by Karl Erick Forsberg for the Typefoundry Berlingska Stilgjuteri AB in Lund, Sweden, it was released the same year in foundry type by H. Berthold AG. A classic old-face design, its generous proportions and inclined serifs make it highly legible.